The Leopard

ALSO BY K. V. JOHANSEN

Blackdog

The Leopard

MARAKAND, VOLUME ONE

K. V. JOHANSEN

an imprint of Prometheus Books
Amherst, NY

Published 2014 by Pyr®, an imprint of Prometheus Books

Cover image © Raymond Swanland
Cover design by Grace M. Conti-Zilsberger

Inquiries should be addressed to
Pyr
59 John Glenn Drive
Amherst, New York 14228
VOICE: 716–691–0133
FAX: 716–691–0137
WWW.PYRSF.com

18 17 16 15 14   5 4 3 2 1

Library of Congress Cataloging-in-Publication Data

Johansen, K. V. (Krista V.), 1968–
    The leopard / K. V. Johansen.
        p. cm.—(Marakand; volume one)
    ISBN 978-1-61614-903-1 (pbk.)
    ISBN 978-1-61614-904-8 (ebook)
    I. Title.

PR9199.3.J555L48 2014
813'.54—dc23

2013047645

Printed in the United States of America

For Chris

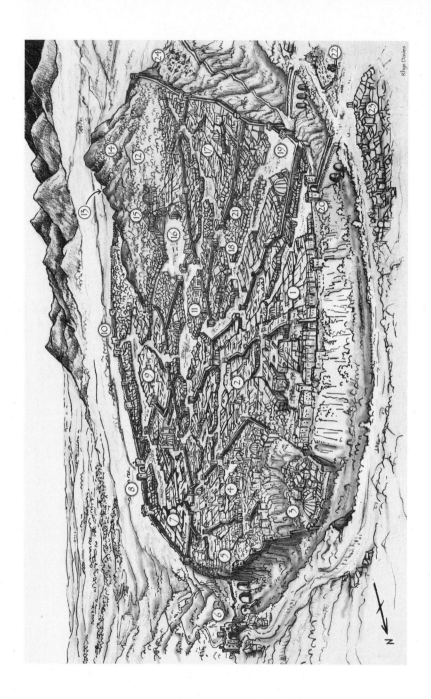

The City of Marakand

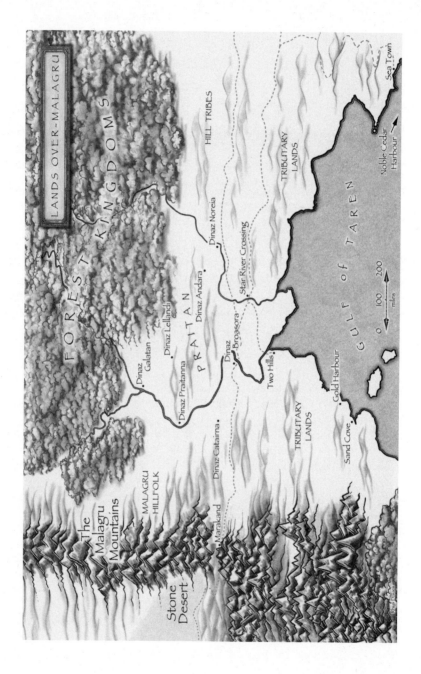

DRAMATIS PERSONAE

Ahjvar—Surnamed the Leopard, a Five Cities assassin suffering under more than his fair share of curses; originally from Praitan, living in Sand Cove in the Tributary Lands.

Akay—A fisherman's widow of Sand Cove in the Tributary Lands.

Andara—Deyandara's god; god of the Duina Andara in Praitan.

Anganurth—A wizard of unknown origins who became the devil Jasberek.

Angress—Champion of Queen Cattiga.

Arhu—A devout priest of the Lady, sent to speak for her in the Duina Catairna.

Arrac-Nourril—One of the Twenty Families alleged to have founded Marakand.

Ashir—A priest, the Right Hand of the Lady, husband of Rahel.

Attalissa—Goddess of the lake Lissavakail in the mountains called the Pillars of the Sky; foster-daughter of Holla-Sayan, formerly protected by the Blackdog.

Auntie—Midwife living with Talfan the apothecary; former nurse of Jugurthos Barraya.

Badger—A mastiff belonging to Deyandara.

Barraya—A Family or clan name in Marakand; one of the Twenty Families, supposed founders of the city.

Bashra—A Black Desert god, god of Gaguush's folk.

Beccan—Sister of Nour, late wife of Hadidu; she died in childbirth some years before this story began.

Bikkim—Serakallashi former member of Gaguush's gang; mortal husband of the goddess Attalissa.

The Blackdog—Thought to be a guardian spirit who bonded with a chosen warrior of Lissavakail to protect the goddess Attalissa; now the Westgrasslander caravaneer Holla-Sayan, free of Attalissa and said by Moth to be the damaged soul of a devil wounded and lost in the world in a forgotten devils' war.

Cairangorm—A king of the Duina Catairna in Praitan; some songs say he was murdered by his elder son, some by his young wife, on the Day of the Three Kings, about ninety years before this story takes place. The songs are still popular among the bards in Praitan, though they are not often sung in the royal hall of the Duina Catairna. It is believed the land and the folk have been under a curse of ill fortune since that day.

Catairanach—Goddess of a spring and patron of the Duina Catairna.

Catairlau—Son of Cairangorm's first wife, his heir, champion, and wizard. Alleged by some to have murdered his father; died not long after him on the Day of the Three Kings.

Cattiga—Queen of the Duina Catairna shortly before this story begins.

Choa, high lord of. Ghu's former master, ruler of a province of northern Nabban.

Clentara—Alias used by Ahjvar in Marakand.

Cricket—Deyandara's pony.

Dann—A Praitannec brigand.

Deyandara—Youngest sibling and only sister of Durandau, king of the Duina Andara and high king of Praitan. Niece and heir of Catigga of the Duina Catairna. Sometimes called Deya.

Django—A member of Gaguush's gang, originally from the Stone Desert, brother of Kapuzeh.

Dotemon—One of the seven devils, otherwise the wizard Yeh-Lin the Beautiful.

Dur—Priestess of the Lady, caretaker of the Voice.

Durandau—King of the Duina Andara and elected high king of Praitan; eldest brother of Deyandara.

Elias Barraya—A senator of Marakand; wife of her cousin Petrimos Barraya; mother of Jugurthos. She was executed in the cages shortly after the earthquake.

Ermina—Second daughter of Varro and Talfan.

Esau—Son of the priestess of Ilbialla and only person from that family to survive the earthquake and the subsequent slaughter of all priests but the Lady's. His name was changed to Hadidu and he was raised by the family of the Doves coffeehouse.

Fairu—A lord in the eastern part of the Duina Catairna.

Farnos—A baker in Sunset Ward.

Feizi—One of the Twenty Families of Marakand.

Gaguush—A Black Desert caravan-mistress and gang-boss, recently married to Holla-Sayan.

Gelyn—A bard of the Duina Catairna, daughter of Queen Cattiga's chief bard.

Geir, Red Geir—One of the first three kings in the north, nephew of the wizard Heuslar.

Ghatai—One of the seven devils, otherwise the wizard Tamghiz, also known as Tamghat, the Lake-Lord of Lissavakail. Father of Ivah.

Ghu—A young Nabbani man, a runaway slave, Ahjvar's servant and companion.

Gilru—Young son of Queen Cattiga, her heir after the deaths of his older brother and sister.

Gisel—A sea-raider and mistress of Red Geir in the stories of the north.

Gurhan—Hill-god of Marakand, formerly served by a clan of hereditary priests.

Guthrun—A Northron caravaneer, camel-leech in Kharduin's gang.

The hag—Ahjvar's name for the ghost which possesses him.

Hassin—Street-guard captain of the Riverbend Gate in Marakand.

Heuslar—Northron wizard who became the devil Ogada, uncle of Red Geir.

Holla-Sayan—A Westgrasslander caravan-guard who unwillingly became the host for the Blackdog of Lissavakail and foster-father to the goddess Attalissa; now one with the Blackdog and a free agent. Husband of Gaguush.

Hravnmod the Wise—One of the first three kings in the north, brother of Ulfhild, said to have been slain by her.

Hyllanim—Son of Hyllau, successor of Cairangorm and Catairlau as king of the Duina Catairna on the Day of the Three Kings.

Hyllau—Second (and much younger) wife of Cairangorm, King of the Duina Catairna. She is said in many songs to have murdered her husband; died on the day of the Three Kings.

Ilbialla—Goddess of a well in Sunset Ward in Marakand, patron of Sunset and Riverbend Wards, formerly served by a single hereditary priest or priestess.

Iris—Third of Varro's and Talfan's four daughters.

Ivah—A wizard, whose father Tamghat was, unbeknownst to her, the devil Tamghiz Ghatai.

Jasberek—One of the seven devils, merged with the wizard Anganurth.

Jasmel—Eldest daughter of Varro and Talfan.

Jecca—A Praitannec brigand.

Jochiz—One of the seven devils, called Jochiz Fireborn; bonded with the wizard Sien-Shava.

Judeh—A Marakander-born caravaneer of Gaguush's gang.

Jugurthos Barraya—Captain of the Sunset Gate fort of the Marakander street guard; son of two executed senators and dispossessed heir of the main branch of the Family Barraya.

Kapuzeh—A member of Gaguush's gang, originally from the Stone Desert, brother of Django.

Keeper—Moth's sword, forged by the demon wolf-smith, inherited from her grandmother. "Keeper" is the meaning of its proper name, Kepra.

Kepra—Moth's Northron sword. For the inscriptions on it, see "The Storyteller."

Ketsim—A Grasslander warleader, formerly among the chief of Tamghat the Lake-Lord's *noekar*, or vassals, and the governor of conquered Serakallash, now a mercenary hired with his followers to take the Duina Catairna for Marakand.

Kharduin—A caravan-master from the eastern deserts, Nour's partner in business and otherwise.

The Lady of the Deep Well, Lady of Marakand—the foremost of the original three gods of Marakand, served by a large number of priests and priestesses. Though the most-worshipped of the three gods, she never appeared to any but her priests. The Voice of the Lady was her intermediary in dealings with the city.

The Lake-Lord—Title taken by Tamghat as ruler of Lissavakail.

Lakkariss—A black sword, which at least looks to be made of obsidian, belonging to Moth.

The Leopard—see Ahjvar.

Lilace—The Voice of the Lady, a priestess chosen to be the shy underground goddess's intermediary with the city, also a prophetess.

Lin—A wandering Nabbani wizard, tutor to Deyandara.

Lug—A Grasslander warrior, one of the mercenary Ketsim's *noekar* and tent-guard. Husband of Chieh.

Lu—A Five Cities caravaneer and horse-dealer involved with Nour and Hadidu in smuggling the wizard-talented out of Marakand.

Mansour—Member of the family of priests of the Marakander hill-god Gurhan; father of Zora. Used the alias Mankul and lived as a street-singer after the massacre of his family and the proscribing of his god.

Marnoch—Queen Cattiga's chief huntsman, son of Lord Seneschal Yvarr, warleader of the Duina Catairna after Cattiga's murder.

Miara—A wizard and friend of Ahjvar's, who died long ago.

Mikki—Moth's demon lover, a *verrbjarn*, or werebear, bear by day and man by night; his father was a Northron sea-raider turned homesteader, his mother a bear demon of the Hardenwald and the guardian of the grave of the devil Vartu.

Mina—A priestess of the Lady.

Moth—A Northern wanderer, wizard, warrior, storyteller; the devil Ulfhild Vartu.

Mother Nabban, Father Nabban—River and mountain, the only gods of the Nabbani empire.

Nasutani—A young Grasslander caravaneer in Kharduin's gang.

Nour—Marakander wizard and caravaneer of the eastern road, brother-in-law of Hadidu, business partner and lover of Kharduin.

Ogada—One of the seven devils, bonded with the Northron wizard Heuslar.

Otokas—A Lissavakaili man, host to the Blackdog before it took Holla-Sayan.

Pakdhala—Name used by the goddess Attalissa as Holla-Sayan's supposed daughter.

Palin—A bard and prince of the Duina Catairna, alleged true father of Deyandara, brother of Queen Cattiga.

Petrimos Barraya—Senator of Marakand, husband of his cousin Elias Barraya, father of Jugurthos; executed in the cages shortly after the earthquake.

Praitanna—Goddess of the River Praitanna and the Duina Praitanna, one of the seven tribes of Praitan; regarded as the greatest of the seven patron deities of the *duinas*.

Ragnar—A Northron caravan-master, cousin to Guthrun of Kharduin's gang.

Ragnvor—A queen of the Hravningas in the north, long ago, descendant of Hravnmod.

Rahel—A Marakander priestess of the Lady, Beholder of the Face of the Lady, wife of Ashir.

Rasta—The elderly master of a caravanserai in Marakand's suburb, where Gaguush's gang usually puts up.

Sa-Sura—A Nabbani merchant lodged at Master Shenar's caravanserai.

Samra—A Marakander wineshop keeper's daughter, wife of Mansour and mother of Zora.

Sayan—A god of the Sayanbarkash in the Western Grass, Holla-Sayan's god.

Sayyid—A servant in Hadidu's coffeehouse.

Senara—Older lady of a northern region of the Duina Catairna.

Sera—Goddess of Serakallash, a town in the Red Desert on the western caravan road.

Seoyin—A Nabbani man in Kharduin's gang.

Shemal—Young son of Hadidu, nephew of Nour.

Shenar—Master of a caravanserai in Marakand's suburb where Kharduin's gang is lodged.

Shija—A priestess of the Lady, Mistress of the Dance.

Sien-Mor—A wizard from the southern ocean who became the devil Tu'usha; younger sister of Sien-Shava.

Sien-Shava—A wizard from the southern ocean who became the devil Jochiz; older brother of Sien-Mor.

Storm—A bone-horse, a necromantic creation anchored to a horse's skull; Storm appears to have ideas of his own, which a bone-horse should not.

Styrma—Storm's name in Northron.

Syallan—Catairnan shield-bearer to Lord Angress, intended to be champion to Prince Gilru; his illegitimate half-sister on their father's side.

Talfan—A Marakander apothecary, wife of Varro, mother of Jasmel, Ermina, Iris, and an infant daughter.

Tamghat—Name used by the devil Tamghiz Ghatai when he conquered Lissavakail.

Tamghiz—Grasslander chieftain and wizard bonded with the devil Ghatai; onetime husband of Ulfhild; father of Ivah.

Thekla—A Westron woman in Gaguush's gang.

Tihmrose—A Marakander woman in Gaguush's gang.

Tulip—Adjutant (and mistress) of Captain Jugurthos Barraya of the Sunset Gate garrison in Marakand.

Tu'usha—One of the seven devils, called Tu'usha the Restless by the Northron skalds; bonded with the wizard Sien-Mor.

Ulfhild of Hravnsfjall—King's Sword of Hravnmod the Wise and his younger sister; wizard who became the devil Vartu Kingsbane. She, however, maintains she did not murder her brother. Once married to Tamghiz; their children were Maerhild and Oern; see Moth.

Vardar—A man of the Malagru hillfolk in Kharduin's gang.

Varro—A Northron man in Gaguush's gang, married to the apothecary Talfan.

Vartu—One of the seven devils, bonded with the wizard Ulfhild; see Moth.

Viga Forkbeard—One of the first three kings in the north.

Watcher—The apothecary Talfan's watchdog.

Xua—One of the Twenty Families of Marakand.

Yeh-Lin the Beautiful—A Nabbani wizard, courtesan, general, and regent, or possibly empress, depending upon which history you prefer to believe; became the devil Dotemon.

Yselly—A Praitannec bard with whom Deyandara travelled as an unofficial apprentice.

Yvarr—Seneschal of Queen Cattiga of the Duina Catairna, father of Marnoch.

Zavel—A Serakallashi-raised Grasslander in Gaguush's gang.

Zora—A dancer and musician in the temple of Lady, daughter of Mansour, the only survivor of the massacre of the priests of Gurhan.

PROLOGUE

*I*n the days of the first kings in the north, there were seven wizards . . .

Mountains rose into a frost-cold sky, but she lay in a hollow of ash and cinder and broken stone. Fire ringed her, lighting the night. She could not move. The dead did not. Her body had faded and failed; well, she had never felt it was hers, anyway. Even the woman she had been before . . . before she was what she had become, when she was only one, weak and mortal, solitary, that woman had not felt she owned her body. It had never been more than an awkward shroud of flesh, a thing wrapping her, a thing that betrayed her, a thing *he* owned. Since she was a child, she had only lived in it, a prison of hip and breast and smooth brown skin. She had longed to leave it behind, and never dared. He would be hurt if she left him behind, and she mustn't hurt him, ever. He had saved her life when they were children, or he a youth on the edge of manhood and she still a child. The war-canoes came out of the south and the king's palace burned, flames rising from its wide verandas, and the great village burned, all the palm-thatched houses, and the fishermen's huts on the white beach.

Who had they been, she and her brother? Noble or servant, tiller or fisher? She did not remember. She remembered the raiders, the folk of the next island but one southwards, the strange accents, the stone axes. She remembered a man with red feathers in his hair and a gold ring around his neck. She—no, she did not remember that. She would not. She remembered her brother, looking down on her, and a spear standing out from the red-feather man's back. Her brother had not said anything, only flung his own sealskin cape over her nakedness and walked away into the night, but she had followed. They had salvaged a canoe and left, going island to island, sometimes staying, taking service here or there, that chieftain, this queen, that king, but travelling, travelling . . . no one liked her brother to stay long. They did not like his eyes. He doesn't blink enough, a woman had told her once, a wizard who wanted to take her as an apprentice. She didn't even let her brother know the offer had been made. She had known what his answer would be. Her brother warned her against the danger of allowing strangers to falsely try to win her love.

Wizards, royal wizards, they had been, before their king and his queens were slain and his palace burned. Her brother said so, and whether it was truth or lie she did not know. It might have been true. It became that. He learned from every master he found, and took what learning was not given willingly. They had the strength, the two of them together. They took the knowledge to make his strength dreadful. He could have made himself a king, but that wasn't what he wanted. In time they came all the way up the islands to Nabban. Such a vast land, not an island, and beyond it, land and land and no ocean, lands even without water, lands where water stood half the year turned by cold to stone, and still he pulled her on with him, never sated. He would learn more, be more. Always. And she followed. Of course she did. He was all she could call hers.

But now she was dead, or near enough. Flesh had long rotted, and it was over. Now she was her own. She could sleep through the centuries, a conjoined soul bound still in the remnant of a human body, a lace of bones buried in ash and cinder, protected by a fire that never died. The Old Great Gods and the wizards allied with them had thought it a prison as well as a grave when they left her here, bound in spells that they believed the seven devils themselves could not break. And that meant even *he*, who was the strongest of them all, could not come at her. She was . . . her own, as the long years did pass, and she knew peace.

But the bonds of the Old Great Gods failed. Not all at once. Slowly, fretted away by cautious and patient work. First one, then another, ravelled them to nothing and stretched again into renewed life, crawled from the grave, walked the world.

Not she. She did not want the world. She wanted sleep; she wanted forgetting. The wall of flame, which would burn so long as the strange gases roiled in the earth and found vents to the air, was no prison but a safe castle, all her own. Her undying fire would hold her, safe and warm, forever, and the spells that bound her in what could pass for death were spells of sleep and safety, like a lullaby woven over a baby. The little soul of the earth that guarded her, a creature of fire, a demon whom she knew only as a flicker lizard-like over her mind, was all the companion she needed. It never spoke.

Her brother called her.

She did not answer. She would not wake. He could not reach her here, safe behind her wall, behind flame born of earth and lightning, of deep and secret wells. Like a little child, she curled her soul-self up small and still, trying to be invisible, intangible. She was dead, but not dead enough. He had found her.

One day, he was there amid the broken mountains, standing on the edge of her flame.

Come, he said, and when she pretended she was not there, he dragged the chains of the Old Great Gods from her interwoven double soul, from her bones, and forced flesh to those bones again, shaping her, not as she had been, not the woman she had grown into, but the girl of the islands, the little sister.

Open your eyes, he ordered. *See me. Come with me. We are betrayed.*

The little demon of the fire flung its flames about him, trying to keep her, to defend her as no one ever had—her gaoler, warder, companion of centuries. Her brother snarled and burned into flame himself, golden, brilliant, furious. He tore down the walls, found the demon's heart, the heart of the flame, and crushed it, reached for her—

Her flames. Her guardian. Her castle of peace. Her abhorred body woke and stirred, and she sang the names of cold at him, of ice, of the deep black of the sea. *No more. Never again. Never, never, never, never, never . . .*

She had never raised a hand against him, never a word in all the long years. He screamed, drowning, freezing; screamed more in fury than in pain, that she, she of all people, she who belonged to him and him alone, should dare.

And he lashed out. He sang the names of fire, the fire of the forge and the burning mountain, the fire that lay in the secret hearts of stars. Her walls of flame roared hot and white, closed in, a fist clenched upon her, upon new flesh and old bone, upon ancient soul and baffled child. *If not mine,* he screamed, *then whose are you? Then whose, traitor?*

His fire devoured her. She screamed and could not scream, flesh consumed, bone flaking to ash, and she burned, burned. Her souls, soul, two spun into one, fled down and down, following the vents of the flame that had not, in the end, been enough to keep her safe. Down to the deep ways, the hidden, secret ways of the earth, down the chain of the mountains, far beneath their roots. She fled and pain followed, but then between the layers of the stone there was water. It was cold, and kind. It eased the pain of her twofold soul, which had not even bone left to feel. Old water, patient water, it waited for the day it could course free again. Could she become water? Without form belonging to the world to anchor her in the world, she would perish. Suddenly she was afraid. True death, true finality, true oblivion held out the arms she had thought she longed to have enfold her, and she fled them. She tried to shape herself to water and could not, but all unexpected the water opened to hold her, to hide her; in pity and mercy it offered sanctuary, embracing her, and the water said, *Who are you? What are you? Don't fear. Rest here, be safe.*

She saw how she could be safe. She could hide within water. Her brother would not see her; he would not know her; he thought he had killed her. So long as he thought her destroyed, she was safe. So long as he did not come to this place or send eyes to this place, she was safe. The water, the old, patient, mild water, all its wild and its wilderness forgotten, held her as a mother holds her child, offering love and comfort.

But then she realized the truth. She was a small, weak, lost thing, an ember, a guttering light with the great cold darkness reaching to her. So was the water. It was only a reflection of broken light, a whispering echo that had not yet ceased to sound. It was *weak*; this goddess was weak. This deity of the water could not offer shelter or mercy or safety. This was a trap. Her brother would hunt her. He would come, he would . . .

But not if he did not see her. She would make certain he did not see her. He would see water. She could wear water. She could *be* water, within the water's shell, within the shape of water, within, within, within, deeper within, burning, where the heart of water lay . . .

And in the days of the first kings in the north, there were seven devils . . .

The Voice of the Lady of Marakand, the goddess of the deep well, was serving pottage in the public dining hall when the ladle dropped unheeded from her hands. The old man whose bowl she had been filling backed away, nervous.

"Revered?" he asked. He knew who she was, of course. Though the priests and priestesses of the Lady of the Deep Well served, in humility, the poor of the city, feeding any who came to their hall for the evening meal, the white veil over her black hair proclaimed her not merely any priestess but the Lady's chosen, the one who spoke face to face with the shy underground goddess and carried her words from the well. He knew also that she—or the goddess who some-times spoke through her—was occasionally gifted with prophecy.

"Lady?" the Voice whispered. Her eyes fixed on the old man, wide and black. He backed farther away, looking around, and the queue shuffling along the serving table, taking bread and pottage and sweet well-water from the hands of saffron-robed priests and priestesses, bunched in confusion behind him. "Where—? Lady? Lady!"

"Revered one," he whispered hoarsely to a young priest hurrying up, a sweating pitcher of water in each hand. "Revered one, I think . . . I think the Voice has need of you."

"Lilace?" asked another priestess. "What is it? Are you ill?"

The Voice flung up her arms before her face as if to shield it, shrieking, and then turned her hands, clawing at her own cheeks. "No!" she cried. "No! No! No! Out! Get out! It hurts! It hurts! It burns!"

"Voice!" cried the young priest, and he dropped the pitchers, spilling the sacred water, to lunge across the table for her wrists.

"Death! Not like this! No!"

Priests and priestesses clustered around.

"Lilace, hush! Not here! And who is dead?"

"Stand away from her, you people."

"Give us room here."

"Go to the benches, sit down, out of the way."

But the line of charity-seekers did not disperse, of course. They pressed in about the clerics, those at the front staring and silent, those at the back clamouring to know what was happening.

"The Voice prophesies."

"What does she say?"

"A fit, she's having a fit."

"My brother has fits. You should lay her down on her side . . ."

"Away, away!" The Right Hand of the Lady pushed through, Revered Ashir, a youngish man for his high office, but balding, easy to take for older. He elbowed the other priest aside and leaned over the table to shake the Voice, which did no good, and then to slap her, which drew shocked murmurs and hissings of breath from those around, but likewise achieved nothing useful. The priestess who had been serving the bread wrestled Revered Lilace from behind, trying to force her arms down, but she could not overcome the Voice's frenzied strength. Lilace's nails grew red with her own blood; she turned on the priestess who held her, raking that woman's face. The Right Hand cursed irreligiously and scrambled over the table, but the Voice, breaking away from his snatching hands, fled, the white veil of her office floating behind her.

"Lilace—Revered Voice!" Ashir gave chase, leaving others to look to the injured woman. "Lilace, what did you see?"

The entrance to the well was covered by a squat, square, domed building of many pillars, the double doors in the entry porch carved and painted with flowering trees. The Voice reached it before the Right Hand and fled within, down the stairs, not stopping to light a torch at the carefully tended lamp, down into cool, moist air, where the walls were carved from the layers of living rock and the stone sweated. The stairs ended at a dark, still reservoir.

"Lady!" Ashir heard her wail as her feet splashed into the water. "Lady, come to me!"

The earth heaved. The earthquake tossed Marakand like a householder shaking dirt off a rug.

It was three days before the survivors of the Lady's temple thought to dig out the entrance to the deep well, to recover their Right Hand and their Voice. Revered Ashir was alive, though weak with hunger. The dome of the well-house had stood firm; only the porch had fallen in the earthquake, blocking the door.

The Voice, however, rocked and muttered, playing with her fingers like a baby, as she had, Ashir said, ever since he dragged her out of the heaving surface of the sacred pool onto the stairs. Her eyes focused on nothing, blank as stones, but she spoke as they carried her to the hospice, which, by chance or the Lady's grace, was the least damaged of the temple buildings other than the well-house.

"Let all the wizards of the temple go to the Lady in her well. She calls them. She calls, she calls, she calls, let them go now, they must go now, make haste, haste, haste, haste, she calls . . . Let the wizards of the library be summoned to her, let the wizards of the city be brought before her, she has need of them, she will have them, she must—they must—No, no, no, no . . ."

In the end they drugged Revered Lilace into sleep to silence her, and prayed for her. The several priests and priestesses who were wizards, the one weakly wizard-talented of the temple dancers, and a son of the Arrac-Nourril, who, being devout, had come to help dig out the temple's survivors rather than those in his own ward, answered the summons at once. All went down the steps of the deep well to face their goddess.

None came back. Not that day. Nor the next, as Revered Rahel sent messengers out to the city and the undamaged caravanserai suburb north and west of the city walls with the summons. Hearing that the Voice summoned wizards in the Lady's name, they came, scholars from the library, both native-born and foreign visitors, scruffy outlander rovers from the caravans, wizards in the service of the Families or soothsayers from the nearby villages of the hillfolk of the Malagru and the silver-mines of the Pillars of the Sky. Some thought it meant a paid commission, involvement in rebuilding and restoration; some for pity and mercy, wanting to use what skills they had to bring aid to the stricken city.

None came back from the deep well.

And after that, two of the three gods of Marakand fell silent, and there was only the Lady of the Deep Well, and the Voice of the Lady to speak her will.

PART ONE

CHAPTER I

The assassin's house was reached by a mud path up along the cliffs from the village; Deyandara, who had been calling herself a bard outright since she left the Duina Catairna two months before, found it by asking a young widow. Not that she asked for the assassin. A mercenary, she said, as she had through all her wanderings. Ahjvar, by name, called the Leopard, a lordless spear for hire, who dwelt somewhere on the coast, at a place called Sand Cove. She had wandered long through what her own folk called the Tributary Lands, where the folk looked like Praitannec folk but spoke a language that was half the bastard Nabbani of the Five Cities and, though they lived under little chieftains of their own tribes, owed allegiance and paid tribute to this city or that. Sand Cove, in either language, was unheard of, though once she reached the south she had been helpfully directed to both Sandy Bottom and Sandy Creek, in the green lands between Two Hills and Gold Harbour. Neither sheltered the Leopard under any guise she could penetrate. He wouldn't be calling himself an assassin; they had law, in the cities, though it wasn't the law of the kings. Everyone knew that such killers for hire flourished, that the lords of the cities hardly dared trust their own kin and harboured assassins among their own household folk, but even so, such a man would hardly deck himself in whatever the assassin's equivalent of the bard's ribbons were, to proclaim his trade.

But finally, south of Gold Harbour, when she was near despairing of ever finding the place she sought, Deyandara met a shepherd who had heard of Sand Cove and then encountered a donkey-cart of seaweed driven by an old man—she never did find out where the seaweed was going or why—and was set on the right path. And finally, the place itself, round, stone-walled, thatched houses that looked almost homelike, a muddy lane meandering through, and a helpful inhabitant.

"Master Ahjvar from the inland hills? Is that the man you mean? But he's no mercenary. He's a man of law, I think. Of course I know him. I send one of the little ones up there every morning with bread and milk." The woman left off her task of spreading laundry to dry over the wall of her yard and propped a haunch on the stones instead, ready to gossip. "He's always being called into the cities by the clan-fathers there, the great lords and ladies. And he has a book of the law, a fat scroll. He showed the headman once, when there was a quarrel between him and his sister over their mother's inheritance. Master Ahjvar settled it fairly and they're good friends again. A wise man, and a kind one."

"I thought he was a fighting man."

The widow frowned. "Oh, no, Master Ahjvar's not that. A peaceful man, and a quiet neighbour. But maybe he's not the Ahjvar you're looking for."

A name of the eastern desert, belonging neither to Praitan nor the Tributary Lands nor the cities themselves; it was hardly common. "He lives in a ruin, I was told—" Had she been told that? She didn't remember it, if so. It unfurled in her mind like a memory only now. "On the cliff, near Sand Cove in the south, on the sea."

The widow—she had already introduced herself as such, as if it were a title, Widow Akay—laughed. "He's on a cliff, that's true enough. And this is Sand Cove. Master Ahjvar has been living in that ruin on the headland to the west there, oh, it seems years now. Since before my husband died, anyway. Just him alone, and now the boy, too."

"What boy? I didn't hear he had a child."

"Ghu, of course. Not his son, at least, I don't think he is. A city boy, a Nabbani. He came along a few years ago to do for Master Ahjvar, you know, look after his horses, cook his meals." A smile touched the widow's lips. "Maybe he's something more. We all thought it a pity Master Ahjvar didn't marry. The sea takes so many men, you know. But wherever he came from, anyone can see they're fond of one another, and the boy's been good for him. Master Ahjvar was—well, he didn't look after himself properly, didn't think about regular meals. You know what men are like when they live alone. Now that the boy's there, he does whatever it is lords can't do for themselves, and Master Ahjvar's the better for it, even if young Ghu is a bit short in his wits. I can't see there's any harm in his being simple, myself, so long as his master treats him fairly, and Master Ahjvar's not a man to hurt the innocent. A quick wit's more likely to grow restless and discontent, when the Old Great Gods' doom for you is nothing but a spade and stewing-kettle, now, isn't it?"

Deyandara smiled, consolingly, she hoped, as one who had never had to face that fate. "Master Ahjvar's a lord? Of where?"

A godless man could not be a lord of anywhere, not among the tribes of Praitan, surely not even among the tribes of the Tributary Lands. And godless he was. The goddess of the Duina Catairna had told her so.

"Where from? That I couldn't tell you. He's never said as much, but we all know. He has that air about him. The north, maybe, by his speech. Praitannec. Maybe you'd know better than I?"

Deyandara shook her head. "He might be the man I'm seeking. He might not be." But he had to be.

"You're a bard, mistress?"

A question asked for mere courtesy, to introduce the topic, with the bard's ribbons garlanded around her brow and fluttering down behind, and the komuz at her shoulder. Deyandara's bow was wrapped and slung behind the saddle, the muddy leathers she wore when she was not about to enter a village cleaned and bundled away. This close to the cities, the tribes were peaceful, and a bard could not afford to look like a straying hunter.

"You'll be coming back when your errand's done? The smith's our headman, and his wife keeps the tavern. Travellers always have a good welcome from them. You'll be heading inland to the chief's hall, of course, but stay a night here, first. If you go to the smithy and ask . . ."

"Tell them I'll be back by this afternoon, then, if not before." Or else she'd have the whole village trooping up to Master Ahjvar's to make sure she didn't escape them. That she was a bard was a lie, of course, but wearing the ribbons seemed safer than not. Still, the woman should have questioned it. Or was she so worn by the road that she looked old enough to be what she claimed?

It was simple ignorance on the widow's part of what it really meant to be a bard, that was all; there were few left among the tribes of the Tributary Lands. They took their news from tramp pedlars and drovers and entertainers from the city, their stories from play-actors and puppeteers. Nabbani stories. These here were a lost folk who had forgotten their own tales. Deyandara's tutor Lin, no bard but a foreign wizard, had said so. She had given Deyandara old stories of the southlands of Over-Malagru, stories from before the colonies were ever planted, from the days when the tribes had had kings and paid tribute to no overlord, from even more ancient times, from the great years of peace under the emperor of Marakand, and back and back, to when the summer rains were frequent and kind, and the forest stretched all the way to the coast and the folk, using only axes of stone, cleared lands in the river bottoms, worshipping the goddesses of the waters. They had feared the darkness under the oaks and burnt the hills of the gods to make new pastures . . . Deyandara might not believe all the tales, but she had drunk them in.

She would give this folk some of those stories back, when her errand to Master Ahjvar was done. And they would not understand it was their own history, and the hill overlooking the bay at Gold Harbour a stronghold from which a queen had ridden to battle and defeat and death, hacked to pieces on the plain of the Yellow Stone, which was now lost under the city of Gold Harbour.

Perhaps whatever god cared for this folk saw no point in keeping old stories alive. Better they dwindled into a peasantry, tilling their fields and guarding their herds and no longer dreaming of past glory, which would serve only to stir up the young and the rash to no good end. Not all the villages of the Tributary Lands were free and governed by free headmen under a chief of the tribe. Nearer the colony-cities, manors engulfed the village fields in walls and legalities, and the folk paid rent to work the lands that had once been held of god and king alone, or traded labour in the vast vineyards and olive groves and wheatfields of the city clans' estates for the right to feed themselves by tilling a scrap of land they did not even own. She had seen it for herself. The kings and the blood of the kings were gone in this land, gone to ash and smoke, forgotten, and the gods diminished, withdrawn, defeated, some even forgotten by their folk, who made their prayers to the gods of the cities, grown in grandeur, adapted to the ways of their new folk. Lady Lin, her tutor, had told her that gods, bound to their hills and waters, unable to flee, must do so when war swept over their lands and their kings failed them.

As Queen Cattiga had failed the goddess Catairanach of the spring of the mountain ash and the tribe called the Duina Catairna in the north? Surely not; to die a victim of murder was not failure. Even the abandonment of the *dinaz*, the royal hill-fort, was not failure but a tactical retreat on the part of her bench-companions. In the hills, they could not be pinned down. Lord Seneschal Yvarr and Marnoch, his son, could not be said to have failed the goddess, not unless and until they surrendered, which Deyandara was sure they would not do. And Catairanach had no intention of relinquishing her folk's freedom without action, un-Praitannec though that action was.

Deyandara gave the widow a Two Hills fish-copper in thanks, mounted her pony again, called Badger from his gossiping with the widow's bitch, and turned to the path that left the fields and groves of the village to climb the rising downland towards the ruin on the cliff. Two miles, she made it. Not a sociable man. A long walk for a child with a jug and basket.

In her own land, Praitan of the two rivers, of the seven *duinas*, the seven tribes and seven kings, part of a bard's duty was to remember and carry messages between the kings of the tribes, but she had never heard of anyone taking a message for a god before. Certainly not such a message, and not to such a man.

The track seemed nothing more than a sheep-path, plodding between hummocks of wiry grass and mats of fragrant thyme and lavender and rue, over patches where the wind had blown the very soil away, rock bare and slippery, fissures opening into mysterious depths. It wound without apparent purpose. Always, though, Deyandara was exposed to the gaze of the ruin on the headland, which was surely only a few more years of gnawing storm from becoming an island. Lin had taught her to look at the very earth that way, as not fixed and immutable but a thing in flux, like the lives of men and their tribes.

She left a stone shed and a thorn-hedged field on her right, inland. Three sleek horses watched her, white and piebald and lion-hued. Looking at the way ahead, she tied her own bay pony to a branch of the thorn, dwarfed and bent by the wind, told Badger to stay there on guard—a whistle would bring the big mastiff running to her defence—and went on foot. The path forked, onwards along the cliff and, her way, out, abruptly down and up again, across the narrow stem of stone that was all that connected the peninsula of the ruin to the mainland. Below her, waves crashed and threw white spume into the air.

Deyandara did not like heights. Wind and heights were worse. It was no comfort that the neck of land was a clear three yards across and that, so long as she kept to the well-trodden track in the middle, she could not trip and plunge to her death without a running start.

"Andara guide my feet," she muttered. She clutched the amulet-pouch on its thong under her shirt, as if the touch could run from the little carved thorn-wood disc away to the god on the Gayl Andara, the hill that rose higher even than the hill of her brother's hall. Then, self-conscious, she let it go. A bard was a free-comer to all Praitans, sacred; that was as true among the folk of the Tributary Lands and the lands west beyond the Malagru as it was among her own folk. And she was on a god's errand. No godless outcast murderer who sold himself to the merchant-lords of the Five Cities was going to see her cringing.

But she did not like heights.

Her bravado was wasted, anyway. No one hailed her. No one

watched. She flicked her braids over her shoulders, made sure her ribbons were secure against the wind, and walked on.

The ruin was fenced with a drystone wall, itself fallen into ruin. Someone had filled the gaps with dead thorn boughs. The servant was hoeing weeds. He only straightened up to watch Deyandara when she coughed, politely—though perhaps he had been watching her crossing, as she stared at her feet, shuffling. She wiped a slick of sweat from her upper lip and pretended it was sea-spray, wishing she could sit down. At any rate, the boy did not seem startled to see her, but gazed with as little reaction as the hens scratching about his feet. His thick black hair was short and shaggy, and his narrow eyes, too, were black, his skin a golden brown. He looked Nabbani, as the widow had said, not colony Nabbani but someone new-come from the empire, without a grandparent from the Tributary Lands to give him height and a sterner nose. He was slightly built, with high cheekbones. Quite . . . good-looking, really. Not quite all there, the widow claimed, and yet . . . what made her think so? There was none of the deformity of face, the slack mouth or dull eyes, to warn of it.

Something was missing, though. She couldn't put her finger on what. He seemed a child, in the open innocence of his gaze, but when she looked carefully, she realized he was older than she by several years, a man and not a boy at all, for all his hairless chin.

"I'm Deyandara of the Duina Andara," she said. "I bear a message for Ahjvar the Leopard of Sand Cove, if this is his dwelling." And she repeated herself in the Nabbani of the cities, what they called trade Nabbani or bastard Nabbani; it slid half into a bastard Praitannec and was the usual speech of the Tributary Lands.

He replied with a bow and a soft-voiced "Master Ahjvar's down on the shore" in trade Nabbani. "He'll be back soon."

He bent to his hoe again and did not offer to show her in or even open the gate to her.

She didn't see a gate to open. One of the thorn-blocked gaps, probably. Deyandara shrugged and seated herself on the wall. She could hear the waves below, like the ocean's breath over the stones. She had no desire to go and look.

Half a dozen speckled hens and a clutch of chickens, in that motley half-fuzz, half-pinfeathers stage, followed the boy's hoe between the young cabbages and onions, clucking with satisfaction over turned-up grubs, while the red rooster eyed her warily from a wind-ragged plum tree. A peasant's garden, a peasant's morning. When the boy straightened up, looking towards the sea, Deyandara turned, though she had heard nothing, in time to see the man appear over the edge of the cliff.

There must be some path there, climbing down. He paused, a shaggy, unbraided head of brass-gold hair that made her think of nothing so much as a lion's mane, gold hoops in his ears, low, straight eyebrows shielding pale-blue eyes, deep-set and startlingly bright against the oak-tan brown of his skin, the sort of eyes that could make a girl forget she had promised her brother to live a chaste and virtuous life if he let her go to the road for a season . . . No. Not this man. Nothing of warmth and playfulness there, as remote as his servant's gaze and not nearly so gentle. His beard needed trimming. He wore a grubby tunic of chequered white and brown and carried a wood-tined fork over his shoulder. If you disregarded the earrings that marked him a man of modest wealth, he looked, in fact, neither lord nor lawyer nor assassin—save for the bleak, winter-sky eyes, so rare among even those light-haired Praitans—but some villager returning, mud-spattered, from his fields.

"Master Ahjvar?" Deyandara rose and bowed. "I'm—" But the

boy Ghu was speaking rapid and unintelligible Imperial Nabbani. She caught her own name and, in Praitannec, "leopard"; that was all.

The man answered in the same tongue. No peasant, indeed. The widow's tale of his being a man of law became more plausible, as who but a scholar of the Five Cities spoke Imperial Nabbani outside of the empire?

"I'm—" she began again, when the boy's introduction or explanation had ended and they were both regarding her steadily, as if waiting, without any great faith, for wonders.

"Lady Deyandara, of the Duina Andara," the man interrupted. "High King Durandau's sister, I take it? And travelling alone? I'm Ahjvar, yes, called the Leopard in the Five Cities, these days. What does the high king want of me? Is his champion and the law of the kings not enough now to keep the peace of the kings?"

She bristled. "My brother has no need of—of your sort."

And she had not given the boy any title. Master Ahjvar was Praitannec enough to know that only a child of the royal house would be named for the god. He simply guessed she was . . . herself. Everyone knew the high king had four younger brothers and only the one sister. Speculation as to which king or heir she might marry had circulated around the tribes ever since Durandau's election to the high kingship three years before. Her name was known to those who took an interest in the shifts of power among the tribes, which even a Five Cities assassin might, as it could affect trade, and that certainly affected the clan-fathers. That was Lady Lin's teaching, making her see the whole branching tangle. She didn't want to have to think about such things. She should have called herself Yselly, as she had on her way south, appropriating the dead bard's name along with her right to the ribbons.

Deyandara tried again, more courteously. "The high king wants nothing of you, Master Ahjvar." She wouldn't call him lord without better proof than a foreign peasant-woman's guess. "My errand to you is from Catairanach of the Avain Catairna, the goddess of the Duina Catairna."

"I know who Catairanach is," he said, mildly enough, but his voice was ice. "And I've no interest in any words from that goddess or that folk. So you can be off."

He came the last way up the cliff, revealing muscular bare legs, black nearly to the knee with mud, and a wooden pail.

"My lord—" That slipped out without her intending. "I gave my word to carry the message."

"Consider it carried." He climbed over the wall. "Now go away. Ghu, is there milk today? We can make a chowder."

The boy spoke in Imperial again and seemed to find whatever he said amusing as he took the pail. The assassin ripped up a fistful of grass to wipe down his legs, scrubbing his hands on the skirt of his tunic after, running still-muddy hands through his hair, defying her to comment. When it seemed he was going to follow the boy into the house without another word to her, Deyandara slid down off the wall into the garden herself.

He heard the movement and turned, swift and balanced and . . . yes, she did think leopard suited. Her heart beating a little too rapidly, she bowed, which she shouldn't have done, since he knew who she was and no princess should be bowing to a lordless exile. "I gave my word to deliver the message."

He said something. It sounded obscene, but Nabbani, so the fact that she could pick out the name of the goddess Catairanach did not need to offend her. "Come in, then, and say your piece."

He ushered her in ahead of him with mocking courtesy. The ruin had no door, only a curtain of hide. She had sheltered in such places before. One of those grand halls built without mortar, in form like a giant stone beehive, which dotted the high places of all the lands Over-Malagru, abandoned, except maybe as shelters for straying cattle or wandering tramps, long before the first colonists came from Imperial Nabban to claim the coast, or so her tutor had said. They mostly stood open to the sky. This one had been inexpertly re-roofed with poles and turf. Even to Deyandara's eye, not used to troubling about such things, it seemed likely to let in wind and rain in equal measure, and probably to come down in a mess of beams and mud in some spring gale.

It didn't look like a home, only a place to camp, despite the hens and the garden.

Ahjvar left her standing and flung himself onto a block of stone with a striped rug thrown over it, part of the wall that had fallen, but he made it look like a throne. A sword, unsheathed, leaned against the wall. A fire burned on a central hearth. The boy squatted beside it, prying the big white clams open with a crook-bladed forage-knife, a peasant's tool. He left off and brought Deyandara a beaker of water from a jar in the corner, courtesy his master hadn't offered. She thanked him and drank, as he went back to his cookery.

Neither man asked her to sit.

Walls thrust inward, dividing the place into dark bays, though there was better light than she would have expected in the open central room, due to a hole in the roof, which might have been for the smoke or might have something to do with a heap of muddy grassroots on the floor.

"Two months ago," she began, "I was in the Duina Catairna, when Queen Cattiga died . . ."

The queen gave a little grunt, almost a mew, and her eyes, meeting Deyandara's across the fire, went wide. Deyandara felt the fumbling, the notes gone wrong, as if her fingers understood before she did. Cattiga, in her great chair draped with a black bull's hide, stared, open-mouthed. Deyandara slung her komuz to her shoulder by its leather strap—she couldn't say why, except an instinct not to drop it—and rose to her feet, mouth open like a mirror to Cattiga's. The queen's chief bard and his daughter Gelyn both trailed off their own playing, a squawk of flute and a soft dying of the great harp, turning to her, then to see where she stared, the shout—or would it be shriek?—still rising in her throat. The queen's champion, Lord Angress, had his sword singing free before Deyandara made a sound, before the queen had begun to slump, the dark flood spreading down her blue and white tunic.

The red-armoured, red-masked priest beside her, courtesy guard to the yellow-robed one who had been bending a knee to speak, the queen leaning forward a little to hear, straightened up. She—a slight thing, so probably she, though the shirt of lacquered scales and the triple-crested helmet with its narrow eyeslits flattened or hid any feature that might say—still held the long, slender dagger an ambassador should not have been carrying in the hall. The yellow priest sprang away, back against the wall, as the champion's sword came around in a swing that should have taken the Red Mask's head.

It did not. The red priest staggered aside, and there was a flare of the firelight so that it seemed her body was outlined for a moment in flame. She punched Lord Angress in the chest with the staff of office the Red Masks all carried, a two-foot-long, carved, whitened rod. It should not have been allowed, but the staff was a sign of their service, their oaths, their honour, and Cattiga, against Lord Angress's advice, had permitted it.

The champion seemed to have been struck with a fist of lightning. White sparks and spiderwebs crackled; there was a stink of smoke, and he dropped.

Gilru, the prince, a brat of nine or ten, red-haired and freckled, had been by Deyandara's feet. Probably considering his chances of tying her bootlaces together. He shouted—she could never afterwards recall the words—and flung himself away around the hearth, running to his mother even as Deyandara grabbed for him. After that it was all swords and spears and shouting, taller, broader people between her and the queen and the boy she was still trying to reach, and the fire gone mad, leaping and twisting and then dying away to embers and choking smoke as if someone had smothered it in wet straw. Lord Marnoch, chief huntsman and the seneschal's son, came down the stairs from the upper room with an axe in his hands and felled two yellow priests before he himself was laid low by a glancing blow from a Red Mask's white staff, something that hit his axe-haft, not his body. One of his own hunters stumbled on him, was struck across her shoulders, and did not get up. The lamps on the posts that supported the upper storey, an enclosed loft, went out then. In the darkness someone's elbow struck Deyandara's chin and she fell.

"Gilru!" she heard Syallan screaming. The champion's shield-bearer was a young woman some few years older than Deyandara, everything Deyandara was not—she didn't tell the assassin that—handsome, skilled, respected and honoured in the hall even though she was the bastard-born daughter of the queen's late husband—loved.

And what followed . . . *Dim light from the embers on the hearth, painting everything in faded red and shadow. Someone trod on Deyandara's hand as she tried to reach Syallan's voice, to be what aid she could to the prince, and then a trampling foot struck her head. Sick and momentarily blind, she grabbed it, heaved, and the man fell on her. He was one of the queen's bench-companions, and as he rolled away a Marakander temple guardsman stabbed down with a Praitannec spear, and the man grunted and spewed blood over her. She didn't dare move, face to face with the dying man, whose eyes, surely, looked beyond her and did not accuse, please, Andara, she hadn't meant—Great Gods forgive her, it wasn't her fault, everything she did went twisted, but that didn't mean she was cursed, it did not.*

One of the queen's household, slain, fell beside her; that was what she told the Leopard, who had his eyes shut, as if he saw the hall and the smouldering light and the dying men and women there. Deyandara had snatched the dead warrior's dagger from his hand—she was lying on her own—and come up onto her knees, driving the long blade upwards with both hands into the Marakander temple guard's back ribs under his short shirt of lacquered scales. He had tried to look around at her and come down on top of her, coughing and bubbling, spitting blood onto her face. His helmeted head had struck hers, a last savage blow at his enemy as he died or plain ill-chance. That second blow to the head had been one too many, and that was all Deyandara had seen of the battle in Cattiga's hall.

By some miracle, her komuz had survived unharmed.

Gilru and Syallan they found in the morning, hacked down in the yard as they tried to flee, the young warrior's body still lying over the boy's, protecting him. It had not been enough against the axes.

And the Marakanders, the red priests and the yellow and the temple guardsmen who had escorted them, were all fled, those that lived. Of yellow priests and guards they had bodies enough, but not a single one of the mute Red Masks seemed to have fallen. The tales of the road called them divinely protected, of course, but no one had thought that was more than poetry.

"Gilru was the youngest son," the Leopard said, opening his eyes again. He didn't seem moved by the tale in the least, now; his voice was quiet, soft, even, as if he feared waking some sleeping child. "What of the older boy, and the daughter?"

He knew the *duina* so well?

"The queen's elder son and only daughter both died last autumn, and her husband and—and her brother as well. The bloody pox, the southern pox." She had the scars herself, scattered white over cheeks and forehead and hands, from an earlier, less deadly outbreak of the eastern pox when she was a child. One could save you from the other. Somehow it was always the bleeding southern pox, which came with the ships from the sea beyond the Gulf of Taren and was almost always fatal, that broke out in the Duina Catairna. "There was a tide of it last year, flowing up the river valleys from the Five Cities, it's said." But he'd know that, living so close, though neither he nor his boy bore the scars of it. "All of the queen's near kinsfolk died. People believe they're an ill-fated family. An ill-fated folk. Every plague, every murrain, every slow cold spring or summer of drought hits them hardest. The old song says, 'A broken branch, a twisted root, and poison in the vein.'" This was how Mistress Yselly would have given the message, anyway, casting in scraps of song, embroidering a great vision in words, but Deyandara wished she had not said it as soon as the words were spoken. The tale of the curse on the royal blood of the Duina Catairna and on the folk itself couldn't be true, because if it were, it meant . . . it couldn't.

What if she were a plague herself and had somehow brought doom to Cattiga and Gilru and all their folk? No. Because if she were cursed, so were they in their own right.

"It came on the ships, last summer," the man offered. "Some captain bribed the harbour-master to clear them out of the quarantine, call something the four-day fever that wasn't." He frowned, and apparently not at that criminal failure in honour and duty. "These priests murdered the queen and her son, and the folk of the hall let them get away? What were Marakander priests doing in the hall, anyway? And armed?"

She did not like the way he sat now, so still, hands fisted on his thighs. She was reminded of that staring frozen stillness that could snap like a string over-tuned and become the snarling, spitting, ripping blur of a catfight.

"They came as an embassy, seeking alliance—so they said, for the benefit of the tribe and Marakand both. The queen and her council welcomed this."

"Fools," Ahjvar said mildly. The boy shook his head. Ahjvar shrugged, and Deyandara was left feeling that there had been some whole conversation in that. The Leopard took up the sword and a bit of oily fleece. He didn't watch her any longer but stretched out his legs, ankles crossed, and frowned over the blade, polishing at flecks she could not see, if they were there at all. Long, strong, brown fingers. The blade had a dappled pattern in the steel, which caught the firelight. Northron work; they were the only ones who made blades with such patterns enfolded in the very fabric of the metal, a demon's art they had brought over the western sea, and a secret jealously guarded by their swordsmiths. Her brother had a Northron-bladed sword, inherited from his father. Even the hilt of the Leopard's looked antique, though, made her brother's look like some merchant's showpiece, no life in it. On Ahjvar's, the grip was carved ivory, a twisted animal-form gone creamy brown with age and . . . stained.

He raised his eyebrows, waiting, and she pulled her gaze from the sword. The pommel was an animal's snarling head, cast bronze dull and smooth, with traces of worn gilding still caught in the fine detailing. A sword for a story, if she could find one it suited . . .

The boy had finished with the clams, setting them in a wide

pot with butter and milk on the edge of the fire. The smell turned her stomach. Now he sat, arms wrapped around his knees, listening wide-eyed, as if it were a tale told for fireside pleasure.

The huntsmen of the *dinaz* turned scout and pursued the assassins. Deyandara stumbled over the word, but Ahjvar didn't react. As if some other will opposed Marnoch and his scouts, opposed what should surely be Catairanach's blessing on their hunt, they lost the enemy in the night, in fog and dark-lashing rain. And then they found the army.

Overrunning the little unwalled settlements in its path, an army of Marakand was coming straight up from the caravan road, following the well-trodden track that skirted the butt end of the hills. The folk, the lucky ones, scattered into the hills with what they could carry and drive before them, while the laggards died amid the looting and the thatch burned. The invading army travelled light, without wagons to slow and mire it in the winter mud. The largest part of the force consisted of warriors of the Great Grass and the deserts, mounted on good horses and camels; a much smaller company were priest-led Marakanders, not so able in the saddle or at travelling cross-country, easy prey. There were twenty or thirty Red Masks. It was not so large an army as all that, sixty-score, a hundred-score—both estimates swore they had lain in hiding to count, so whether one was in error or whether it had divided, and when and where the other part was, no one reported, but either way it was large enough to threaten the *dinaz*, especially in the wake of last autumn's plague, which had killed so many. If all the spearmen of all the lords could be summoned in time . . . they could not.

They lit the hill-beacons, but of course there was no time for the lords of the outlying regions to come down the valleys and over the hills with their warriors. Dinaz Catairna was only a day's hard ride on a good horse from the caravan road, and though the Marakanders weren't advancing quite so swiftly, they were not dallying over-long at their looting, either. Deyandara was sick with headaches, throwing up whenever she moved too quickly, though the queen's physician said her skull was sound and she had taken no permanent harm. She had strange dreams, of the Avain Praitanna, the western of the two rivers of Praitan, rising in flood and carrying her away; of drowning in a bog, a great weight on her; of a burning roof falling in on her while she screamed and beat at someone she could not see, who held her down by the wrists and shrieked with laughter. Fever, Lord Yvarr told her.

The assassin stirred restlessly. Yes, this wasn't meant to be her story.

There had been no warning from Catairanach their goddess. Her spring on the hillside, where the clear water welled up into a pool of mossy stones overhung by three mountain ash trees, still naked and winter-grey, was troubled, cloudy with sand. When Yvarr knelt on the flat stone where the kings stood to call her, there was no answer but a skirl of wind and a spatter of rain, like tears, from an unclouded sky.

"Nothing but tears," he reported back to the old bard in the hall.

"A goddess may mourn as much as a man," the bard said.

"But we need her. If men crawled away and hid in their grief, the world would soon fall to ruin. If she would speak to someone, anyone . . ."

Marnoch was appointed war-leader, in default of any other, before the lords could begin quarrelling over that right. He led out a war-band to nip at the army's heels, test them, harry them in the twilight and by night. He didn't have the force to meet them in the open. Before long he was falling back on the *dinaz*, though they still made harrying attacks on the Marakander camp in the dawn and dusk, and few of the enemy scouts got far when they left the protection of their main body. But he could not hold up the advancing Marakanders for long. The nearby lords who answered the summons of the beacons had come with the bare minimum of spears, thinking it no more than a raid out of the Tributary Lands south of the road.

Who went to war now, in the cold rains of the lambing season?

A city folk. Mercenaries, with no land and no god.

And the Duina Broasoran to their east would not come to their aid, would not set old quarrels aside and stand together as Praitans should. Yvarr sent a messenger, but without much hope. There was outstanding between them the matter of a raiding party led by Queen Cattiga's late brother, he who had died last autumn of the southern pox, and a woman of the Broasorans carried off from her husband, who was kin to the Broasoran queen. The Catairnans said it had been elopement, the woman a willing conspirator, but folk of the husband's household had died in the pursuit, and the woman had died of the southern pox as well, so there was blood between them, and they had not agreed on asking a wizard to divine for the truth, neither tribe trusting the divination of the other.

If truth be told, they had expected either a demand for a combat of champions or outright war with the Broasorans to follow the lambing and spring planting. That did not mean they were ready for Marakand; maybe it was the threat of the Duina Broasoran that had led Cattiga to listen when the Marakander priests falsely spoke of alliance.

Lord Yvarr sent couriers bearing messages, pleas, to the high king in Dinaz Andara as well, but that was a ride of many days. Dinaz Andara lay east and north, between the two great rivers of Praitan, the Avain Praitanna and the Avain Noreia, and quite far north of the caravan road that was the southern boundary of Praitannec lands. Deyandara signed them, as Yvarr asked, and then she went away to the queen's bower, a separate, stone-walled building, hung with tapestries from the distant east, where it was quiet. There she carried on turning words, discarding words, making a song of the death of Cattiga and Gilru. But they fell stiff and leaden, never the ring of true silver. She was not a poet. She thought she never would be, and there was an ache in her heart for that lack in herself, heavy as the weight of Cattiga's death.

What followed was her own story. She did not need to tell the assassin how, when Marnoch returned to the *dinaz*, she, with Badger at her side, met him at the gate, watching as the file of men and a few women threaded their little horses up the twisting path between the earthen banks. They eyed her warily, wearily . . . knowingly. It was late afternoon, and the sun slanted over the hills, touching gorse-flower into golden fire. A few of the lords reined aside, once through the gate in the innermost dyke, the outer face of which had a drystone facing and was topped with wooden pales. They were already preparing to burn all that would burn, including the wooden gates, and flee, not to be penned up here like pigs awaiting slaughter. The lords milled about between the low-eaved roundhouses, as if waiting. Deyandara's stomach had grown tight and sick. She wasn't waiting for them; she had only come to see that Marnoch was safely returned. He rode near the last, muddy and tattered; he would have gone out with the scouts, she knew, war-leader or no. He was a fox of the hills, not a wolf. But maybe a fox was what the folk needed, now. For a moment she had thought that she should tell him so. There was defeat already in his eyes. But he saw her and swung a leg over his horse and came down to fling his arms around her, which startled them both. She pulled away, heart racing, and cursed herself the next moment for the look on his face, gone careful and closed.

"My lady," he said. She had always been Deya, before. "When I left, I feared I'd come back to find you'd joined the dead."

"It was only a knock on the head," she said, and felt the blush burning from her breasts to the roots of her hair. "I'm—I didn't come out here to be in the way. I wanted to see you were safe, you all were safe." Damn her tongue for adding the last.

"Those we didn't leave on the hills," he said. "The Marakanders are close behind. They'll be here tomorrow." He crouched to scratch Badger's ears, and the dog leaned into him, tail stirring welcome. "I should go to my father." He eyed the hovering lords, sought Deyandara's eye, which dropped to her boots; he waved the lords on. They went without a word, though they leaned heads together and whispered.

"We need to talk, lady," Marnoch had said. "You and I and my father."

She nodded, with a sick churning in her stomach that had nothing to do with the headaches that still chased her. She should have ridden with the first couriers sent to her brother, but had been too ill. And now . . . before she died, Queen Cattiga had spoken to Lord Yvarr about Deyandara and what she had sought in the Duina Catairna. Of course she had.

"Once we've started readying the folk to flee to the hills," he said, "we'll talk. The land's lordless; Catairanach can't like that."

She had licked her lips and nodded; he had given her a weary smile and gone away.

It had not been only Yvarr and Marnoch waiting for her in the queen's bower, later. The old bard and his daughter, all the lords and ladies who had answered the beacons, they all stood, waiting, when she came, hesitating in the doorway, a hand on Badger's head for courage.

"Lady," said Yvarr, "we need to know. Are you our—are you kin to our queen?" He looked around, a challenge, but no one disagreed. "All the hall has watched you all the winter, ever since you came in the last of the autumn. All the hall could see it, when you stood by the queen, like enough to be her sister. All the hall," he sighed, "knew Prince Palin, and there have always been rumours out of the Duina Andara. Your mother was sent back to her own people after your birth, was she not?"

And died of a broken heart within a year. Deyandara nodded, took a breath, and looked up.

"I didn't know," she said. "Nobody told me. I was supposed to be a seven-months' baby, though my nurse says I was born fat and hale. But—but if I had been carried the full term, then my father, my mother's husband, was away beyond the river fighting the eastern hillfolk with the Duina Noreia at the time I should have been begotten, and—and the bard Palin was in Dinaz Andara, they say, then." She hadn't dared ask the god the truth; she had been too angry with him, angry at all the hall, at all her kin and the lords who had kept this from her all her life. By the time anger cooled, she was with Yselly in the Duina Galatan, far from Andara's land. And after Yselly died . . . "I came here to ask Prince Palin the truth."

And came too late, on the heels of the bloody pox, to find him dead, and the queen's husband dead, and the queen's two elder children dead, and here she was, the high king's sister, or half-sister, almost claiming to be the queen's niece and next heir after her only surviving child, as if she wanted, as if she hoped . . . but all she had wanted was to know, to understand if that was why her mother's husband, for all he claimed her and gave her a royal name, possibly just to spite her mother, had shoved her out of the way all his life, and taught her brothers to do likewise, to call her clumsy, unlucky, a lodestone for mischance.

Tainted with the curse on the royal blood of the Duina Catairna, she understood now.

"What did Cattiga say of it, lady?" Yvarr asked gently.

She took another steadying breath. "Cattiga said it was all too likely, knowing her brother, but that none other of his bastards had ever survived their first year; they were born sickly and never did thrive. He thought it was the curse and treated it as a blessing, freeing him from responsibility. She put our faces side by side in her mirror and said, 'No one can doubt it.'" Red hair, golden-brown eyes, the dusting of freckles; that was something a score of women within a day's ride might claim. Deyandara had her mother's longer face, darker lashes, but the nose, the chin, the set of her mouth, were all doubled in Cattiga's mirror. "'I don't wish another heir,' the queen said,"—with sorrow in her eyes, because she knew and Deyandara knew that one child was not enough to safeguard her line—"and I said I was not looking to be one, that I wanted only to find my kin, to be—to be among friends." She raised her chin. "So. Yes, she acknowledged me her niece. And no, she did not publicly acknowledge me her next heir after my cousin Gilru. Why should she have? She was still a young woman; she would likely have other children; she knew the need to remarry soon, whatever her grief. I didn't come here for that. I'm a bard's apprentice—" Still that lie. "I'm not of age. I'm no warrior, no wise old woman, I'm not the queen you need."

"But you are the last descendent of King Hyllanim," the seneschal had said.

"A bastard," had been her harsh retort.

"Some," the old bard said, with his fingers touching the strings of his lap-harp, waking no sound, "say that King Hyllanim was likewise."

Silence greeted that. White-haired Lady Senara, lord of a valley in the north of the *duina*, coughed. "Well," she said, "at least his father was *a* king." And she chuckled. Marnoch made a face as if suppressing a smile, but most looked disapproving, blond young Lord Fairu outright shocked. It was not a story in which the folk of the Duina Catairna took any pride. Deyandara didn't much care who Hyllanim's father had been. He was her great-grandfather, and it was a long time ago.

"I don't want to be queen. I'm not fit for it. I wasn't educated for it." She wasn't educated at all, till these last few years after her acknowledged father's death, when her brother Durandau realized he had a pretty and potentially useful tool for alliance-making on his hands, who was running wild as a feral cat about the *dinaz*. He'd inflicted a tutor on her, an elegant and ladylike Nabbani wizard who'd been travelling through the *duina*, and tried too late and all at once to make her a princess of the folk. Letting her have one season travelling with a minor bard of her mother's folk had been a concession he proposed to stop the fights about learning court Nabbani, the accusations that he meant to sell her to some foreign merchant of the eastern desert. Her quarrels with brother and tutor—to herself she admitted she had thrown outright tantrums—had far more to do with the secrets no one would discuss than with any lessons of Lady Lin's. She had never been Mistress Yselly's apprentice.

"There's no one else," Marnoch had said. "Deya—my lady. We need you. We need to be able to summon the lords, the ones who think the *duina* is already lost, the ones who didn't answer the beacons. And Deya, you know the high king as we don't. My father's already sent to him, in the name of the folk, but if we beg aid in your name—will your brother come?"

A good and dutiful and half-educated little sister, who had no idea how to be a queen, and needed counsellors and officers and . . .

"He'll come," she said wearily, and looked around them all. "Even if he won't come to save Catairanach's land from Marakand, he'll come to make me your queen."

After a moment, Yvarr had said, "Lady, you're already our queen." Though that wasn't quite true, not without the approval of the lords and the blessing of the goddess.

After the letters were written and she had signed them, and the messengers who would carry them to Dinaz Andara had come and gone, she had gone herself to where her pony was penned with others of the royal hall, meaning only to check on him and on her gear in the stable, since she would be going wherever Yvarr and Marnoch fled to make their new fastness, no doubt of that, now. But in the dusky twilight of the stable there had been water rushing around her, a wind in her ears . . .

"The night that Lord Marnoch returned," she told the Leopard, "the goddess Catairanach drew me into a waking dream and gave me a message to carry. I seemed to be at her spring below the *dinaz* walls. The boughs of the mountain ash over me were heavy with creamy blossom, and the bees . . ."

"Leave out the bard's embroidery. I know the place. What did Catairanach have to say for herself?"

"She said that the Marakanders dreamed of drowning, and darkness, and storms off the hills in the night, and that their hearts were heavy, but that the Lady was stronger and overwhelmed her."

She stands in water to her waist, though the deepest part of the pool is no

more than knee-high, and the current buffets, threatening to sweep her away.
The eyes of Catairanach are golden-brown like water-covered pebbles in the
sunlight, but her hair, satin-brown like the bark of young twigs, is wild
and twisting and flows into the water, wrapping Deyandara's legs, hobbled
and heavy in a formal gown of blue and white, and the weight of the cloth
threatens to pull her under. "I will have no child of another land rule my*
folk," Catairanach says. "No tool of Andara of the Gayl Andara, no high
king's puppet, bastard blood of my blood or not. I will have revenge on the
ruler of the city who murdered my Cattiga, my sweet Gilru. I see my way and
you will be my messenger, child. You have come lying to this hall, claiming a
bard's rights. Fulfil now a bard's duties . . ."

"She charged me to say—" Catairanach had said more than she
remembered at the time, Deyandara found, when she began. Words
came she had not known she had heard. "She told me to travel to Sand
Cove on the western coast of the bay to find Ahjvar the Leopard, to
carry this message. She said, 'As the Voice of the Lady of Marakand is
a mortal woman chosen to carry out her goddess's will in the world,
so will I also choose a champion. And now Ahjvar the Leopard is
all that is left to me. Let him go, because this was murder and foul
treachery and a war without justice. And tell him, that as a king's
champion should, he is to be justice and judgement and the sword
in the open court, and as he has chosen to walk in the darkness and
be the knife in the night—'"

The man made some noise of protest.

"'—I also name him to be my blade in the darkness, for there are
shadows in the deep well of Marakand that I cannot see, and he may
find that the time for a trial of champions in the open court is past.'"

"Long past, by the sound of it," Ahjvar muttered.

"She says, 'By day or by darkness, in open battle or in secret
death, make an end to this Voice who has taken from me the last

of my royal children born to my land. Leave the Lady bereft as I am bereft. Kill her Voice, and the priests who planned this, and the lords of Marakand who sanctioned it, so many as you can. But the Voice first of all, because she will be the nearest and dearest to the Lady, her chosen one, and her death, most of all, I demand in payment for my queen and her son.'"

And what else she had said, before Deyandara, in a dream, a trance, hardly knowing what she did, saddled Cricket, taking bread and a skin of water from some scout's untended pony to ride unchallenged out the gate in the fog that had crept up the hill from the spring and the narrow brook it fed, was entirely between Deyandara and the goddess.

Come back to me when your errand is done, and we shall see then if you are worthy of the duina *you would claim.*

"Selfish," Ahjvar said. "She doesn't mention the sufferings of her folk, I note."

Deyandara frowned. Had there been more? "She says, say to the Leopard, 'You will not do this for me. But you will do it for the Duina Catairna. You will do it for the drovers and the shepherds of the hills, and you will do it for your own honour, lest the Duina Catairna be called slaves of the city of Marakand. And you will do it, because when it is done and you stand before me I will give back all that I have taken, and I will take back what was put upon you, and you will be free.'"

So. The man was an outcast and an exile of the Duina Catairna, clearly, but beyond that . . . it wasn't her business to understand, only to convey. Deyandara flinched as the sword thudded into the earthen floor before her feet.

"You won't get an answer to take back to her," Ahjvar said. The sword still shivered. She stepped away.

"I wasn't charged to bring any, my lord." Catairanach had not said she was to carry an answer, only to return. And she had done it again, giving him honours she had no reason to believe he owned. "*Master* Ahjvar. I suppose . . . I suppose my duty now is to reach my—to reach the high king at Dinaz Andara as swiftly as I can." Though she would rather ride in almost any other direction. He was bound to be searching for her. Maybe after all she should go back to the Duina Catairna, as Catairanach had demanded, but to ride alone into an occupied land—no. Even she was not that much a fool, whatever the goddess wanted. She would go to Durandau and, if he had not by then raised all Praitan against Marakand, add her voice and her arguments in defence of Marnoch's folk.

Her folk.

"The high king should already be on the march, depending on how long it took him to win the other kings to moving." Ahjvar frowned, calculating the time, it seemed. "This war should have been fought by now, though the kings might prove reluctant, or the gods themselves may be so. They'd turned their backs on Catairanach, and all that's hers, at one time."

"That's an old story," Deyandara protested.

"Has anyone asked them if they've forgiven her?"

"For what?" she protested. There were different songs of why Catairanach had fallen out with the other patron deities of the Praitan kingdoms, everything from a curse she herself had loosed on all of them, to some quarrel over who should hold the high kingship, to a disagreement with Praitanna herself, the greatest of the seven, over a man. It seemed somehow as though it ought to be connected to the curse of misfortune on the royal family and the folk, but no song had it so.

"There's the curse on the *duina*," Ahjvar said, not answering her question, "Maybe Praitan would be better off without the Duina Catairna, that's what some kings and their counsellors will say. Let the Catairnan ill-fortune pass to Marakand, lest it spread."

That at least had a known cause, a dying wizard's curse, though who the wizard had been, varied. Some songs even had it one of the seven devils, the Northron Ogada, who had wooed some long-ago queen, or Tu'usha the Restless, who had fought a wild goddess and a band of demons in the Malagru, though why she would then have cursed the Duina Catairna was not clear. "No wizard could ill-wish an entire folk, even if he put his death into it," Deyandara protested. "That they were cursed is only a story."

"And you, a bard, say so, yes? After saying yourself its kings are ill-fated? 'A twisted root and poison in the vein,' you said. Only a *story*. But you're not a bard, are you? Not in the marrow where it counts. You're a lady of the Duina Andara, a king's sister. You get to enjoy a few years of running free. When the way gets too long and the road too cold and your bones start to ache in the night, you'll let your brother persuade you to be useful, to be off to some prince's bed, be a lady of the royal hall again." The Leopard bowed, on his feet, sweeping her towards the door. "Good day, Lady Deyandara. Go sing them a song at the tavern. Give them a clown's wedding."

She was scrambling back over the garden wall before she knew it, face burning. How dare he? How dare he speak to the high king's sister so? A godless, outcast murderer, by Catairanach's word and his own failure to deny it, a city merchant's hireling, that was all he was . . . and everything he had said was true but hurt threefold because it was unjust. She wasn't a bard; she hadn't taken on the pretence to claim undue honours but as a shield for the road. She looked back and the assassin was in the garden, watching her, arms folded, with the naked sword tucked in against his body, the hilt against his cheek.

A bare-legged peasant come in muddy from the struggle for his daily meal. The hem of his tunic was ragged, and the sun was gold in his hair. She blinked and swallowed and looked away, straightened her shoulders. He didn't look someone to creep up walls and murder fat old merchant-lords in their beds on behalf of impatient nephews.

He looked some king's champion, awaiting the summons to enter the circle, with the judgement of the Old Great Gods to prove in the outcome of battle, and his own death waiting.

Deyandara hardly noticed the height of the cliff, the waves that crashed and the flying spray. Her hands were shaking as she knelt to Badger's greeting and rested her head on the dog's shoulder, blinking. She shouldn't be ashamed that the assassin was right and she was no bard, for all she could sing, and play the komuz and the harp. She *knew* she would never be one; she loved the music, but the long years of study, the secret alphabet of the trees, the true histories that lay behind the songs, the long, so long chants of the kings—she didn't have the mind for it. Like her mother, shallow and inconstant. She had tried to learn all that Yselly was willing to teach, being no true apprentice and so cut off from many secrets, but Yselly must have known, too, that she was fit to be a tramp-singer, nothing more. A princess could be nothing so commonplace, not if her brother knew. All she really wanted was a dog and a horse and place by the fire, the feel of the strings beneath her fingers, her voice rising.

"Come on," she told Badger, freeing Cricket from the thorn bush. "They're waiting for us at the tavern."

In the rough-cobbled yard under the grape arbours by the smith's house, all the tavern the village offered, the story of the last queen of the land before the ships came from Nabban fled her, came out ragged and stiff and lifeless. She hurried it to its end for her rest-less hosts, put away her komuz for the drum, and gave them the old comic tale of the fox-demon and the shepherd's daughter instead. A clown's wedding.

Ahjvar sat on the garden wall, watching the sea.

Ghu vaulted over to sit cross-legged at his feet. "You weren't very kind," he pointed out, leaning back, head against Ahjvar's leg.

"She was too full of her own worth, unearned."

"You don't know what she may have earned."

Ahjvar shrugged. "I don't like red-haired girls, and that child was over-stuffed with her own importance. Let her go away and think about whether she's to be a bard or her brother's sister."

"She never mentioned it till you did."

"It was in every word she spoke and every glance down her little upturned nose."

"If you hadn't left her standing, she wouldn't have had to look down on you."

"She's not old enough to have earned those ribbons she wears. And I didn't like her face."

"I thought it was her hair. And it was a rather pretty face."

"I don't think there've been any marriages between the royal lines of the Duina Catairna and the Duina Andara. Though there was some rumour about a Catairnan bard, that wild brother of the queen of the Duina Catairna . . . I don't know. The king's wife of the Duina Andara was sent back to her own people after her last child, this girl, was born." Ahjvar's mouth twisted. "It almost caused a war with the Duina Lellandi, I think."

"But that there was once rumour of a bard of the royal Catairnans doesn't make the lady his daughter, even if she does have orange hair. If you think it's so, send her to her brother to be made queen, and tell the goddess she has an heir and no need for vengeance on the city."

"You think she doesn't know already, if it's so? Don't wish that on the child. The Duina Catairna is truly cursed, whatever she believes."

"Who cursed them?"

"I did." Ahjvar hurled a chip of stone out over the cliff. It was a long time falling, and the splash was lost in the rising tide. "When the hag killed me. I told you that." He added peevishly, "You make me tell you things. I don't know why I do. I don't know why—"

He didn't finish that thought. *Why I can't get free of you?* because the obvious answer was that he could. Ghu dead could not dog his steps. Such thoughts came too easily, too lightly, and it was likely to come true, though the boy—man, now, but he seemed so young still, save for the unguarded eyes that strangers never saw—had survived four, or maybe it was five, years with him and had never been . . . never been in the wrong place at the wrong time. But Ahjvar was careful, too. He wasn't so far gone in madness but that he knew such thoughts shouldn't be his own. And there was work enough for the clan-fathers of the Five Cities to feed the madness. Assassination wasn't law and it wasn't justice, but it was . . . not innocence, either. Their lords had bodyguards, and wizard guards, and the ones who hired assassins expected assassins. There was a code, of sorts. It was warfare of a different type, maybe, and it kept the blackness eased and quiescent and . . . how, by the cold hells, was he to get to Marakand, on the long road, with Ghu by his side?

There was a time, a long time, lifetimes, when everything was dark and nothing mattered, so long as he kept within the walls he made himself, let nothing in, and ran away from anything that tried to get in, or pushed it away, or—Ghu was a cat. He always found a way in.

Going away didn't seem to be an option. The man would simply follow.

How, Old Great Gods forgive him, did he end up keeping Ghu, when he wouldn't even let himself have a dog to care about, to see innocence defiled by loving him? The boy—and Ghu had been a boy, then, though the tale he told of his life packed too much into too few years—had followed him all the way from Gold Harbour, had sat on the garden wall in a spring gale, wet and shivering and turning blue, until Ahjvar dragged him in by the collar of his ragged robe and dropped him by the fire. Feed a cat and you were stuck with it.

"So . . ." Ghu rose to his feet, stretching. He wasn't all skin and bone and hollow eyes now, anyway, but compact, taut muscle. And no gang of street-toughs was going to be able to work him over for their own amusement ever again; Ahjvar had made sure of that. Nobody hit Ghu but him, these days. The man refused to learn the sword, though. *Someday I may have to learn to kill. Not this day.* Ghu hadn't meant it as reproof. Sometimes it sounded prophecy, what fell from his lips. "That's why we're going to Marakand? For Catairanach and what she offers?"

"*I* am going." Ahjvar frowned. "Not for Catairanach." But because he did take her at her word? Maybe. But more, because the goddess who'd flung him out to damnation knew him. He would not see the Duina Catairna made subject to any foreign temple.

He shrugged. "Maybe they'll kill me at last, for good. These Red Masks sound . . . a challenge. But you're not going."

"You need me."

"I don't."

"You do."

"I don't need you. You followed me home, remember?"

"Because you needed me."

"I needed you to hold my horse. For an hour or so. I paid you a quarter-gull and that should have been that. I don't remember at all, I really don't, saying anything like, 'Why don't you trail me home and move in with me and convince all these good folk, who think I'm a nice respectable man of law, that I've brought home a half-witted beggar's brat as a catamite? I'm sure I'd remember if I'd said anything of the sort. It's not the kind of thing one says in passing and forgets."

Ghu walked to the cliff's brink, staring out past the sea, beyond the horizon, into what depths or heights Ahjvar couldn't think. Ghu's soul wandered, and sometimes he seemed nothing but a shell, a little, hollow child, waiting. To be filled with what?

"There is death, in Marakand," he said abruptly, but his voice was still soft, gentle, sleepy, even, and very far away. "Death and deep water. Death and fire. Death and ice."

Ahjvar shivered. A thing said thrice bound itself into the world.

"Death," he said, "you should have learned to expect by now, chasing after me." And he strode off barefoot, inland to the hills. Ghu didn't come after him.

He shouldn't have come back, but slept out in the open. He should have expected what followed. The nightmares returned that night. Ahjvar woke shrieking, soaked in sweat, striking out blind and mad at Ghu, who withstood the blows to pin his arms and whisper stupid soothing nonsense into his hair like he was a wild and panicked horse. He ended up curled, shivering, with his head on his knees, pressed against the cold and reassuring wall, solid and rough and real, and had he hit Ghu's head against it? He thought so, but the man was still on his feet and moving.

"Stupid," he said, and his speech was slurred, because sometime between then and now Ghu had forced more than one beaker of straight distilled barley-spirit on him. "Told you, get out of the house when I start screaming."

"It's all right."

"It's not all right." He squeezed his eyes shut on the little bard's face gone to stretched black skin, crackling on a grinning skull.

"Go to sleep." Ghu pushed him over and squirmed down to lie against his back, pulled one blanket over them both, an arm around him like a mother holding an infant against the night. And then he lay there singing Nabbani nonsense lullabies in a voice barely audible. Maybe they were charms, for all the man denied being a wizard, because Ahjvar slid away into deep sleep, and that night there were no more fires in his dreams.

In the morning, Ghu had a scraped cheek that needed tending, and Ahjvar a thumping headache that he ignored, because he thoroughly deserved it, seeing the state of Ghu's face. They stuffed the hens and chickens and the protesting rooster into two sacks and tipped them out in the widow's garden as they rode by. The sun was barely rising. Only the widow's dog saw them go.

When Deyandara returned to the assassin's house later that morning, having remembered in the midnight with a jolt a part of her errand unfinished, she found the hens gone and the ruin abandoned.

CHAPTER II

The high road, a succession of rambling tracks and drovers' trails, followed the snaking course of the Praitanna River, which was the Avain Praitanna in Praitan, north from the great port of Two Hills to the caravan way that ran from Marakand to the distant east. Even that was not a highway, not once it left the mountain pass, but a braided trail of many threads, wandering up and down to this walled *dinaz* and that village of watering-places and camping grounds, crossing and recrossing. Some threads, drovers' tracks, mostly, swung away south again to the other ports of the Five Cities, where the coffee and incense and ivory came up into the Gulf of Taren from the southlands beyond the sea, and the iron of the hidden forest kingdoms, the wool and tin of northern Over-Malagru, the olives and wheat and wine of the Tributary Lands went to the lordly dark merchant-princes of the ships.

Ahjvar set his course to the northwest instead. He took the wild paths, the ones only the locals and the wanderers knew, the steep climbs where winter rain stripped the thin soil from the stone between the thickets of myrtle and spiny gorse, humming with bees, the green hidden valleys known only to the herd-folk of the little chieftains, the wild heights of juniper and naked stone where even the shepherds rarely ventured, and the wooded ravines of laurel and holm-oak between the bare hills. He avoided the wider valleys, where villages were common, and the heights where gods dwelt and local folk might gather to them. He did not want to meet strangers, and yet . . . better strangers than Ghu, when the darkness came. But maybe they would reach Marakand first, where he would have an enemy to hunt, a focus, and that would be enough to satisfy it, knowing that a death lay at the end. He hoped it would hold off so long. He thought it probable, or he would have sent Ghu on some errand to the city, to be rid of him before he left.

The poison in his soul had no steady tide, no warning moon. It came, like the four-day fever, with only a little warning, a growing fret once the signs were known, but there was no bitter bark from out of the southlands to head it off. Stalking a clan-father of the Five Cities, a man well guarded by steel and wizardry, who knew his enemies hired assassins against him, killing and coming through alive, could drive it away, often for as much as a few months. Time enough to ride to Marakand. It had fed—call it that—well enough in Gold Harbour lately, as the elderly governor had died—not of natural causes, although perhaps three walls scaled and two wizard guards and a devoted young swordsman dead was natural causes for a wily old Five Cities clan-mother. The merchant-lords and clan-fathers sorted out precedence and alliance in their usual way, choosing her successor. The Leopard had been much in demand by several factions and had spread his favours impartially, as befitted one who sold his body—for whatever use.

There was no one but Ghu and the occasional shepherd or pedlar on the paths they took. One night Ahjvar found himself unable to sleep, restless, and came to himself pacing, prowling. By the stars, an hour had passed unnoted. Bad. The black tide was rising again.

So soon. Too soon. Weren't all the deaths in Gold Harbour enough to keep it satisfied? But he should have remembered that the nightmares could bring it on. Sometimes he thought it made him wilfully forgetful, hiding itself, to . . . to sneak up on him.

He was mad, and sick in his soul, and he should have been mercifully slain like a mad dog years since. That had to be done, if a wizard was not handy to drive the sickness from its blood. Well, he'd had a friend try that, too. Both the latter and the former, back when he had still stupidly dared to have friends. And she had died, by his hand.

He woke Ghu. The man was all edged in shivering light, which might be *her*, starting to see the world as ghosts saw it, or might be some headache illusion. There was no face within the tracery of light. His own hand looked the same but darker, a dirtier smudge of fire. "I'm leaving," he said. "Don't follow me. Take the horses and go where you will."

Ghu was silent a long moment. Ahjvar could imagine the wide-eyed, lackwit look. Then the man took his sleeve, and at the touch the light faded, leaving nothing but darkness, shadow and deeper shadow, night as it ought to be. After a moment, as if sense had slowly to seep back into him, Ghu found his voice. "There's no one out here."

"That's why I'm going."

"It will be all right," Ghu said. "You won't hurt me."

"I have hurt you."

"Barley-spirit?"

"I've drunk myself insensible. It doesn't help. It doesn't stop it. Opium doesn't help. I've tried. It makes me slower, maybe. That's all. I've told you."

Ghu considered. "I could hit you on the head."

"Then do it now."

He saw the movement as Ghu rubbed the back of his hand over his mouth, considering, maybe, the practicality of hitting a much taller, stronger man over the head while he was crouching above and Ghu himself lying flat on his back.

"Do it now, because later you won't be able to." His voice shook.

Ghu sat up, yawned, and put both hands on Ahjvar's shoulders. "It won't be tonight," he said. "Go back to sleep." And he took his own advice, rolling over on his side, a hand still out, resting lightly on Ahjvar's ankle. He was asleep again almost at once.

Ahjvar left him, took his sword, and set off walking for Marakand. They were good horses. Ghu could sell them and live off the money for a long while—if he didn't give them away to the first beggar who looked like he needed a ride.

Ghu overtook him around noon the next day. Ahjvar had left the tracks entirely and climbed juniper- and heather-grown crags to follow another ridge, then cut down through a dense growth of pines and across a bog. The man was, by his own admission, a slave born on an estate in northern Nabban, a horse-boy, then a runaway, a stowaway, a sailor, and a beggar in the Five Cities, where for all their sins, slavery at least was outlawed and the runaways of the empire found sanctuary. None of that allowed for any fieldcraft, and yet he tracked Ahjvar with no particular effort and appeared over the skyline riding the piebald with the white and the lion in a string behind him, unmuddied, unhurried.

Ahjvar shrugged defeat and took the yellow gelding's reins. "I should have taken the horses myself and left you to walk back overland to Nabban." His head ached. He smelt smoke on the edges of the wind. Heavy, thick smoke, acrid, and the sweet scent of roasting meat. Bad. It coiled in the corners of his eyes. "I'd tell you to kill me, but it won't let you, and it would end with me killing you."

Ghu kept silent. It was his amiable simpleton's look, listening without any word seeming to sink deeper than the surface of that vague, sweet smile.

"I walked off a cliff once, you know," Ahjvar told him. "Years ago. Fifty years, maybe. I woke up in the rain. Bruised like I'd rolled down a hill. It was a cliff. It should have smashed every bone in my body. Woke up in the rain and an old man asking, did I have the falling-sickness? The four-day fever? I could hardly walk. He tried to take me home. I told him not to, I told him to leave me, to run away. It was rising, I could feel it. It keeps me alive, you know. She keeps me alive. She's watching. She wants me to kill you. I knocked his arm off me and I staggered away into the hills again, with him shouting behind me to come back. But I guess—I found them—later. I buried them under their threshold. There was an old woman too, his wife, did I tell you that? Did you know? I set their cottage alight after I buried them and I tried, I tried—I can't walk into a fire, I can't, not fire, I tried."

"Hush," said Ghu. "I'll tie you up, tonight."

"Devils have mercy." It was half a groan, half a laugh, but at least it brought him back to some edge of reason. "Ghu, that won't . . ."

"I'll tie you up," Ghu said complacently. "And then I'll hit you over the head with something if I have to. We'll be fine."

"It's no wonder all Sand Cove thinks you're only half there, you know." But it might, it might be safe. It might get them both to Marakand, where he could hunt the Voice, who sought to make the city an empire and sentenced wizards to death in her Lady's waters. So long as he was actually hunting, it would sit, watchful, but leave him in peace to his work, leave him in sanity, and Ghu would be safe.

And it would be over? Did he trust Catairanach to keep her word, to pluck the curse out from his soul? And then? It would be over and he would die, maybe. Fall away to old bones and dust, as he should have been by now, in the mound of his fathers.

How many more nights to Marakand? They had been travelling for ten days now, and sometimes from a high ridge they could see pale peaks floating, a smudge of mist on the western horizon. North of the westward weavings of the road lay the Duina Catairna, but Ahjvar was not crossing that border.

"Do we have rope?"

Five nights. It was a nightmare, but Ghu had lived nightmares before. Ahjvar's wrists and ankles were torn raw and bled, slow and sluggish, night and day now. He rolled his sleeves because the touch of cloth even through bandages was an agony. He wouldn't let Ghu leave the bandages on when he bound him at night either, saying even that much give in the rope was too much. Ghu thought that at least wrists and ankles should be enough, but Ahj insisted, so when the sun sank near the horizon he tied him wrist and ankle and knee as well, and left him lying in some open place far from fire and rock and sharp stone. He took the horses, too, and rode on to make his own camp. And went back at dawn, to find wherever Ahj had crawled to, untie him, bandage him, make him eat and drink and put him to bed, because he needed rest even more than the horses, who suffered this additional nighttime back-and-forthing with patient grace. At noon they would break camp and travel on, Ahjvar silent, grim, and sometimes muttering, too low for any words to be heard.

Ghu had been in the lands of many gods since he left Nabban, where there were only two, Mother Nabban of the great river and Father Nabban of the holy peak. It did not seem a natural state for all the godhead of a land to have drawn into only two beings, too great to know all their folk as they should, but Ahjvar's talk of Catairanach showed him the other side of godhead, how dangerous it might be for a little god, an unwise god, to sink to the level of the folk she ought to have nurtured as a wise aunt, guarding and guiding. She had become as locked in petty, passing daily life as they, tormenting her folk through her unwisdom. A goddess should be impartial, patient, and thoughtful, slow in judgement, broad in love; encompassing all her folk, not favouring; devoted, not impassioned.

During the sixth day of Ahjvar's madness, cloud rolled up from the distant sea, low over the hilltops, smothering the sky.

"Now," Ahjvar said. "We have to stop now." It was the first he had spoken all that day. Even his muttering had ceased.

"It's not sunset yet."

"Soon enough. She's not waiting for full dark."

He did not like it when Ahjvar began talking of the curse as "she." It raised the hairs prickling on the back of his neck, as if the very words brought some other presence with them, some stalking ghost. He could see ghosts, usually. This one—Ghu did not doubt it existed—but it never came out where it could be seen.

"All right," he agreed. "But it's going to rain tonight."

"Good."

"At least let's find a tree to give you some shelter."

"No."

"You'll end up with catarrh or water on the lungs, lying out in the open."

"Good."

"Ahj—"

"Now, Ghu." And his teeth were clenched. Ahjvar flung himself from the horse, unbelted his sword and hurled it away. He dropped his cloak, too, kicked off his high riding boots, and held out his seeping wrists. "*Now.*"

Last night's ropes Ghu had burned, every length of them blood-soaked, fly-crawling by dawn, and the knots pulled so tight there was no untying them. He had needed to cut them out of Ahj's swollen flesh. His hands ought to rot off. They wouldn't, Ahj said. Rope. Ghu hadn't thought they would need an anchor-cable's length of it. They had leather harness-ties and spare straps, but those might stretch or be gnawed through, Ahjvar insisted. Well, the mountains marched closer. Another two or three days would bring them to a main branch of the caravan road, by Ahjvar's reckoning, and they would turn west towards the dry valley where the coulee came down from the pass, carrying a remnant of mountain snowmelt in the spring. And then, on the rising, straight road, three days at most after that, Marakand. Ahjvar swore that he was safe, once he had prey to hunt. He would not be a random monster in the nighttime streets, at least. It might even be justice, Ghu supposed, for a change. The kings of the Praitannec tribes had champions to fight for them, to settle disputes short of war—though that was only rarely to the death. Why not the gods? But a goddess should not hunger after another's folk. It was wrong, though. An elderly priestess was not much of a champion to set against a warrior who did not die.

Ahjvar knelt, head bowed, like a man awaiting execution, and Ghu cut new lengths from the coil of thin rope to bind his arms behind his back. Ahjvar hissed and clenched his fingers white and said, "Tighter. Damn you, make the knots tighter."

"We could try what happens if I hit you," Ghu said doubtfully. "I didn't really mean to do it, but if you think I can't kill you, I will, only I wouldn't want to be the one to prove you wrong. About not dying, I mean. Your wrist is festering, Ahj. There are maggots in it."

"Knocking me out wouldn't last the night. Pour the barley-spirit on the wrist to clean it; that's what I brought it for. In the morning, not now! Wet rope will stretch."

"It's going to rain."

"Then tie the damn knots tighter!"

Ahjvar was trussed to his satisfaction at last, lying amid long grass on the hillside, eyes clenched shut. Shivering, but he said he wasn't cold. He felt fevered, in fact. Too hot, skin dry, as if he lay near a fire.

"Go," he muttered, as Ghu still crouched, doubtful, a hand on his forehead. "See you in the morning. Smoke's getting thick. Go. She's waiting. She's coming. She's here, Ghu. Go!" He cried out, a sound like a tortured animal, and kicked at Ghu with his bound feet. Ghu grabbed up the swordbelt and sprang away to the white mare's back, dragging the weary horses into a trot down the hill, along the stream at the bottom. There was a track there. Too well-trodden for his liking. They were getting into a settled land again; some village must lie nearby. He rode on, till he could not hear Ahjvar's screaming any longer. There were words in it, but he did not want to hear them. It was not truly Ahj anymore. He would have made camp there—the horses desperately needed rest—but it was not nearly far enough, he knew Ahjvar would say, and there was something on the wind. Smoke. Not the ghost-fire of Ahjvar's madness. Smoke and roasting meat.

He rode on, a little, as the rain began, a swift and rushing patter, drowning even the noise of the stream. Willows lined the valley, and when he heard voices even above the rain on the leaves he went back a ways, into shelter under the oldest of the trees, unbridled and unsaddled the horses and fed them some of the grain they carried. He didn't bother to tie them. "Stay here," he murmured, patting each smooth cheek in the darkness. Ahj laughed at him for speaking to the horses so, but they always did as he asked. Ahj pretended not to notice.

Then he went on afoot. An outlying herdsman's hut or a travellers' camp, maybe. Whoever it might be, they weren't likely to go roaming the hills in the dark and the rain, but he should keep an eye on them, in case.

No dog barked to announce him as he worked his way up the ridge again, which argued against herdsmen. The fire was out-of-doors, a high blaze. He went over the hillcrest on his belly and lay to watch it. Five dark shapes in close, or six, and only one small horse, no shelter but a great chestnut tree. Chunks of meat were angled in over the fire on sticks. They didn't look likely to go roaming, to stumble upon Ahjvar. Five sat close together under a shelter that was only cloaks or blankets sagging on propped branches. The sixth sat apart, hunched. Another stood up, crossed to it, and struck it in the face. Ghu bit his lower lip, frowning. Still on his belly, he worked his way in nearer. The standing figure hit the other several times more.

"Leave her alone, so long as she's quiet," a woman said. She spoke Praitannec, and her voice slurred.

"She's not quiet. She's snivelling." But the man who had done the hitting went to sit by the fire again, taking something from another—a jar, drinking. He held one arm, the one he hadn't been hitting people with, tight to his chest.

"Let her snivel, then," said the woman.

"You should have left her alone in the first place. She's a *bard*." That was another man, reaching for the jar. Ghu was close enough now to guess at four men and a woman. By the voices he'd heard so far, too loud, too careful, they were all drunk.

"She'd have gone to the chieftain's hall and told them she'd seen us." That was the whining man, who had hit the bard. Ahjvar's bard? Ghu thought so, without any more reason for it but that he felt something like the shape of her, the scent of her. His dog-sense, Ahj called it.

"If you hadn't dragged her off her horse, she'd have said 'Good day,' and passed on, never thought twice about us."

"With all the countryside raised against us now, and all the chieftain's spears out after us? She was following us. And her damned dog attacked me."

"What did you expect, when you grabbed her like that? You're lucky it wasn't your throat."

"At least I did for it," the whiner said, with satisfaction. Ghu growled softly to himself, just a breath.

"She was going the same direction as us, not following. It's not the same thing, and you're a fool," said the woman.

"What are we going to do with her?" one of the men asked, an irritated complaint.

"I can think of lots of things to do with her."

This time the woman hit the whiner. He shrieked. Maybe she had hit his wounded arm. Good, as Ahjvar would say.

"Kill her and get out of here, head south?" she suggested.

"My brother will ransom me," the bard said. Her voice shook. Terror, certainly, but fury beneath it, and grief. She was Lady Deyandara; he had been right. "I'm worth a lot more to you, alive and unharmed."

They ignored her.

"Sell her, if we're going south."

"They don't have slaves in the Five Cities, idiot."

"Hah, everyone knows there's ship-captains sailing for the empire who do a bit of that trade on the side. People go missing in the Five Cities. 'Specially pretty boys and girls."

"We can't let her go," said the woman. "Not with the hunt up against us as it is, thanks to you. And we can't cross however many miles it is between here and the coast with her making trouble all the way. We have to kill her. You should have done it then and left her with the dog."

"She's a bard. If she gave her word not to tell . . ." one of the men suggested. An older voice, which hadn't spoken before.

"You want these kingless tribesmen to take your head? Because that's what's waiting if they find us. You killed that young swine-herd, you clumsy bastard, not us, but we'll all pay for him. And one murder, two, it doesn't make a difference. It's death. Hers or ours. She'd tell where she'd last seen us, no matter what she swore."

"You're Praitans. So am I," Deyandara said. "Listen, the high king will pay a ransom to have me back unharmed. But if you kill me, not all Praitan and the Five Cities will be big enough to hide in."

"Shut up, or I'll cut your throat like your brute's, here and now."

"We're not quite that stupid." The woman again. "One of the high king's bards, way out here in the west singing in the Tributary Lands—right."

"How do you think he gets news of other folk and other lands but through his bards? Who carries word between the kingdoms? Fools yourselves. He's my *brother*. If you kill me, even running as far as Nabban won't save you."

The whiner flung himself staggering around the fire and hit her again.

"We can't kill her," said the one who had wanted to let her go. "Catairanach save us, not the princess of the Duina Andara—every god and king of the seven kingdoms would be against us."

"You don't *believe* her?"

"But there was a lady of Andara at Dinaz Catairna last winter. Didn't you hear?"

"Great Gods, why did you give me a fool and a drunkard for a brother? If there was, she's dead with the rest of the lords who didn't have the sense to run from the Marakanders. And if she escaped and it's true, what she's saying, more reason to be rid of her now and quickly, because she's right, they won't give up till they find her, and slipping off over the border won't be enough to lose the hunters this time. If you won't do it, Dann will. Or Jecca, since he's so keen to do something with her."

"Do it yourself," the whiner said, though he'd been eager enough before. "I say we take her to the cities. And maybe she can show herself grateful for being spared, on the way."

"You weren't that squeamish about the dog. Just use the axe and get it over with."

"Gods, leave it till morning, at least," said the old-voiced man, "when we can see what we're doing. We're safe enough here for now. No one will be out in this weather, and I don't want to spend the night sleeping by a corpse."

Ghu felt around in the grass, until he found a pebble down in the roots. If he had his sling . . . but it was long-lost and he hadn't made another. He raised himself up on one arm and shied the stone, striking one of the brigands. There was a sharp cry. Ghu squirmed backwards till he was over the hillcrest and then ran, bending low. Some of them followed. Two? Three. Good. So long as the remaining two didn't decide to kill the lady then and there.

He took care to break some branches, let others spring back with loud swishings and snappings. Grabbed the sheathed sword from where he had leaned it against the saddles and baggage, leapt on the white mare, turned her with his knee and sent her plunging up through the willow tangle, more than enough noise, the horse gleaming as lightning broke over the hills. The other two raced with him, good beasts. And if it pleased Mother Nabban to hold her hand over him, none of the brigands would have thought to snatch a bow.

He was well ahead, and had probably lost them, but—the important thing—they were between Ahjvar and the lady.

Thunder sent the yellow horse shying off, vanishing into night. Rising wind drove the rain in waves, flattening the grass. He'd left Ahjvar—where? Lightning. The white mare reared as a darkness rose up out of the grass at her feet. Ghu slid sideways and grabbed Ahj around the shoulders as he passed, ending up on top of him. Still bound, but the man thrashed over, trying to drive him into the ground. Ghu elbowed him in the chin and rolled away to his feet.

"Ahj!" he shouted. "Ahjvar!" He smelt smoke. Sullen firelight seemed to hover on the edges of his vision, not an afterglow of the lightning. It looked like Ahjvar, it moved like Ahjvar, coming up onto its bound knees and then rocking to its feet, but that dog-sense that said the hunched sixth figure had been Lady Deyandara said this was not Ahjvar. "Catairlau . . . ?"

That didn't work either. Worse. It did not like that name. It hissed. There was a horrible emptiness about it, a soul in abeyance, a ghost-ridden shell. And killing fed it and kept it from waking. He had never seen this, Ahj had made sure he didn't, and now that he did, he wished he hadn't. Worse than seeing someone you loved come to mindless, drooling dotage. This thing was all mad hatred. He couldn't talk to it, and he could talk to almost anything. The eyes were on the sword, and he thought they saw it through fire. He dropped the belt, caught the white mare again by her mane and turned her.

"There are men," he said. "Wicked men, brigands. They murdered a boy, they said. Four men and a woman. Do you remember the bard? Can you hear me, Ahjvar? You didn't like her, but it wasn't her fault. Remember that. She's afraid. The wicked men have her prisoner. They're going to kill her. You can find them first, if I let you go. But you can't kill me." Was this monster like a little child? Could it understand better if he made the words easy? He thought so. It had become a thing of simple thoughts, twisted, evil thoughts, but simple ones. "Ahjvar thinks the bard is heir to the Duina Cataírna. *You* don't want to kill her, do you? Ahjvar wants to kill her." Except he thought Ahj didn't, not really. "You don't. Not your own last heir."

Probably a lie. Probably it knew it for a lie. It gave him no words. Maybe it could not speak, maybe the cursing and obscenities before had been the last of Ahjvar as the darkness took him. But it made no move towards him. Good.

"Good," he said aloud. "And you don't want to kill me, because then Ahjvar will be in his right mind again, and—and he will be so, so angry with you. He might kill the lady then, your heir, out of hate for you. So you can't make him angry. You can't kill me. All right?"

It stood very, very still. Maybe that was too complicated. Maybe it was going to spring, bound though it was.

The mare was dancing and jerking her head, as if even she smelt the ghost of a bed turned funeral pyre. Ghu wound her long mane about his wrist, a good way to break it, maybe, or pull his shoulder out. "Come with me," he told the horse, speaking Nabbani, which the ghost probably did not. "Good girl, my pearl, my queen of mares, quiet now. We'll get him back, we will. Come."

He had his own belt-knife in his hand, a thin, sharp blade. His heavy brush-cutting knife was back with the harness. He moved slowly, keeping the horse tight at his side. The thing that was not Ahjvar watched the place where the sword had fallen, hungrily, like a dog eyeing dropped bread.

"I'm going to cut the ropes," he said. "Don't move."

It swayed towards him as if it would use even its teeth, if it could.

"I'm probably going to cut you, Ahj," he added. "Sorry."

It hissed again, jerked as the blade touched it, but stood. Hot—even soaked with cold rain it was radiating heat he could feel. Quivering, fighting its own urge to kill, to devour whatever element it was that it took of the departing life. Enough intelligence left in it to fear the threat of the bard's death? To care? Or just enough to know it couldn't kill him easily with its arms behind its back.

Probably that.

He trailed the knife down, caught what he hoped was rope, and slashed it. Dropped the knife and vaulted up as the mare took off running at the scream the thing gave, a hand's edge striking for his throat.

But he was out of reach. He brought the mare to a reluctant, sidling halt, turned enough to see the shape that was and was not Ahjvar already free of its remaining bonds and running, knife in its hand in the glare of another lightning bolt. "Sword, Ahj!" he shouted. "Before they kill her."

Then he gave the horse his heel and got out of reach again, heading back the way he had come, a wary eye out for the brigands, or the piebald, which he had also lost in the lightning with no idea where it had run. Trusting to Father Nabban to spare him marmot holes, as he had in the first wild ride.

"I see him! Dann—!"

"Tell him where we are, why don't you?" The voices ceased, but he heard their panting, even over the beating of the rain on the earth.

Ghu circled widely enough that the white mare's shimmer would disappear; he came down on the fire from the opposite direction. They hadn't tried to put it out. The pony raised its head and whickered, giving him away, and at first he didn't see the bard, only the two nervously on their feet, one with a bow. That one shouted, but Ghu slid down and slapped the mare's flank, ordering, "Away, find the others," as the man loosed an arrow. It hissed overhead as he crawled in towards the light. He found the lady with his hand, flat in the grass, before he saw her. His heart jolted in fear even as her muffled gasp told him she lived. Her hands had been tied before her; she was crawling like a lizard, flat, on her elbows, escaping while she could. White light burned the air and the thunder crashed almost on top of it.

"Come," he ordered in Praitannec. He tugged at her shoulder, and after a moment, she followed, farther from the fire, where two alert brigands crouched, listening for their fellows. No knife now. He sat hidden in darkness with the bard, worked at the knot with his fingers, wriggling it loose, and finally pulled the cord free. The lady clutched him close, muffling a fit of sobbing on his chest. She was pleasantly soft.

A scream away in the night. He sighed and found the lady's hand, squeezed it. A death. They would be all right now. It was Ahjvar, not the monster, who would come for the two at the fire.

Of course, Ahj might not know anything of the brigands. He would think he had found some innocent tribesman benighted in the storm . . .

"Ghu!" The bellow made the archer shoot another arrow, blind in the dark.

Ghu cupped his hands, rose up on his knees to call, "Outlaws, Ahj, five of them." Small chance they spoke good Nabbani. "Two here, three out looking for me. I have the lady safe beside me."

"Shut up!" Lady Deyandara wrenched her hand from him and tried to cover his mouth. "Andara help me, you're—what's your name, the Leopard's Nabbani servant?" She tried the pidgin of the Eastern Road. "Be quiet. They'll find us." She spoke too loudly, making each word stand alone, as if he were deaf as well as simple.

She was right, of course, about the danger of shouting, but he had meant to crawl quickly away afterwards. Wrestling Lady Deyandara's hands off his face delayed that moment too long. Lightning betrayed them.

An axe wavered at him out of the night, moving in a stench of sour beer.

"Is it the girl, Jecca?" the woman called, safely behind. "Don't let her get away."

Ghu kicked the man's feet out from under him, rolled over, dragging the lady, pulled her up and ran, while the man groped around for his lost weapon.

"They're all around!" someone wailed in the distance. "Dann, is that you?" A shout that ended in a breathless cough. It hadn't been.

Pounding hooves, a shriek. That was three. The man and the woman found the axe at the same moment and tussled for it. The man won. The woman yelled, "Damn you!" and grabbed one of the sticks of meat. Ghu wished he had a stick himself. Hands and feet weren't much defence against an axe. He dragged the lady over to the tree, put her behind him with her back to it. The woman knocked the make-shift tent of blankets flat and began turning in small circles, watching all ways, afraid to leave the firelight, as if that were somehow safety. The man, in the stupidity of drink, seemed to have one thought only, to make sure the bard didn't escape. A beer-muddled belief that her death now would save them from being found.

"Help!" the bard yelled suddenly, catching a sound. "Over here!"

The piebald loomed into sight, and the long sword, red in the fire-light, swept the brigand-woman's head from her shoulders, spraying the white-mottled withers black with blood. The horse turned, and the last of the outlaws, raising the axe, screamed high-pitched like a wounded animal, for the brief moment he still had a voice to scream with. Ahj ran him through the ribs and carried on around the tree, dragging his sword free, the body, ripped and spilling, tumbling to a heap almost at their feet.

The lady whimpered and tried to press herself into the trunk, as if it might open up and hide her. Ghu couldn't say he blamed her. Ahjvar looked more a brigand than the outlaws had, barefoot, hands and feet blood-glistening on the blood-spattered horse, without saddle or bridle, and his face deathly grey, a skull-mask with the deep shadows of his eyes. He came sliding down the piebald gelding's shoulder and didn't quite pitch forward onto his face, ending up on his knees, a hand braced against the earth, never losing his grip on the sword.

Ghu caught him. He was cold and wet and shuddering and couldn't seem to speak.

"It's all right, it's all right now. They were going to kill the lady."

Ahjvar shook his head.

"Yes, it is all right," Ghu insisted. "Whatever chief governs this land has his household warriors hunting them, they said themselves, for murder and brigandage. You would have fought them anyhow, because they had the lady; they were going to kill her." And he thought that though he did not believe it was yet his time to decide on the life and death of men, he had. Turning Ahjvar loose in his madness was as much a choice as slashing a man's throat with his forage-knife. He sighed. Father Nabban, was it right, ever, to kill a man? But it was a worse wrong to stand by while a bound prisoner was hacked to death with an axe.

"It's all right," he repeated, and Ahj finally found his tongue.

"My head aches," he muttered, and pushed away from Ghu, standing up. "What have you done with the rest of my horses?"

"I'll find them. You look after the lady." But maybe that was not a good idea, just now. It was Ahjvar who needed looking after. Lady Deyandara with her red hair and turned-up nose was not the one to do it. "Just . . ." He couldn't expect them to stay here. The storm seemed to be passing; the wind had dropped and the rain dwindled to a light drizzle, almost a mist. Ghu pulled a burning brand from the dying fire. "Take this. Stay together. Go down into the valley. Make a fire. I'll find you." He didn't wait to see if Ahjvar obeyed, but clucked to the piebald and walked off, with it following like a dog.

Pearl was easy enough, a soggy white shape under a skyline tree, fool beast, but the lightning had passed. She whinnied when she smelt the piebald, followed. No sign of Ahjvar's favourite. He found a body, headless, and the piebald came on the head and shied away. He whistled it back and hesitated. Different folks had different customs or even laws about the violently dead. In the empire, to send on the soul of a slain man before the emperor's wizards could question it about its murderer was a crime itself, even if you had nothing to do with the slaying. Among others, it was a cruelty not to give a body a little earth at once, to free the soul to the Old Great Gods. Well, the dead did not easily lie; the man would have to speak the truth about his deeds. He did not want there to be any mistake, to have Ahjvar taken up for murder.

"Bide a while," he told the ghost, which crouched small and whimpering and near-senseless in its terror. "The chief's bench-companions will no doubt find you and send you to your road." The ravens would alert them.

He did not try to find the other two, who must also lie out on the hills somewhere. It was his belt-knife and Ahjvar's boots he wanted. And Ahjvar's horse.

The golden gelding eventually came to his whistling, with its silver-cream tail knotted up with burrs.

"Such foolish horses," he told them. "You know it's me who has to comb your silly tails." But he was glad to find them all safe. He found the trampled grass where he had left Ahjvar bound, and after much blind searching in the sodden and torn grass, retrieved boots and cloak and his knife. After that, he went, with the horses following, down to the stream again, to harness them by feel in the dark, and load them.

They were not happy. They stumbled at roots and plodded like weary buffalo after a day under the yoke. No rest for anyone through the day; Ahjvar would not want to wait to meet the spears of the local tribe, out hunting the swineherd's killers.

Lady Deyandara had made a little smouldering fire, with wet sticks tented steaming over it, under a stand of towering elms in the valley bottom. Her pony was tethered close, still saddled as the brigands had left it, as though she thought she might yet want to flee into the night—though the east was greying. Ahjvar, soaking wet as if he had plunged into the brook fully clothed, as perhaps he had, sat apart, cleaning his sword.

"Good," he said hoarsely, when he saw the horses.

"Go to sleep," Ghu told him. "I'll cook."

"We're not staying here."

"I know. That's why you should sleep, now. Just till the morning comes. The horses need rest, so you might as well take some too. I won't let you have nightmares. I'll wake you if you even twitch." He added in Praitannec, for the bard, "It's safe now. Go to sleep."

"Do dogs walk?" Deyandara asked, in a low voice. It was Ahjvar she looked at. He was startled into glancing up.

"They killed her dog," Ghu explained.

Ahjvar shook his head. "I've never seen a dog's ghost." Most people who were not wizards didn't see ghosts at all or saw only those of close kin. "Animals go to the earth, like demons; they don't take the road to the stars. I've heard it said that sometimes a dog, maybe a horse but usually a dog, waits after all, to join its master on the way."

"Dogs are patient," said Ghu. "He'll wait. Buried or unburied."

"I don't know where he is. They took me across country, all day. I never had a chance to fight. I fought in the hall when the priests killed the queen; I killed a man then, and I'm not useless, whatever my brothers say, but they—they came up and gave me good day, and then, then they just—Badger knew something was wrong, he was leaping at the same moment the man pulled me down and—"

"He'll find you," Ghu said.

Ahjvar gave him a look that was more like Ahjvar, a bit sarcastic. He hadn't meant to say that. He hadn't meant to speak of her own death as a comfort. The lady should go east, to her brother. She would be safer there. But she watched Ahjvar now with a sort of wary fascination, which wouldn't please him, when he noticed.

"Go to sleep," Ahjvar ordered, and she listened to him, wrapping herself in a blanket from her bags and curling up on some flattened ferns, wet, but out of the mud.

"You too," Ghu said. Ahjvar just grunted, but he sheathed the sword at last and flung himself down. He was asleep almost the same moment. Ghu covered him with everything dry he could find and yawned. But he couldn't sleep himself; he had promised to watch. Someone had to.

He made porridge and let it sit, keeping warm, as the sun crept up a murky, rain-heavy sky. He found coffee and made some for Ahjvar's headache, and tea for himself, because despite the fire he was shivering with cold, soaked to the skin, and his cloak of oily wool had stopped shedding water and begun drinking it like a sponge sometime in the downpour. The coffee woke Ahjvar, who at first seemed vague on what had happened and needed to be told why the bard was sleeping by their fire, why he hadn't woken bound hand and foot on a hilltop. While Ahjvar drank his coffee to the last of the revolting thick sludge, saying nothing, eyes shut, Ghu cleaned Ahj's wrists and ankles with the barley-spirit and bandaged them again.

Ghu didn't ask if he had done the right thing. He had done it; it was his burden to carry, right or wrong. But Ahjvar grabbed him as he reached for the kettle of porridge and pulled him close a moment, face bowed to the top of his head, breath warm against him. "You did right," Ahj muttered into his hair. "Lesser evil, anyhow. But Great Gods, Ghu, don't do it again. I could have killed *you*."

The lady woke and sat to watch them.

"You were wounded," she said, as if it were an accusation, and Ahjvar let him go, tugging his sleeves down over his wrists.

"There's porridge," Ahjvar said. "Probably thick enough to break spoons. His always is."

Ghu shrugged, grinned, and found they had only two horn spoons. He and Ahj shared.

"You've come entirely the wrong direction, if you're looking for the high king's hall," Ahjvar said. He was washing the pots in the brook while Ghu, belatedly, checked over the horses' legs and feet, dealt with the yellow gelding's burr-matted tail, and cleaned the blood from the piebald. Luckily the burrs were the worst harm any of them had taken. "What are you doing here?"

"Looking for you," the bard said. "I needed to find you. I forgot—" She swallowed, stood and bowed, a deep bow, Nabbani-fashion, hands together. "My lord, I am sorry. I was ill-tempered and hasty and I forgot a part of my charge, and I haven't thanked you yet for last night."

Ahjvar waved a hand, ducked a grim face over the porridge-pot.

"Keep your wrists out of the water," Ghu said sternly, speaking Nabbani.

"I owe you—and your boy—my life."

"You don't owe us anything."

She didn't hear the anger. "I owe you everything. My brother will do you honour, if you come to Dinaz Andara."

"I won't. What is it you forgot? Tell me and you can be off. You can reach the hall of the chief of this land by noon. It's away to the east; you'll find the track a few miles over there." He pointed. "Don't mention which way we're going, that's all the thanks we need. Say we were travellers heading south."

Her lips set, but she didn't argue then. She reached into the neck of her tunic for an amulet-pouch, opening it as she spoke. "Catairanach gave me this, to give you. At least—it was in my hand, after I dreamed of her. She said, 'Say to him, That which was taken, I give back, as token that I mean to honour what I promise. He will have need of this before the end, if I foresee truly.'"

Deyandara held out something on the flat of her hand. Ahjvar came to take it and then recoiled as she was about to drop it into his hand.

"Ahjvar?" she asked, and frowned at what she held, looked up again, puzzled. "It's just a blessing-piece."

"It's—Ghu, take that from her."

Ghu dropped burrs and snarled horsehair in the fire and held out a hand. The lady, still frowning puzzlement, gave him what she held. At first he had thought it was a coin, but he was wrong; it was a disc of unfired clay, about the size of a bronze half-ounce dolphin-piece, but fatter in the middle and tapering to its edge, as if it had been pressed between the palms. It was not stamped with any design but scoured deeply with a few of the slashing, hen-scratching characters the Praitannec bards and wizards used. He couldn't read them, but then, he couldn't read his own folk's writing, either.

"It's from the goddess," the lady protested. "I was to give it to you, Ahjvar."

"What is it?" Ghu asked in Nabbani. "What's to fear in it?"

"It's not a blessing-piece," said Ahjvar, using the Praitannec word. "It's a seal. The bards give the characters different values than we—than wizards. I don't think she's read it rightly if she thinks it's a blessing, but I don't think she's much of a bard, anyway."

"You shouldn't insult her when she can't understand you; it's not polite. But you couldn't stamp ink onto paper with that. Could you? And it's too rough; wax would stick to it."

"No, it's a *seal*. It seals." Ahjvar, whose barbarian-accented Imperial Nabbani was usually impeccable, had been using the wrong word.

Ghu ducked to hide his smile. "What's it sealing?"

"Nothing that should be let loose yet. How can a goddess be so *dim*? You think you could have tied up a wizard, Ghu? Last night?"

"Ah," he said, and closed his fingers over the disc. It felt hot now, as if it pulled heat from his hand and held it.

"Keep it for me," Ahjvar said in Praitannec. "It's safer with you."

Ghu nodded. He didn't carry any kind of token of his own gods, no amulet. He knew he belonged to Nabban, wherever he went. He wrapped the little thing in a wisp of wiry grass to cushion it and tucked it down inside his purse, which held no coins but did have several long cork-oak acorns and half a dozen interesting shells from the shore.

Ahjvar nodded satisfaction and looked back at the bard. "Now, Lady Deyandara—we'll be on our way. Had the brigands robbed your bags before Ghu found you, do you want to go up the hill and see what's of use left in their camp, or can we give you anything to aid you on *your* way?"

"They hadn't bothered to search me or my saddlebags at all, beyond taking the jug of beer the last village gave me. They were too busy arguing over what to do with me," said Deyandara. "And I'm not going up there again for anything. I'll come with you to Marakand."

"You will not."

She raised her chin. "I will. The high king will know everything that I could tell him long before I could reach him."

The Praitan high king should have been able to summon his warriors and ride to throw the city folk out by now, but if he had, the lady would probably have heard of it in the villages, now that they drew near the caravan road. So perhaps the high king of the Praitans did not much care about a folk so far from his own.

"And I can't go back to the Duina Catairna. I can't." She repeated that to herself, as if for some reason she only now realized it. "I can't. They'll think I fled them. They'll think I betrayed . . . but you're going to Marakand as the champion of Catairanach," the lady plunged on. "In a way, you're going as the champion of all Praitan. And there should be a witness there, to take word to Catairanach— she did tell me to come back, afterwards—and to her folk, and to the high king. Maybe I—I haven't seen my duties clearly, before now."

"No," said Ghu, and wondered at himself.

Ahjvar's eyes narrowed. "Ghu says not."

"You'll let your—your groom rule you?"

"Call him my shield-bearer, if groom's not grand enough. I generally listen to him."

Ahjvar did not have a shield among his gear. He said there was no point. But it meant something else to the Praitans: an esquire, a young warrior serving a senior.

"He's—" Whatever she had been going to say might have been

interesting. It made her cheeks flush. "You're using him as an excuse.
I am coming. It's my duty."

"If you go to Marakand, you go on your own. Ghu." Ahjvar
jerked his head to the horses and kicked ash over the embers of the
fire, turned his back on the lady and acted from then on as if she were
not there.

Her mouth clenched to a narrow line, but her eyes shone too
bright, angry tears welling. Ahjvar had hurt her, and she hurt already
from her grief for her good dog and her fear. Maybe she was honest
that she saw it her duty, and maybe she wanted to prove to Ahj, who
had come riding out of lightning with the fire gold on his hair to
save her, that she was not a girl, a child too young and thoughtless
for the weighty calling she claimed. Or for other things.

Well, it was her choice, where she rode. Ghu would not make it
his. He kept silent as well and saddled the horses, giving the piebald
the baggage this time.

When they left, the lady followed. Her bay hill-pony stood not
too much shorter than their horses, and she had no trouble keeping
them in sight. They couldn't outrun her, not without abusing their
own weary mounts. Ahjvar settled for pretending he did not notice.

But there were wolves calling away towards the mountains that
night. While Ghu was cooking a stew of dry ham and broken wheat
and some greens he'd gathered—how did the Praitans grow so tall
when they ate everything boiled to mush?—Ahjvar stalked off to
Lady Deyandara's distant twinkling fire. After a while it went out,
and he came back leading her pony, with her walking nervously triumphant at his side.

The very next day they came to the great road, and as they travelled
it, the cleft between the low range of the Malagru and the towering
Pillars of the Sky rose slowly over the western horizon before them.

CHAPTER III

The last day's journey on the climbing road to Marakand was on a paved highway, which ran along the north bank of the ravine, hemmed in by steep-rising mountain walls, all shale and juniper, or outright cliff. The previous time Ahjvar had ridden to Marakand, forty years ago, the road had been disappearing beneath an accumulation of dust and dung, cobbles missing, kerbs cracked and fallen away. The city was reclaiming its highway. He wasn't sure he liked to see that. Marakand had been a great fortress once, seat of an empire that ruled all Over-Malagru and the Stone Desert—or so a wandering wizard of the Kinsai-av had told him when he was a boy. Nobody had taken it for anything but an evening's tale, though there were a few songs that told the same history, if only people would listen to them properly. Ahjvar thought he might believe in the old forgotten empire. The fortress at the eastern end of the pass and its mate at the west, which he'd seen long ago, were built of vaster stone, harder lines, than any other part of Marakand, like the work of giants. The repairs of later masons showed like woollen patches stitched on a tattered silken robe. Even now, Marakand was as great a city as any in this part of the world, larger than Star River Crossing on the edge of Praitannec lands at the ford of the Avain Noreia, larger than Gold Harbour itself, even not counting the dusty sprawl of caravanserais outside the city walls. Deyandara was certainly awed by the distant looming mass of the eastern fort, long before they ever approached it, or perhaps she was grimly comparing it to a royal *dinaz*, and calculating the chances of the Catairnans ever reclaiming their land. The few travellers they'd talked with since joining the road spoke of the Duina Catairna as a conquered land, kingless, its lords scattered, its folk abandoned.

Ghu was less impressed by the fort, but he'd been in the Golden City of the emperor.

"Ghu," Ahjvar called back, "you're in charge of keeping the *bard* out of trouble."

Ghu gave them both a slow smile. The girl looked insulted. Ahjvar reined in the yellow gelding, dropping back between them.

"Understand," he said. "You weren't invited, my lady. You'll be more trouble and stir up more trouble trying to follow than if I keep you where I can see you, that's all. And Ghu, whatever you think of him, is good at surviving in cities. You're not."

"You don't—"

"Ah, you've been to Marakand before?"

"No, but—"

"You've been to Two Hills? Star River Crossing?"

"No."

"Then you stick with Ghu and do what he tells you."

She pursed her lips and said nothing. Stupid, stubborn, silly *child*. Anyone but a bloody-minded child would have gotten fed up with being so clearly unwanted and taken herself off days ago. She held fixed to the notion he had belittled her honour as a would-be bard; she was going to prove him wrong, prove herself right to herself, maybe, by seeing this foul business through and making a poem of it.

He'd have to change his name again. Head for Noble Cedar Harbour, maybe, the easternmost of the Five Cities, where they didn't know him. Though if Catairanach kept her word, he shouldn't have to. He couldn't quite believe that, but he tried. It was the only hope anyone had held out to him, gods-rejected as he was, in decades.

Deyandara should be still toddling at her master's heels, carrying his pipes, learning her trade. She was too young to be on the road on her own.

"Ghu," he said, turning his shoulder on her, switching to Imperial, "don't get yourself in trouble looking after the girl. If she runs afoul of any city authority, you don't need to know her. Just someone you met on the road coming up the pass, all right? I'll drag her out of whatever messes she falls into later, if I can."

Why, when the brat gave him nightmares so that he hardly dared sleep, even when Ghu lay with an arm flung over him, trying to keep his dreams away. Convincing the girl of all sorts of things that were—probably just as well, given the way he caught her watching him sometimes. A few days travelling together didn't make him responsible for her, and she wasn't—he didn't *know* she was any responsibility of his. Besides, it was her brother the high king who should be looking after her. He didn't even like her.

Ghu nodded solemnly, which didn't mean he agreed or would obey. He'd packed away his travel-stained plaid Praitannec tunic and looked a proper Over-Malagru servant of some prosperous small trader, respectably but not richly dressed, colony fashion: a short wrapped gown with a broad sash, wide-legged trousers tucked into soft boots, a round felt hat with a tassel, the colours all modest grey and brown. Only his hair, unruly as a hill-pony's mane, spoiled that well-groomed illusion.

"Horses, I think," said Ahjvar, switching languages yet again.

He had made sure this morning to look as respectable as a lord's horse-buyer ought to, scarlet tunic over a shirt of bleached linen, blue trousers, and the twisted gold bracelets, which hid the pink and healing skin of his wrists.

"You won't sell my mare."

"*My* mare. Which you bought with *my* money. No, we're buying. Say, desert-breds for our lord, let's say a lord of the Duina Galatan; it's a good long ways away."

"What?" asked Deyandara.

"You met us on the road, a week or so back. When we saved you from brigands." He scowled at her. "Which lets us deny you nicely if you make yourself a liability." He added fairly, "And the reverse, of course. Feel free to insist to anyone who asks that you hardly know us. And don't go claiming you're kin of the high king."

"Why not?"

"Because even though he doesn't seem to have done so yet, or at least word hasn't run ahead of him this far, the high king ought to be doing something to raise the tribes to take back the Duina Catairna. He has to, if he doesn't plan to see Marakand gnawing away at all Over-Malagru. Claiming to be blood of the Duina Andara might bring you to harm, especially if your brother's gone to war." She should have seen that herself.

She frowned and bit her lip. "Just . . . Deya?" Expecting him to object?

"Good."

Deyandara flushed prettily and broke into a dimpled smile, as if the word were effusive praise. Cold hells. Ahjvar urged his horse on ahead again, leaving them to follow, as befitted groom and hanger-on.

There was more traffic on the road here: a caravan of mules coming up from Over-Malagru; a small string of a half-dozen camels heading east, one carrying its own calf in a sort of cradle on its back, led by a white-haired Five Cities woman, escorted by young men who were probably her sons; an ox-cart piled high with green fodder, wobbling its way into the city; other carts and donkeys and ponies heading home to the hill-villages from city markets. It was late afternoon. A long-distance caravan flowed towards them from the fortress's reaching shadow; ponies and donkeys, ox-carts and all, they crowded off the road. A river of camels, each a hillock of goods: Marakander silver, Northron furs and sea-ivory, mountain gems, dyestuff of Tiypur, which would come back again as Nabbani silks, Westgrasslander wool and leather . . .

They drew aside themselves; there was no contesting the right of way with that. The piebald, carrying the baggage this morning, decided to take fright at the great, grunting current, till Ghu slipped down and held his head, whispering. The outriders called out and laughed with one another, full of good cheer at being on the road again or replete with the pleasures of the city. Ahjvar was looking forward to a bath-house himself.

Ghu, leaning back against the white mare's shoulder, took it all in with a look of serene enjoyment, as if it were a play laid on for his entertainment.

Finally the road was clear, and they were able to ride on. The ruin of a wall stretched before them, anchored north and south against precipices, once guarded there by lesser towers, derelict since before the present city ever rose. The wall, in its day, would have completely barred the riven valley between the Malagru mountains running up to the north and, to the south, the steep and snow-capped Pillars of the Sky, which made the Malagru look like hills. No, call it a half-ruined wall, rather. New work was raising it again, gangs of labourers at several points, spreading down from the shells of the lesser towers. A road of churned mud wound along it. Personally, he would have repaired his walls *before* attacking his neighbours, but in the event, it didn't seem likely a Praitannec army was going to come storming up the pass any time soon, so perhaps there was no hurry. Going through the long gaps where the wall had fallen or settled into a broken ridge, easily climbed even with horses, would be simple enough at night, but by day it was overlooked, and for an army or even a small war-band to get itself past the eastern fort would do little good. The city itself had walls and gates. You'd only be trapped in the narrow valley, with the garrison of the fort at your back.

The fort itself was no ruin. Squat, square towers straddled the road, sharp-edged, unweathered by sand and frost, and the gates— never closed except in tales of near-forgotten wars—were faced with beaten bronze, dark but uncorroded, patterned with bulls and camels. Even the river, which had once flowed from the south to curve around the city, tumbling down the pass and out to lose itself in other rivers Over-Malagru, had once been guarded, forced into a narrow channel, swift and deep, overlooked by towers. The riverbed, all broken stone and tangled greenery, had been mostly dry even when he first came to Marakand. An occasional spring or autumn flood from the mountains might turn the ravine along the city's north side into a shallow lake, for a time, until the thirsty stone drank it, but little water from it ever reached the lower hills, and it never flowed for long. If the river had ever had a name, the Marakanders did not remember it. They called it only "the ravine" and carted their street-sweepings out to it.

Ahjvar reined in again as they drew near the gateway, letting Deyandara draw level with him once more. "Marakanders," he observed, "like to write everything down. They make lists of what caravan-masters pass in and out and what they're carrying, and anything else they think noteworthy. At the moment, Praitans might be noteworthy. Keep your lies simple and consistent."

She nodded, lips set, as though preparing to lie valiantly. Ahjvar sighed, thinking of Lady Deyandara tied up in a sack like Ghu's hens, dumped on the threshold of some respectable chieftain's hall, while he and Ghu galloped away into the night. Snickered. She gave him a disapproving scowl.

The fodder-cart, which they were just overtaking, passed in under the cool tunnel of the arch without a glance from the guardswoman propped against the wall. She looked the same sort that had lounged at the gates decades ago, a young woman in a short grey tunic, bare-legged, wearing sandals, with a two-foot staff swinging from her belt and a spear, the better to prop herself up. Her helmet was only a cap of stiffened leather with a metal frame; she wore no armour but did have a rectangular shield, which she had leant against the wall. Within the city itself, the guards carried no weapons but their short staves. The Marakanders did not permit weapons of war on the streets except for officers and the few bodyguards allowed to a senator or head of one of the Twenty Families, the rulers of the city. Sensible, in Ahjvar's opinion, when you had so many people of no high honour so close together, though he would rather that it did not apply to him.

Deyandara had reined in and was frankly gawking, staring up at the gates.

A mate to the first guard slouched in a sentry's niche opposite the woman, eyeing them thoughtfully. A third came purposefully out of a dark doorway under the arch, angling over to intercept them. A clerk, maybe. He clutched what proved to be a waxed tablet and had a brown band to his tunic-hem. Deyandara shut her mouth and twitched her pony closer. Ahjvar gritted his teeth and resisted the urge to lean down and clout her.

"Good afternoon, master. Your name, and whence you've come?" the man asked, in the caravan-road version of trade Nabbani, stylus poised over his tablet. Everyone in Marakand seemed to speak both bastard Nabbani and the Stone Desert dialect that was the language of the western caravan road, and to slide from one to the other without conscious effort, sometimes halfway through a sentence, sometimes conducting a conversation, one party in one tongue, another in the other.

Ahjvar gave the clerk a nod that was remote courtesy. A lord's retainer, a horsemaster, was nearly a lord in his own right and had no need to humble himself to common guardsmen. No point trying to bribe him not to take down their names, either. The man would no doubt be happy to oblige, if given enough to share with the other witnesses, and then, unless he was utterly without initiative, would tell someone off to follow them and find out where they lodged, to find out why they had felt the need.

"Travellers from the Duina Galatan in the north. My name's Clentara."

The soldier set that down in quick, neat colony-Nabbani characters. He wasn't interested in Ghu; his eye flicked over the Nabbani and shrugged him off as only a lesser servant, didn't even ask his name. Lingered on Deyandara, obviously another Praitan. "Your wife?"

Ahjvar flinched. "She's only—"

"Deya," said Deyandara, before he could say anything about a chance-met acquaintance of the road. "A bard of the Duina Galatan."

Silly, *stupid* girl. A bard—she immediately made herself the noteworthy figure in the party.

The soldier-clerk set that down.

"You've been to Marakand before, Mistress Deya?" he asked.

"No," she said brightly. "But I wanted to learn songs of the western road, so I—"

The clerk didn't want to listen to explanations. "Then make sure your men know that it's forbidden to carry weapons inside the city walls. Even for a bodyguard, going armed is forbidden, for outlanders. He'll need to pack that sword away in the baggage once you leave the caravanserai suburb."

She nodded.

"And wizards are forbidden in Marakand. On pain of death. You understand?"

Deyandara blanched and flushed red, guiltily, under that look. "I'm not a wizard. Truly. If I were, I wouldn't come to the city. I know of your law and I've no wish to offend your goddess."

The clerk shrugged. She had been warned; it wasn't his business. He flipped the cover of his tablet closed and waved them on.

Ahjvar resisted the urge to drag Deyandara away by the ear.

"You—" he began, and clenched his teeth. The long archway was dark, cool after the sun outside; but doorways opened into the towers of the fortress, and they weren't alone, anyhow, another cluster of home-going Malagru hill-farmers ambled to meet them, some riding, some driving, some leading ponies. They wore embroidered jackets and pleated white kilts, a tall, pale-skinned, dark-haired folk, worshipping other gods than the Lady for all they paid taxes to the city; they talked together in their own language, laughing raucously at some joke. Passing the guards, they fell silent.

Emerging into sunlight, Deyandara put Ghu between Ahjvar and herself, and then raised her voice to nevertheless be heard. "You're not really going to want to be spending a lot of time dickering over horses, after all, and this way—"

But Ghu broke into song then, obscuring her voice and startling her into silence. Just in time, too. A lower wall edged the road here, part of the fort's enclosure, and its gate opened for a rider on a stocky pony. With a curious glance at them, the rider, a guardsman in a scarlet tunic and dark leggings, kicked his mount on ahead.

Useful to find out what the colours meant. Ahjvar had forgotten, if he'd ever known. He didn't think he'd seen street guard in red in his day. Deyandara had said something about the temple guard, which hadn't existed forty years ago.

Ghu broke off his song. "That," he told Deyandara, "is called 'The Turtle's Sisters.' It's about a girl given to the river . . ."

Deyandara seemed to get the message. She fell back again, and Ghu with her. A boy on a donkey almost hidden under bundles of reeds from some wet pool of the ravine scrambled up onto the road to join them, heading into the city. He chattered happily in trade Nabbani, wanting to know who they were, where they were coming from, and if the tall grouchy one was Deya's father. The three began trading songs, while Ahjvar rode ahead, studying the landscape. Across the ravine to the south there was cliff-topped city wall, not nearly so old as the ruined wall of the pass, and in better repair, though still crumbling and vine-grown; there were no gates in the city wall until the Riverbend, over a mile distant at the northwestern corner, where the ravine made a sharp bend from the south and the sprawl of caravanserais along the road began. Here the northern flank of the road was scattered with the paddocks of dealers in animals, but the bulk of the suburb stretched from the city graveyards for a mile or so west along the road towards the distant second fortress, which watched the pass against the desert tribes; the six gates of the city ran from Riverbend around two of its three sides, the last, the Fleshmarket, in the east. There was not a single one along the ravine;

the earthquake hadn't led to any major changes there that he could see.

Deyandara began one of the shorter—which meant you could get through it in a mile of riding—ballads of Cairangorm, king of the Duina Catairna, and his murder by his faithless wife, stopping after every verse to translate the story for the enthralled reed-cutter. Ghu came up at a sudden canter to put himself and the packhorse between Ahjvar and the girl again. "I only thought to hush her before she told all the passers-by we were liars. Let her sing and stop scowling; it won't do any good. Do we go into the city or stay at a caravanserai?"

"Harder to find stabling within the city proper, I imagine. For a singer, since we're stuck with that story, either would do, but out here there'll be a lot less notice of odd comings and goings. Caravanserai."

With relief, he saw the first of the two bridges ahead, its three spans crossing the empty riverbed, and the square tower over the Riverbend Gate.

The boy urged his donkey into a reed-rustling canter and, safely out of reach, turned back to blow a kiss at Deyandara before bouncing onto the bridge, leaving them, finally, alone.

"Good," Ahjvar said under his breath. "You, *Deya*—" No, he didn't trust himself even to speak to her yet.

After one look at Ahjvar, she hunched her shoulders, losing all the bright pleasure that had lit her face while flirting with the reed-boy.

Good.

Deyandara still trailed warily behind them as they passed an enclosed triangle of dusty, pockmarked earth, a small field between three roads. A graveyard, with a charnel-house crouching four-square and heavy at the west end, a man trundling a wheelbarrow of old bones into its pillared porch from an open pit. Beyond, on the western road, between steep-rising mountains to either side, lay a straggle of dusty lanes and caravanserais. There were inns and stables hugged around smaller yards, taverns and tea-houses, of course, bathhouses. No god, though. The three gods of the city had all dwelt within the city walls, and now two of them were dead or faded away. There was a blockhouse for the city guard garrison that kept order in the suburb, too. In the old days, it had even had its own magistrate. Probably still did. City law kept any shanty-towns of caravan-parasites from growing, though some of the taverns, last time he was here, had seemed to employ rather a large number of servants who didn't spend much time serving, not wine and bread, anyway.

He didn't really want to stay in a caravanserai. They tended to watch their gates very closely, with all the caravans' goods and gear and beasts within to defend. An inn would be better, but first he paused in the road to seize Deyandara by the arm, when she incautiously rode within reach.

"If you say one word to embroider that story any further, I will beat you."

"Let go!" She tried to pull away. "You're hurting me."

Ahjvar didn't slacken his grip. "Do you understand me? Did you ever stop to think I had a reason for what I said?"

She glared, white-faced, every freckle standing stark against her pallor.

"If they take me, and I am yours, they will kill you too," he said, and shook her for emphasis. "They will drag you up to the palace plaza and hang you. They will probably torture you first. You won't be able to say you just met me on the road; you don't know anything about me. You won't be able to say your royal brother will be angry, because they won't care about that, unless it's to use you as a hostage and hang you later, once they've got what they want from him. Hanging is not a nice death, and not always a quick death."

Her eyes filled with tears, but he thought it fury, not pain.

"We're blocking the road," Ghu said, low-voiced warning. Ahjvar turned the girl loose as a party of caravaneers afoot came by, all dusty coats and headscarves and the rank reek of camels and sweat, arguing with one another about whether to go to the bathhouse or find food first.

He chose an inn not quite at random, a place with the usual flat Marakander roof and a useful accretion of porches and galleries. As the aristocratic bard's retainer, it made sense for him to handle the money, and the girl's fuming silence could be mistaken for lordly disdain. A private room, stabling for four horses, a meal to be brought to them. Mistress Deya was obviously a woman of wealth, about as much in keeping with a youthful bard as having her own sworn spearman. Ghu disappeared with the horses as befitted a responsible groom, which he would have done just the same if he'd been emperor of all Nabban. He reappeared, draped with the last of the baggage, to find Ahjvar staring out the window and Deyandara, arms folded, face tear-stained, squatting with her back against the wall.

"I didn't touch her," Ahjvar growled, looking around, though there was no accusation in Ghu's face. The girl's brief outbreak of weeping had been silent and private. Anger, definitely. A better outlet than shouting or throwing things, when it was him she was angry with. But maybe it was herself. He wasn't feeling sorry for her. She'd been a fool, and folly could get her killed. She was so damned young.

Ghu nodded, dropped the bags and patted the girl's head in passing, joining him at the window. A rap at the door announced a servant hard on his heels with a tray of filled dumplings and a jug each of wine and water.

"Eat," Ahjvar told them. He couldn't face the food, himself.

He needed to think. To walk. Somewhere well away from anyone he wanted to hurt. "I'm going out. Ghu, you explain things to her again, in nice easy words so she can understand, and then take her out and trot her around to wherever a bard might reasonably go, if she were hunting new stories. Don't forget to lock the door and bar the window-shutters. There's a porch roof right below, easy to get in." Or out. "You keep the key, not her. Keep her out of fights and don't let any drunken caravan-mercenaries fondle her." What else? He tossed the man a purse. "In case you need it. Don't give it all to beggars. Don't buy any more horses."

"Sword," Ghu said.

"Who said I was going into the city?" He didn't plan on it, not yet. But he unbelted the sword and handed it over. "I should be back before too late. Don't come looking for me if I'm not."

Ghu gave no answer to that. He would, of course. Ahjvar left without a word to the bard.

"Dumplings," he heard Ghu saying to her. "Here, try. They're good. Spicy."

There were a few purchases he wanted to make, anyway. The caravanserai district was always a good place for picking up odds and ends. And he needed a new rope.

Travellers new-come to the city would find themselves a bathhouse, have their linens laundered, find a tavern, hear the news. Not in necessarily that order. Ahjvar walked, and kept his ears open. He bought his rope, then picked up a cameleer's coat in a lean-to against a caravanserai wall that functioned as a pawnshop, in another, a couple of the striped shawls or scarves of the sort caravaneers so often wore swathed about their neck and shoulders, ready to pull up over head and face against the dust. Deyandara wore a scarf, but it was a very Praitannec weave and too memorably bright. He bundled it all up and found a tavern serving something claimed for Northron-style beer, though he didn't see many Northrons drinking there, and the host was a woman from the Great Grass. Tasted it and thought he knew why his was the only blond head in the place. Listened, asked a few questions. They'd travelled so swiftly and secretly, keeping well away from even outlying farmsteads, dodging other travellers until they were on Marakand's own highway rising to the pass, that he'd had no news out of the east. Even with an army, the high king could have been in the Duina Catairna by now, if he'd set out as soon as he had word of the queen's murder. If Durandau had taken such swift action, Ahjvar wanted to know.

This tavern was full of gangs come in from the west who knew nothing of the Duina Catairna and cared less. Useless. Still in his role as Clentara, he wandered on, tried other places. Picked up a rumour here, a word there. Had a worrying thought about the rider in the red tunic, as the red did mean temple guard, and it was couriers who rode ponies between the eastern and western forts and the city. Temple courier. Watching for Praitans? Not much he could do now if they had been. What he really wanted to know about was the Voice, though. She kept to the temple and was never seen in public, these days. Was she the real power in the city? No one knew. The other chief priests weren't spoken of as if they were rulers; nor was the Lady herself. It was always *the temple* and *the Voice*. Maybe Catairanach had identified her enemy accurately after all.

No curfew in the suburb, though by full dark the place had quieted down, most gangs gone to their rest. He found a wineshop full of stragglers, edged into them, asking about the road, as anyone might, and the army the city had sent to the Duina Catairna. He'd had to leave his homeland out in the east, not their business why, was it? Wandering a bit now, took service with a lady to get here, but didn't think much of her. Wondering if there would be much profit in going back to join this army, was there any land promised . . .

There was not, he was told, and no hope of it. The temple had hired the war-band of a Grasslander chieftain last winter, and they had their own temple guard and their own corps of holy warriors, the Red Masks, as well. The Grasslander warlord Ketsim might take him, if he really thought he wanted to take oath to Ketsim, but he wouldn't get any land out of it.

"The same godless bastard that was governor of Serakallash after the Lake-Lord took it, and we all thought he was dead when Sera retook her town," said a Red Desert man with a horse-tattooed face. "And up he pops here, not so long after, with far too many of the Lake-Lord's scum trailing after him. Collected them on the way, I guess. They'll sell their spears to anyone. The temple bought them and sent them Over-Malagru."

"It's the temple will be getting what land's going," someone else said, leaning in from the shadows. "No hope for you, friend. Go home and marry a rich widow, if you want land."

Someone threw in a story about someone they knew who'd done just that, only to have the first husband turn up, not lost with his caravan after all, and how the threesome settled down together, back in the Western Grass . . . After a while, Ahjvar asked a question or two about the Voice. Goddess and queen of the city, wasn't she?

Ignorant tribesman. The business of setting him right took another two jugs of wine, which somehow he ended up paying for, and a platter or two of greasy flatbread and salty cheeses, likewise. Not only was the Voice neither the goddess nor a queen, she was possessed, she was mad, she was the power ruling the city, she was a hermit living in a cave beneath the temple, she was kept locked in a tower above the ravine—this though anyone on the road could see there was no tower—she didn't exist at all. The Marakander-born mistress of the wineshop grew fed up with them and squeezed in on the bench between Ahjvar and the Red Desert man. He flinched away from her, losing the thread of what he had been saying. He hated being trapped, hated being touched at all. He let nobody but Ghu that close to him, and pinned against a heavyset Grasslander, he had nowhere to go when the woman spread herself contentedly, thigh against his, to set them all straight over a third? fifth? jug, for which nobody seemed to need to pay. He ducked his head, shut his eyes a moment against the panic, the racing of his heart, forced his breath to slow, hands to unclench on the table. Pay attention, now that he'd finally worked them around to what he wanted to know. The Voice of the Lady was not the ruler of the city. The goddess of the deep well, the Lady herself, was; she spoke for the Lady, that was what *Voice* meant. And no, you could not go and ask her to tell your fortune, she wasn't some hill-folk soothsayer, she spoke only to the priests.

"And it's a base lie that she's mad." The woman glared around the table. "She's a pious, holy woman living a modest, secluded life, not like some of the priestesses you hear about in foreign parts."

A few sidelong glances, a few shrugs. Grass and desert folk; their gods and goddesses had no priests.

"She lives in an apartment in the old hospice along the ravine, where they used to tend the dying in my father's day. I should know; my own brother's wife's sister is a cook there. Towers and caves! The Voice spends her day in meditation and prayer, and the world would be none the worse if a few more did likewise."

"What about the Lady, then?" Ahjvar—or Clentara—asked. "Have you ever seen her?"

Shock. Only the priests and priestesses, and the Red Masks, were permitted to visit the Lady. Not like some gods, out carrying on like everyday people.

"Goddess in the mountains took a human husband," a darkly tattooed Westgrasslander man said, and started a wandering tale about a battle up in the Pillars of the Sky and a lake-goddess there, wizards, demons; the human husband never did get into the story. Hard to say what his point actually was, as he kept forgetting what he had said, repeating himself, interrupted by the Red Desert man; it became a muddle of horse-goddesses and sandstorms and warrior-priestesses. The wineshop-keeper's hand was doing some wandering too. Ahjvar let the conversation go and tried to shut her hand out from his mind, since he couldn't do much else about it without drawing attention to his doing so. They were on—he'd lost track, but it was someone else paying now, and he hadn't even been drinking, really, since the first cup. A lot of gesturing and sloshing took care of most of it. His good tunic, too. He caught the woman's hand and pulled it up to the table. Avoided her eye. She wasn't getting the reaction she hoped for, and he kept thinking of how a knife between the bones of the wrist would keep her damn hand on the table where it belonged, which wasn't quite the shape of his mind, Great Gods, please. It was a plump, beringed hand, clean nails, and it turned, fingers closing over his. She oozed a substantial pair of breasts around his shoulder, lips hotly crawling on the back of his neck.

Sliding under the table as if drunk to insensibility would just leave him stuck there getting kicked for the next hour or so. Leaning over to the desert man and saying, "Here, I don't want her, she's all yours," might get him kicked too, more maliciously. A graceful exit, that was what was needed, now that they were onto the merits of Serakallashi horses, and the Voice was a topic long in the past. Before he turned the table over and killed someone, without even the madness to blame it on.

"Here," he said, and squirmed out from under the wineshop-keeper. "You talk to my friend. Ou'side a moment. Be back."

He staggered away, bouncing, he hoped convincingly, off a few other tables, making a wide circle around a boy collecting empty cups. Found the street door by fumbling his way along the wall. He stumbled down the steps from the porch. Movement in the corner of his eye, shadow on shadow in the black corner by the door, scent of a body.

He continued unsteadily along the dusty, churned-up lane, turned the corner of the building, as a man might in such need.

Another corner. Around that too. He waited. Waited. Finally heard breathing, cautious movement, and then saw the hint of solidity in the darkness. He shoved the heel of his hand into where a face should be, kicked high as the shape reeled back with a grunt, and heard the man fall, followed by the reassuring moan of a body that wouldn't be getting up in haste.

Thief, preying on drunken caravan-mercenaries? Working alone didn't seem too wise. Most of them would be leaving in straggling gangs. A spy set on to watch the little band of Mistress Deya, because of all wandering Praitans a bard was the most obvious agent to be gleaner of information for her high king? Fast work, if so, but his party was perhaps not so hard to find. He left the man curled up groaning and slunk warily back to the inn, where the young porter wasn't any too pleased to be woken to let him in, but since he'd left by the door, better to return by it as well.

Ghu had, of course, given up the one bed, easily big enough for three, not that he'd intended to allow her into it, to the girl's modest solitude. Ahjvar stripped off his wine-reeking tunic and shirt to join him on a thin mat on the floor.

"Nice evening?" he asked. Deyandara seemed to be asleep. He didn't much care if he did wake her.

"We met a family of Stone Desert singers. They juggle knives, too, and dance on a rope. Deya told a few stories."

"Kept her out of mischief, anyway."

"About the Duina Catairna, mostly. It seems to be on her mind, and of course, people are interested, since Marakand's at war with the Catairnans. She was looking," said Ghu, in his ear, "at your sword. I took it away from her. How about you?"

"I was nearly ravished by a woman with an enormous bosom." It was funny now, yes. He could make it so by telling Ghu.

Ghu's hand found his face, a light touch, no more. Ghu knew it wasn't funny, not deep in the marrow. He'd told Ghu too many things in the dark nights.

"It's your yellow hair. They can't help themselves. You should stay out of taverns."

"It was a respectable wineshop, I thought. And someone was following me."

"Did you kill him?"

"He might have just been after my purse, so—no. I bought you a coat."

"Do I need a coat?"

"In case you need to turn into a caravan guard. It has nice big pockets you can put things in."

"Ahj, you sound drunk."

"I'm not."

"You smell drunk."

"I spilt a lot of wine."

"Wasteful." He could hear the smile in Ghu's voice. The hand slid down to his chest. Not possessive, not intrusive. Just . . . there. "You must have spilt some of it down your throat, I think. For such a big man, it doesn't seem to take much to make you silly. Go to sleep."

"I'm leaving in the morning. Soon as I get a little sleep. I think Mistress Deya and Clentara had best have had a falling-out. Better yet, you can hint delicately that I'm just some godless mercenary she took up with on the road. Blame it on yellow hair. And once I'm gone I want you to take her and get out of here."

"Out of this inn?"

"Out of Marakand. Head back east. Wish for a different clerk on the gate. Don't make it an obvious rush, but go tomorrow. I'll give you a day before I do anything to stir anyone up. Try to time it so you're going out with all the home-going market-folk, lots of bustle, right? You know what you're doing. We've done it before."

"Leave you a horse?"

"No. And devils take her tongue, put her on the best horse and some baggage on the pony. Someone's bound to question if she's really the one in charge, otherwise. Get the lot of them good and dusty. Better, sell them and buy yourself a couple of hill-ponies. Or if you think you'll have to run, desert-breds, but don't buy pretty ones. You have appallingly lordly taste in horses, for a slave, y'know. Change her name. Call her your wife. Put a scarf over her shiny hair. Tell her I'm going to kill her if she opens her mouth at all before you're a day's ride from the eastern fortress. I don't like the attention we've gotten, and I'm liking less, the more I think of it, that someone tried to tail me coming out of that wineshop."

"I'll come back after I find someplace safe for the lady."

"I wish you wouldn't."

Ghu made no answer to that and seemed to fall asleep, close against him.

Ahjvar did not. The girl's breathing was too loud, too—present. It hadn't been so bad when they camped, she on her side of the fire, he as far from her as he could be without making it obvious, and Ghu choosing to lie close by him. Under a roof, within four walls, he could hear her, smell her. She and Ghu had found a bathhouse; they both smelt of soap and scented oil, but she had chosen poison jessamine, not jasmine. He could *feel* her there, between him and the window, which he didn't like, which was foolish, when he could throw her with one hand.

Don't be stupid, he told himself. You're used to her by now. She's nothing to do with Hyllau; red hair and upturned nose or not, she's never heard of Hyllau but in a song; she certainly doesn't know what scent the hag wore. Go to sleep.

He did. But the smoke stole into his dreams.

Not here, he said. Not now, not yet, but the words made no sound. A blackened claw of a hand bright with the wineshop-keeper's rings seized him, pulled him down, rolled onto him, heavy flesh that crackled, skin flaking, and Deyandara grimaced above him, face contorted in what could have been a grin or a leer or a snarl of agony, hand wound in his hair, pinning his head down, forcing her mouth onto his, and the flames roared louder than his screaming. A sudden sharp pain in his ear.

Not his screaming but the girl's, and Ghu had an arm around his throat, was gripping his wrist with his other hand, dragging his arm back, hissing, "Ahj, Ahj, wake up! *Wake up!*"

He froze. Night. Dark. Not sure where he was, where they were, not sure for a moment of anything except that Ghu had him, Ghu was safe, his ear hurt, and the stink of heavy smoke was fading. It was only nightmare, only the old nightmare, back too soon, but not the sick burnt-hollow feeling the curse's tide left behind when it swept through, consuming him, not that yet, not yet. He didn't remember dreams then, didn't remember anything, which might be a blessing. Some would say so. Not knowing what he had done, whom he had slaughtered to feed *her* could be worse. But he remembered the dream, so he hadn't been killing. *She* stirred, but didn't wake. Not yet. He was not empty, not hollow, scoured, burnt to a husk. Not yet.

He was muttering that under his breath. *Not yet, not yet, no.*

"Ahj, are you awake?" Ghu asked.

He sighed, which the man took for answer enough. Ghu's arms relaxed, turned into more of an embrace, a hand sliding down to his, a gentle pressure prying his fingers loose . . . he was gripping his sword, and he had not even known where Ghu stowed it after he gave it into his hands in the afternoon. "You can let go now," Ghu said, his gentle, talking-to-idiots-and-horses voice. "It's all right, let go."

There was a whimper, just a breath, hardly that, and far too close. Ahjvar flinched and dropped the sword, found he was standing with one knee on the bed.

"Ghu . . ."

"It's all right. She's all right." Ghu spoke Praitannec, then. "You didn't hurt her. You only scared her a little. That's all."

"Scared . . . ! Seven d-devils!" Shadow of an indignant squeak. It turned into a stuttering, gulping chain of sobs. Ahjvar slid boneless to the floor, sickened. Ghu let him go and crawled onto the bed. By the sound of it, he was being thoroughly wept-upon.

"It's all right now, it's all right." More of the horse-soothing voice. "He has nightmares."

Ahjvar made some inarticulate noise, head bowed to his knees, shivering. Nightmares.

Someone rapped on the door. "Mistress Deya? Mistress Deya!"

Another frozen moment. He hauled himself to his feet, sword in hand again. "What?" he snarled.

"A woman screamed," said the voice on the other side of the door, warily. "I—I'd like to speak to Mistress Deya."

"The lady has nightmares," Ghu called. "She's well enough now. Thank you."

"Nevertheless . . ." That was a second voice, the innkeeper himself, not the young porter.

Ahjvar ground his teeth on obscenities. Good people, brave people. No idea where the sword's scabbard was. Ghu trod past him and kicked it skidding his way over the floor. It hit his foot as the door opened onto lamplight. He sheathed the blade, hoping it would look as though he had merely grabbed it up at the unexpected knock.

"I beg your pardon," Deyandara said, and she came forward too, wan and dishevelled and shivering, wrapping a blanket over her nakedness. She'd undressed fully with Ghu in the room? But she no doubt thought him uninterested. Not, Ahjvar was fairly certain, the case. There'd been something between the boy and the Widow Akay's eldest daughter, nighttime walkings-out unknown by the village and the girl's mother, that first year he'd come to Ahjvar, till the girl up and married a fisherman down the coast.

"It's . . . it's been an affliction since childhood," Deyandara almost whispered. "I thought it had passed off for good, but . . ." An embarrassed smile, apologetic, ashamed, directed half at the floor. "I do thank you for your concern."

The innkeeper peered around warily, careful not to look at her too directly, undressed as she was. Nodded, said gruffly, "Well, then. Sorry to disturb you." Took his boy firmly by the scruff of the neck— the porter had no courtesy to match his master's and was frankly gawking at the girl's smooth shoulder where the blanket slipped. Ghu held them up a moment, lighting the room's lamp at theirs, and then they were gone. He dropped the bar of the door again.

"They'll ask us to leave in the morning," Ghu said matter-of-factly. "Disturbing the house."

Ahjvar swore and crossed to the girl in a stride, seizing her by the shoulder. She stifled her shriek, gone stiff, wide-eyed and trembling in his grasp. He ran a thumb over the darkness at the base of her throat, not shadow in the tiny flame of the lamp but slick blood. A nick, no more. When he dropped his hand, she fled back to the bed.

He sat down with his back to the door, sword across his legs, watching his hands on the cracked red leather of the scabbard.

"There was a woman who killed me once," he said at last. "You look like her. It's not your fault. But you get into my nightmares."

"Who killed you . . ." Deyandara repeated. He heard Ghu crossing the room, the creak of the ropes supporting the mattress as he sat by her.

"He thinks he's dead," Ghu explained. "It's all right. He isn't really."

"It won't happen again." Ahjvar got to his feet again, wearily, found himself a clean shirt and the tunic chequered in muted greens and greys that he'd worn most of the long road since the south, the dull brown trousers likewise, still stiff with mud and dust, a headscarf of the caravan road. In the corner of his eye the girl was huddled, watching, wrapped in her blanket in the half-light of the lamp. Well, Ghu was in his drawers, too, and was probably a more pleasing sight to her, under the circumstances. He unpacked, found knives, a wider assortment than it was politic to carry on his person, other gear, and repacked, so he had one small but heavy bag. He hung the belt of his sword over his shoulder as well and slung his cloak over all. Usefully dark.

"Did you bite my ear?" he asked, not for the girl's understanding.

"It woke you up. I didn't dare let go to do anything else."

"You—." Ahjvar almost laughed, but couldn't, quite. "Go first thing in the morning," he told Ghu. "Don't wait. There's too much smoke in my dreams. I can't trust I'll be given time. I'll find you when I can."

Ahjvar unbarred the shutters and dropped lightly down onto the porch roof. Ghu, silent, closed them again, locking the lamplight away behind him.

Any footpad fool enough to jump him now was going die. He'd kill of his own will if only some useless thug would give him a halfway honest excuse. Feed it, stave it off a little longer. But the night didn't oblige, and he hiked to the ravine without a human soul seeing him. By then, the east was lightening, dawn creeping near, and he found a way through the scrub of the riverbed easily enough. Hard to avoid disturbing the birds, but there were feral dogs, foxes, some long-snouted cat-beast, and no doubt other creatures to explain the birds' stirring as he passed. It was treacherous underfoot, stones tilted, broken. The rubble of the earthquake must have been dumped here, what could not be salvaged or built over, and no flood great enough to settle it or fill it in with silt had ever come down out of the mountains. He saw no sign of human passage save one well-trodden track that ran lengthwise, broad enough for three abreast, lush with nettles and honey-scented angelica towering to either side, sweeps of daylily, the night-closed buds like cold fingers stroking over him as he brushed past. A patrol-route, almost certainly. The trees along this stretch were mostly willow and poplar woven with grape and blister-vine, which he recognized by its rank scent in time to avoid crushing it with more than a boot.

Little sign the patrols ever ventured off their beaten track.

By the Riverbend Gate, city wall topped the ravine. Along most of Riverbend and Greenmarket Wards, the cliff was enough of a defence, and likewise in much of East Ward. Along the temple, though, the level of the ground dropped. The last time he had been in Marakand, the low-lying temple precinct had been fenced from the riverbed by a combination of city wall and temple buildings. He remembered a hospice, a pleasant white-plastered place. His quarry had gone there to make a donation for the temple's charitable works, all part of winning over some son of one of the banking Families with whom she sought an alliance. A marriage that would have destabilized the delicate balance of the clans in far-distant Sea Town, where he'd lived then, under a Nabbani name. It was the woman's own father had hired him, he remembered. He hadn't killed her there, merely followed, watching, followed her through a week and shot her in the twilight from a rooftop as she walked up the steps to her new betrothed's Family manor. She would never have exposed herself so carelessly in Sea Town.

Dusk or grey dawn twilight, Ahjvar was certain he could get up the cliff and through the jumble of houses that made a tight wall along its brink. He could see small gaps, alleys, with mounting mounds of nettle-grown rubbish and street-sweepings beneath. But from what he had seen of the wall the day before, he could just as easily climb it and get right into the temple grounds, or get in through one of the buildings that formed part of the wall and had looked half-ruined themselves. He found himself what was not exactly a cave but a narrow darkness under a lip of stone in the shelving cliff. There he crawled in and lay down, with his dark cloak pulled over him, making him a shadow behind a screen of olive saplings, as near invisible as could be. Sleep. He hoped. And if he did have nightmares here, there was no one to hurt. He'd probably just brain himself on the ledge overhead.

The smoke had faded. He'd go scouting come evening, before it grew full dark. Find out if the wineshop-keeper's description of the Voice's so damned convenient living arrangements were true. He rather wished they weren't. Too simple. Not enough to keep *her* entertained for long. Simple execution, no long stalking.

Though the Red Masks might make it more interesting, if there were any about. Not a word he wanted Ghu to hear him use of it. Interesting, Great Gods forgive him.

And if Catairanach kept her promise, what then?

He would die as he should have, gone to dust long since? Well enough. But if he'd thought of that, he'd have taken a longer farewell of Ghu.

The truth was, he didn't believe her. He would kill the Voice, and, assuming she was the ruler of the temple as Catairanach believed—which he still doubted, but it made no difference to what he did—maybe, if he killed some other powers of the temple too, that would sow enough confusion to give time for a strong lord to arise from the Duina Catairna. The Marakanders would be thrown out, Durandau would confirm some lord in the Catairnan kingship, with or more likely without Catairanach's blessing, and in a month, or three months, the smoke would steal into his dreams again, he'd find a victim or *she* would take one, and the nightmare would cycle round again. And maybe Ghu would be there, the only person he had willingly let near him, body or heart, since Miara, and that was eighty years, trying to convince him there was yet some grace in the world. And maybe he wouldn't.

A man could crave simple human touch as he could water.

It was a good time to run, while Ghu had the girl in his charge.

He could go west, to Tiypur. Escape Ghu, force him to get on with his own life. Let Ahjvar vanish and take a new name.

He'd miss Ghu.

Never feed a cat.

He fell asleep, exhausted, and if he dreamed, it was only to twitch a little, as a dog might, unsettled.

CHAPTER IV

The Leopard had not returned and the cut on her throat still stung. Deyandara pushed barley porridge about the bowl and watched Ghu, who had climbed out the window, squatting on his heels on the roof of the porch. He hadn't touched his own food, though he had been up at dawn, requesting their breakfast, seeing that the horses had theirs. Apparently Ahjvar had ordered them to leave the city. She hadn't even seen it yet; this dirty sprawl that served the caravan road was not Marakand of the golden-roofed library, the markets where the goods of the world were bought and sold, where you could hear songs in a dozen languages from the folk of two dozen gods, just walking down the street.

Ghu did not seem happy with his orders, if that was what they were. She touched the rough and still sticky scab and felt it move as she swallowed. Ahjvar could have killed her. A little more pressure . . . Nightmares. He had been going to *kill* her. There had been a noise, and she had thought she smelled smoke and woken out of some horrible dream to hear what sounded like Ahjvar and Ghu fighting. Ghu had shouted at her to get out the window, but she had been too sleep-muddled to even think where the window was. The sword had been cold, pressing her skin, but the hand that held it shaking—

"Ghu!" she called. He didn't respond. She'd learnt that over the past days; he might be Ahjvar's servant—or whatever. He certainly wasn't hers. He went deaf whenever she gave him anything approaching an order. She went to the window. "Ghu?" And uncertainly, off-balance, because . . . because whatever had gone on last night, Ghu had saved her. He had been the one with the quick and believable lie; he had been the one holding all in balance, and . . . and he was not quite what she had thought him. His voice, not her screams, woke and mastered the madman. "Can I come out there?"

Ghu looked back at her then. It was the same mild, simpleton's look, but . . . had she ever truly seen his eyes before? Black eyes, not mere poetry, not dark brown: black like the night sky and deep enough to drown in. He still said nothing. She took that for an answer, of sorts, and climbed out to join him, sitting down carefully. The tile roof sloped.

"There's something wrong with him, isn't there? Beyond being—what he is." Godless and lordless, she meant.

Ghu looked away again.

"He was afraid," she persisted. "He really did not know what he was doing."

"No," he agreed at last. Nothing more. And then, "There's something bad in the city," Ghu said.

"What?"

"I don't know. Something. Something old. Ahj isn't safe."

That he wasn't, in any sense of the word. She had been coming to think him tame, a short-tempered man who was no unwelcome companion to have on the road, a reassuring strength, however irritable. She had wanted to see some kind of honour in him, too, the champion the goddess Catairanach named him, like her brother's man Lord Launval the Elder. That vision in blood and fire, the savagery of the night he, *they*, had saved her, had faded swiftly to almost a dream, the whole affair of the brigands had, except when she reached to touch Badger's head, and the mastiff was no longer at her knee, no heavy head weighing down her ankles and groaning complaint when she rolled over in the night, no grinning shadow looking up at her whenever she glanced aside.

"You're worried about him. You said he told you to take me away. He thinks I'm an idiot."

Ghu's smile startled her. "He does, yes. He thinks you're very young."

She bit her lip. "Maybe I am."

He did not rush to contradict her.

"Would he beat you, if you disobeyed him?"

"*Ahj?* He never hits me. Except by accident."

"By *accident?*"

"He has nightmares." As if she hadn't learnt that this past night. And he said it as though it were of small import. "Lady, Ahjvar needs me. Will you go back to your brother? We can find a caravan going east; you could travel to the lands of the Duina Broasoran in safe company and ask escort of the queen there."

"I—" She shut her mouth on indignant protest. "I'll come with you."

"No. There's death in the city."

"There's death everywhere," she snapped.

"True. But—there's death on your heels, most of all. Better you go."

"I don't want to go to my brother."

Ghu's head tilted. "Why?"

Deyandara shook her head.

"Why?" he repeated gently.

"I'm their—they want me to be their queen. The Catairnans." It was suddenly easy, telling Ghu, laying the words at his feet as if he could somehow carry them for her. "But their goddess sent me away. She—it was a dream. It seemed like a dream. But then I was out in the hills, and the night was around me, and I heard voices, the speech of the western road. The Marakander mercenaries. I didn't know where I was, and I was afraid. So I went on. South, through the Tributary Lands, back and forth, to within sight of the walls of Two Hills, then down to Gold Harbour and around it. Wandering, doing what she had told me. Going to you. To Ahjvar, I mean. And I followed you because I couldn't go back, not after what I'd done, running away, and to run and then go back with my brother, as his, his tool . . . I didn't want to do that. But Marnoch will—they'll think I ran away no matter how I return."

"Did you not tell Catairanach it was wrong, to make you go when it was not your will?"

Deyandara shook her head, about to protest that she couldn't have, not refused a goddess, no, but she could see Ghu doing just that, saying wide-eyed and simple and kind, as if explaining the obvious to a child, "But I don't want to. I won't."

If she had tried—had she thought to try? Had she tried to wake, as she led Cricket out to the gate, Badger running ahead? Or had it all slipped into her so easily, because it was what she wanted, because it was easier, to run and to be able to say, it wasn't my fault? Catairanach wanted me for a messenger, not a queen, it's her fault, not mine?

Her eyes were watering, and she would not cry like a scolded child. She blinked furiously.

"I don't know what to do." It was a whisper. "Ghu, what should I do?"

His arm was around her, holding her, and she wanted to lay her head on his shoulder and weep for loneliness, but that wasn't right, and how had he turned into someone she wanted to lean on, anyway? She wound her hands together in her lap and took a deep breath, blinking at the city rising over its walls away beyond the caravanserai. House piled upon house, it looked, steep tiers of flat roofs and roofs with shallow domes or red tile, all yellow-mud plastered or lime-washed and gleaming in the sun. She could even see the glare of what must be the famous library, a golden roof that burned the eye. Real gold, or some illusion? Hadn't the senate palace fallen during the earthquake, killing all the rulers of the city? She turned her head and found Ghu studying her, far, far too close, and if she leaned just a little more . . .

His smile was sweet, like a little child's. But then he looked away. "Do you see that man, down the street?"

Deyandara shaded her eyes. "The one sitting in the doorway?"

"He's waiting for us."

"You don't know that. Why would he be?"

"I saw other Praitans ride down the road. He didn't watch them. He doesn't think they're all spies. Just us. Just you, maybe."

"Me? If he's looking for anyone, it's Ahjvar. Even the goddess of the Duina Catairna knew he was an assassin."

"Catairanach knows him. No one else Over-Malagru who knows him knew we came here. I don't think Catairanach would sell him to Marakand when she sees the death of the Voice as her only possible vengeance for Gilru who should have been king. The Marakanders only know Master Clentara, who came to the city with you. They don't know the Leopard. They may know Clentara attacked a man following him last night."

"Did Ahjvar kill him?"

"No."

"Why not?" she demanded.

"Because he's not that kind of man."

"He's an *assassin*. He murders people for *money*."

Ghu hushed her, took her hand in both his own. They were warm and rough, a servant's hands, distracting, overwhelming, and she shivered, as if he'd touched her far more intimately. She wanted to shut her eyes and just . . .

"He isn't meant to be that kind of man," Ghu amended. "Does your brother know you went to the Duina Catairna?"

"No! Yes." She swallowed, opening her eyes again. "He would by now. Lord Yvarr sent letters, in my name as queen, asking him to raise the tribes. It's—it's a king's right, a queen's right, when the threat is to all Praitan Over-Malagru. Our right to ask aid of all the *duinas*, and the high king's duty to give it. The messengers had left before I did."

"So he'll have had the messages by now. He'll know you've declared yourself queen."

"But I haven't!" But in signing those letters and setting Cattiga's seal to them, she had.

"And he may have heard you're missing. And your folk—"

"Not my folk. I'm not fit to be their queen."

"Your folk—your lords, at least, know you are their queen, and that you are gone in the night. They may think you went to your brother, following the messengers. They'll have sent to him again to find you."

"Yes, but even if, even if they did, and a messenger was captured by Marakanders and made to talk, they didn't know I was coming to Marakand. *I* didn't know I was coming to Marakand."

"But even if no messenger were captured, someone else may have been taken and told the Marakanders that the high king's sister was wandering alone in the west of Over-Malagru. A girl alone, a bard too young to be a bard, with hair like copper in the sun."

That was—nice. Copper in the sun. His finger was tracing the lines of her palm.

"They might keep an eye out for such a one, in the event she crossed their path. A hostage against the high king, perhaps. Or perhaps to kill, as Cattiga and Gilru were killed. The Voice of the Lady of Marakand wants your land for her own, and she does not seem to care what offence she does to the goddess of the land to get it." He frowned. "Though I do not think your goddess is a wise one, to have sent you away, and in secret from her lords and yours. Ahj calls her a fool, often." He considered again. "And worse. With cause. Lady, what do you want to do? What's in your heart, now, if you could choose, now and for the rest of your life? Where would you be?"

She swallowed. Somewhere on the hills, with Cricket and Badger, the strings of harp or komuz singing under fingers, afterwards, and a song in the friendly firelit dark of the hall. Could she ever grow to be a bard, a scholar, with the history and the wisdom of the seven kingdoms in her head? Probably not. She certainly couldn't carry the weight of a *duina* as a true queen should.

But there was Marnoch. There was Yvarr. They gave her trust. Where else had she ever found that? And she shattered it. Everything she did went crooked.

"I belong to the Duina Andara by my birth, but I need to be of the Duina Catairna," she said. "It—it felt like home. Whether Catairanach wants me or not, the folk need a queen. Not to lead them. I don't know anything of war, or justice and the laws. They need—they need someone, just a name, for Marnoch to stand behind as he leads them, to stop the lords turning each one to make their own bargains with Marakand. But the brigands, the ones that killed Badger, they were Catairnan folk, my folk, and they said the lords were all dead!"

"Outlaws. They may not have known. They may have been excusing their own brigandage. You can't ride alone to find your Marnoch. You can find your brother, though."

"He'll just use me as an excuse."

"If it drives Marakand out of Praitan, then let him. And then be a queen for your own folk, make them your own folk."

"Catairanach doesn't want me," she repeated dully.

"Catairanach," Ghu said, with sudden hissing vehemence, "is no goddess worth your worship. Find your folk a new god."

"What?"

But he seemed hardly to know what he had said. He blinked at her, vague and quiet, closed his hand over hers and stood, pulling her up with him. "Better you go to your brother than stand so near Ahj as I do. Hyllau may not care for the comparison."

"What?" She had been telling the story last night, Hyllau who killed her husband Cairangorm, or for whose sake he was killed, depending on the song, and the day of three kings, that ended with Deyandara's own great-grandfather Hyllanim the infant king.

"I'll find you safe company to Dinaz Broasora; the queen's folk there will know where the high king is."

He drew her back into the room and released her, which, Andara damn him anyway, should not make her feel as if she had suddenly been cast adrift, dropped into deep water. Or launched, like a hawk, into the empty and unsupported depths of the sky.

Someone rapped at their door. They both froze. Not Ahjvar returning, surely not.

"Lady Deyandara?"

The innkeeper should not know that name. Besides, it was a woman and speaking foreign-accented Praitannec. The latch jumped, but the door was barred. Ghu jerked his head to the window, but Deyandara, belatedly, recognized the voice, though how it came there she couldn't imagine. She crossed to the door and lifted the bar, ignoring Ghu's aborted grab at her sleeve.

"*Lin?*"

Her brother's Nabbani wizard greeted her Marakander style, clasping both Deyandara's hands in her own. "Lady Deyandara," she said, as if they had merely met crossing the stone-flagged yard between the hall and the maiden's bower.

Deyandara stepped back to admit her. No spearmen, no bench-companions of her brother followed her. The woman was alone. "Ah, we were just . . . we were . . ."

Ghu stood with one hand behind his back, watching, gone utterly blank, eerily like Ahjvar in some moods, when he stared and there was nothing but darkness behind his eyes, eerily like Badger, smelling the danger she didn't realize, just before he had gone for that brigand. She burned red, she could feel it, like a girl caught misbehaving with her young man in the byre, but surely Ghu didn't look like someone's secret lover; he looked like someone's groom. Almost. Someone's very handsome, very clean groom. And not a simpleton at all. There was only the one bed. And her neck was wet. She touched a knuckle to last night's wound. The scab must have pulled.

"It's all right," she said, and heard her voice shaking. "It's all right, Ghu. This is Lady Lin, one of my brother's wizards."

This was Marakand. The word could get Lin killed.

Lin said nothing. Of all Durandau's servants, Lin was the only one who might say nothing to him, if she thought Deyandara had run off with a lover; be sarcastic in private, yes, lecture her on a woman's responsibilities and the thoughtlessness of bringing a child into the world unwanted, yes, she would that, but not feel it was anyone's business beyond Deya's own. Hard to believe, especially now, as the wizard gazed past Deyandara to Ghu, expressionless as a statue. She looked dreadfully respectable, dreadfully regal, like a queen herself, elegant as always, beautiful even with the weather-lines of age creasing back from eye and mouth, her hair, cut at her shoulders, a sheet of iron grey here, shot silver out in the sun. She dressed, almost always, in the Nabbani fashion. More: she often wore vast wealth in silk brocade, though she kept not a single servant. Even here, where she must have travelled the caravan road, her short, wrapped gown, though slightly dusty, was blue brocade, great sprawling peonies in red and amber over all the breast and shoulders, and her leather leggings were dyed deep crimson. The red-tasselled Nabbani sword at her shoulder looked a queen's weapon, too, even the scabbard patterned in anemones and set with jade about the mouth. Carried to assert her status among a warrior people, maybe; Deyandara had never seen her draw it, and she made no move to do so now. Or to spread her fingers into the signs whereby she drew her wizardry from the air.

"You're not of this city," Lin said to Ghu. "This isn't your place. What are you doing with the king's sister of the Praitans?"

"You can't have her."

"I don't want her. Her brother does." Lin's eyes narrowed.

Whatever Ghu said next was in Imperial Nabbani but harsh with menace. Deyandara put herself between the two of them, which was a mistake. Ghu grabbed her as roughly as Ahjvar might have and thrust her behind. *Strong* . . . His hand went back to the hilt of his curved knife, but he still didn't draw it.

Lin spoke in Imperial too, but she sounded amused now, not—

no, she had never sounded angry. Startled, at first. Shocked, even. Definitely amused, now. Ghu shook his head, denying something. Demanded something. Repeated it. Lin's answer was disdainful.

"Lady," he said, without glancing aside at Deyandara. "You know her, truly? Is this truly your brother's wizard? Do you trust her? Is she a woman of her word?"

"She's served my brother Durandau for three, no, four years," Deyandara said. "She was my tutor. Of course I know her. She came from Nabban before that. She's not from Marakand, if that's what you're afraid of. She swore fealty to him."

Did she trust Lady Lin? Did she trust anyone of her brother's hall? In some things yes, in some no. Ghu didn't wait for her to decide.

"How did you find her?" he asked, of Lin, this time.

The wizard held up a hand, smiling now, touched what seemed to be a ring of pale, thin cord on her forefinger. "She left her big harp behind, but she played it often till then. I took a string. It's a simple spell, once I was close enough. It led me to the very door."

"What do you mean to do with her?"

"Ghu . . ." Deyandara protested.

Lin ignored her, answered Ghu. "Take her to her brother."

"Who is where, now?"

"And why do you need to know that?"

Ghu said nothing.

Lin shrugged, a rasp of heavy silk. "The high king's army is at Dinaz Broasora, as it has been some time, waiting for the kings of the Lellandi and Galatan to join us. Yesterday we finally had word from a man sent, I think somewhat belatedly, by Lord Yvarr of the Duina Catairna, that Deyandara was no longer with them, though they had sent out letters to her brother in her name. They hoped she had gone to meet him, this messenger said. In his defence, he had had to go up into the Duina Praitanna and had travelled all the way to Dinaz Andara to find the king gone. Durandau was quite upset. We divined for the girl again and found that though she had been roaming far south of the road, as far as the coast, she was now in Marakand. Much to Durandau's horror, as you can imagine. He sent me to fetch her back, and so far as I know, he's still at the queen's hall in Dinaz Broasora, with a few rather irate caravans detained in his train, lest news of his advance should run ahead to the city. I trust I do have your word you will not pass that information on to the temple?"

Ghu didn't answer that. Maybe he thought there was no need. "Her brother should have sent you seeking her months ago. Will he do well by her now, do you think?"

"He'll do . . . as a high king must."

More Nabbani followed, but Ghu took his hand from the knife at the small of his back and went to sit cross-legged on the bed. Absurdly like a king holding court, like Ahjvar in the ruin, with Lin standing before him, legs braced, arms folded now, tilting her chin, raising her fine eyebrows. Deyandara felt her anger growing. Was she being haggled over, sold, transferred from one guardian to another? The Leopard's *horseboy* had no right.

Lin abruptly drew her sword. Deyandara yipped and backed a step, but the wizard only clasped her own hand around it, held up her palm with a thin red line blooming, spoke, hissing, now almost angry. But Ghu nodded and smiled suddenly at Deyandara, the open smile of the simpleton, with nothing behind it at all.

"She swears she means you no harm, lady. You can go with her safely. It's better so. Ahj and I might be the death of you."

The high king's wizard was making oaths in blood to the assassin's groom. Deyandara quelled the urge to stamp her foot and scream at them, settled for sarcasm. "Thank you for asking what I thought of it."

"I didn't," said Ghu. "I need to find Ahjvar. You should go, before the guard finds you."

"What guard?" Lin demanded.

"He thinks the Marakanders are looking for me," said Deyandara in disgust. "He says there's someone watching the inn. He's the one who came to town with an assassin, but—"

"An assassin?" Lin frowned, snapped more Nabbani.

Ghu shrugged, bland, blank. "But you say you are nothing to do with whatever is in the city," he said, in answer to the question Deyandara had not understood. "So you should not care. I do. I care for him very much. You can tell me, and maybe I will answer. But what he is and what he does I will not tell, not you."

Lin's lips thinned.

"Or you cannot tell what you know," said Ghu kindly. "We'll find our own way."

Lin turned on her heel. Deyandara had never seen her disconcerted before, not by anything. "I know nothing. Do you have a horse?" she demanded.

"Me?" Deyandara asked. "Yes, still Cricket."

"I need to find—to buy a horse."

"You *walked?* All that way? It's, what, ten days' or a fortnight's ride."

"I did not. I was with the king yesterday, as I said. I wish you would learn to listen, child, and more, to think. You don't need to live down to your brother's expectations, you know. But you can't travel as I do."

"Ah," said Ghu suddenly. "Mistress Lin, you could borrow Ahjvar's horses. Borrow."

Lin turned back, and Ghu frowned, but only as if he were puzzling over some detail. "Can you ride a horse?"

"Of course I know how to ride."

"Did I ask that? Will you hurt my horses, to do so?"

"I *like* animals," Lin said. "I am not wantonly cruel to beasts."

"No?" That was definitely a question. "Use them well, then. We'll ask them of you later." Ghu frowned again. "I will. If I can. If I need to."

"And how are you going to travel, then, after you find Ahjvar?" Deyandara demanded of him. "No, you have to come with us. Ahjvar told you to leave the city, too."

"Ahjvar is not my master." That didn't even sound like Ghu, stern, reproving. He smiled. "He's *mine*, to care for. Whatever he thinks."

"And you're needed elsewhere, my lady," said Lin. "Master Ghu's company would be, I think, awkward for you to explain." And she bowed again. To which of them, Deyandara wasn't certain.

And awkward? Her face burned. "We—I didn't . . ."

Ghu seemed oblivious. "I can always find horses," he said, and his smile now was a fox's, seeing an unguarded flock of hens. "When I need them, I find them. Come with me. The innkeeper's to be paid; then I'll tell them they go with you."

The white mare put her ears back when Lady Lin stroked her neck, and the piebald pulled to the end of his rope to get away, but the golden gelding only shuddered his skin under her hand and lowered his head to the bridle. He was used to Ahjvar, Ghu said, as though that explained something. Whatever it was, it made Lin frown.

Ghu had overseen the packing of the saddlebags, making his own belongings and Ahjvar's, and another heavy purse Deyandara hadn't known they had, up into a roll, tying it over his shoulder. He had also put on a somewhat tattered caravan guard's coat, hiding the forage-knife at the small of his back beneath it. In the inn's yard, the horses introduced to Lin to his satisfaction, he wrapped a scarf over Deyandara's hair, too, a great striped earth-coloured shawl. She had not braided in the bard's ribbons this morning. Just as well; she would have blushed with even greater shame under Lady Lin's knowing gaze, caught in that lie.

"Your death is still on your heels," he said, with no more weight than if he mouthed some conventional blessing for the road. "Perhaps it isn't Ahj, after all. Go warily. Pray for Ahj. Someone should." For a moment, as he stood with his hands on her shoulders, she thought he would kiss her and was quite certain she would not mind if he did. But he only brushed his thumb over her lips, which made her shiver again, and stepped away.

"You will look after her. Your blood and word," he told Lin, and was gone, trotting out of the inn's gate.

Lin turned the yellow gelding in a neat circle. "You didn't sleep with him, did you?" she asked. Her Praitannec was good, but she had an odd accent, not of the Five Cities. Ghu had no accent at all; he might have been Praitan-born, in the west. Ahjvar's accent. Catairnan.

"No! He's a groom." Deyandara added, flustered, "Anyway, he's in love with Ahjvar, I think."

"Do you think so? Ah, well, perhaps you'll be given another chance. He'll have to come collect his horses, after all."

"Ahjvar's horses. And the only reason he gave them to us is that he thinks Ahjvar's going to die, and he wants to go die with him."

"The mysterious Ahjvar. Yes. I must meet him someday soon. However, let's be off for now. If these stalkers of yours do give chase,

I'm going to cut your pony loose, child, so I do hope all the important baggage is on the piebald."

There was hardly any baggage but a few blankets, her change of linen, and some socks that needed mending, anyway. The komuz she had slung on her back, the bow and quiver handy behind the saddle. Little food. Had Lin thought of that? Hunting would delay them, and the horses, if not the hardy pony, would need grain if they were to travel swiftly. Deyandara patted Cricket and whispered, "Keep up" in his ear. Ghu talked to horses as if they understood, after all. The white mare turned to eye her as she settled in the saddle but set out willingly, a long, fluid stride. Nobody was going to catch *her*, at any rate.

Ghu had vanished, though Deyandara looked for him. They rode past the man he had claimed watched them, still sitting idly in a doorway, whittling. When she looked back, he was gone too. It didn't matter. He couldn't outdistance them when they were heading straight for the Eastern Wall.

They rode in silence, and the city wall of Marakand beyond the ravine's green river of scrubby forest seemed to taunt her. Fetched home in disgrace, like the silly little fool she was. No. Maybe she was a fool to have tried to travel alone, so inexperienced, so—ill-fortuned, as fate proved to her, time and time again. Not a fool to have wanted her freedom, to desire to be more than a petty afterthought in her brother's hall.

"I'm not going to Durandau," she said.

"No?" Lin turned to look at her.

Deyandara took a breath. "I'm not going back to Lord Yvarr and the duina in my brother's shadow, his, his dog at heel. He'll have been sending scouts west into the *duina*, won't he?"

"Naturally." She eyed Deyandara sidelong.

"If you were really with him so recently, you know where the Marakanders are, as well as his war-leaders do, or better. You can divine for them."

"They're in Dinaz Catairna," said Lin.

"But Marnoch was going to burn it."

"The Marakanders rebuilt."

She pictured herself slinking along the caravan road south of the Duina Cataírna and into Broasoran lands, a laggard, a truant, rounded up by her brother Durandau's scouts, brought humble before the high king, with whatever other kings and queens had assembled there to witness her scolding.

"Do you know where Lord Yvarr and Lord Marnoch are?"

"Alive. They've gone west and north into the hills, we think. There's their *dinaz* deep in the Red Hills, but I haven't heard if that's where they've made their stronghold or not." Lin eyed her sidelong. "But I can find them for you."

"Can we get to them, instead of going to my brother? Without being taken by the Marakanders?"

Was that a smile, a fox's glint of tooth, like Ghu contemplating horse-theft?

"We can make the attempt. This Ketsim, the Marakander captain, seems not to like the steep hills and the woodlands."

"Good." Deyandara bit the word off and wondered why it echoed in her mind. Ahjvar.

"I am," Lin said, a bit hesitantly, "yours to command, my lady. Not your brother's. I swore so to your pretty-eyed friend just now."

"Oh."

"You've been travelling in dangerous company."

"Ahjvar's not—He's—he . . ."

"I meant the other one."

"*Ghu?*" Deyandara coughed to hide her squeak of protest, coughed more earnestly and pulled the scarf across her face. Lin had gotten them mixed in with the tail of a caravan. The horses blew at the dust. "Dangerous? He's not dangerous. He's the most gentle . . . half the time I think he's not even all there!"

"Yes, I wonder where the rest of him is? Anyway, I did not promise anyone to make you a queen. If you did run away from that fate, you don't have to lie to me about it, and if you decide to run away again, I fear I am bound to run with you, though how we then get these horses back to your assassin and his tame—his friend, I don't know."

"You swore an oath to Durandau when you took service as his wizard."

Lin waved a hand. "I've sworn lots of oaths in my time, child. Some I meant to keep and some I didn't. You're allowed to think, 'Perfidious outlander,' if you like. I am."

"So why would you keep an oath to Ghu, then? He's only Ahjvar's groom."

"Oh, child. Answer me. What do you mean to do?"

"Go back to Yvarr and Marnoch. They needed me, they said. If they still do . . . then I'll be what they want me to be."

Until the Marakanders murdered her too.

She needed to find them, to tell them she hadn't intended to flee. She owed them that for their friendship. She owed herself, to prove she was no coward, to prove that she could keep faith after all. That if the goddess pushed her again, she would demand to know why. She would push back.

Lin coughed. "Why did you go south, anyway? I traced enough of your trail to see that you did, eventually. If you were afraid, and didn't want to go to Durandau, running to the *duina* of your mother's father would have been much safer."

Deyandara sighed and told it again. "Catairanach came to me, right after Yvarr had spoken with me and those couriers had gone out with the letters in my name. Right when the *dinaz* was being abandoned. She told me she couldn't fight the power of the Lady of Marakand, and that she would not have a queen born to another tribe, and that she wanted me to carry a message to a Five Cities assassin. Ahjvar. They call him the Leopard. She wanted me to tell him to kill the Voice of Marakand for her. And by the time I seemed to be thinking my own thoughts again, I was heading south in the fog, and there were Marakanders between me and the *dinaz*."

"Oh." And that seemed to silence Lin at last.

The road might have been paved, but it was not swept and for the most part they travelled in a cloud that caked the nose and tasted of old, dry barnyard on the tongue. To swing out and around the caravan would have been easy enough, as the caravanserais thinned out to a straggle of horse-pens and fodder-sellers' yards. Lin showed no wish to do so, keeping them in the dust.

"Come nearer," the wizard ordered abruptly, and Deyandara obeyed. Lin leaned over to her, spreading her hand, fingertips pressing cool on her face. They moved, some pattern made.

"Improbable that they would be looking for you rather than for Catairnan Praitans in general," Lin said. "However, your young man is not someone whose vision I would fault." She snorted, most unladylike. "He sees all too clearly. Keep your eyes down and stay quiet, and nobody will notice you."

The towering fortress of the gate drew nearer, floating in the haze. The dust died away as the camels trod clean stone, wind-scoured now as no buildings lined it; the day was growing hot, the sun beating down the pass.

The city guards in their grey tunics took no interest in the departing caravan, beyond noting the master's name and the number of beasts and running a cursory eye over the caravaneers as the camels ambled by. No, they were summoning one man at the rear out of line. A pale-bearded Northron, he called them names, amiably, and when two guards in red tunics rather than grey, and scale-armour shirts as well, came out to question him, he settled into grumbling, growling Northron speech, baffling and annoying them, till they tried to drag him from his camel. One got a boot in the face and the other the butt of his spear, and like wasps when the nest is disturbed, the caravan guards closed in to defend their comrade, a seething mass of camels, shouts, spears blocking the gateway.

"We should maybe go back?" Deyandara suggested. "Wait till later?"

Lin considered. "I wonder what he'd done?"

Been mistaken for Ahjvar—for Clentara—was Deyandara's thought.

The shouting swelled to a triumphant baying and yelping, as of hounds, and the camels surged on their way, the Northron caravaneer in their midst. Lin gave the yellow gelding a touch of her heels and cantered after. Deyandara followed, glad of the concealing scarf over her hair. Guards tumbled out of the doors behind which they'd retreated from the caravan, grey tunics and red, arguing. Two of the red tunics, whose numbers had increased since the caravan's escape, stepped out into the broad roadway and snapped an order to halt in the language of the western road. Easy to tell what they meant, even without understanding the words. Lin reined her horse back to a walk and turned her smile on them all.

"Barbarians," she said cheerfully, speaking trade Nabbani. "What was that about?" She failed to halt. Deyandara, therefore, didn't either, but the reins grew sweaty in her hand. Both men in the roadway, big men, had spears, and a woman to the side of the gate a bow. She had her own bow and quiver close to hand now, but a move to take it up would be a mistake.

"*Some* fools can't tell a Northron from a Praitan," said one of the grey tunics. "*Some* fools need to get out of the city a bit more, maybe, and see the real world." One of his comrades scowled him to silence; they made no move to stop Lin or even ask her name.

But, "Where'd you get those horses?" demanded one of the red tunics.

"A dealer," said Lin, her face going just the right degree of wary.

"What dealer?"

"Are you suggesting I stole them?"

"No, mistress. I want to know who you bought them from."

"Some dealer at the horsefair."

"What horsefair?"

"By the north gate."

"North gate? There's no—"

"In Star River Crossing," Lin added helpfully. "I don't remember her name. It was months ago."

"Told you," said one of the red-tunics to his comrade, stepping away. "A woman and two men, it was, anyway."

And Lin hadn't even worked any wizardry, not that Deyandara could see. People believed what she wanted them to.

That was worth considering, when she trusted the woman so unthinkingly.

"A white and a silver-maned lion and a piebald," said the other, hesitating. "And a Nabbani servant-boy. This one's Nabbani."

"Servant!" snapped Lin, with no smile at all now. "*Boy!*"

"Apologies, mistress," said the guard. He even managed a bow. One of the grey-tunics hastily hid a smile behind her sleeve.

"It's 'lady,' not 'mistress' to you, and I should think so. Come."

Lin crooked a finger at Deyandara as the yellow horse broke into a trot, the piebald the wizard led following, bunching close. A shadow moved in the doorway of the tower, flowed forward and detached from it, a darkness becoming a man, a woman, a slight figure in a long, faded red robe, with a shirt of lacquered leather armour the colour of old blood and a helmet equally red, the face completely masked, rising into a triple crest of flaring fins, like waves or flames. The grey tunics withdrew hastily towards the other end of the archway. The red tunics saluted. "Revered One?"

Red Mask. A light flared over the priest, a dirty red light that crawled along the edges of the armour segments, up the sweeping crest of the helmet, made the air sizzle on the pale carved staff she carried. The white mare, ears flattening, head up, skittered sideways. A wash of panic roiled through Deyandara's stomach as though she looked down to find herself at a cliff's edge.

"Cold hells!" a man hissed, and a woman almost whimpered, "Lady bless, Lady bless."

"Revered One," said the nearest red tunic, his voice shaking now, backing away, right to the wall of the arch. Deyandara found her teeth were chattering. Nightmare. Nightmare. She had thought the story of the Lady's divine terror some city boasting; they had shown no such power at Dinaz Catairna, only the white crackle of their staves, only . . . Cricket kicked and bolted, the leading-rein jerked free. He took off after the vanishing caravan.

"The much talked-of blessing of the Lady, I see," Lin murmured. "The divine terror of her presence. Indeed."

Deyandara couldn't think. She couldn't move. She clutched the saddlebow to keep from falling, and the thing reached out a hand in a red gauntlet. The white mare squealed, reared, and Lin's sword hissed, the tassel floating like a bright banner. Lin and the sweating, eye-rolling yellow gelding suddenly thrust between Deyandara and the Red Mask, the priest's grab turned to a two-handed strike with the white staff against Lin.

"Ride!" the wizard snapped, but if Deyandara's fingers, her body, had not been frozen, locked up like a sleet-entombed branch, she would have slid boneless and shivering to the ground. The mare bolted a few steps and turned with her tail to the wall. The piebald fought his rope. A white fire blazed over the Red Mask's hands, over the length of the staff, as the priest swung not at Lin now—the first blow had somehow failed—but at her mount. The wizard interposed her own left arm, shieldless, and Deyandara choked on a cry as the blow—again—failed, held on a shadow, a smoke in the air that sheeted between wizard and priest, a slow and lazy drift of eddying grey. The Red Mask recoiled and Lin brought the gelding around, left-hand fingers flickering. Her own sword's edge sparked white as she shifted to a two-handed grip and struck the priest's head from shoulders.

The body crumpled; the yellow gelding flinched away sideways. Lin gathered up her reins while Deyandara gulped bile and found she could sit up straight again, though her heart still raced and her skin was cold with sweat.

"Huh." Lin frowned at the corpse, then swung to face the gate guards, her bright smile sweeping over them, as if she had completely forgotten Deyandara was even there.

Deyandara snarled, "Lin—ride!" and kicked the mare, who took off with good will now. No looking back for the battle-mad wizard; she didn't slow her mount's pace until Cricket, grazing by the road-side, panic forgotten, came lurching up out a stand of reeds after them. Then Deyandara trotted, circled, caught his trailing rope and made it fast again. Andara and the Old Great Gods be thanked he hadn't tangled his legs and broken his neck. Only then did she think to fumble her bow free, trapping it between knee and saddle to string it. Lin cantered up, holding her bloody sword off to the side.

"She didn't bleed much," the wizard said.

Deyandara couldn't speak, but she pointed at Lin's dripping blade, hand holding the bow still shaking a little. The pony shied away, nostrils flaring.

"Oh, *they* bled," said Lin. "But the Red Mask did not. A little, only. Very strange. Unfortunately she was the only one. A Red Mask prisoner might have proven very useful."

There were several scattered mounds in the roadway at the gate, grey and red.

Deyandara found her voice. "You killed the guard? All of them!"

"No, two fled into the tower and I thought it was better we run while we could. One had a bow," Lin added. "She missed. I'm sorry; she shouldn't have had even the one chance to shoot. I'm out of practice. We should ride; they do keep courier ponies at the forts, I think, to carry messages into the city, and it's possible the Red Masks will come hunting us. I wish I had thought to take the head."

"The—why?" Deyandara asked weakly. She wanted to scream, *I thought you were a wizard only, I thought your sword was for show, you're an old woman, not a warrior. I thought the Lady's blessing on the Red Masks made them immune to wizardry and why weren't you frightened, why didn't you fall down quaking in terror, when even the horses and the guard did and I think I wet myself and then the panic just—stopped.* But she swallowed hard and straightened her fingers, shaking her cramping hands to ease them, first one, then the other. Swallowed again. "What would the head tell you?"

"Whatever I asked it, perhaps," said Lin, and gave her a grin like the one she had flashed on the guards. "No, sorry, dear. That was a joke. But I'd like to find out why she didn't flood the road with blood when she fell. In my experience people usually do, when you cut their heads off."

Had Lin great experience in cutting off heads? She didn't dare ask that. "Does Durandau know you're such—such a swordmaster?"

"What does he need another champion for?" Lin asked. "He has Lord Launval the Elder, whom I would not for the world discomfit. Besides, I'm not so young as I once was." She coughed. "You're supposed to say, no, no, you're not so old as all that." She eyed Deyandara, who was not at all in the mood to play along. The wizard sighed. "Well, I think this proves your pretty friend right. They are looking for you or rather, for the company you've been keeping. Suspicious Praitans, you are, obviously. Or . . ." her voice went slow and thoughtful. "Or perhaps this Voice of Marakand dreams true dreams, and they were troubled by a vision of the heir of Catairanach's land. I really should have taken that head." She grinned again. "Next time. Now let's make what speed we can, lest these Marakanders find good horses or camels somewhere, and men capable of riding them."

But the wizard dismounted to clean her sword first and rode with the reins slack, fingers weaving patterns in the air. A fog began to smoke from the dry riverbed, from the stagnant pools and the hot stones. It crawled over the road, overtook them, filled the rift between the mountain walls and wrapped them from sight.

"Better," said Lin. "Now we ride."

CHAPTER V

By noon Ahjvar was awake again. He wanted coffee, but since he wasn't going to get any, he made do with a broken biscuit and a drink from a drying, algae-slick puddle in a hollow of the stone ledges, the last of some rain. He couldn't see the road for the broad band of ravine-scrub, and if patrols used the path along the ravine bottom, none came by that afternoon. He could have been alone in a wilderness, rather than squatting on the edge of a teeming city. He made a foray into the trees, found cherries already ripe, which made a better meal than the very stale biscuit baked by Ghu on a stone at some campfire days gone, and wondered whether the city folk were forbidden the ravine or only afraid of it. The reed-cutter of the previous day had not acted as though he had been about any illegal harvest. Perhaps it was fear; here under the trees he thought he felt the dead. Not ghosts, unburied, no lingering trapped souls, but death nonetheless, a grave-hill's calm. The river had dried long ago; the stands of fruit-trees amid the willow scrub, the silver-leafed, whispering poplars, were all only just come to maturity. Let grow since the earthquake? His foot, kicking at the mould of fallen leaves between the broken stones and plaster, turned up broken bone, a human jaw. So they had dumped not only the ruins of the city here but its dead of the catastrophe. They might fear to eat the fruit or burn the timber that grew from their parents' bones, yes.

He retreated to the crevice, lay half-drowsing, waiting for the dusk, and slept once more, dreaming. It was not a bad dream, as dreams went. Miara. Not her death. Just Miara, a long time ago, and no pain in the dreaming, no murder, but he woke with damp eyes and thought about dropping from the top of the cliff, once he climbed so high, or a roof, but he would somehow survive, battered and broken maybe, but still, by miracle and luck, as alive as he was now.

It was having sent Ghu away brought that on, but at least the man would never haunt his sleep. One death he needn't carry.

The lengthening shadows made black pools of the wooded ravine. Ahjvar set out, while he could still see enough to stop him turning an ankle in a crack or blundering into a tangle of blister-vine. The cliff to his right dropped lower, topped here with crooked buildings, some roofless, abandoned. He skirted a heap of nettle-grown rubbish that was just asking to be used as a ramp, and the cliff, dropping lower, was again surmounted by a stretch of wall. The temple grounds occupied what might have been a bay of the river once, or perhaps some earlier earthquake had made the land sink, a depression like the hoofmark of a giant's horse, stamping down. Here the south shore of the ravine rose in shelves of stone and steep banks of broken rock intermingled to meet crumbling wall and the blank backs of temple buildings, all the lower windows bricked shut, most of the doors, though not all, likewise. Some of the doors that still might be usable from within were overgrown with vines, though, or opened from empty space, landings and water-stairs long crumbled. Between buildings, the temple's wall was in even worse repair than that of the city. An old man could climb it. He did, as the last of the red-tinged twilight wrapped around him.

Lying flat atop the wall, the faded black cloak pulled over him, Ahjvar could see into a courtyard. It looked abandoned. Dry weeds grew between its stones, and the laurel trees at the four corners were scraggly and unkempt, wind-broken twigs and dead weeds littered around their feet. The building that backed onto the yard seemed in better repair. Light glowed through piercings in its carved window-screens. The building which made the eastern end of the courtyard was roofless and looked to have burnt long ago. Perhaps this was the abandoned backside of the temple, the equivalent of old out-buildings left in case they came in useful someday. There had been talk in the caravanserai suburb of rising tolls and duties; the money wasn't showing here. But then, Grasslander mercenaries probably did not come cheap. To the west, the wall on which he lay abutted the old hospice. He recognized its placement, at least. Four storeys high, with wide windows for fresh air, and a pitched roof. There had been arcades running along the east, and if he remembered correctly, the unseen south, the front. There had been wooden galleries above the arcades, too, but on this eastern face they had been stripped off. It was blotched now as if with bruises, plaster crumbled away, and what was left dirty, stained with dust and soot, fading into the night. Abandoned, maybe, despite the wine-seller's tale, but it was a place to start.

Smoke. But there would be a kitchen somewhere within the temple grounds, and the night air in this hollow was damp, carrying scents. It was only kitchen-smoke. Looking down into the ravine, he could see the paleness of a night-mist rising.

She stirred, and it wasn't the kitchen fires any longer.

Not yet.

Bells rang. Ahjvar flinched, though he had been expecting them. It was only the city curfew. Sunset, officially, but the temple lay lower than the city, and darkness pooled here earlier.

In addition to the gleams showing through the carved screens opposite, there was a little glimmer of light in the hospice, a wink of it moving past shuttered windows, as though someone carried a candle up on the fourth storey, into one room and then the next and the next, then vanishing, so maybe the wine-seller's rumours had been worth the groping. He had hooks and rope and had planned to get in by a high window, but the arcade roof was not even his own height below. Ahjvar kept a grip on the edge of the wall as he tested it, thinking of the missing galleries, ready to pull himself back up if it were too rotten to bear his weight, but it seemed sound enough. The scent of smoke abated. He could spend days stalking, scouting, planning routes, learning his quarry's routines and customary defences, and *she* would wait. She enjoyed it. Like a huntsman taking pride in his hounds, perhaps. It let him choose, anyway. Made him the guilty party. It was still cleaner.

He tested the shutter of the nearest window. Solid. They were meant to open inward, no hinges on the outside that he could tell, but there was no give at all in the centre: not merely latched, which would be easy enough, but perhaps wedged shut? No sound within. He moved along, trying them. All firmly fastened, even the one in the centre, which came down to what had been the gallery floor and had functioned as a door, once upon a time. Keeping people out, or in? Out, and probably the shutters of the higher windows, which did not have a convenient thieves' walkway beneath them, would merely be latched and he could slide them open with a thin knife. If they were keeping someone in, though, even the less-accessible would be more permanently sealed. The rumour of the Voice's madness made him consider that not utterly unlikely, and there was no sound at all within, no light. A warm summer night, not one against which to close the shutters.

He tried a small noise, a rap on the wood with the hilt of a knife. No stir of a disturbed sleeper. He slid the blade up, found a latch and flipped it, found another, and still, as he had thought, the door did not open. Near the bottom, and again at the top, an immovable block. Barred? Nailed? If so, it seemed nothing that he could move either up or aside with the knife. He retreated along the arcade roof to the outer wall again, and pulled himself back up, considering. He had time. It didn't have to be tonight; he hadn't planned on that. The hag slumbered again, easy, quiet. He felt utterly alive, every nerve and sinew alert, and the slow weight of the bleak years burnt away like mist in the morning. The hospice's river-doors might be barred, or merely locked and forgotten. Worth checking. Back down the wall, feeling his way carefully in the dark, remembering his route, then along the edge of the foundation, feeling over the wall for traces of the old stairs, the old landings, whatever had been there that would mark a door above him. He remembered seeing one, yes, and then he felt it, where the stonework of stairs still clung in broken fragments. Enough to climb, warily, till his fingers pressing through the thick clinging vine—grape, he was certain—found wood instead of stone.

The door's hinges were on the inside. The latch-handle was still in place, and there was a keyhole, so it might not be barred within. Crouching on a protruding nub of stone like a cormorant hunched on its rock over the sea, Ahjvar went through his bundle by feel, eyes closed. There was nothing to see, anyhow, in the black night, not even starlight to gleam on metal, clouds rolling down from the mountains. Closing the eyes brought greater sensitivity to the fingers, he always found. Something—a grappling hook—slid and slipped, and grabbing blind he caught it before he lost it clattering down the stones of the once-riverbank. Found a set of cast bronze hooks and wrenches, long-stemmed, delicate, but heavy enough to press the weight of an iron lock without bending, strong enough not to break when twisted. Chose those which seemed the best fit for the size of the lock's hole and felt his way into it. Seized up, he decided, not surprisingly. He had oil and ink-brushes in several sizes. He tried to sit without thinking, without feeling, with an angler's patience, waiting for the oil to do its work, to break the seal of rust and float the dust free. He usually could be still and calm once he was about such work. The concentration brought a sort of peace that he only found elsewhere with Ghu's arm over him, with Ghu's breath in his hair. He'd never been one to find other men particularly attractive, but Ghu was—a comfort. Leave it at that. The Old Great Gods knew he hadn't let himself have the faintest glimmering of desire for anyone, woman or man or even Ghu, since he surfaced from the madness to find Miara dead, strangled, and the spells she and he both had thought would hold him, would kill him—Great Gods, such a thing to ask of the woman who loved you—sloughed off, shattered, and gone to ash.

It was not wizardry had destroyed Miara's spells; neither he nor *she* had that to call on now, by Catairanach's blessing, the one mercy—or piece of common sense—the goddess had shown. It did not balance that no wizardry seemed to have a hold on *her*, though. If he could ever find a way to kill a god . . .

But he was fretting after Ghu despite telling himself he would not, and if he did not find that stillness, that quiet hunter's centre, he was going to make mistakes, and fools would try to kill him, and more people would die. None of whom would be he, no matter how he suffered. Even the cage in Sea Town, when they'd taken him quite justly for the murder of some poor sailor . . . he ought to have night-mares about that, but he didn't, didn't remember much of it. He'd been willing to see how long it really could take him to die, but *she* had risen, someone must have come too close . . . the Tzian clan-fathers had thought a man who didn't seem capable of dying could have his uses. That set him on this road. They were all dead now, with one thing and another. Him, mostly. They'd managed to fail to hang him when he started to scare them more than their rivals did; bad luck, ill chance, or a miracle in the failed knot. That was after they'd found he couldn't be poisoned. Made very sick and angry, yes, but not poisoned, not to death.

Even the brightest stars were veiled, and the night was not cooling off as one expected in the mountains. The first whisper of storm? The key-hooks again, a slight give, maybe. More oil. He gave it as long as it took him to silently recite the alphabet of the trees, with the three sacred blessings of each letter's namesake as the Praitannec wizards Over-Malagru reckoned them, asserting some discipline over his wandering mind, and then the hooks moved, the thin wrench was able to turn. The lock clunked, loud enough to make him freeze motionless, listening. Nothing stirred.

The door might, of course, also be barred.

It wasn't, though he had to give it a hard shove. The hinges creaked.

Another silent waiting, with no stir. He rolled everything up again, including his cloak, and belted on his sword properly. Even if he told himself he was only scouting this night to find if the Voice were here at all, there were still Red Masks to consider. He tried to do as little damage as possible to the vine, weaving his way in like a ferret.

He was in a fairly broad passageway, Ahjvar judged, feeling along either wall. Two doors to one side, one to another. Two opened stiffly into rooms that smelt, like the passage, stale. Windowless. The other led to a descending stair from which a cold, damp air arose. He didn't venture down. The passage ran to another door, which did not squeak, and beyond the air was better. There was even light. He edged out cautiously, but it was only a silver lamp sitting in a wall-niche: some night-light, which at least told that the building was in use, and that people would not be unexpected in this—entry hall? Maybe. Double doors, unbarred. He tried one, and it opened smoothly. A courtyard beyond, not the same one on which he'd gazed down earlier, a dark hedge running along the buildings that framed it. So . . . he could have gone around and come in the front door. Right. It didn't seem to be guarded, but it was overlooked by buildings that showed here and there a glimmer of light, and lamps burned at this door and at an archway opposite. Visitors might be expected? He left the lit areas, found more disused rooms, all smelling of dust or mould. Some were furnished, simple bedframes stripped of mattress and blankets, jumbled anyhow, shoved out of the way. He thought for a moment he had trodden on bone, stooped to pick it up and found broken crockery. He felt over the window. A lath had been nailed along the sill to keep the shutters from being swung inwards. He shook them. They did not rattle, but the wood felt old, dry, rain-damaged. He could smash through them any time noise ceased to matter. Good to know.

But the lamps were lit for something, for someone. Finally he found stairs and started up. Lamps burned in wall-recesses at every turning, polished brass or silver, not clay, and the oil was scented, an incongruity with the abandoned rubbish below. It was the fourth floor on which he had seen the moving light, but Ahjvar checked each as he came to it, listening, smelling, wary for the faintest gleam of illumination, before he ever opened any door. The second-storey rooms were empty, as were those of the third, except for one, which was scattered with wooden chests and lacquered boxes. It smelt strongly of mice and mouldering cloth. The fourth floor, then.

The central passageway of the fourth floor, when he cautiously let himself out onto it, was carpeted, silent, and well-lit. It felt lived-in. He opened doors more warily, no need to go in and feel his way around, with the puddles of light shed by the passage lamps. Empty. A storeroom, but a neat and tidy one, clearly not abandoned. A . . . library? A wall that was floor to ceiling with what looked like nest-boxes, anyway, each filled with scrolls, and another wall with shelves of codices, a table of waxed tablets for notes and drafts, paper and reed-pens and pots of Westron ink, a tall writing-desk by the window. He went in. These shutters pulled open easily. He looked down on the mist-filled ravine. The taller trees made floating dark islands above it, and moonlight turned the fog to a flowing ghost-river. He closed the shutters, as the breeze threatened the orderly papers on the table.

A woman's wail checked him in the doorway as he would have slid out into the passage. He stepped back and closed it to a crack, keeping an eye to it, dagger in hand. Wordless, the cry rose to a howl like that of the newly and suddenly bereaved, helpless, without hope of comfort.

The door across from him opened. Two women hurried out, both in white nightrobes, the younger struggling into a grey caftan, the elder shielding the flame of a lamp with her hand. They pattered barefoot down the corridor to a farther room on the ravine side, and the elder, with a key on a long cord around her neck, unlocked a door.

"Revered One? Revered Lilace, Voice, what's the matter?"

He felt the satisfaction of the lock turning over. The wine-seller's tale had been truth. The Voice lived in the old hospice. But locked in. A prisoner of the temple, or mad?

Either way, he thought, not a power to make war, murder queens, and steal a kingdom. Not the fit object for Catairanach's vengeance. Not his place to point that out. He was no champion, whatever the goddess said, to question his king as was any free Praitan's right and a lord's duty. An assassin of the Five Cities with a commission did not protest that a particular killing was bad policy. And the goddess had promised him an ending in return for this. So. Though she had demanded others, too, and he might serve damned Catairanach and his—her—folk, better if he found, afterwards, who truly set the temple's course and dealt with them as might the Leopard, if not an honourable champion of the *duina*.

"I will go," a voice wailed. "I will go, I will go, I will go now, oh, spare the child, don't heed her do not heed me I will not—I will have youth I will have beauty I will have the dancer the orphan girl to be my daughter my child my beloved my own my beautiful queen and he is come for me let him come let me go . . ."

The voice trailed off into sobbing once more, and another said, "Set it down, when she speaks, set it down."

"But Dur, she's said all that before, this afternoon, in the pulpit."

"Even subtle differences can have significance. Go fetch a tablet, girl, and set it down. Always bring a tablet. You'll have to learn that, if you want to keep this position."

The younger woman hurried out—and where else was she going to find a writing-tablet but in this library?

Now or later. This had been scouting. He had more than half meant to return to the ravine, to plan his way once he knew the place. To draw it out over days. Odds were the priestess would fling open the door, dash in, dash out, never see him if he kept still in the corner behind it.

Great Gods, he didn't ask for mercy, just let there be an end to this. A few more murders and an end.

Ahjvar caught her as she darted in, a little slip of a thing, hand over her mouth. She struggled and bit him but, pinned against the wall, couldn't get herself free. He slashed the thin cotton of her night-robe with the dagger in his other hand, then ripped the whole hem off and stuffed it in her mouth to gag her, tying it with the sash of her caftan, which he dragged free one-handed, forcing her to the floor. More or less sitting on her, both hands free again, he tore further strips of the night-robe and bound her hand and foot, propped her in the far corner, comfortable as she could be, and left her with her caftan decently wrapped over her naked legs for her modesty. Sheathed the dagger and went swiftly, then, to the door, shutting it quietly behind him on her terrified eyes.

The elder priestess—nursemaid or secretary or perhaps both— had not yet called in impatience to hurry her on.

In the Voice's apartment, the lamp burned on a low table, surrounded by cushions in the fashion for desert dining. The room's carpet muffled his footsteps. There was a bed, high and ornately carved in the Five Cities style of fifty years ago, all animal grotesques and squinting faces peering out of foliage. The shutters were open, but the window was barred. The Voice, surely the Voice, an elderly woman of desert ancestry, brown-skinned, black-robed, tall and gaunt, white hair the dingy yellow of old cotton all in flyaway wisps, knelt on the floor by the bed, rocking her body back and forth.

"It will be done it will be done it will it will I do *not* will I did *not* see I see I see him now I will not will have him take her let her go she is done she is finished she fails she is yours I will have youth oh let me go let me go let me go—"

Old Great Gods have mercy. Spittle bubbled at the corner of her mouth, and the priestess crouching before her, hands on her shoulders, did not move to wipe it away but merely said, in an echo of Ghu's talking to horses and nightmare-mad fools tone, but with all the kindness worn away, "Speak more slowly, Revered Voice, I need to remember your words till the clerk returns. Who do you see?"

The Voice's dark eyes glanced aside to his and what was almost a smile twisted her face. "Now I will escape you," she whispered. Her rocking stilled, hands, writhing and fluttering, settled to her lap. "Now, now, now, you cannot keep me now not now not here but oh why oh why oh why my lady where is she where is she where are you?"

"Mina, what kept you? I'll set down what you've missed—"

The priestess climbed stiffly to her feet, a hand held out for the tablet even as she turned. Ahjvar was already crossing the room. He punched her, hard below the ribs, before her mouth was halfway open on a cry. Too hard, maybe, for an ageing woman, when a blow like that could lay out senseless a well-muscled man in his prime. He caught her as she crumpled, lowered her to the floor; she still breathed, anyhow. The Voice continued to gaze up at him.

"I'm tired," she whispered. "Did you know she is mad? The Voice is mad, the Lady is mad, the city is blind, and you should kill her too. Someone should."

That sounded halfway sane.

"You should be quick," she added. "Dead king of the Duina Catairna, she sees you, she dreams the Lady dreamt she sees you she wants you she says no gods but the Lady in Marakand and you brought him here I see him I dream him if she does not no wizards in Marakand no powers in Marakand she eats wizards so you will be hers she will make you hers no champion but hers and you will be high king under the empress of Marakand and she will feed the death that lives in you on her enemies on the enemies of Marakand on the wizards of the tribes and the cities will fall but we will stand against the west that is coming the death that is coming, the sword that is coming out of the north but he will destroy her tell her the west is death is—*No*—we will build the fortress here and hold the east and he will break against us against the swords of the tribes against the fleets of my cities against my king who cannot die who carries death who—" She screamed abruptly and bit her own arm, wide-eyed, rocking again. "Let me go!"

He had stood, shocked, when he had let nothing of this victims stay him, distract him, move him, not in long years. He crossed to her in a stride, with the thin waxed strangler's cord in hand.

"I am sorry for the girl, though," he thought she said. She reached to clutch not her throat but his hands, not struggling, holding them as if to make sure he didn't leave her, till her fingers grew slack and fell away, and *she* uncoiled. *She* embraced the death, the torn moment when earth touched the road of the heavens, and rose stronger, and the fire felt like it would split his bones, but she fell away like the slumping dead priestess, like a sated snake, to sleep. A little while.

Ahjvar didn't die. He hadn't really expected to. Hope had gone to ash long ago. Anyway, Catairanach wanted more than the one. And the Lady had known her servant was about to die. He ran for the door, drawing sword and dagger, but they were already crossing the threshold, two priests in red armour, faces hidden by masked helmets, naked swords in hand. A third came behind them, armed with a white staff. An eerie light crept over them, like slow lightning, sullen red.

The damned wizard-hunting Red Masks the Marakanders all feared so were wizards themselves. Didn't the city *know*?

The first struck towards him, low and fast with a short stabbing sword, the usual Marakander weapon, and he turned aside, in close, caught the arm on the left-hand dagger, grating on bone; their armour had no sleeves. The priest jerked free, and he met the other's slashing blow; that one, taller, had a long Northron blade. He let himself be forced back so he could turn and get the wall behind him. More of the Red Masks slid into the room, silent, all of them silent, and fluid as water in their movements. These were unarmoured, carried only the white staves. Armour turned his sword, blade skittered on blade, the smaller priest was still using his torn arm strongly as ever. They seemed to care little for defending themselves, pressing in, till he stabbed through an eye-slit of the shorter priest's mask. He lost his dagger, but that one fell without a cry, becoming a hazard to them all—devils forbid, trying to stagger up again, which was not right, not with a handspan of steel in the brain, but she or he failed and sprawled, clutching at Ahjvar's foot, and the red light faded from the body. Faded from them all, first one, then another, but it didn't stop them. Some wizardry they had collectively and silently decided was worthless.

Catairanach's champion, was he? It became like that, a duel between him and the taller Red Mask with the Northron-style sword, and he wished for a shield after all, gripping his bundle to guard his left side, but even if he did cut his opponent down, the Lady of Marakand would hardly accept it as the judgement of the Old Great Gods in Catairanach's favour and let him leave. And it could not be a judgement to mere blooding, because the damned Red Masks didn't seem to bleed. He should have noticed that sooner. He should have jumped for the window instead, but in the lamplight he wasn't able to see if the bars were wood, with a hope of breaking, or unyielding iron.

The robed Red Masks circling around were as faceless as the man he fought, wearing long, dull red veils, thick enough to show no shadow of feature, thick enough to blind them, but they didn't move as if they had any difficulty seeing. Wizardry.

He bled, if the Red Mask did not. Arm and ribs. The other's armour was torn, gown slashed, a warding arm sliced half away, hanging, Great Gods, and only sluggish dark blood congealed on the wound. He made no sound, nor faltered. Ahjvar beat the other's stroke aside with the bundle of his cloak and gear, drove forward for the damaged segment of armour where the stitching showed, and ran him through, falling forward, missed footing on slick stones, dizzy, his own blood, and the dead priest underfoot. He recovered, dragged sword free with both hands, makeshift shield abandoned. He swept at a veiled one's neck, seeing a path to the door, a chance, as they stood about like onlookers to a tavern brawl, but they closed in, half a dozen of them; they had merely been waiting, watching, testing. There was no guarding against all the blows that beat him down.

CHAPTER VI

The main road of the caravanserai suburb forked at a triangle of land uncultivated and pitted, enclosed by a low drystone wall; the graveyard they had passed yesterday, with a charnel-house, its plaster flaking, squatting at the westernmost end. Ghu, who had melted into the shadow of a doorway as the lady and her wizard trotted past, took the right-hand fork. He could see in the distance that the Malagru-folk, if those were the pale, dark-haired country people who had been passing through the Eastern Wall yesterday, seemed to be taking the bridge to the Riverbend Gate with their produce. Most of the caravan-folk heading in to the city did as well. The southerly, right-hand road joined one coming down along the city wall from the south, and the folk there seemed mostly to be Marakander peasants, dressed in shawls and caftans, and not so free-moving and proud as the people of the Malagru. Well, if your goddess ruled you as an emperor through a corrupted viceroy, you probably learnt to walk warily, and cowed. Why Sunset Gate? An impulse. He trusted such impulses as a dog trusts its nose, not to keep him out of trouble but to tug him along to where he ought, or perhaps ought not, to be. Sometimes it was better to be where you ought not, if you meant to change the flow of the world.

The bridge over the ravine was empty as he walked across, pausing to lean on the parapet and gaze down at the broken stone and lush greenery of its bed. No water. Not even any reeds, here; it was all thorny fruit-trees and creeping vines, busy with birds. A garden, but an untended one. This bridge was not old stone but new, barely wide enough for a single cart. The ruins of a broader one framed it on either bank. He went on, thoughtfully. An empty river, but not, not quite godless yet. There was the faintest trace of some presence. Perhaps only a memory? A ghost. Nothing he could call to. It was a sorrowful thing for a god to die, but the living world, even the world of stone and water, was not eternal. It had its currents and its tides.

This Sunset Ward gate, if he remembered what Ahj had told him on the road, when he was sane again and the lady was travelling with them, was the one that had fallen in the earthquake. Unlike the gates of the pass in the Eastern Wall and the distant Western down where the caravan road dropped to the Stone Desert, the city gates were closed at dusk and opened at dawn. Ghu strolled along the fringes of a party not of peasants but of grander folk, a bulky, jouncing carriage like a box on wheels, with four armed men walking beside it and four horses to pull it. A swirl of writing on the tiny door and the same badge painted large between the shoulders of the men's capes probably meant something. A senator? A clan-father or whatever the senior lords of the great families were called here. No one looked out the tiny, cloth-covered slit of a window. Miserable way to travel, when you could be out under the sun. There were great manors up along the southern road, Ahjvar had said, where servants and tenants of the lords of the Twenty Families or of the temple grew some of what fed the city, and where the lords of Families went to flee the summer's heat. The carriage was followed by a swarm of hangers-on, a cart piled with baggage, servants on foot, one carrying a fluffy little dog that sighed and looked longingly at Ghu, envying him the freedom to use his feet. Even these servants wore long caftans; only the guards and the boys who led the ponies went bare-legged in short tunics, though the day was gathering to hot. Half of them had Nabbani-black hair; the folk of Marakand were descended from the folk of many gods. Ahjvar should maybe have thought to get him a caftan rather than a cameleer's coat, but then, Ahjvar had not wanted him to come into the city. He should have thought of it himself.

"May I pet the dog?" he asked, as they came up near the gate, and the woman who carried it looked over at him, then back at the carriage she followed, before smiling.

"If he'll let you. He has a temper."

Ghu would have a temper too, if he were forced to be carried everywhere so that he grew too fat to walk if he wanted, and to wear his hair tied up in a topknot of ribbons. But the panting dog leaned into his fingers as he scratched around its ears. It even licked his hand, so that the woman laughed and said, "You're somebody special, I can see." He strolled through the darkness of the gate hearing about how the dog always threw up in the carriage, past the bare-legged street guards in their grey tunics, armed only with staves, and nobody paid him any heed as a brown-haired man with a black band on the hem of his tunic and his russet cape and a short sword on a baldric came out from a square stone building, his helmet under his arm, to bow to the carriage. It didn't stop, just passed on through. Ghu did likewise, just another servant of the carriage despite his western-road garb, then took his leave of the dog and its bearer, sauntering off.

Marakand was more like the Five Cities than the capital or the ports of the empire, although even its main streets seemed unplanned, grown up from wandering paths, where the colonies were orderly. The broad road from the gate, lined with what he guessed were warehouses, windowless on their ground floors, was paved in stone and swept clean, though the morning's traffic was already leaving it toll of dung and dust. It ended very quickly at an open market square, filled with rugs spread on the ground, bright awnings, and arrays of baskets, mostly of produce. Interspersed with such displays were carts piled equally high, whose oxen switched their tails against flies and chewed their cud in unhurried peace, while the donkeys drowsed. The houses surrounding the square were mostly plastered golden with clay or washed bright with lime. Narrow streets and narrower alleys divided them, a web fanning out in all directions with only two broader roads fit to take a cart that he could see. Even those were dark, almost tunnel-like, overhung with balconies and galleries that almost touched. It made the market brighter, like a pool of sunshine.

There was a weight to it, too, a heaviness drawing him down, as if it were water sweeping to some drain. Not in the centre but towards the southeast corner there was a single building, a squat, barrel-vaulted stone square. Ghu threaded his way towards it almost unthinkingly. Something ancient, something deadly, something that was no goddess of clean water, however diminished from her river.

There was power in that stone building, which had no entrance he could see. Not power within, but power laid in the stones, in mortar, in the incised script that stalked along the frieze. What lay within he couldn't tell. It was not an emptiness, though. A blindness. But he felt that only as he drew closer, close enough to read the script, if he had been able to read at all. No, the weight, the wind that stirred the market, the dangerous thing that drew him, was another woman, standing with the odd building at her back.

He stopped, stood, heart running a little too fast. He had seen wizards, servants of the emperor, about their business. They wore an air of power that pressed against the world a little, as though they held more space than other folk. He had met demons, a time or two, and they swam in the currents of the world and were all that it was and all that made up the land of their heart, and the gods of the high places and the goddesses of the waters, too, had a weight and a presence, much greater than that a wizard carried. He had thought the wizard who called herself Lady Deyandara's was a goddess, at first, when she came to the room in the inn, maybe the Voice or the Lady herself, and he would have felt her approach sooner if he had not been so distracted by the distant brooding threat within the city. No goddess, he had known almost at once, but she might be some halfling god, some child of a rash goddess or hill-god into whom too much of her parent's divinity had been permitted to flow. Perhaps. But there were stranger powers in the world, not all indifferent or well-disposed to humanfolk. He did not think she was a dragon. But she had sworn protection to Lady Deyandara, and she had meant her oath, and she had seen enough of him to be wary. Not that he wished her to have done so.

And now all in one morning here was another such, within the city where the darkness brooded, and he did not think, he did *not* think she was what Ahjvar had come seeking, either.

"There is a cycle of tales told by the Northron skalds, and they begin like this . . ."

The storyteller wore a bright shawl, black with patterns of red and brilliant blue, trailing over one shoulder, looped over an arm, flashing scarlet and kingfisher as she gestured. He had seen such patterns of jagged lines and borders in the cities, exotic soft yak-woollens of the Pillars of the Sky. The storyteller appeared to be no mountain woman, though, but a Northron, one of the *skalds* she spoke of, maybe, a bard of the north, a weaver of poetry, a singer of history.

A power, choosing to appear road-worn and shabby, who would blur and fade from mind the moment she removed that brilliant shawl.

The bard didn't sing but chanted in trade Nabbani. Her eyes, grey as storm-clouds over the sea, held Ghu's a moment. He made his way towards her, reluctant. A necessity, being here. Maybe. And if she were truly a storyteller, and only some wild godling child throwing off sparks all unwitting of threat, well, he had heard few stories from the kingdoms of the north, and perhaps he should hear one now. Nabban had looked inward too long. Besides, the sense of heavy menace underlying the city was not lessening, but his urge to hunt down Ahjvar, drag him away, hold him safe was being overruled by common sense. Ahj would be scouting around the temple, and it would be unwise to draw the attention of the Voice of the Lady. Just because the clerk at the Eastern Wall had set nothing down when he glanced over at Ghu and dismissed him did not mean that someone would not remember that the Praitans, who had most certainly drawn attention, had had a Nabbani servant with them. That courier who had galloped by so soon as they passed through had given them a studying look.

Ahjvar would certainly shout at him if he came searching now. But something lurked, like a beast, waiting. He did not think it was this storyteller . . . but he was not absolutely certain. Another reason to listen.

"Long ago, in the days of the first kings in the north . . ." The storyteller watched him as she did not watch the others drawn round her amidst the bustle of the market; her eyes flitted over them, and her smile was swift and practised, entirely belonging to her art, like the sweep of her arms, the flash of the scarlet and black and king-fisher blue, that invited them closer, to squat at her feet. He joined the others who had settled near, old men and women with little to do, children truant from errands, a few curious market-goers with their filled baskets pulled warily close against thieves. The woman was tall, lean, almost gaunt, a warrior's, a traveller's hardness. Neither young nor old, with the strong harsh bones of the north, a skin much lighter than the Praitannec tawniness he was used to seeing with pale hair; her long plait a faded silveriness that wasn't due to age. She made no concession to the fashions of the land in her tunic and narrow-legged trousers, all brown and grey and shabby. A dark cloak was slung down carelessly on the ground at her side. Her open-handed gesture indicated the little wooden bowl at her feet, a small and lonely coin its only offering. None responded. She pulled a face at them all, sighed, shrugged, folded her arms, fallen silent and looking at the sky.

A grinning imp of a boy carefully broke the corner from a loaf in his basket and tossed the crust to join the coin. He sat on his knees, ready to run if she swooped to box his ears, and Ghu almost held his breath, ready to hurl himself between her and the child, but she put her hands together and bowed deeply, Nabbani-fashion, as much in Ghu's direction as the boy's, and suddenly grave and formal, went on:

". . . who were Viga Forkbeard, and Red Geir, and Hravnmod the Wise—there were seven devils, and their names were Honeytongued Ogada, Vartu Kingsbane, Jasberek Fireborn, Twice-Betrayed Ghatai, Dotemon the Dreamshaper, Tu'usha the Restless, and Jochiz Stonebreaker. If other tellers tell you different . . ." she raised her brows, shrugged, ". . . they are ignorant singers not worthy of their hire. And these seven devils escaped from the cold hells, where the Old Great Gods had sealed them after the great war in the heavens."

Even in Nabban they had their stories of the seven devils, mostly fantastical. Wizards who flew on the wings of the wind, horses of bone, the dead rising from their graves to follow their lords to battle, a princess buried alive to call a demon from the sea . . . Dotemon had conquered and ruled Nabban until the gods themselves rose up to throw her down—but he knew that one was true.

So was a devil truly a creature of the cold hells or merely some name, some excuse, for a wizard grown over-mighty and taken to lording it over his fellow men?

"And in the days of the first kings in the north, who were Viga Forkbeard, and Red Geir, and Hravnmod the Wise, as I have told, there were seven wizards. Two were of the people of the kings in the north, who came from over the western sea, and one was of a people unknown; one was of the Great Grass and one of Imperial Nabban, and two were from beyond far Nabban, but the seven were of one fellowship. Their names were Heuslar the Deep-Minded or, as his enemies named him, Heuslar the Cunning, who was uncle to Red Geir, Ulfhild the King's Sword, who was sister to Hravnmod the Wise, Anganurth Wanderer, Tamghiz, Chief of the Bear-Mask Fellowship, Yeh-Lin the Beautiful, and Sien-Mor and Sien-Shava, the Outcasts, who were sister and brother. If other singers tell you different, they know only the shadows of the tales, and they lie." A stern look at the boy who had tossed the crust, as if he were suspected of believing such ignorant singers.

"These wizards were wise, and powerful. They knew the runes and the secret names, and the patterns of the living world and of the dead. But the seven wizards desired to know yet more, and see yet more, and to live forever like the gods of the high places and the goddesses of the waters and the demons of the forest and the stone and the sand and the grass.

"Now the devils, having no place, had no bodies, but were like smoke or like a flame and not of the earth at all. And these seven devils who had escaped the cold hells hungered to be of the stuff of the world . . . They made a bargain with the seven wizards, that they would join their souls to the wizards' souls and share the wizards' bodies, sharing knowledge, and unending life, and power."

Ghu joined those making themselves comfortable on the ground. This made the building loom in his vision, not comfortably. The inscribed frieze kept trying to pull his eye away from the storyteller. It . . . prickled. The woman swam in his vision, edged in shifting light. Her eyes found his again, a singer's trick to gather her audience in, now this one, now that, except he did not think she looked at any but him. It raised the hairs all down his neck, and he wondered what she saw, in turn. That was twice in one day he'd seen such eyes, old eyes, too old, hot with suppressed fires. Yet he stayed where he was, listening.

"But the devils deceived the wizards and betrayed them. The devils took the souls of the wizards into their own and became one with them, and it is said they devoured them."

A sandalled foot pressed against him, someone shifting nearer, out of the flow of people passing, slowing, yet going on their way. He glanced up, into striking amber eyes that flicked down, and the young woman muttered something, apology, maybe, in the speech of the western road, folded her arms and stayed to listen. He was suddenly only half attentive to the Northron woman. Amber eyes and a rope of blue-black hair, a heart that, like his, ran too fast—with fear? Afraid, and she paused to listen to a story?

She settled down by him, one knee drawn up. Her caftan was a dull pink, with a pattern of faded black diamonds in the weave, the elbows patched with a streaky red that did not match. She should wear crimson, and the golden-brown of her eyes, and the blue of the evening twilight. Her right cuff was ink-spattered. A clerk, a scribe, and not one who could do better than a second-hand caftan. A market letter-writer? He eyed her hands sidelong. Bitten nails and further ink-stains, but old scars, too, of cut and callus. Not indoor hands. He shut his eyes; her heart was silk banners and horses running, an ocean of grass and a sabre, fear in the darkness. A great weight, a great sin. She was a wizard, too, magic pulsing with her heartbeat. He opened his eyes, and the storyteller was watching the both of them, sombre, unsmiling.

"Now this tale is from the saga of Red Geir and concerns the wizard Heuslar, who was brother to King Geir's mother, and who was at this time become the devil Ogada. And it concerns the sword of Red Geir, which he cursed with his dying, that ever after, it betrayed the one who claimed it, so that there was blood between him and one dear to him, either to slay or be slain, witting or unwitting, murder in the dark night or an ill-chancing accident."

The young scribe's fear eased. To be a secret wizard within Marakand's city walls must be to live in fear, and yet it was what the story might have been, and was not, that had worried her.

"And it concerns the lady Gisel, a sea-rover owning no lord, who had borne a child to Red Geir, all unknown to his wife. For Heuslar loved Red Geir's wife . . ."

It was a different style of storytelling than one met on the caravan road, with no place for the clown and the broad jest, not within the tale, though her knowing asides had somewhat of the same effect, lightening the telling, as the story spun out into spell and curse and tragedy that echoed down the generations. Ghu listened, entranced, forgetting, mostly, his apprehension of the city and the storyteller, forgetting the young woman sitting so close he heard every catch of breath as the story ensnared her too. It came to its end, if it could be called that, in vengeance and death and a war between brothers, with the promise of more to follow another day. The scribe sighed, as one returning out of dream, and the storyteller bowed, not mockingly but a Northron ducking of the head, hand to her chest. Coins rattled in her bowl. She sang, then, without any instrument, not even the drum that any storyteller of the Five Cities would carry like a part of themselves—he saw her with a harp, and a high-raftered roof of straw, and a fire leaping against the cold night. He saw ice, and shadows like old blood, murky brown and thick. It was maybe part of the story, untranslated, a music of language that ran both harsh and soaring, and was soon over. She swept up the bowl and the coins and swung the dark cloak about herself, hiding the eye-catching shawl.

He would have expected the listeners to press her for another tale, a song, though she would of course refuse; whatever else she was, she was bard, *skald*, or whatever the Northron word was. He knew market-storytellers from every city he had ever seen, and they always left their listeners to look for them another day, not growing fretful and stiff with sitting. But their listeners always asked. Instead of doing so, the audience faded away into the passages between the carts and awnings and booths, as if she had already gone.

Only he and the scribe still stood, risen expectant to their feet. The storyteller studied him, head a little to one side. He'd seen such a look before, though not—all thanks to Mother and Father Nabban—directed at him. He'd had the one master his whole life, till he ran. It was the look of a buyer in the slave-market, considering utility.

"What do you see?" she asked suddenly. "Here." And she raised a hand, touched the inscription behind her.

She spoke Imperial Nabbani, her accent strange but not precisely foreign. Ghu glanced at the scribe, who frowned and answered in good court speech. "I—" and that was a royal *I*, where *was* she from that she knew no better than to use that? "—can't read it. Is it some Pirakuli script?"

The grey eyes were back on him, and there was an odd light in their depths. The hairs on the back of his neck prickled again. Ghu shook his head, wide-eyed, innocent, young, and harmless. "I can't read." He didn't think that was what she wanted to know. He should have taken warning by the scribe's fear and gone his way sooner. "Lady," he added, to be safe. He gave her a little bow and smiled, made to slide out of the glare of her attention. Dangerous, very dangerous to have such focussed will upon him.

"I do see you," she said.

And I see you. Almost. But he didn't quite let that thought float to the surface. He hoped.

"Tears and fire and binding," he jerked out, pinned there. Steel catching firelight, that was the colour of her eye now. "The slow death of a god, smothering. Starving. Cut off from the earth."

The scribe turned on him, a hawk's fierce stare, just for a heartbeat, before moving away, making it clear they did not stand together. "I know your name," she told the woman. "I figured it out. I know my father's name, too. All the road does. And they say the Red Masks can smell wizardry." Her voice shook a little as she dared. "If you sent those folk on their way and didn't just drive them off by growling in Northron at them, you'd better leave. Stay away from me. I have to live here."

"Do you?" The storyteller didn't seem much to care. "It wasn't wizardry, Ivah. I'd be interested to see what it does bring. But what is this thing? I asked and was told it was Ilbialla's tomb, built by the

Voice. The man I asked admitted that much and scurried off as if he'd seen a devil." She grinned wolfishly. "Who was Ilbialla and why is she sealed within?"

"She was one of the goddesses of the city," the scribe said, edging back still farther. Ivah. Not a Nabbani name. "Don't you know even that much of Marakand? Where have you been the past year? It's not so long a road from Lissavakail—as the hawk flies."

"In the mountains," the storyteller said shortly. "We were in no hurry. A wild god in the Salt took a dislike to me. And Mikki was ill. The deserts were too hot."

"Who?"

"You never met him." Another smile, self-amused. "Just—a bear I know. We lost ourselves for a while, wandering out of the world, nearly, up into the heights. There are valleys in those mountains, streams and caves no human has ever seen. He slept. We went fishing."

That seemed to puzzle the scribe as much as it did Ghu. She frowned, shrugged, dismissing it. "There's another tomb, a sealed cave, up on the hill." Ivah nodded to the south. "Gurhan's tomb. Those two gods are supposed to have betrayed the Lady, some thirty years or so ago. Plotted with wizards to destroy the city by earth-quake and died. The old people believe it's a lie, though they won't say so. What does the inscription say?"

"I can't read it either." The storyteller considered. "Not all of it. We've been camped up there by Gurhan's cave a couple of days now, and we can't make anything within hear us. There's such strength in the binding, as if all the wizards of a land had worked it together. I've never seen anything like it, except maybe some of the great imperial works in Nabban, and the words I can read—aren't ones you or any wizard could. Tell me, was it the Lady built these tombs or the Voice?"

Ivah shook her head. "They're the same thing."

"I wonder. And you, son of Nabban, you say, slow death—" She broke off, looking past them. "I came down the road from the south, through the silver mines. We didn't travel with any gossiping company to learn much of the city. What's a Red Mask?"

Ivah turned a sickly pallor and spun on her heel, but her colour came back almost at once. "The Red Masks are an order of warrior-priests who serve the Voice and the Lady. They're the ones they send to arrest wizards, and no magic works on them. They can kill with a touch, it's said. They dress all in red and never show their faces. I've never seen one; I lie low when there's even a rumour of them passing out into the city. *Those* are simply a pair of street guard from the gate-fort, and—and the *licensed* singer who usually lays his rug down just over there." She nodded across to where a couple were doing a brisk trade in greens and eggs from the back of a high-wheeled oxcart. "He was standing over there, just listening, till almost the end. I suppose he was busy learning your story to make it his own, but figured on balance, better to make his own ending for it and be rid of you. Did you apply for a licence?"

"For what?"

"This is Marakand! You can't just stand on a street-corner and tell stories. It doesn't much matter what you're doing, you have to prove your skill to some guild or other. You have to register and buy a licence."

"It's the middle of a market, not a street-corner."

"Yes, and that old singer decided he didn't want to start a fight with you for taking over his pitch. He's decided getting you hustled off the street is worth the bribe it'll have taken to get the guard to pay any attention. They're going to ask to see your licence, and when they learn you don't have one, they'll arrest you and lock you up till

you or your friends can pay their fine, and the one the guild of entertainers will levy."

"Huh," the storyteller said. "I never did like cities." And she
turned and walked away.

Ivah started to stride off as well. Ghu, he wasn't sure why, took a
few steps after her, but the male street guard grabbed him by the arm.

"You the outlander storyteller without a licence?"

Ghu looked up, wary, docile, and timid. The guard's grip on his
sleeve slackened.

"It was a woman," said a withered old man with a flat drum
tucked under his arm, puffing for breath. "I told you. An outlander
woman, a tall one. I don't know what she was. Something up from
the caravanserais. Stealing the bread from honest men's mouths. No
better than a beggar."

The street guard let Ghu go, held up a warning finger as he
began to sidle off. Ghu ducked his head meekly and stood still. The
storyteller had vanished. The other street guard, a young woman,
had followed Ivah and was greeting her by name.

No, Ivah hadn't seen where the beggar had gone, either. No,
she couldn't really describe her. Tallish. Foreign. She smiled apolo-
getically. She needed to get back to work herself. It was getting near
noon, and she was expecting a trader's clerk with a sheaf of contracts
that needed copying . . .

She didn't look back as she walked away. Why should she?

The lawfully licensed storyteller went off to unroll the rug over
his shoulder on the ground beside the oxcart, looking disgruntled.
Ghu faded back a step or two. It didn't do to run at such times. If you
ran, you were noticed. If you were noticed, you were chased.

"What was that runner from Riverbend fort saying to the adjutant about a Nabbani man at the Eastern Wall?"

The woman guard shrugged, returning from her talk with Ivah. "Arrest him, I think?"

"What, every male Nabbani who comes through the gate? Waste of time," the man grumbled. "Better we let him go and have nothing to report, don't you think?"

"But what if he is the one they're looking for? An enemy of the Lady?"

"He can't be, not unless he outran the couriers."

Both street guards unfortunately looked over just as Ghu was sauntering behind a basket of green nakatis and the shawl-wrapped woman selling them.

"You! Stay put!" the man shouted. He plunged after Ghu, who in the eyeblink of decision chose to run. He'd never fared well in the hands of any sort of city watch, and it was harder, these days, to endure being beaten. He dodged a pair of hobbled donkeys and the array of baskets piled with radishes and onions just out of their reach, doubled up a narrow aisle of carts and awnings and thick-pressed folk, squirming, twisting sideways. Behind him, someone clanged a handbell. Plenty of almost-Nabbani faces here, but not so many desert coats, and his Five Cities dress was going to stand out if he dropped the coat. He swarmed between legs, rolled under a cart, came up startling a dog on the market's edge and had a clear run for a narrow street, darkly shadowed with the balconies above. Let him get into narrow alleys that would twist between enclosing walls, and he would lose them, find some dark crevice, and they would miss him. He could be still, still as a wild thing, and unseen as his hunters trod within arm's reach.

He went sprawling, landed rolling. The male guard had been closer on his heels than he realized, under the cart and all. Now he had hurled his short staff like a spear to tangle between Ghu's feet.

The man was on him as he bounced up and staggered, his ankle failing him. He pinned Ghu's arms, lifting him onto his toes. Ghu dropped his weight, but the guard was ready for that, twisted his arm up so that pain burned in his shoulder as well as his ankle and he had to stand where he was put, favouring his right leg.

A donkey brayed shrilly, and someone else began to screech what sounded like protests, with the clanging of the bell and a woman shouting, "Make way, street guard, get that damn beast out of the way."

The guard glanced towards the noise of his partner; only a moment's inattention, but it was enough. Ghu wrenched himself free and hurtled back into the market, down the line of houses facing it, ignoring for the moment the pain in his ankle, but it slowed him. He sidestepped a pony laden with empty baskets and a crowd of running children who broke and re-formed, giving chase, shouting. When someone seized his arm again he swung with the heel of his palm at her chin, turning the blow aside when he saw it was the scribe who had stood by him to hear the storyteller. She didn't waste words, just hauled, so that he went staggering through an open doorway, under a low lintel and down a sudden drop of three steps, into a cool room that after the glare of the noon outside was all shadows and softness, dappled with light from the carved screens. The woman dragged him between low tables and people seated on cushions, talking over coffee and pastries, quiet murmurs, a sudden burst of laughter, intense indignation and placatory shushing . . . but none seemed at all startled by his sudden entrance. None looked around at all. They crossed the length of the room in silence. The room smelt of coffee, but the woman of honeysuckles and wizardry. Ghu submitted to being towed, though he was gritting his teeth on the pain now and wanted very much to sit down. Still in silence, they passed between two empty, dark rooms to either side, then through another doorway, this one hung with a bead curtain that shimmered and clattered like falling rain. A short passage opened out into a kitchen, swelteringly hot, where a thin, bearded man squatted by a clay stove built like a bench along the wall, just lifting a frothing copper pot from the fire. Even he didn't seem to notice them, nor did the boy and girl arranging cups on a tray. Only a second man, with his brown hair in long braids, looked up. He wore a Marakander caftan and was seeding raisins, but his sun-lined face told of the caravans. He frowned, looked around, towards another door through which daylight streamed, and went back to his raisins. The scribe tugged Ghu across the red-tiled floor and to a narrow flight of stairs. He hobbled up as quietly as he could, sweating now with the effort of it, clutching her hard enough to make her stagger with him.

It was very dark, and they went up two flights and along a passageway, till she shouldered open a door and they both stumbled into a narrow room. If he had had his wits about him he should have gone out the back into the coffeehouse's yard, where there would be sheds or a gate or a wall to be scaled, more streets and allies into which he could disappear, not this dead end of a room, to condemn the scribe when the guards came searching.

"Sit," she said, and he did, because he couldn't stand once she let go of him. The bed was a thin quilted mattress on the floor, neatly made up with a striped blanket over it, and at the head, a carefully wrapped and strapped bundle that looked not so much a pillow as something to be snatched and fled with when some long-awaited emergency arrived.

Ghu sat, and sighed, and remembered the balconies of the houses, thrusting out over walls and streets, all enclosed with wooden walls and carved screens or shielding wickerwork. "Is there a balcony? I can get out there. Could I climb to the roof?" And jump down to another house's roof and make his escape, but not with this ankle, no.

"They won't follow," said the woman. Since first grabbing him she had touched him only with one hand. Now she breathed on the other and wiped it on her caftan, leaving a dark trace of ink. She fished strings out of her sleeve and began weaving a cat's-cradle. "I hope," she added. "Here, hold this loop."

He did so and felt her pulse in the string, but maybe it was his own, from his racing heart to his fingers. The crossing and recrossing strands trapped his eye. He was falling into it, circling down . . .

"Not you," she said. "Don't look, if it does that to you." He looked at her instead, biting her lip as if she found what she was doing difficult, and yet the pulse was hers, making the world shiver. Her fingers flashed and plucked confidently, swiftly, at odds with the expression on her face, and then she shook the pattern free.

"Ivah," he said, tasting the name. Not mistress, not lady. Just Ivah. She looked startled. A heart-shaped face, pale from an indoor life that did not much suit her, he thought, and he smiled. She flinched and looked away.

"That—the storyteller knows you," she said. "Who are you?"

He considered. "Ghu. I don't know her."

"Why did she think you would know anything about Ilbialla's tomb?"

"I don't know anything."

"She thought you might. Why?"

"You should ask her," he suggested gently, "if she's your friend."

"She's not my friend. She's . . ." Ivah shook her head. "I don't even know her name." She frowned. "No, I know a name. I doubt it's one she's using now. What did you do, to have street guard after you?"

"I'm not sure. They want a Nabbani."

"Oh."

"A man," he added, and touched her hand. She was frightened again, and she had been so bold. But she had been working wizardry in the Voice's city, and the Red Masks would kill her for simply being what she was, and where. "But you're not a man, and you're . . ." silk and horses and that bundle pretending it was a pillow had a sword's length to it. A sabre's length. That was what he saw. "Are you of the western deserts, or the Grass? You don't belong to this city."

She looked startled. "My father was of the Great Grass. I was born on the Grass. My mother was from the empire, a—she was from the empire, yes."

"Still not a man. They shouldn't look for you."

"But what did you do?"

"I don't know."

People usually believed him. She didn't. He saw the disbelief in her eyes. "I'm going back down to my desk in the front room before someone steals my brushes. The street guard should be thinking you've lost them in the market."

"Thank you."

Her face closed up, and she backed away, rose to her feet. "If they do find you, I'm going to scream and hide behind Master Hadidu and say you must have got in from the balcony.

"Yes," he agreed, without asking who Master Hadidu was, and watched her leave.

His right boot came off only with difficulty, and his foot-wrapping hid an ugly, livid swelling. In his time he'd had a broken arm, cracked ribs . . . he didn't think this was in the bones. Nothing—when he clenched his teeth and moved it gingerly—grated. Ghu began bandaging his ankle.

And since he could do nothing for Ahjvar at the present moment, with the guards no doubt still keeping an eye out on the nearby streets, when he was finished he piled his own bundle atop the scribe's and lay down with his feet up, hands folded on his chest and forage knife laid by his side. He shut his eyes and let himself slide into that place between sleep and waking, where there was rest and the slow rhythm of the world's tides carrying him. The river waited. The mountain watched. They were always there, a breath away.

Ivah wrote one letter for a neighbour of the coffeeshop, an application to a magistrate in Silvermarket Ward to adopt a cousin's son from there, and worked her way through the stack of blank copies of various contracts one of the ward magistrate's overworked clerks had brought her, with the names and details to be filled in later. She was fortunate to get the work, being both a newcomer to the guild, licensed only about nine months and lacking the web of connections the relationship between master and apprentice brought, as well as an outlander, a barbarian Grasslander. All her life she'd been called Nabbani, and when her father was angry with his mistress, or his daughter, it had been an insult. Nabbani whore. Now, in a city where half the folk seemed to have Nabbani ancestry—one of the founding Twenty Families had been Nabbani adventurers, long before the colonies of the Five Cities were ever planted, back in the days of legend—they looked at her tawny eyes and heard her accent when she used the tongue of the western road or bastard Nabbani, and called her a Grasslander.

When she spoke the Imperial Nabbani she'd learned at her mother's knee, they affected not to understand her at all. She'd begun to think . . . she didn't know what. To doubt every tale her mother had ever told her, till the storyteller addressed her in that same speech,

and the young caravaneer, and she'd felt for a moment as if the landscape had suddenly shifted about her and she was home. Moreover,
the young man made her heart run too fast, as if he were some deep,
swift current about to pull her off her feet and sweep her away. She
wasn't sure she even liked men, beautiful or otherwise. At least she
could admire a beautiful man; he wouldn't be the first. But that
didn't mean she had to want . . . And why was she even thinking
about such things?

Ivah wiped the brush carefully and switched to a finer one for a
new page, with two extra clauses to be added. It was dull work but
demanding of meticulous care. Master Hadidu, unasked, brought
her a tiny cup of coffee. She smiled wary thanks as he set it on her
desk. All the regulars at the Doves thought he was courting her, in
his shy way, seeking a stepmother for his little boy.

She certainly hoped he wasn't, but she couldn't tell, so she pretended not to notice. Ivah wasn't good at things like that. And he
wasn't a beautiful man, just a thin, worried, gentle one, with a beard
that was beginning to grey at the corners of his mouth, though he
wasn't so old as all that.

Ivah worked the afternoon away, until the shadows were too
slanting through the high slit of a window in the front parlour and
she would have to pay for lamp-oil or make mistakes. She put her
cleaned brushes, her inkstone and papers away inside the desk, with
the finished contracts carefully wrapped in a square of old cotton.
Beneath the hinged lid, the desk was a tidy tray of compartments:
brushes, inkstones, inksticks, a corked jar of liquid ink, reed pens,
a knife, a jar of sand for drying, paper in various sizes, a wax tablet
and bronze stylus for notes, a couple of candle stubs, several codices
on calligraphy and its history, copies of obscure and dull treatises,
purchased from the booksellers who set up every day in the great

porch of the palace library . . . All innocent possessions of a conscientious new member of the guild of scribes and letter-writers. Under the sheet of stiff waxed cotton that lay beneath the dividers were other papers, some with a careful copy of the inscription on Gurhan's tomb, the walled-up cave near-forgotten, hidden in the forested folds of the senate palace hill, and a less confident copying, from memory, of the frieze around Ilbialla's tomb, some with her attempt to translate. Since few of the characters showed up in even the most ancient Pirakuli alphabet that she could find, and that was her best guess as to what writing it might be, she was not making much progress. If even the so-called storyteller could not read it all . . . The Northron's name was Ulfhild, and she was the devil Vartu. If the stories of the Northrons were true, she had been Ivah's father's wife, once upon a time.

And whatever the stories of the road might say about the Blackdog, she knew Ulfhild Vartu had been her father's killer. She didn't know how she felt about that.

Ivah locked the desk, though a child could turn the lock with a broken knife, and on one memorably inky occasion had, and borrowed a bowl from Hadidu's kitchen. She walked down the street to the nearest hot food shop, where she bought a heaping dish of spiced chick-peas with eggplant and a couple of rounds of fried unleavened bread. Back at the Doves, balancing the food atop her desk, she carried both away up to her room with a nod to Nour, lounging unsmiling in the doorway to watch her. He was Hadidu's brother-in-law, a native Marakander despite the scorpions tattooed on the backs of his hands, and a caravan mercenary with a gang that worked the eastern road; his caravan had come in a few days earlier. He seemed to mistrust her. Afraid, maybe, that she aimed to marry Hadidu and take his dead sister's place.

Nour watched her all the way up the stairs.

Ghu was gone.

"Great Gods and damned devils . . ." Ivah dropped to her knees by her bundle, but the knots sealing it were still intact. It would take a wizard to untie them. She did and checked over, carefully, like one mistrusting a treasure's safety, all the things rolled in her coat, her other self: boots, sabre, short horseman's bow and quiver, her mother's purse of three silver oracle-coins and the scroll of *The Balance of the Sun and the Moon*. Since she had the coins in her hand anyway, she threw them, twice, four times, six, thinking all the while of Ghu, but "What is he?" and "Where did he go?" ran together, and the hexagram, when she checked it in the book, doubting her memory, told her that *The Mountain and the River hold the Land*, which ran to three hand-spans of commentaries, none seeming to be of any immediate use.

Lame or not, there was no point to her chasing him through the streets. He had hardly run off to betray her to the Red Masks. She lit a candle stub with a quick sketch of the character of fire, took a blank page and set down, in small, neat clerk's characters the words Ghu had spoken when the devil asked him what the tomb was. *Tears. Fire. Binding.* Fire—that resonated with something else. She lifted the ink from its compartment, slid some older papers out from beneath, and laid the book on the history of writing in Pirakul before her, chasing meaning through the night.

It kept the darkness at bay, while the night grew hotter and thunder growled, promising rain. Eventually, when she realized she had been staring unseeing at the page for far too long, ink drying on her brush, all inspiration fled, she cleaned up, undressed, put on a thin shift, and lay down to sleep.

It did not seem so very much later, but perhaps she had slept deeper and longer than she thought, that the sound of smashing wood, muffled by distance, awakened her.

Time passed, and Ivah did not return. As the room began to grow evening-dim Ghu stirred into life again. There were questions he wanted to ask her about the storyteller, but there were questions she wanted to ask him, too, no doubt, and he did not think that he wanted to answer them yet. There were questions he should have asked the storyteller, but perhaps . . . perhaps she had already answered them.

He did not think Ahjvar could kill a devil.

Ghu gave up on getting his boot back on; he had gone barefoot most of his life anyway. He added the boots to his bundle, tied it firmly across his back again, and considered the passageway outside. Sounds of laughter floated up from the kitchen, and a small boy, about waist-high to him, came suddenly hurtling up the stairs, waving a carved wooden camel and shouting for someone called Sayyid to come see what Uncle had made for him. Ghu slipped back and shut Ivah's door firmly.

"Sayyid's gone out to the market!" a distant voice called, and footsteps galloped past again, down the stairs.

He followed, warily, down to the floor below, where the rooms seemed more in use. In the second one he ventured into he discovered what he wanted, a balcony screened by curtains of reed. He pushed the screen aside and found he was above a narrow alley. He could drop to the ground quite safely, if he hung from the edge and landed only on his left foot. The little boy came tumbling into the room just as he did so. He didn't think he was seen. Maybe. No one shouted after him, anyway.

From Sunset Ward he had to find a gate into Riverbend, and

thence, remembering Ahjvar's descriptions, to Greenmarket and
Templefoot. He wrapped his scarf to hide his Nabbani-black hair
and walked, halt and slow and hobbling, mostly using a hand on
whatever house-walls edged the street, towards the north, as straight
as any narrow street would let him go. Eventually found the ward-
wall, a low, crumbling thing visible only because of the lanes that
ran dead against it. Weeds climbed it. Cats basked in the last of the
sun. He could climb it too, but not, perhaps, at the moment. There
were people about, sitting on doorsteps, gossiping with their neighbours as the day drew to its close. They watched him suspiciously.
He gave them his most inoffensive and innocent smile. Just a poor
bewildered caravaneer. Eventually he found a gateway through to
the next ward. He was barely into Riverbend when bells began to
ring out and most people disappeared indoors. On the broad street
on which he found himself, sweepers were hastening about their
work, filling donkey-carts and hand-barrows with dung and other
trampled detritus, chasing off the poor thin dogs that nosed through
the garbage. He might as well be crawling on his hands and knees;
he would get there faster. He sat down on the doorstep of a ruined
house, deep in shadows, to watch and wait until the sweepers passed.
His ankle throbbed wearyingly. It would be easy to slide into sleep,
so as to leave it behind. He used to do that, just fade away, when the
world hurt too much. It wasn't a good idea, now. Sometimes you had
to run away, and sometimes you had to bend your neck and endure,
and sometime, someday, you would have to fight. Perhaps not yet.
Anyway, he'd had worse. This was merely troublesome.

When the sweepers were gone and night had fallen, Ghu went
on, still hugging the walls, a shadow within shadows. It was a
dark-striped coat, a dark scarf. Ahj thought of such things, and the
shadows had always been kind. In Greenmarket Ward he took a

wrong turning, down a lane that ended not at city wall but a broken cliff, with a rubbish dump below it in the ravine. He nearly stumbled over the edge in the dark. It had begun to rain, quietly and steadily, and the air was growing swelteringly hot. Bells rang again. That would be the second curfew; some professions were allowed the first hours of the night, Ahj had said. The city was dark and mostly silent. A brief chorus of dogs down in the ravine set off barking in the streets around him, which rose and died. He shivered despite the heat. Turning away, his ankle betrayed him and he fell. He groped his way up another doorstep to sit a long moment, too long. The longer he sat, the more terribly getting up and going on loomed. He shook out the bandage and wrapped his ankle again, trying to ensure it would not fail him if he had to run. The swelling was far worse, now; his foot bloated like a frightened toad. He needed a crutch, but crawling down the cliff into the ravine in search of a bush wasn't something he wanted to try by feel in the dark. He would end up at the bottom with a broken leg or neck.

What was he going to do, anyway? Ahjvar didn't want him around when there was killing to be done, and he could hardly persuade him to simply abandon Marakand and what little hope Catairanach's doubtful promise had held out. He wanted to keep the man safe, safe and his, in the ruin on the cliff's edge by the sea, and that was hardly his right, or right at all, when it damned Ahjvar to possession, to the cycle of madness and murder. He made Ahjvar into an excuse to stay as he was, where he was, made him a refuge from . . . the vastness of what might come. He used him, that was the truth of it. And did not Ahj deserve better, out of love, out of common humanity?

Distant and deep under the temple, he could feel the presence of the thing that was not a god, though he might have taken it for godhead had he not twice in this day met a similar shape of power, and had a name that might belong to it given to him in a story. Finding Ahjvar, trying to persuade him this Voice was something beyond his ability to kill, beyond the reach of any single small goddess of the earth such as Catairanach, would simply suggest to Ahj that maybe death was within *his* reach at last.

Maybe that would be so, and if it were, did Ghu have any right to stand between him and an end, however it came? Right, no. Need, yes. He needed Ahjvar. He did. He couldn't let him go.

Which was what mad Hyllau had thought, yes? Mine, mine, mine.

He sighed and turned back to find a street heading more towards the temple. Though how he was to get over the temple wall with a foot so swollen and blindingly painful when he put any weight on it, he didn't know. Knock at the gate with an urgent need for prayer? That, at least, would bring him swiftly to the Voice, if it did not send him straight to the deep well. Perhaps there would be some easy stretch of wall. The ward-walls seemed half-abandoned; perhaps the temple wall would be in no better repair, or one of the patches of old ruin that crowded cheek by jowl with inhabited houses would provide some easier way to scramble up.

And then?

He shoved that thought away angrily and felt himself sliding down into childhood again. Child's thought. Slave's thought. Child's words, slave's words. Simple words for simple thoughts. Later didn't matter. Later wasn't his. Nothing was his but here. Now. Here and now, he wanted Ahjvar safe and away.

He'd learnt harder words and harder thoughts, and values harder to hold, maybe, and had anyone asked him, would you, will you, before they took him and said, be ours? Well, the ones who had claimed him had asked, he couldn't pretend they hadn't, and he'd said, yes, not understanding, maybe, what he took and what he gave. Was it fair, what they'd done? A child's question. Most things weren't fair, though they should be. Was it right? Was it needful, for what was right? Ghu who had been a horseboy in the stables of the high lord of all Choa, Ghu who had been Mother Nabban only knew what poor girl's secret and sorrow, thrown into the river to drown before he'd hardly drawn breath, to be caught in the reeds and fished out wailing by a horseboy watering his charges, couldn't say. He'd been, if not utterly a simpleton as they called him, simple enough, till he'd gotten benighted on the high slopes seeking a foaling mare in a spring snowstorm. He had come down with mare safe, and foal, and a fever the head groom had thought he'd die of. Maybe he had. The world had been broken, melted down and reforged for him, in those few fevered days when the river and the mountain's snows had flowed together into light.

The bout of fever, the head groom said resignedly, had done simple Ghu's wits no good at all.

He couldn't go back to that place. Wear it as a cloak, yes, carry it as a shield upon his road, yes, but he couldn't crawl back inside that boy. And that meant he could not go on staggering blind and thoughtless in pursuit of Ahjvar this night without thinking why he did and what he meant to do, and what greater harm he might bring to what was already set in motion, drawing the eye of the Lady, the attention of the Red Masks, upon Ahj.

He passed from Greenmarket into Templefoot Ward through a gateway with houses built over it and had to fold himself into a doorway as a patrol of five street guard came by, led by a man with a lantern on a pole. They clattered along, hobnailed sandals loud on the street's stones, hoods pulled up against the rain, grumbling, never glancing his way. But when he went on, because he did not know what to do if he stopped now, there was a sound behind that wasn't the noise of the guardsmen. A scuff without the ring of nails, a grunt, hastily stifled. Someone had walked into something in the dark. A moment's hesitation. The house alongside was another old earthquake ruin; even in the night apparent as a jagged shell, barely rising above its first storey, its windows black pits and the plaster mostly flaked away, so that it hulked darkly between its paler neighbours. Door, somewhere, but he couldn't see the shadow of it.

Thunder broke over Palace Hill to the south, streaking the street with white and black, shadows running too swiftly for the eye to catch before the night took everything again and left him blinded by the glare.

It wasn't a knife or club that came at him out of that moment of blindness, which he'd been expecting, but a fist. He trapped it between his hands as much by luck as anything, and hopped sideways from the kick that was probably following, jerked his attacker towards himself and punched hard. He missed the face in the dark, hit solid, bony shoulder and was flung back into a wall. Playing the innocent fool didn't work on people who attacked without warning out of the night, but he dropped to the ground anyway, not cowering but not where he was expected to move. His attacker lurched off-balance as his following punch met air and then, with a suppressed hiss, the wall. The man crashed down, his legs hooked out from under him, but before Ghu could get him pinned he rolled away, striking out as he went. He hit the swollen ankle. Ghu gasped and curled up small, for a moment unable to think. He'd been ignoring it, floating on the pain, all night; he didn't need it brought to his attention now. He hit out in anger, then, wanting, just for a moment, to hurt, and the man, back on his feet, doubled over. Ghu swept his legs out from under him again and dug fingers into his throat. He had his forage knife out. Picking up bad habits from Ahj.

"Don't," he said, as the man tensed. Lightning showed the blade. His attacker held no knife. Think why. He didn't want Ghu dead; he wanted him captive, and he was neither thief nor street guard. Someone he'd seen, briefly, this day; there was that familiarity in the feel of him, the air about him. He was the man from the kitchen of the coffeehouse; not the thin worried one, the other, who had thought something stirred and looked around for it, when Ivah led Ghu to the stairs unseen.

Ghu felt movement, the man's arms moving stealthily, or hands, whispering under his breath. He felt the magic gathering, dropped his own knife and grabbed for hands and mouth, put the knee of his bad leg over the man's throat instead, pressing a threat, fingers clapped to his lips over wiry beard.

"Wizard," he whispered. "Hush. You're from the Doves. I thought you were the guard."

A stillness. He lifted his hand slightly. The wizard should have been trying to bite; he would have been.

The man rolled. Ghu sprang back and let him go, leaned with the wall behind him, balancing on one foot and a toe, his knife in hand again. They were washed in lightning, and he saw the man standing, wary, arms spread, a short knife now in hand. Desert-braided hair and a cameleer's coat, not the caftan of earlier.

He waited for the thunder to die. "What do you want?" he asked. "I stole nothing from your house. I'm only looking for my friend."

"Why call me a wizard?" Was it fear that underlay the voice?

"Because you are," he said.

Now he knew the man's fear, yes, in the catch of breath, the utter stillness.

"Red Mask," the wizard said then, not even an accusation, just a whisper. Resignation, as of one who knew his own death.

"No! I'm not from the temple. Anyway, I thought they didn't speak, or is that a lie you tell to foreigners?"

"Who knows what you do, when you lay your veil aside and creep out spying in the city?"

"I'm not from the temple," Ghu repeated. "I only came to Marakand today. To the suburb yesterday. Truly."

"Why come sneaking around the Doves, spying on us? Don't deny you were there with her, and both of you hidden. I smelt her perfume cross the kitchen. I felt the air move. I should have hunted for you there and then, but I thought it was nothing, imagination, till my nephew at bedtime said a man jumped off the balcony. It took me far too long to pick up your trail, and that's not natural, either. You or Ivah, one of you's still hiding you."

Ghu admitted, "I'm hard to see. I know. It doesn't make me a Red Mask. It doesn't make me anything. I'm not even a wizard."

"So what are you to the lying scribe, then?"

"Nothing. No spy. The scribe hid me from the street guard."

He saw it, felt it, rather, in the man's gathering tension, like a bow being drawn. Ghu might be a temple spy or he might not, but now he had to die, because he, a stranger, knew there was a living wizard in Marakand.

"No," he said. "You don't have to do that. I'm no enemy to you or yours."

But the man came at him, not to capture this time, and he was a caravan guard, a fighter. But the forage-knife was a wicked tool and used for butchering as much as cutting brush and green fodder. The man knew it, left him wary room till the last. He could have laid the man's arm open as he guarded his face, but he only knocked aside the sudden slash from the darkness and punched for the arch between the wizard's ribs with the knife reversed, the hilt a weight to knock the wind and maybe the sense out him, but the man was already rocking back and out of reach, slipping aside in the dark. The rain poured down, no thunder, just the dark curtain of the water and the night, the drumming of it loud on the stones. Ghu didn't dare move from where he stood braced against the wall, because to fall now was to lay himself open to the wizard's knife.

This wizard who only wanted to keep his family safe, or Ahj— did it come to that choice?

No, it was this wizard or himself. Ahj's fate lay beyond Ghu's grasp.

"I'm not your enemy," he tried again. "Wizard, can't you tell truth from lie?"

Movement he didn't see. The knife bit, slashing a sleeve and his arm beneath. He seized the hand that held the blade and smashed it into the wall, almost easier to feel, to know where the blow came with his eyes shut rather than straining in the dark. He heard the grunt, the thin noise of the knife falling, and let go before he was jerked off balance. Wet arm, but his sleeve was wet anyway, and he hardly felt the cut. Did the man have a second knife? He didn't follow with any second blow. Maybe he thought he'd missed. Ghu slid his own knife away to its sheath once more.

"No weapon," he said, a bit breathless, a bit desperate, voice raised reckless over the rain. "Look, take my hands, see? Trust. For the sake of the Old Great Gods, trust me, work your spells and see that I speak the truth."

No answer, just a rushing body. The night became desperate scuffle, Ghu grabbing the wizard as he flung himself in close, both of them on the ground, locked together. The other had the advantage there, a greater weight and resolved on killing, but Ghu was fast, at least, and had a better sense of his enemy's body in the dark. He jerked away from the hands that closed around his throat and for a moment the uppermost body, got a thumb against the other's eye, a grip on the edge of bone, enough to be real threat. He pinned one hand down where it could do no harm.

The other came up against Ghu's throat, not to seize but a nail scratching, a word gasped, and there was a ringing in his ears, a muffled rushing, as if he were drowning, fainting. He let the other go, rolling to draw the knife one last time, to use it, at last, because he could not die here. The wizard's spell might be only to hold him senseless a moment, it was not so easy as all that to kill with a simple working, but he judged the man was desperate enough to cast honour aside and kill an unconscious enemy.

The tramp of nailed sandals and of boots was abruptly louder than the rain, and he shook off whatever half-formed spell it was that slowed his movements, slid off the wizard and dragged himself to darkest shadow, tumbling down the sunken doorstep of a house, a pit of black with jumbled uneven stone. The door of the ruin. Lantern-light made hazy gold of the rain down the street to the east and the wizard came after him, a hot, blood-reeking body pressed against him, hardly even knowing he was there. The man was shaking.

Ghu felt his way up the door, which was still closed, found the latch and pressed it down, pushed with his shoulder until it opened. He laid a hand on the wizard's shoulder, tugged him. The man had the wit left to follow silent, despite the terror near unmanning him. The door closed as softly, as silently behind them, in good shape for a ruin. Ghu put his back to it, holding it shut against any investigation. The air stank of rats and dirty humans.

Light spilt in through a window-hole, jogging to clattering foot-steps. The wizard had his head up, wide-eyed, teeth unconsciously bared, and still he shook. Ghu pointed at the window, urgently. He didn't dare move, clumsy on his one leg, and if they tried the door with him sitting against it they might think it locked. The wizard, with no small effort, moved to where he could see out, crawling over rubble, rotting beams and plaster and bricks. The remains of the floor above roofed only the far side of the room. Here, rain misted down, gentle now, soft and warm. Ghu rubbed at his throat, not certain what life might still linger in whatever mark the wizard had put there. Enough to draw a Red Mask? Or was it only more street guard, passing on patrol? He doubted the caravan wizard would be so unmanned by fear of a mere street-patrol's passing.

The last lantern bobbed on by, the last light faded. There had been other faces raised as well, three girls, two men, and a baby, all in a nest of rags in the far corner. Beggars who had claimed this place, but they were silent, not protesting the invasion, not yet.

"What were they?" Ghu asked softly, when the sound even of their feet was gone and there was nothing but the rain.

"Two patrols of temple guard, and Red Masks with them," the wizard said, as if they hadn't been trying to kill one another a moment before. Ghu warily shifted so he could open the door.

Still nothing from the beggars. Well, there had been light enough to show them two bloodied and battered caravaneers, and he knew what came to beggars who drew the attention of armed men.

"Sorry," he told them and, "Thank you. Gods bless you."

He edged the door open, stood half in, half out, listening, but there was no sound other than the rain, and the light had gone away west, into Greenmarket Ward. The wizard was at his shoulder, pushing past, reaching back to take his arm, half dragging him up to the street level again. The man was cut after all, hand, sleeve, wet with blood, worse than Ghu's own. He didn't seem to notice.

"You've really never been in Marakand before today?"

"I don't lie."

"All you had to do was call to them."

"No." All he had had to do was cut the wizard's throat.

"I still don't trust you."

"Don't then." Ghu sighed, too tired to argue. The pounding pulse of his ankle was deafening him to all else. "Go away."

"What are you doing?"

"Looking for my friend. I told you."

"At the Doves?" The man drew him farther up the street, not letting go, and he was glad enough to let the wizard take some of the weight off his foot. He sank down on a doorstep, no windows near for eavesdroppers, and leaned back against the doorpost.

"The street guard were told to look for Nabbani men," he said wearily. "Your scribe hid me. I left when I thought it was safe. That's all."

"Why are they looking for Nabbani men?"

"They think I'm a Praitannec spy."

"You say, 'I.' So it's not Nabbani men in general they're after; it's you yourself."

Ghu shrugged, which the wizard probably didn't see. "Yes, but they didn't know that."

The wizard sat down beside him. "Nour," he said.

"Ghu."

"Are you a Praitannec spy?"

"No. My friend," he added, "is a Praitan. Someone followed him last night, when we came in to the suburb. He lost them, but maybe they're still looking."

"Is he," Nour said with the patience of one talking to a child, "a Praitannec spy?"

"No." Ghu didn't mean to fall away into himself, into simplicity again. He was just so overwhelmingly tired all of a sudden. There was something wrong, something . . . there had been something wrong in his world for a time now, something lost to him, slipped from his grasp . . . "His goddess sent him to kill the Voice."

Nour's silence was deep. "How?" he asked at last. "With the hand of the Lady over her, how?"

Not "why," not horror, and he was a Marakander born, Ghu judged.

"He'll find a way." But after, but after . . .

"Even if he does," Nour said, "it won't change anything. The Lady will appoint a new Voice. Nothing will change. Nothing ever changes, nothing ever has, in thirty years."

"Is there a Lady?"

Another deep silence. "I do wonder," Nour said. "A conspiracy of priests, maybe. But if that's so, I don't know how they can be killing wizards. And there's some divine power behind the Red Masks."

"I think," Ghu said, "there is a devil in your temple. One of the seven from the stories. Maybe claiming to be the Voice. Maybe claiming to be the Lady. I think . . . I think Ahjvar is . . ."

Gone? Gone, sometime in the night.

"The Voice certainly acts like one, the way she sends folk to their deaths," said Nour, not believing him. "I think," he added, "that you'd better come back to the Doves with me. I'm not certain yet that I trust anything you say. I want you where I can see you. You and Ivah both. She's very good at meekly getting her own way, and there's wizardry behind that. She bespelled Hadidu into giving her lodgings, I'm sure of it. He's not so besotted with her he'd risk his only child's life on trusting her within his household, otherwise. And I'm very surprised, now I think about it, that I haven't done something about her before. I've been home for a week. I wonder if she's been working on me, too? You, at least, I'm going to send out to my gang-boss, tomorrow night when I can get you over the city wall unseen. He can keep you safe till I figure out what to do with you."

Ahj was . . . lost. And the wizard thought he had Ghu a prisoner. It didn't matter.

Dead. But Ahj always had said he was dead. Ghu bent over, his head on his knees. The Voice of the Lady was dead, and so was Ahjvar, and he had not believed that Catairanach would keep her promise, he had not, he would not have let Ahj go without him if he had, he would not, he would not have let him be alone. He did not want to be alone.

"Come," Nour said, and touched his shoulder. "Give me your arm, Ghu. No wizardry to hide us, not with Red Masks prowling, Old Great Gods keep whatever poor souls they've been sent out for."

Ghu let himself be helped up, arm around the other's neck, and shut his eyes. It was easier to keep walking that way. If Nour turned him loose he would sit and wait for the Red Masks to find him. He wanted simply to fall, down into that emptiness, that darkness, after Ahjvar. Easier than going on.

CHAPTER VII

Light burned through his eyelids, red and hot. Ahjvar turned his head away, tried to drag an arm up to shield his eyes before he forced them open. Too heavy. Even the weight of his eyelids seemed too much to force against the light and the kicking of the horse inside his head. Light blurred and swam and faded. A fire, which rose and fell with his pulse.

Not dead.

King. Champion. Sword. The words whispered in his head, confusingly. Something the Voice had said before he killed her? The light must be a torch. Ghu? No. The light, whoever carried it, was probably not his friend.

Darkness returned. He tried, then, to sit up, but the horse that was kicking in his head had evidently trampled over him a few times first. Fire arced across his ribs as he twisted, hunched himself up. He managed to get sitting in the end, but a mewl of pain escaped him, and his breath came loud and gasping. If they were listening . . .

They weren't. Whoever they were. No rustle, no breath, no scent of a body. Where was he, anyhow? Someplace cool and damp, with his back against a wall that curved up from the floor, all rough stone, it felt. It smelt of mud.

Cave, he thought, but could not think why he would be in a cave. He had lain up for the day under a ledge, dry rock. Not a cave.

He tried again and this time did get his eyes open. The world was not much different. There was light, a distant dim yellow. Tunnel. A tin-mine . . . he was not in a Duina Praitanna tin-mine. He tried to pull himself upright, using the rough wall as support but ended on hands and knees. Good. You had to crawl before you could walk. He blinked, licked lips that tasted of blood. Had they thought him dead and dumped him as so much refuse? Wouldn't be the first time. But his sword was in front of his nose, the leopard of the hilt staring at him, accusing. *Dead king.* Who called him that? Sword, and dagger too, cast down beside him. Refuse they couldn't be bothered plundering? Not very likely. Saved him going back for it, though. He didn't abandon that sword. Stuck to it, empty defiance though that was. His, himself, when everything else was gone.

Everything else *was* gone, even his tunic and boots. He was barefoot, in trousers and a torn shirt. But they left him his sword? Stitches in his gashed arm, and the blood-filthy linen in tatters. Stitches on the deep slice under his breast, and the shirt sodden, edges sticky, not yet dry. Recent, very recent. Whoever had sewn him up had left with their torch only as he woke. So. Follow them.

Dagger in belt. Sword in hand. Knees, good. Hand on wall again, up. On his feet, ears ringing, a bit light-headed, not falling. Better if he just crawled into a hole and lay quiet a few days, like a corpse or a toad buried in the mud against the cold winter rains, while his curse put him back together, restored its wounded and aching shell. That was all he was, a much-darned and patched sack to give the curse a home . . . and obviously a delirious one at present, as well. He didn't need Ghu here to tell him that.

He headed for the light, moving like an old man, feeling every year since his birth. Bare feet told him the floor was stone, coarse-grained but water-smoothed, seamed with earth. Natural, this tunnel, at least it had been, once. The walls were jagged with the work of the picks that had heightened and broadened it.

By the time Ahjvar reached the mouth and the light, he was walking without leaning on the wall, and the sword was no longer an unwieldy bar of iron he could barely lift.

He looked out into a rounded cavern. A mist of rain pattered down onto a muddy patch of floor from some shaft open to the sky. It was still night. A crack in the floor stirred darkly, some breath of moving air touching the water. No, there was no breeze at all, and the air was heavy with the smell of rotten wood and damp stone. Something dark humped and rolled below the water, and a man, a Red Mask priest still in his armour, spread arms on the lip of the crack, the well of the Lady, surely, and heaved himself out, dripping, a beached seal. Then he got a knee under himself and stood, shaking his head, water coursing down his chest from under the mask. For a moment, the eye-slits of the mask turned Ahjvar's way. Then he crossed the chamber out of sight. Ahjvar leaned out, saw him climbing stairs without another glance, leaving a dark, wet trail in the light of the torch affixed to the wall at the foot of them. No chance he hadn't been seen.

He had killed that man. He knew he had, the tall one with the Northron sword. But this one had two strong arms, and he had shorn the other's left nearly away. But the same. The water-dripping sleeve had been in tatters, the scales over the breast twisted and rent apart.

Mist had followed the reborn, recovered Red Mask from the well. Now it rose, shaping itself to a pillar.

Dead king.

No words. A whisper in the mind. Ahjvar was on his knees without willing it, too weak to stand. He had no right to stand before this.

No bloody way did he kneel to gods, not foreign ones and not his thrice-cursed own, either. Hands on the hilt of the sword, he lurched up again, put his back to the wall and leaned there.

She stood between him and the well. He hadn't seen her move. He shut his eyes and opened them again, and she was closer, the mist coiling around her feet, her knees. No, he hadn't seen her form herself.

He saw *through* her. A reflection on water, a heat-shimmer on the baking dust of the road. She was naked, her skin burnished gold as if lit by firelight; her eyes caught and held it, blood and flame. Young. A girl just turned woman.

"Dead man," she said, and saluted him, flat of her sword to her forehead. Her smile was quite, quite mad, like a little child that took pleasure in tormenting weak and helpless things. Hyllau, her foster-father had warned him, warned him to warn the king when Cairangorm first began to watch her in the hall, Hyllau as a little girl had penned frogs in stone in the sun, he said, to watch them die, she had taken a kitten . . .

Pay attention! The Lady had not held a sword a moment before. It was a single-edged slashing weapon, wider towards the point and red in the firelight, like her eyes, and she was solid flesh, not mist and shadow. He drove straight, two-handed towards her while she still posed elegant, smiling faintly, and did she think her body distracted him? More fool she. He had the longer reach and longer blade, and the leopard-dappled steel, demon-forged, they said, took her, as he leaned from her downward slash, felt his stroke meet flesh, grate bone. But though she could not have moved so fast, she had opened his ribs again, and he was on the damp floor, a wind rising in his ears that was his own blood failing him, fleeing him. She held his sword by the blade, slick with her blood, disdainfully. He hadn't seen her withdraw it from her flesh. She rubbed the place below her breasts with the fist that held her own sword as if it merely itched, no gout of blood, no wound at all but a faint smear, and then set her point at the angle of his jaw.

"Wasteful, when I had you so nicely sewed up," she said.

The cavern was lit briefly white by lightning. The patter of the rain intensified, and distant thunder cracked the unseen sky.

For a moment she changed. Still naked, her hair now a streaky, shadowy brown, loose down her back, her skin dark enough to be a child of some sailor from south across the sea, but her eyes were blue as his father's, calm as some summer sky in the light, she seemed to shed herself, a memory of daylight, bright dawns. She was no longer young but wide-hipped, heavy-bosomed. Her body sagged, face lined, mouth and eyes grey-shadowed, as if with long illness.

"Praitan," she said. "Warn them. They must not listen—"

Then the golden girl smiled down at him again, until he felt as if it were he who were naked, wanted to cover himself, to crawl beneath some blanket and get on with dying in peace.

Except he wouldn't, of course.

"Oh yes," she said. "I do want you, we do want you are the one I have waited for Marakand waits for you I have seen you dreamed you made you mine. We will take you into the well and you will be ours."

There was smoke in the cave.

She licked her lips, squatted down beside Ahjvar. There was blood on her hand, her own life-blood from his blade, though she had faded again to mist, a reflection on water, yet still she cast a shadow in her own light. She sucked a finger thoughtfully. "He's a wizard," she said, "but a wizard who is not a wizard who is not death not our death not *his* eye, not his spy, no. A wizard behind walls."

Two Red Masks, veiled and robed, walked from the tunnel. Ahjvar shut his eyes. He was tired of the lot of them. The pain welled up around him, thick, smothering, clouds of it like pillows, a deep mattress, water into which he sank, mud, choking him. A sudden sharp burst of fire. The Lady had slapped him with the flat of her blade.

"Open your eyes, dead man."

They were open. She wiped bloody fingers over his lips, forced a way between them as he panted, found his tongue, her fingers obscene. Her blood tasted of old dead fires. Shadows chased over her face. A pretty face, girlish, with long-lashed eyes, dark with secrets. Her saffron-hued robe was silk, and lent warm lights to the eyes. Was this any time to notice such things? She had been naked a moment before. She made him see them, as if she thought such things could have any power over him; she stole his pain and gave him the thoughts she wanted him to have. Her shaven head was repulsive, slick and bony, her skin blistered, black in patches, like bread from a too-hot oven. He tried to shut his eyes and he couldn't. Her hands fluttered, spattering blood, and she flung his sword away, standing up. Her own had vanished. She swooped down on him, the beautiful firelit girl again, hand behind his head, and kissed him, tongue searching where her fingers had gone. He tried to turn his head away, couldn't, too weak, and her grip was iron. Then she found his ear, whispered, "King's champion, were you? Where were you when he died alone in the night, calling for you?" Or was that his own thought?

She kissed him again. The mist wrapped around him and dragged him into the well.

There was fire, and he burned. Again. Still.

CHAPTER VIII

Another month until the anniversary of her acceptance, the end of her seventh year, and Zora would be free. What would she do then? Seven years as a temple dancer. She had had the best education someone not born to wealth in the Twenty Families could get in the city. Clerk, scribe, musician with a wealthy patron, library copyist, tutor of mathematics and literature . . . A dancer's education fitted you for any of those.

She could even join the priesthood.

It would be a fast way to die. A priestess, unlike a dancer, was taken to the deep well to be made known to the Lady. Best, perhaps, not.

Thunder broke over the mountains. Zora turned, beat her pillow into better shape. She couldn't sleep, and surely the night must be half over by now. The rain had begun not long after the bells for second curfew rang over the city, in a jagged ripple spreading from the temple, two hours after sunset. She had been listening to its steady drumming on the roof for what must have been another couple of hours, but rather than cooling, the air was growing heavier, more stifling. The dance of the morning prayers would be the sort that left you stinking, robes stuck to slick skin, face-paint prickling and itching with sweat, left you longing for the bath-house. She had three youngsters to give a lesson on the zither afterwards, as well, and they would be cranky and stupid, with the heat weighing on them, unless the storm had washed the city clean by then. It didn't seem likely. No wind.

At this rate dawn would find her still wakeful in a nest of wrinkled and sweat-damp bedding. She needed to sleep, to stop stewing in her worries. She wasn't supposed to have any worries, an innocent girl, content in her place. She forced herself to lie flat on her back, hands folded below her breasts. Breathe. Breathe slowly. Relax. Count breaths. Put all thinking aside.

Sleep still failed to take her.

Had she heard footsteps, earlier, on the stairs? A hushed stir from the rooms at the end of the corridor, where several unmarried priestesses lived? Someone taken ill?

Revered Shija, Mistress of the Dance, was pushing her to take her vows and stay, promising that she would be made Shija's own assistant. Zora couldn't say that every year, on her anniversary, she made her way to one of the several abandoned and half-ruined buildings down along the ravine—out of sight of the former hospice where the Voice was kept, shut up like a demented old auntie to stop her embarrassing the family before neighbours—and danced a solemn prayer of thanks for another year's survival. That was all she hoped for, each year when the day came around. One more year.

That the god she danced for was unaware of her prayer was irrelevant. She prayed, that was the important thing. She remembered. Thus she was not forsworn, not of the promises that mattered, regardless of what other oaths she had falsely taken since, a dancer's vows of chastity—well, that one she kept—and obedience and service to the

Lady. She was promised, long before, to her father and to her god. It was their service that brought her here.

Her father's story was the foundation of her own, the root of all she was. He had told it to her often and over the years it had become real, until it seemed she must have been there, must have seen him, skinny, dreaming, love-stricken boy, younger than she was now.

On the evening of the great earthquake, the rambling compound of the priestly family that had served the god Gurhan since before there was ever a city at all (or so they claimed), came down in rubble. Dogs howled, mothers and fathers ran shouting, cousins wailed. Young Mansour, who intended running away to the caravan road as soon as he could persuade the daughter of a certain wineshop-keeper in Spicemarket Ward to run with him, was at the god's sacred cave in a narrow folded valley of the many-folded hill, composing not a hymn but a love-song, with Gurhan's tolerant and somewhat amused assistance in the rhyme. He was shielded by Gurhan's own body shimmering into solid flesh as what seemed half the slope above and a copse of silver-leafed poplars slid down in thunder on them both.

"Run!" the god said. He was over the ridge and in the priests' compound before the youth, shifting stones with his own hands, easing pain, keeping life in broken bodies that might yet mend, if the first shock did not sever soul from flesh. Others there was no saving; Mansour was an orphan by the time all the family of priests were dug free and the god left them to do what a god of the earth might do throughout the rest of the Palace Ward, in the wailing dark of the night.

It was some nights later that the servants of the Lady came, and all the family of the priests of Gurhan were dragged out into the yard of their compound and butchered, men, women, children, babes, and dogs, their bodies left lying, and the children, as if even the servants of the Lady could not face what they had done, thrown into the well.

Mansour had been in the city, seeking the comfort of Samra, the wineshop-keeper's daughter.

Mind you—and Zora rolled over, head on her arms, though she had long ceased crying in the night about it—at nearly nineteen, she knew her father's plans for folly, and worse even than folly, if more blameless: the dreams of a mind losing its reason, as his final illness claimed him. Get into the temple. Find the truth of the Voice who rules us in the Lady's name. Find the power that commands the Red Masks. Find who has imprisoned our gods.

And?

And *what?* What then, Papa?

What had she thought, what had *he* thought? That she would discover the Voice to be some human tyrant enthroned, whom she could denounce from the steps of the senate palace, raising the city in revolt?

It would have to be the senate palace steps. There was no senate palace any longer. There was a senate, but the elders of the Families who sat in it were appointed by the Voice, or by the Right Hand and the Beholder of the Face in the name of the Voice and the Lady. It met in the Hall of the Dome, with the Right Hand and the Beholder watching all in the Lady's name.

The work of recovery and salvage after the earthquake had gone on through the dark, her father had told her, and it was only afterwards that the folk of Marakand truly realized what had come upon them. The gilded dome of the library of the senate palace still stood, triumphant over all in a red dawn haze, but the great basilica adjoining it, with its pillars of black marble, the famous mosaic floor and the green copper roof, was gone, fallen into jumbled stone and twisted metal. That had seemed, to many, the symbol of it all. Marakand was its senate, its folk. No kings, no princes, no priests ruled them, but the folk, ruling itself, or at least the folk allowing itself to be ruled by its most noble and deserving and gods-blessed representatives, the elders of the founding Twenty Families, Barraya and Xua, Arrac-Nourril and Feizi, and the rest. In theory, everyone had some adherence to the Families, based on ward or distant blood or adoption, and so they all, in theory, belonged and were spoken for. But in the earthquake the basilica that was the heart of that rule had been utterly destroyed. The senate had been meeting with the Over-Malagru Five Cities clan-fathers, and the bickering over customs duties had stretched into the evening. Those very few senators who had survived had been truant from the debate or had been fortunate enough to have their benches at the north corner, where not all the pillars had fallen. The god Gurhan led searches to find them on the second day. Nearly all the Twenty Families had lost their most respected, or at least most powerful, elders in that one ruin.

Who governs the city? the folk had asked. *Listen*, her father said. *This is important.* The young magistrate Petrimos Barraya, who had lost father and mother, becoming thereby head of the two most powerful branches of the wealthiest Family, had said, "Let the gate-captains and the wardens of the street guard rule the wards. Let them do what seems best to keep peace and order, to save what can be saved and look to the dead, for a ten-day, and then the Families must meet here, in the open air, with the gods of the city, and convene the senate anew."

And it had been done. Because they were the folk of Marakand, and Marakand's folk was sovereign still.

The senate, the survivors, the successors, had denounced the Voice and the temple, a few months after the earthquake. They had met on the steps of the palace . . . how had her father put it, his voice falling into a priest's, a storyteller's cadence? . . . *as was the tradition when great matters were debated and the wards were summoned to send a man for every hundred, to cry yea or nay. And they voted to censure the temple*

*and demand that the Red Masks be disbanded and return to their plain
yellow robes and bare their faces to the city like honest men and women. Red
Masks marched to arrest them. There were no trials. Cages of iron were set up
in the plaza at the foot of Palace Hill, and the rebel senators, as they are set
down in the temple's histories, were thrust into them, Petrimos Barraya and
his wife Elias first of all. By the third day without water, all were dead,
and it was said the flies could be heard before a man ever entered the gates of
the plaza.*

So had her father believed she could somehow bring the true senate
into being again, with some word or revelation? Or had he believed
that she would find the gods themselves, Gurhan and Ilbialla and the
Lady, in some locked room, and a bull-headed, wolf-fanged monster
devouring wizards, while the corrupt priests and priestesses knelt before
it in servile awe?

Her mother, Samra, had died of the wasting cough when she
was small. What took her father several years later was something
subtler, unseen. First he had lost the sight in one eye, and his hand
had gone clumsy, devastating, for a street-musician. He still sang,
but it had been she who earned the most, singing and dancing with
the tambourine while he played the drum, which did not betray him
as flute and tanbur did. He had begun to sweat in night-time fevers,
and talk, too loudly, sometimes too publicly, of the god, his god, lost
Gurhan, till she persuaded him he had to stay within doors, for both
their sakes. He turned that into conviction they were in danger of
betrayal, not from his own wandering words but from their friends.
They moved several times from ward to ward, hiding not from the
enemies that might truly threaten them if the singer Makul claimed
to the wrong ears to be Mansour, the last priest of Gurhan, god of the
Palace Hill, but from those who might have helped her care for him,
those who already knew his secrets: Master Hadidu of the Doves,

Hadidu's wife Beccan and his brother-by-marriage, the wizard Nour. They ended up lodging in a hot and foetid room over the wool-shed at the back of a weaver's yard in Greenmarket Ward, and there, finally, blind and shaking and stuttering, her father died.

Gurhan would make himself known to her, Mansour had said, that last long night. Gurhan whispered still in his dreams; he could hear the god's voice, now that he could no longer see. Gurhan said that their enemy was in the temple of the Lady, hidden in the temple, within the temple, under the temple, and they must fight, or the city would perish.

Promise. Swear to me you'll do what I cannot, and find the truth within the temple. Trust no one, not your mother's family, not Hadidu, not Petrimos. She swore. She didn't even know any Petrimos, unless he meant the Barraya senator who had died in the cages. Someone long dead, anyway. And her mother's family had disowned Samra when she ran away to marry Mansour; Zora didn't even know their names.

As for Hadidu . . . but she had sworn.

Now, seven years older, she could understand it was the illness, whatever killed Mansour from within, leaving him bereft of sight and, ultimately, reason that had extracted that promise, not her father in himself. But then, she had been a child, and she had always been loved and protected and expected to learn and obey and hold secrets, too, because when he was gone she would be the last priestess of Gurhan, and someone must remember the old songs, the old dances. Someone must carry Gurhan in the heart. So she was used to secrets, to obedience; their survival depended on it. She trusted him. What did she know, in those days, of how the brain, the seat of thought, could be overthrown and broken by illness, just as surely as the heart or the lungs or the bowels?

There had been no one to help her do any of the necessary things when his breath finally stopped. She had used her last coin to pay the oilman next door for use of his handcart and dragged her father's body out to the pauper's graveyard in the Gore where the roads from Riverbend Gate and Sunset ran together, and then, having returned the cart, she left everything behind, like one walking to execution. She had gone to the temple, to audition for the dancers.

Zora had never had any doubt they would take her. She knew she was beautiful, even at an age when the body was all arms and legs and flat as a stack of bricks. That she could already sing and dance and play flute and tanbur was mere gilding.

She had passed the Doves, Hadidu's coffeehouse overlooking the Sunset Ward market square, both going out to the Gore and trudging back. She hadn't even thought of going in to ask the last priest of Ilbialla for help, still tangled, then, in her father's web of fears.

Maybe it was time. She never had gone to the Doves on her monthly free-days, at first because she had promised her father and she half believed that he must have known some truth, that Hadidu was unfaithful, would betray them to the temple in return for, what, amnesty for Nour, who was a wizard? And then because she was ashamed, and she was a temple dancer; Master Hadidu would see her scarlet robes and think she betrayed *him*.

And then, even later, because she was shy, and she did not think he would know her.

Should she go and say, *Master Hadidu, I'm the daughter of Mansour and Samra, who were once your friends, and my father made me promise to enter the temple, so I did. I found what I'm sure you already know, that the Voice, in her own person, is a senile old woman, that even the priests fear the Red Masks, who never, ever raise their veils, and no servants ever enter their hall. That the wealth that pours in goes out again at the Voice's word on walls and warriors and gifts to false senators who approve whatever Revered Rahel the Beholder of the Face tells them.*

I can tell you that the Voice truly speaks with the Lady's voice. I have heard her, hiding where I should not have been, and sick to my stomach with fear. If there is a monster in Marakand, it is the Lady herself, and though my father claimed Gurhan whispered to him behind the darkness of his eyes, my god never comes to me, to put thoughts into my head. Does yours?

She would. She had to. It was that or spend her life tutoring Family brats in calligraphy and music, dance and geometry, forgetting, as the city did, that there had ever been a god of Palace Hill. Not that she could see how mere remembering did anyone any good.

Zora tried stretching and then curling up small. It didn't slow her rat-scrabbling thoughts any.

No getting up before the rising bell was sounded outside the dancer's dormitory. A discipline priestesses did not have to keep. No grey showed at the dormitory window. How long till the dawn? Thunder still grumbled distant over the mountains, and just when she thought the storm must have passed from the city, the world lit white again and it sounded as though the clouds smashed together like falling rocks. Had she dozed after all, as she lay thinking of Master Hadidu? He had had some plan, he and Nour—and her father, back before he began to fear them and cut himself off from all his friends. The gods were not dead, they believed. And they could be freed. Nour travelled the eastern road with a caravan. Nour sought something that could help. That was all she knew. If there was something her father had wanted her to do in the temple, to further that end, he had never made it clear to her.

Perhaps he never knew himself.

Whisper, scuff of sandals and slippers, the hushed rustling of bodies. Zora's nerves prickled to the alert. Again? Had one of the elderly widowed priestesses gone to the Old Great Gods? But their rooms were all on the lower floors, to spare them so many stairs.

A narrow crack of light widened, as someone opened the door at the far end of the dormitory. Zora blinked at it and sat up before she could wonder if it might be wiser to pretend to be asleep. A dozen priests and priestesses came in, rustling, scuffing, all the noises of people trying very hard to be silent. Several carried lamps. Two Red Masks followed. Her heart lurched. For Red Masks to come into the girl-dancers' dormitory . . . that had simply never happened in all her seven years in the temple. A sickness rose into her chest, and she felt her pulse racing—*they know you, they've found you out*—but she swallowed down the panic, kept her voice merely puzzled.

"What is it?" she whispered, and a few of the other girls, waking at the stir, repeated the question.

Startled, the clergy whispered among themselves, which gave everyone else time to wake. The Red Masks stood aloof, but then, they always did. Zora frowned at them. One at least was definitely a man: tall, broad-shouldered. A pillar of menacing, fluttering drapery. Red Masks walked in her nightmares.

"What's happening?" she demanded, as anyone might, no longer whispering.

"The Voice . . ." a priest murmured, but there was still a whispering among them, as if they debated, not certain.

If the Voice had warned of some danger, the priests shouldn't stand muttering together in the girls' dormitory. There shouldn't be *priests* in the girls' dormitory, on the upper floor of the priestesses' hall.

If the Voice had revealed a traitor, a spy in their midst . . . But why now, after almost seven years, and she'd been into the forbidden building, the old hospice, she'd seen the Voice stripped of her robes and mask and veils, seen her vacant, slack face, and no goddess had woken in pitiable Revered Lilace to shout denouncement then.

"How many girls here are orphans?" demanded Revered Rahel, Beholder of the Face of the Lady.

A few hesitant hands were raised. Zora's was not among them. "Why do you ask, Revered?" she asked.

There was no answer, but fingers pointed. "Zora's an orphan too."

"Yes, our senior dancer," Revered Rahel said. "What's your Family, dear?"

Zora shook her head. Her father's family had been here before the city, her father always said. Not that she was about to make that fact known.

"Well, where are you from? What ward of the city?"

"Fleshmarket Ward, Revered." That was in the entry register next to her name, along with a note that, since she was an orphan, the ward magistrate's permission as her guardian had been obtained.

"Very well, very well." Revered Rahel glanced over them dismissively. "You may put your hands down now, girls." Those who were orphans did so. Half of them were Family, not merely by name. Bastards and orphans. Was Zora imagining it, or had Revered Rahel not bothered even to glance at those?

"And, Zora, you are accounted by all the most beautiful of the dancers."

That didn't seem to be a question; just as well, because how could she answer? Her mother's dark, narrow face, soft black hair that rippled in waves, when unbound, to her waist, Samra's dusky, long-lashed eyes as well—her father's slender musician's hands. Beauty, she saw, in the polished black pillars of the Hall of the Dome, but it was not something a decently modest girl ought to say about herself.

"Through her blessed Voice Lilace, the Lady has said, 'I will have youth. I will have beauty. I will have a dancer. Let the orphan girl be my daughter. Let the orphan girl become my child, my beloved.' Zora, dear, a great blessing has fallen upon you. The Voice of the Lady has risen from her labours here and set out upon her road. Her final act for our Lady was to name the one who should take her place."

Zora sat dazed. Did Rahel mean . . . ? The Voice of the Lady was dead, and they wanted her—

She licked her lips and tried to swallow, but her mouth felt paper dry. "I . . ."

"You will be the next Voice of Marakand," said Revered Ashir, Right Hand of the Lady and husband of Revered Rahel.

"But I'm not a priestess, Revered." The words croaked.

"Beautiful and beloved," whispered the Mistress of the Dance. "The Voice of the Lady has spoken."

And what other rubbish did she spew? Zora wondered. Measured by her thundering heart, it seemed to take a very long time for them to come farther into the long room, with its double row of beds. To stop blocking the door. Her own bed was farthest from that door, under the window, privilege claimed by the senior girl. The window, unfortunately, was blocked by a wooden screen and on the uppermost storey. Even within the holy grounds of the temple, certain precautions had to be taken when one had thirty of the most beautiful maidens of the city under one roof.

The other girls stared, blank, startled, awed, horrified . . . envious?

"Come, Zora," said Revered Ashir. "The Lady awaits you in the deep well."

A long breath. She went. Down the centre aisle between the beds, then up, bounding bed to bed past them, nightgown hitched above her knees. Out the door and down the stairs, long strides.

To reach the main gate meant crossing courtyards and gardens and dodging around other buildings, then passing up a sloping tunnel and beneath the compound's outer wall to the higher level of the city. They'd be expecting that, and the gates were defended by temple guard, locked at night. But she could hide; there were deserted ruins even within the temple. She knew the grounds in the dark. Few of the priests could say the same.

She heard them shouting behind her for torches. Lamps blew out as they ran, and most of them were old, puffing; even the young lacked a dancer's fit body. She might have a chance.

But they took her in the end. The Red Masks ran swiftly as she, anticipated her, more coming, bearing torches, to cut her off, blocking her in on the landing of a stairway. Revered Ashir pushed past the silent red priests, trying to seize her by the shoulders as if she were a naughty little girl, to be shaken into sense. She kicked him where it hurt, knocked another priest's legs out from under him, punched some grey-haired senior priestess in the eye, and was brought down by a blow between the shoulders from a Red Mask's carved staff. Nobody escaped the Red Masks. Certainly not she. They hauled her up, Revered Rahel shouting at another priest to take her legs. Revered Ashir was being sick in the corner.

"Thankless beggar's brat," the Beholder of the Face was almost shrieking. "Impious trollop's bastard, is this how you show gratitude to your Lady for the great honour given you?"

Shija, the Mistress of the Dance, was sobbing. None of them looked happy, except possibly Revered Rahel, who wiped her mouth and gave a mirthless grin of satisfaction at Zora's now-useless struggles.

"If it's such an honour, you go to her," Zora spat. "Go on! Tell her I'm not looking to be anyone's daughter."

Revered Rahel slapped her. Zora yelled and twisted but could not break free.

She stopped yelling when yet another pair of Red Masks came. These two wore their armour, and the light of the Lady shone on them. They set her on her feet, but she fell to her knees again. The priests themselves backed away, tight against the walls.

Go now. She should go now, run, run run . . . Get up. Knock them over. Run. They're not ghosts. They're not devils. They're people in stupid vestments. Run.

But the divine light of the Lady shone from them, muddy scarlet edging eyeslits, nostrils, crawling slowly over the helmets and chest-armour like ripples in dark water. The watching priests crowded away. One priestess whimpered under her breath.

Run! Zora screamed at herself in the silence of her mind. But her joints had gone watery and her teeth chattered and she couldn't move.

The armoured Red Masks each took her under an arm, the merely veiled falling in behind. They dragged her out the main door, past a stern-faced portress there to protect the virtue of the dancers and the other unmarried women, across the rainy courtyard walled by the married priests' apartments, past the scriptorium and the house where the Right Hand and Beholder of the Face lived in splendour befitting their rank. Across the public courtyards, glistening with puddles, under the colonnade of the Hall of the Dome. The hall of the Red Masks stood near the sacred well-house, fortress-like, windowless on its ground storey. They all hurried down the uneven steps into the well-house courtyard, the old level of the temple grounds before the rubble had been built over. There were more Red Masks watching from behind the screened upper windows of their hall, from within the dark mouth of their doorway; she felt their eyes, burning, and even the priests hunched and kept their faces averted, as if their grim colleagues might read some hidden guilt in their thoughts. The two Red Masks holding her set her on her feet, still gripping her by either arm, and Zora walked stumbling. Revered Rahel unlocked the well-house door with an iron key a handspan long.

Zora had never been within. Even priests did not approach the Lady unbidden by the Voice, and dancers never descended to the well and the Lady's presence. Inside, the building was a single room with a stone-flagged floor that was merely a ring around its outer edge. It was roofed with a dome, the open eye of which let in a plume of rain. A gilded lamp burned in a niche, shedding just enough light to show that most of what should have been floor was a dark and gaping pit. They started down a stair that descended in a great spiral, without railing or banisters. It was carved of soft rock; the treads were worn into hollows, cracked and crumbling, damp. The air grew cool and moist. Four of the priests carried light now, two ahead and two behind. Zora was in the middle, in the pool of shadow. The Red Masks held her up whenever she slipped. The stairs were slick. Zora tried to catch the eyes of the Mistress of the Dance when she looked back.

Revered Shija looked away.

The stairs were abruptly newer, sharp-edged and less carefully matched, some with narrower treads or shorter rises, so that Zora was not the only one stumbling, though a torch burned below them, at the foot of the stairs. The walls here showed no sign of working. They were in a natural cavern deep beneath the temple. The deep well. The sacred well. Except it was no well; it was a dank cave. Zora's legs were trembling so that the Red Masks had to take all her weight. She couldn't have run even if they had taken their hands off her.

This was what they worshipped? She wanted to scream hysterically at them, *It's a cave, an empty cave*, but she could not. There was something. She felt it.

The priests fixed their torches to brackets spaced along the wall, spreading the light. The floor of the cavern was natural rock, uneven but water-smoothed, a mottled pallor stained with streaks of green and red, fissured with dark earth in which a few pallid, straggling weeds had sprouted to grow beneath the dome's eye. A rotting boat, its planks crumbling, caked with a white paste of mould, sat near the foot of the stairs, long abandoned on the stone.

A veiled Red Mask stood guard, back against the wall on the far side of the cavern, unmoving.

There was a well after all. Of sorts.

Centre of the cavern. Mud and slick damp stone, and an edge of black water, reflecting torchlight. A crack in the floor.

The water rippled as though something beneath were stirring, breaking the firelight into jagged shapes. Mist began to rise. Zora sagged to her knees and the Red Masks let her down, into mud. There were six of them now, seven with the motionless sentry. Where had they come from? Darkness. Cavern mouth. Could she run for that darkness, hide, escape? Not if Red Masks could walk out of it. Not if she could not stand.

Her god was not this. She held that thought. This terror was not how a god should be.

"Holy Lady," Rahel said. "Great Lady of Marakand, we have brought you a devout and beautiful and virtuous virgin to be your Voice."

Nothing spoke, but tendrils of mist reached out towards her.

"Do you hear us, Lady?" someone else asked, speaking not to the well but to Zora.

She did not answer. Neither did anything else. Nothing happened. The Red Masks waited patiently. The mist wrapped around her. Her head ached, badly enough to make her queasy. That was all.

It was cold, and she shivered from that as well as fear. The Lady's divine light faded from the armoured Red Masks and the miasma of terror they carried ebbed with it. It was her own honest fear that kept her trembling. Zora clenched her hands to fists. Prayed, never giving her prayer a name. *Guide me, hide me, . . . save me.*

Eventually, "It's been so long. How did the Lady used to approve her Voices?" a priestess asked in a whisper.

"She came to them in dreams," an old priest said. "She came in dreams and called them to her. They woke knowing they were called."

"But it's all different now. This girl's not even a priestess. Are we wrong? How do we know?"

"The smoke," said Revered Ashir, who must have hobbled after them. He stood propped on a younger priest. "It's the smoke that makes the Voice receptive to the Lady."

"Well, you should have said so before," Rahel snapped at her husband. "We need to do this in the Hall of the Dome instead."

"The Lady will receive her Voice in the deep well," Ashir said, satisfaction in his voice. "I have all that is needed here."

"Prepare it, then," Rahel said. "Do you have the mask?"

Ashir made a noise of impatience. "The mask is for dignity, for respect of the Lady when the Voice ascends the pulpit. We'll do without the mask. Shija, assist me."

The Mistress of the Dance nearly scurried in her haste to obey, to not be seen hesitating any longer. Zora tried to crane around to see what they were doing, but a priest moved between them, backing away from the crawling mist.

That was *not* how you should feel about your gods.

"There's . . . there's nothing to fear, child," murmured an older priest, a man who had taught her to play the zither. "The smoke helps you to open yourself to the presence of the Lady, that's all. Then she will enter your mind and you will speak the words she gives you. It is as though . . . as though you are the trumpet, and she the musician. She will fill your mind with holiness and make you Marakand. It is a blessing. A blessing." But he looked down at his feet as he whispered, not meeting Zora's eyes.

"Lady of Marakand, you who hold the waters of the deep well in your cupped hands, be with us. Lady of Marakand, whose blessing is in the deep waters, protect us from all evils. Lady of Marakand . . ." Revered Ashir, pausing often to gasp for breath, was praying.

The Lady is not Marakand, said her father's voice in her memory.

I am not the Lady's, Zora told herself.

Revered Shija, a sleeve held across her face, came to her with a censer wreathed in blue smoke.

"Breathe," said Revered Rahel, and forced Zora's head down almost to touching the perforated brass globe, as Shija dangled it before her. "Breathe deeply. You will be the vessel of the Lady, filled with a holiness you could never deserve."

"Just breathe, Zora," whispered the Mistress of the Dance. "It won't hurt. It will be easier. The Lady knows what's best, she must."

"Breathe," said Ashir, and his hand on her hair was possessive, caressing. "Be the daughter of the Lady."

Zora struggled, almost freeing herself, until the Red Masks moved even Ashir aside and held her, pushing her head into the thickest smoke. It stank. She tried not to breathe, but it seemed to crawl in by her eyes, up her nostrils, between her clenched lips, until finally she had to gasp. And once she did that, breathing was easy. Slow and easy. She was dizzy almost at once.

Whatever poison it was, it was swift. Poison. Remember that. Poison. Not holiness. She began to feel drunk, her body slow and heavy, but her arms strangely light, floating at her sides, though the guards gripped her as if their fingers would meet in her flesh. Her head sagged. Drunk. She'd only been drunk once, celebrating, celebrating something . . . One of her free-days, going with a friend to visit her family, and they had been celebrating a brother's betrothal. The hangover had put her off unwatered wine altogether.

This was bad. She floated, muttering prayer. It wasn't the Lady she prayed to. Had the priests heard? This was very bad. She felt . . . something. Touching her. Finding out the shape of her, like a woman holding up a garment, wondering if it would fit.

She had seen the Voice. There had been no room left in her own mind for herself, that was what had come upon that pitiable woman, the day of the earthquake. The Lady had ceased to speak to her, to whisper words for her to pass on, and had taken her, wearing her skin. And now Zora was going to die that same life in death. She would dribble and drool and shamble empty-eyed, while the Lady put on the husk of her to rant and froth in the temple.

"Papa!" she cried, because who else was there to come to save her? He couldn't save her. He was dead.

"Hadidu—No! Not him. No!"

"What did she say?"

"Nothing yet. It's just the smoke speaking."

"Smoke smoke smoke." She was babbling already and was there nothing in her mind but herself? It was her mind, her place, her palace, a cave within which she dwelt, alone, darkness, waiting, until the day she could open the door and let the secrets fly free.

"Fly," she said. "Not yet. I didn't—I didn't tell—not yet." Something brushed over her. "So beautiful," she giggled. Her own voice, not her thought, was it? "G-Great Gods," she said, and clamped her mouth shut. She was a child of—a child of—the Lady could not take that from her, could not, could not, she was afraid, and there was a hand reaching for her and she took it, a man's hand, broad and strong. Papa? His hands had been narrow, callused fingertips but delicate, musician's hands, don't think that don't think it, don't give them his name. She squeezed her eyes shut too, watering in the smoke. Eyes, she remembered, dark eyes and restless energy, he was never still, even sitting by her mother's bed as she gasped and choked her last, hands drawing music from his tanbur, soft and soothing, at odds with his burning anger, till when the end of his own life came he had lost even that. He had stared with wide unseeing eyes, arm twitching, unable to make music even with a drum. She took his hands in hers and held them clasped together, feeling them hot, hot, hot, as if he burned. Don't think of him. Mankul, a street-singer, died of a brain-fever. Nothing more.

What more is there? Voices murmured in the distance of her mind, one so faint she could barely hear it. One was her own. One laughed, greedily.

Mansour, of Gurhan's Hill. He died mad, of a growth in his brain. He sent his daughter here to die.

Child of Gurhan, I name you the Voice of the Lady of Marakand. Hear me. Hear me. In Gurhan's name. Tell my city, warn them, the Lady is not the Lady is—

Let go now. Let go let go let go. You will fall. I will catch you. I will hold you, close under my heart, my heart, you will be my heart, mine.

She clung with both hands, digging in her very nails, but the big rough hand was gone, as if she had grasped smoke. She fell.

Zora went limp, as the words poured through her, a flood.

"Oh, you have lied and lied and lied and you think you are not mine but the city is mine, my city, he is dead he is gone he is fled he is buried he cannot have you lying cuckoo child—Shall we tell the priests what you are who you are what you do who are you—

"My city, mine, none other, tell them tell them tell them—

"She is dead she is dead she is dead. Let the child speak for me, oh let the priestess speak . . .

"—the child will be my child my daughter no other my daughter mine good daughter good girl to speak for me she will be my daughter—

"Treachery deceit and lies and lies in the mouth of the cuckoo child and you hate me you betray me and they will come back for me—

"Close too close death is coming."

She—who was she was not Zora . . . she saw him, standing, smiling at her, as he had stood all her life since she was a little child, but then he was only a shape, a man-shape, a hole in the air, outlined in yellow-white flame. She saw *her*, smoke and scarlet fires twisting into a pillar. She saw a sword like a splinter of stone, spinning frost across the stars. "Death is walking the road of death of dreams of walking death is sleep is ice is death—"

Hide!

Voices. Her own. Two. Three, screaming in her head, vying for her tongue.

"Papa!" she screamed, and once started could not stop— "Papapapapa—" until she choked on mud.

"My daughter, my Voice. Hear, Marakand, our Marakand. No other god, no other power no goddess no mother none but me no no god no—"

I see your heart, traitor child. I see. Secret servant of Gurhan, who was too weak, too small, too blind to defend your city. What can your little gods do, when death comes in ice and flame and great armies of godless men? I see your lies, and lies upon lies. And they are coming he is coming he must be coming a Red Mask died this day you see as I see you know as I know but do you understand? A Red Mask died who cannot die, cut down at the Eastern

Wall and she the killer rode away. You know. He it must be he plans to take the Praitans from me, but we need them, we will have them, they are meant for ours and one by one we will have them. All our enemies gather. You, my enemy, my daughter, close under my heart. You thought to see my secrets, you thought to know my truth, to betray my truth.

"No!"

I have sought them. I see them now I see them now.

No, someone wept, and it did not seem to be her own voice. *No, no more death no more no more.*

"Traitor!" she cried. "I see him now, the traitor—traitor of long years, slow treason, slow rot, slow poison. He betrays the city, he betrays me, you betray me, dreamer of empty dreams—you cannot see—you cannot free them—you cannot see them you are mine he is—he is—he is—he the worm in the heart of Marakand the enemy the rebel gods dead gods no gods but the Lady—

"No!—

"The daughter of the priest of Gurhan the daughter my daughter fool no threat no threat a whisper a dream too weak—

"No!—

"Before me bring me the man Hadidu of the Doves he will stand before me—he will stand will stand he will know he will hear himself condemned out of your mouth out of my mouth. I see him now I know him now. The priest of Ilbialla lives he plots to be my death to free the feeble gods to be our death—no!—and now I see him I know him I hear him—"

I see him in your memory, Mansour's daughter, do you know yourself a traitor now?

"—there is a wizard visits his house who dares to creep within our gates my gates are closed against him bring him bring me the wizard to face the Lady in the deep well as is my law my word the Lady's word—

"*No!*

"We are betrayed betrayed betrayed," she shrieked, and the words piled atop one another, tumbling, cascading. A woman, somewhere, wept.

Consternation among the priests. Two Red Masks started up the stairs to meet others from the barracks. They would go, even if the fool priests did not hear her did not understand needed more to understand—

"They plot against us against us Gurhan stirs Ilbialla cries out I drink their dreams I see their dreams my children of Marakand in the deep caves in the secret water she sees she knows the sword brings night we cannot see beneath the river of night brings fire brings ice the sword of the ice the ice brings death . . .

"The Doves, the priest of the Doves, the hidden priest, he hides a wizard who comes to him he hides his secrets he hides his goddess they mean our death our deaths his death is ordained the Lady speaks. Bring him to me."

Whispers. *A priest of Ilbialla? But they all died after the earthquake, the whole family, didn't they? What's the Doves, what does she mean? Some wineshop, some caravanserai, a tavern, the guard will know, send to the commander on watch . . .* A younger priest was sent scurrying up the stairs to wake the commander of the temple guard. No need to summon the Red Masks; the priests knew the Lady would send them where she would, without any need for word from the Right Hand or the Beholder.

Somewhere a girl was crying, not she-Zora. Weeping, voiceless, no sobs to shake her, to betray, just the slow hot tears that gathered, pooled, and rolled down her face, and the heavy arm over her that pinned her down.

Somewhere a weary old woman keened, arms hugged tight about

herself. *My city my folk my sister my brother, ah, Marakand, Marakand, hear me, Marakand, save me, let me go.*

"Let me go let me go let me go—"

Somewhere a woman stood guard, sword in hand, stood on a city wall, watching the road to the west, and in her mind she saw it black with moving bodies, spilling from the road, filling the pass, and their minds were filled with love of him and fear of him. He was coming to make the world his own, no rivals, no allies, no friend or lover or kin would stand by him; he burned the air and he would open the road with the dying of the world and the gates of the cold hells would be shattered and the very stars would fall, but she could save them, stop him, she could hold the east . . .

"Get out!" Zora cried, and the priests pushing close around her backed away as she clawed at her face, till a Red Mask crouched to seize her hands.

Zora. Cuckoo's egg, cowbird's nestling, Gurhan's lost servant, but you are strong, strong as Lilace was not, will you be Lilace, will you be a Voice as Lilace was, a broken instrument? There is another way, a better way. She was unfit, unworthy, and it was not yet time but the time is come the time is here.

No, no, no, no, no . . . Let me go let her go let us go . . .

There is a better way, an easier way, a stronger way. To be honoured, not pitied. Worshipped, not loathed. To be strong, to be Marakand . . . hold me. Take me into your heart.

No! She tried to fling herself away, to run, and was trapped in Red Mask arms.

"What's she saying? Bring the censer nearer, Shija, she needs the smoke. She's growing too wild. Voice, Revered Voice, what does the Lady say?"

Lilace broke. Lilace was burnt away. She was only a priestess, a speaker for the Lady, a messenger who carried words to the well and back. The ribbon that bound them was too thin, too delicate, the thread the lightning followed. She was weak; she shattered. She was the Voice of the Lady, but she could not bear the weight of the Lady once the Lady became great, became strong, became me . . .

. . . she lies, I am not . . . she is not . . . oh, hear me, let me go.

But I am the Lady and the Lady will pour through you, empty you, scour you clean with flame and you will be the Voice be Lilace be what she became . . .

Or will you join with me? Will you let me in of your own will? To be whole and strong, worshipped and loved and feared, yes, is it not the better way, the truer way? How will you serve your god, through infantile decades of death in life, a mouth for the Lady who cannot dares not must not be seen—

And she saw, she saw the Lady form of mist, she saw her waver, falter, shiver, young and old, dark and golden, beautiful and homely. A red light struck her eyes and her priests fell back and one cried, "She is not the Lady, she is—" but it was only her fear, only imagining, only what might yet be, for the priests had no faces, they were nothing but saffron robes with masks, the silver moon-mask of the Voice in the temple, which hid her slack and twisting features.

No! And the vision was rent away, not for her, not that thought for her but she had seen and the old woman the Lady said, *See? Child of my brother Gurhan, see, be strong, seek truth.*

Yes, see this truth.

Zora saw herself, a bloated, grey-faced, sagging creature, grown stiff and heavy. The weight of her hair, dry, brittle, dull, dragged her down. She sat in a chair in a locked room. The windows were barred, and she rocked and rocked and rocked her body and spittle dribbled down her face and no one came to wipe it away, and she rocked, and her hands twisted and fought one another, and her face bore old scars, pale scars, where she had tried with her very nails to peel it away.

No . . .

What will you? She saw again the woman armed, the woman strong and beautiful and clean, and Ashir bowed and Rahel, Rahel was afraid, Rahel rubbed her hands together and said, "Lady, what will you?" And she said, "Let the senate palace be raised again, let the senate meet, let the wards choose elders of wisdom to sit with them. Let the guilds be for the folk, not the folk to feed the guilds." She saw the ruined houses of the great earthquake, the ones enmeshed in Family claims, landlords holding, waiting, never building, while the poorest paid all they earned for a room lightless, airless, hot in summer, damp and cold in winter, and the fevers took them, and her mother coughed herself to death. "Build," she said. "The temple hoards, when it should build. The Families pile wealth upon wealth and there are children who sleep huddled in the ruins and the street guard are sent to drive them out. Let us build . . ." And Marakand was great and golden again, and the senate met in wise and solemn dignity, and the houses gleamed with plaster white and golden and there were flowers laid at Ilbialla's tomb and Gurhan's, in memory of gods that once had been, honoured dead. She rode out of the city with the folk crying blessings upon her, and they threw flowers beneath her horse's feet . . .

Horses scared her.

. . . And there was a hospice built where the compound of Gurhan's priests had once stood, all green and airy gardens and white paths and sweet-scented plants, and low, cool, bright rooms. The poor lay in white beds, while physicians in the yellow robes of the temple tended them, or they sat on benches in the sun and grew strong again.

And Zora who was the Voice as Lilace had been the Voice . . .

Her body sagged and hung in heavy folds of fat about her, breasts dragging, heavy, belly flaccid, overhanging her private parts; her vast thighs shuddered as she moved, but her feet, her slender, her shapely feet were still her own, though her swollen ankles settled heavily on an anklet of dancer's bells. Shija and Rahel dressed her in the black gown of the Voice, and she gasped for breath with the effort of moving the great grub she had become. Her lips whispered the flowing thoughts of the Lady's mind, the jabber of her own fears, "No, not me, this isn't me this mustn't be me this is death in life is death let me go . . ." She watched—with loathing for herself, with hunger—as they brought the mask, the silvered moon-face, delicate, beautiful, with its tiny eye-holes and the slit in the rosebud lips through which she drank the smoke . . . she hungered for the smoke and licked her lips, as they settled the helmet-like mask of lacquered paper over her, showing her beautiful face her mask the face of the Voice to the world, and draped her in the veil of white silk tissue, that fell to her knees behind and before, and they settled her into a chair, not a closed carrying-chair such as senators and the wealthy of the Twenty Families used to travel about the crowded streets but a gilded throne that needed six strong temple guard to take its poles, because she could not walk so far, not from the Voice's hospice on the bank of the ravine to the Hall of the Dome and the high pulpit where she would drink the smoke, bathe in the smoke, open herself to the Lady's will and speak in answer to the questions of the priests, or to judge the accused, the blasphemers, the traitors, the rebels, the wizards who sought her death . . .

Oh, she hungered for the smoke . . . but in the back of her mind she was still Zora, still Mansour's daughter, and she wept and beat her hands against the prison of her flesh, and still she cried, *No, I am not yours I will not be yours you will not have me.*

And she was the Lady, riding her gleaming chestnut horse with a sword at her side against the barbarians who had slain poor pitiable Lilace, who raided the caravans of the road, her road, or levied tolls they had no right to, and threatened her city, who could be tamed and turned to good and virtuous folk of Marakand, to become her armies when the dark tide flowed up the pass . . . and the folk threw flowers beneath her feet and loved her. Was that so bad? And in the hospice on the hill, Gurhan's hospice, in memory of Gurhan who had faded and died, honoured and remembered, as gods did fade and die, a woman who might have been her mother lay in a white bed in a sunny room and put an arm around the little girl who stood by her bed, a little girl in a clean, neat caftan, and said, "I'll be coming home soon, my darling."

Choose, said the Lady.

Zora wept.

I cannot force you. Choose. You must ask me in ask us in, to be one with me with us, to be strong, to be free, to be wise and great and ruler of the city, to make the east great and save your folk Gurhan's folk all the folk of all the blind gods of the east against the death of the world that comes. Or not, and be still the captive Voice, a defiant soul a broken slave a prisoner in your own repulsive body in your own rotting mind as it slowly burns away.

Choose.

"Yes," she whispered, crouched on the floor.

She felt the surge of joy, of hunger, and almost cried again, "No!" but she saw her hand on the muddy stone, the fine bones, the lean strong fingers, her father's hand, and she saw the skin stretched to bursting over obscene, fat, grey-hued flesh, the knuckles twisted, swollen, fevered, the hand grown to a feeble claw that pawed with nails chewed ragged at her own face.

Strength, the Lady whispered. *Unity. Power, to build, to save, to make anew. Understanding, yes, clear sight. Come to me. I cannot stand before so many.*

They would see, too many would see, would fear, would suspect, if she failed to be their Lady, the grave, shy goddess to whom they sang their songs and danced their prayers—they would see as the true Lady fought for a toehold in the world, for a moment's meeting with her folk, they would fear . . . The thought was snatched away from Zora, but she hardly noticed. She was shivering, trembling, shuddering, retching in her fear.

"Is it yes?" she asked, the Voice of the Lady asked the Voice. "Do you choose, do you choose me choose us choose to be?"

"Yes." Her teeth chattered.

"You must come to me—

"Do you give yourself to me?" her own voice asked. Was that not a part of the vows of marriage? Did she marry the Lady, then? That was the mad babble of the Voice's thought, and the Lady laughed. *Do you give yourself to me, Zora of Gurhan?*

"I—"

The Lady waited. The priests, kept away by Red Masks, waited, not certain for what. For the Voice to gather herself, to prophesy, to give them the Lady's will. Or for the girl to pass out, overwhelmed by the glory and blessing that had come upon her, so they could carry her off to her apartments in the hospice where she could not disturb them, so they could haul their rheumatic bones from this damp cavern where the rain once more sheeted down from the open eye of the dome far above.

"I do." Not her mother, in the bed of the new hospice. Too late for her mother. Some other mother. Some other child.

She crawled to the lip of the crack in the floor.

"Stop her!" Revered Ashir cried suddenly. "She'll drown herself!"

Shija moved to grab her, but Red Masks were swifter, putting themselves between the Voice and the priests. Zora crouched, shivering.

"You must come to me," the Lady whispered through her, patient, kind. "Come to me in the Lady's well."

Zora rolled over the edge, into dark water, and she fell.

She drowned. The goddess poured into her, ripped her soul open and fastened claws, flayed her and crawled in and wore her skin. Fire. Burning. This was how wizards died, she thought. Died, yes, and were forged anew. The water was fire, surrounding her, pulling her under.

The deep water, the heart of the goddess. The weight of nothing-ness beneath, sinking down, down, drowning down, burning in the secrets. Marrow, sinew, bone, heart and blood, the taste of cold water, stone on the tongue, the fire behind the eyes, the ice, the prisoning ice and the light of the stars that called, that flowed in her veins . . .

No, no, no, the Lady of Marakand cried, a faint voice, a prisoner, a cyst within.

We are you are I am.

Black ice. Copper sky, murky, the moon low, moons. Sea, the out-rigger canoe dancing on the waves. Long journeys. The white roads of the empire. The seas of sand, the seas of grass. The hunger that drove them—her brother's, not hers—to know more, to be more, to hold all in his hand. A new folk, a new magic, a strong magic, a folk come like he and she over the sea, but the sea of the cold grey north. What could they learn from them? The magic of blood. The wars, the folk dead in the valleys, the Great Grass stirred to war, to spill to sweep over the land, to slaughter even the babes in arms and the cattle in the fields, the north in flames, as they fought one another, rivals, friends, lovers, and the world itself the prize once one should make his empire there. But the gods and the wizards and the kings found strength and stood, and summoned the Old Great Gods, and they were thrown down, and slain, insofar as such as they could be slain, and the Old Great Gods bound them, chained them, and set powers of the earth, gods and demons, to guard them, and the world was safe.

Not the Lady. No, she was not the Lady. She wore the mask of the Lady; she was a parasite engulfing the Lady, a worm grown great, holding the Lady within. She had taken Lilace through the bond of love that bound servant to goddess, she had used her because it suited, because the temple would obey, when the Lady spoke through the Voice, and she had begun to shape her Marakand.

Our Marakand.

My Marakand.

Not the Lady. I was Sien-Mor, and I came over the warm, sweet, killing sea of the south and up the chain of islands in my brother's shadow. I am Tu'usha the Restless, and the cold hells could not hold me. And if the madwoman of the southern islands taints me though her bones are burnt to ash, you are not she and I am not what I was. I was Sien-Mor, but I am Tu'usha, and I am Zora, and we are one.

CHAPTER IX

They had to hide twice more from patrols of street guard, but at least no further Red Masks passed them on their slow and halting progress back to the Doves. Ghu did not want to be going to the Doves, but for the moment, he could only drift, rudderless.

"Smoke," Nour said uneasily, as they staggered their way along a narrow street overhung with buildings. Ghu blinked, waking out of a nightmare doze. Yes, smoke. Nour dragged him on a little more swiftly.

They hesitated on the edge of an empty openness, the Sunset Ward market. Not empty enough, though stalls and carts and awnings were gone. Lantern-light bobbed a pallid yellow, flung back at them by puddles and the slick, clean-swept stones. The street before the Doves was crowded, guards in red, with spears and swords, guards in grey with short staves, lanterns on poles, several flaring torches. The door of the Doves stood open, gaping dark. Behind the pierced window-shutters of the upper floor, though, firelight flickered red.

It was all strangely still. No crowd of clamouring folk, no urgent calls for water, for buckets. No onlookers at all, though the weight of them pressed, huddled fearfully behind shutters, on rooftops, behind doors just ajar. Still, but not silent. Grey tunics and red seemed to be arguing. A grey tunic with black ribbons trailing from his helmet turned away. He wore a sword, which the other greys didn't. He said something, and a slim girl in grey took off running, crossing the square, disappearing down the broad main road towards the gate-fort.

"I forbid it, I said I forbid it, Captain Jugurthos, I'll have you dragged before the bloody Voice herself if you interfere in this— leave it to the Revered Red Masks!" That was a red tunic, also with black ribbons on his helmet, shouting.

"And I'm not standing by to see my ward burnt down!" the grey roared. "What did you want to go starting fires for?" He said something further, not shouting quite so loudly, and waved his sword around at his guardsmen, who scattered to begin banging on doors. "Fire!" they called, men deep, women shrill. "Curfew's lifted, fire, in the Lady's name!"

"Anyone sets foot out of doors will be arrested for curfew-breaking!" shouted the red captain. "This is temple business!"

A child's wail pierced the night, and it came from the Doves. "Oh gods, oh Great Gods," Nour breathed, and took off running. Ghu, dropped and abandoned, almost fell. He caught himself on the corner of a house and took a few tentative steps after Nour, but he couldn't hope to overtake him, or to fight his way through those clustering temple guards, waiting to arrest anyone who fled out, he had no doubt.

Nour hit them with a shout. They yelled and scattered back, taken unawares, till they saw he was only one. Then they closed in, but Ghu saw a temple guardsman go down, punched in the face, and another kicked in the belly, before Nour vanished through the dark doorway.

"Leave him!" the temple captain shouted, as his men rushed to follow. "The lieutenant can deal with him, or the Red Masks. Get those people back indoors!" People were creeping out now, some with pails and jars, as if waiting for the fire to spread. It gave them an excuse, maybe. Nobody dashed into the burning coffeehouse with their water.

"Who has a cistern?" the street-guard captain shouted. "You all, get up to your roofs, start wetting everything down. Get axes, cut away any balconies that catch."

The heat would crack the adobe of the roofs and walls, given time, send tendrils of flame down the beams, but the wooden galleries which so nearly touched, house to house, would take no time at all to catch and spread, despite the night's rain and the drizzle that continued to fall.

"Curfew!" shrieked the temple captain. "Get back inside. Stay off your roofs. Close your shutters. This is the Lady's business."

A bell began to toll from the gate, five strokes, a pause, and five, repeated over and over. It seemed to embolden the onlookers. Still none made to carry their water into the Doves, where it might do some good, but more appeared from further houses; window-shutters were flung back, one group came running with a ladder and stopped halfway, in the middle of the market, uncertain. The temple guard tightened up, outnumbered now. Even women with little children in their arms turned out, staring, muttering among themselves, shifting from group to group. The general intention seemed to be to get everyone out of the nearby houses, to move folk farther away and to wet down all the nearby wooden accretions to the buildings. People ran back and forth on the flat rooftops, pulled down the reed screens in the galleries. The temple guards seemed uncertain of how far they ought to go in driving them back indoors. They closed on one group only to have everyone fade away, but to other, more distant clusters. A few threatening spears weren't backed up with any rush.

Ghu couldn't fight his way in the front door as Nour had done, not with the nervous temple guard so thick about it now. The child's distant wail was abruptly cut off, muffled, he hoped, against some loving shoulder. Surely they could get out the way he had or up to their roof. There would be doors, ladders . . . Ghu set off at a halting trot, dodging from crowd to watching crowd. Not the front door. He went up the narrow alleyway nearest to the Doves, barely wide enough for two men to pass without rubbing shoulders. It was a tunnel, overhung with galleries, close and silent, unswept, the muck underfoot muffling his footfalls. He turned down another, just as narrow. This ought to run behind the Doves and the houses facing the market. Gates, doorways set into house walls and high yard-walls, but which? There, a flicker of red behind upper windows. Locked or barred, naturally. He leapt and caught the upper edge, swarmed up and rolled over, into a clean-swept cobbled yard, with a large cistern and a grape arbour, and a shed where a goat tugged bleating at her rope and hens roosted, hunched together, undisturbed as yet. He cut the goat free as he paused for thought. She forgot the scent of smoke, headed for the pile of green fodder in the corner, so he grabbed her and shoved her out the gate, closing it again to keep her out, but leaving it unbarred. A cat fled over the wall and away. No humans, though. He'd half expected—hoped—to find the back door open and everyone dashing out. Warily, he tried the latch of the house-door. It opened. He edged through into the dark kitchen and froze.

There were two figures standing, one kneeling, dim shapes half seen. Something lay prone on the floor between them. Nour, at a guess. It felt like him.

The triple crests of the Red Masks' helmets turned, all of them, towards him, though he'd been silent. He could feel something pressing at him, a great will, a weight of fear that tried to tell him he was tiny, a weak and twitching mouseling, exposed naked and blind to the hunting fox. He frowned at it as it flowed over him, a summer's breeze, sensed on the skin, but nothing he had to bow to, nothing that could move him. The fear wasn't born of the Red Masks themselves; they merely carried it. They . . . stank. Not to the nose, no. But there was a foul air about them, a corruption of the soul. A price they had paid for sharing their Lady's power?

No. Oh no, not that, not that at all. The stink of death, faint, like a memory. The echo of a scream more animal than human, wordless, born as much of despair as of pain. Red firelight flared along the eye-slits of the masks, and his stomach turned, but it wasn't the unmanning fear their goddess desired.

I see you, Great Gods have mercy on you, I do see you, but you don't see me, he told it, the thing that lay behind the firelight. *I do not will that you see me. Not here, just a stranger, a wizard, maybe a wizard, that's all, another wizard . . .* And he stepped sideways, not so smoothly as he would have liked, when circling some crazed beast, drawing his forage knife as he moved. He came up behind the kneeling Red Mask while they still stood uncertain, merely turning to watch him, jerked the helmet back, and slashed the exposed neck, parting the cords of the throat with a blade a hand's breadth wide.

"I'm sorry," he said. "Go, be free, find your road in peace." He let the body fall, empty, but shoved it aside from falling on their victim, who groaned faintly and stirred.

"Stay down," he warned, and blocked a blow that he barely felt coming. The white staff crackled against his knife like a cat stroked in black mountain winter. The other had a sword. He could see their eyes, glowing, but little beyond that. The man underfoot was a hazard.

Light, he wanted light.

Methodically, he kicked a Red Mask, ignoring the flare of pain in his ankle, and sent it reeling back, hooked the tip of the knife under the other's helmet edge and jerked it off balance, staggering as clumsy as he, heard a cry but couldn't look around. He followed and managed to slash that second one's throat, enough to let it know it should be dead. "Go," he told it. "Take your road, if you can. Find yourself. Be safe."

It was in tatters, what soul still clung to it. Rags of memory. It crumpled.

Steel skittered on armour. It was Nour, on his feet, swaying drunkenly, and he had a sabre. His left arm hung a dead weight at his side. The Red Mask sprang back, lacings cut, lacquered plates gaping and a flake of bone exposed. It drove swiftly forward again, but Ghu lunged after it. The Red Mask went down as it stabbed with a guardsman's short sword, intending to run Nour through, but Ghu had severed the tendons of the knee. Again, he cut its throat to be sure it knew its death, sent it on its way. Nour fell forward on top of it.

"Light?" Ghu asked. He didn't want to see, but he needed to.

After a moment, though the wizard didn't speak, his hand groped, drawing on the floor. There was light, a lamp on the table suddenly sparking to life, a clean, white-gold light. Nour knelt, grey and swaying, teeth set. One side of his face was blistering, oozing dark as if burnt.

Ghu tugged the nearest Red Mask's helmet free. A brown face, desert tattooed, bearded, a young man's face, black-haired, but the staring eyes were white with cataract.

"Ilbialla save," Nour panted. "How'd you—? Nobody kills Red Masks."

"How many?" Ghu asked urgently. "Upstairs?"

"Hadidu. I called. I heard them. 'S on fire. Temple up there. Red Masks."

Nour was going to be no help, and how many could Ghu sever from the will that gave them this perversion of life before they overwhelmed and hacked him to pieces in turn? But there were living folk upstairs yet, he felt them, and maybe they were temple guard, and maybe they were Hadidu and Ivah and who knew what servants of the house, still, and the little boy with the carved camel.

"Get yourself away. I'll see."

"No blood," said Nour, but he was bleeding; it dripped from his fingertips, seeped to colour his face.

Ghu looked down. The Red Mask's throat oozed blackish sludge, old, sick, dead blood, though the yellowish fluids of a weeping wound ran swifter, staining the edge of a white shirt. "No," he agreed. "They don't bleed. They're dead. Get outside."

"'ll watch your back," Nour offered. "I'case more guard come in." He half-stepped, half-fell towards the bottom of the stairs, ended up on his knees there, sabre laid before him.

Ghu stepped around him. "Don't wait too long," he said. "They may be long gone over the roofs."

"Go." There was a puddle dripping by Nour, not any wound from his brawl with Ghu earlier.

"Tie that," Ghu advised, and went, haltingly, left hand on the wall, into darkness and the edge of torchlight. Maybe he grew too used to men who could not die.

"Master Hadidu?" he called up the stairs, but there was no answer.

The far end of the passageway dividing the second floor was crowded. There was light from the temple guard lantern, but also an odd, dim firelight, as if it were leaking around a curtain. A Red Mask in the passageway turned towards him, but five or six temple guards clustered, looking away, up the narrow stairs to where yet another Red Mask stood, staring up, like a cat at a mousehole.

The one that had seen him charged, white staff in one hand, a short sword in the other. The forage-knife was no weapon to meet that. He lowered his hand, as if terrified, numb, but he floated in the calm of snow and deep water. The Red Mask moved so slowly, it seemed so simple to duck under the white staff raised like a shield to guard the stabbing sword, to come up embraced in the Red Mask's arms and spread his other hand against the chest, feeling the man's heart, the cold, dead heart that still pulsed in weak sympathy to some slower rhythm than a running man's should. He spread fingers over it, seeing, for a moment, a young man's pride that he could do this thing, summoned to aid the Lady in restoring the city, he whom his brothers had thought a feeble, book-bound scholar, unfit for the rough world.

"You're dead," Ghu said. "Know it again. Go. Be free. Find yourself if you can and take the Old Great Gods' road." He clenched his fingers, twisted the fiery umbilical that was not quite only poetry for what he felt.

The Red Mask folded up at his feet, and Ghu went down on one knee, propping himself on the body, which was cold. His arm hurt, his ankle hurt. His heart hurt; he wasn't sure he could stand much more, in any sense.

"Wizard!" shouted a guard, a one-ribbon woman, who with her patrol had turned to watch, crowded tightly as frightened sheep, as fearful of the Red Masks as he had been meant to be. Slowly, too slowly, Ghu pulled himself back up the wall. He couldn't fight six living human folk. The sullen fire on the one remaining Red Mask was only a reflection of the odd firelight; the Lady's divine terror was fading, and with that the temple guard grew more menacing, spreading out, courage and will returning.

The last Red Mask—he hoped the last—seemed to have no interest in the slayer of its companions. It still stood halfway up the stairs, staring towards the web of darkness barring the way at the top. The glow of the fire leaked from beyond. It raised a hand. Smoke suddenly began to pour along the ceiling like a river, cascading down the stairs, too, a strange waterfall, as if some barrier had given way. Smoke shouldn't sink and crawl. There had been wizardry at work, barring passage to the upper floor. He could hear the fire now, hungry, feel the air of the house stirring with it, hear the roar. The Red Mask left off staring, or listening, or whatever it had been doing, and started up the last few steps.

A yell, a screeching cry. Something came flying down the stairs, careening off the Red Mask, knocking it sprawling. All black silk and firelit steel. The temple lieutenant fell, neck half-severed and spewing blood like a fountain. The rest came tumbling back in panic, into Ghu, knocking him into the wall. His vision went dark and dizzy, but the black silk whirled and another guardsman fell, and then ribbons were floating, knotted ribbons, loops of cord flung high and caught between fingers and teeth. The sabre slashed in front of her face, towards her own ribbon-stretching arm, and stopped short. Ribbons parted. The temple guards fell senseless, all the three or four of them left.

The Red Mask sprang up. The fury in black silk was only Ivah, panting, with a banner of dishevelled hair hanging half in her face, in knots to her knees, and a gory sabre in her hand.

"The red priests won't die," she gasped, as the smoke rose, flowing upwards now, as it should, on a wind sucked through the passage. The web of wizardry that had been blocking the doorway was torn, dissolving away, and the fire roared above them. The Red Mask picked itself up and turned to face them, weaponless, no sword, the short staff still hanging from its belt. Ivah put herself between it and Ghu. She was shaking, though the red light on it was only fire from above and the poisoning fear was in abeyance, as if judged useless and not worth the effort.

"No." He limped after the wizard, put a hand on her arm and edged past. "Me," he told the poor dead thing. "I'm the one you want. I'm the one can let you go."

It swayed, as if about to spring down the stairs.

"Come," he invited.

He met it again with his open hand, staggering back, falling with the force of the body that was abruptly dead weight, as he told her, "You died, years ago. Remember. Find yourself. Find your road." She had come in secret to the library, a scholar of Two Hills, not a wizard, she told them at the gate, oh no, just a woman of the law, seeking certain books. She had trusted the fellowship of scholars, but a librarian had reported her to the temple because those books, though they were still to be found in the lists of the great catalogue, were ones that had been burnt by the Voice's decree; they were books that wizards had studied, on the nature of godhead as the fount of wizardry. She had been arrested by Red Masks, whom her magic could not touch. They shed her spells like water, and they clubbed her with their white staves and bore her away senseless from the library. She woke gripped between them in a great black-pillared hall, with yellow-robed priests in curving ranks about her and a dome over-head shedding broken blue light from the stained glass pattern of its eye. A woman in a black robe, with a white veil over a silver mask, swayed and spoke, a child's sing-song in a high carved pulpit. *She is wizard she is damned she is not his she may be his she may see she may know*

she is wizard she is dead let her be drowned dead deep in the deep well . . .
And her nerve failed her, and her knees, and her bladder, and they
dragged her because she could not walk, into another domed house
and down, and down into darkness and damp, a cave. No priests followed, only Red Masks, and torches lit it, water stirring in a crack
in the floor, slopping into glistening oily puddles. A goddess grew
from mist and stretched out her hands, crying, "Tell them, warn
them, see me—" but the mist crawled and the face of the goddess
changed, and she said nothing, only smiled and licked her lips and
reached to the wizard, reached inside her, took her beating heart and
said, "No wizards in Marakand, my servants, my dear and loyal soldiers, my Red Masks, my own," and something tore. It wasn't her
heart. She thought it was her soul, and she cried out to the twin gods
of Two Hills as she drowned in the well, but water brought her no
release, though it was one of the clean burials. Her soul was ripped,
and braided, and knotted, and some flung away to drift broken and
screaming in the caverns and the cracks of the stone, and some woven
into a web that centred on the Lady who was not the Lady, and some
knotted into her bones, reins, chains, with hooks that tore and . . .

"Go, little sister," Ghu said. "Peace."

The corpse folded up, empty, and he sat, head back against the
wall, eyes shut, not caring that there was fire over him.

"Ghu!" The Red Mask knocked against him as the body was
dragged aside. Ivah seized his hands.

"They don't die," he said. He thought he spoke quite clearly
and sensibly, but perhaps not, if that was his voice. It wavered and
wandered and faded to a whisper. "They don't die, because they're
already dead and they don't know it; they're just rags, broken husks.
You have to cut them off from what's feeding them and holding
them here. Let them go, let the ghosts go."

He shook the last trace of the poor Five Cities wizard from his mind, the poisoning madness of the Lady with it, and opened his eyes.

"Necromancy, then," Ivah said. She was wearing only a short cotton shift. It was scorched, though she had the bundle from her bed slung over her shoulder, intact. Miracle her unbound hair hadn't turned her into a torch. "Who? Not Ulfhild, she wouldn't—"

"Who? The necromancer? She's in the well. The Lady."

"Not the Voice, then." Ivah offered a hand, heaved him up, and got an arm around his waist as he slumped against her. He fumbled to clean his knife on his trouser leg and sheathe it, clutched Ivah to keep from falling.

"Is she really the Lady?" the wizard asked.

"Yes. No, what they call the Lady is she, but I saw . . . the Red Mask saw, when she died, not now but then, when she was taken— the goddess is . . . not quite dead. Not so dead as the Red Masks. Nearly. Ivah, your storyteller. What is she?"

"Ulfhild."

Hazily, he wondered why that was an answer. But Ivah *had* answered "what." The storyteller had answered. *In the days of the first kings in the north, there were seven wizards . . .*

Ivah, almost drunkenly, giggled, the hysteria of being alive after all. "You could call her my stepmother. After a fashion." And choked on a moan. "Oh, gods and Old Great Gods. What are you, Ghu? What have I done, coming here? I just wanted to run away."

"From what?"

Something crashed. A beam.

"Down," he said. It was a furnace up there now. There could be nobody left alive. She was already trying to run, dragging him for the stairs.

"Temple guard started the fire?" he asked, choking. What kind of people burned out a house with children in it?

"I did. I didn't mean to. I heard—they smashed the door open. They were shouting. It wasn't me they were after at all. I thought I'd brought Red Masks by hiding you, but they were shouting about rebels and heretics and the priest of Ilbialla. 'Take the priest of Ilbialla alive for the Voice, take the wizard for the Voice, but kill the rest.' Hadidu got his son and his servants into the room where the girls slept, to try to get over next door. He was shouting for Nour, but Nour didn't answer."

"City. With me."

"Oh. Temple guard went after them and Shemal—the little boy—was screaming. They'd grabbed him. I ran out of my room behind them. I felt the Red Masks coming up the stairs, like some kind of—some kind of death. I panicked. I cast a fire on the guards who'd come up first—I couldn't think of anything else—and they dropped the boy and started shrieking and blundering around, and everything started burning, the beds and the rug on the floor and the doorframe. It was a—a strong fire. Not easy to beat out. It wasn't meant to be. I wanted them dead. I didn't think. Hadidu grabbed his son and the rest all came running with him. They'd all come back, just children themselves, and they'd all come back to help when the child started screaming. They could have gotten away. But the gallery was on fire and it was too late. Hadidu started them up the ladder to the roof, and I blocked the stairs, to stop the Red Masks coming up while Hadidu got everybody out, but the spell wasn't holding. As fast as I wove it, the priests seemed to just—just melt it. And everything was on fire behind me then."

"Held a while," said Ghu. "And they say nobody casts spells on Red Masks."

"Nobody kills them."

He shook his head.

In the kitchen, smoke was feeling its way over the ceiling with long fingers as they came down the last steps. Nour crouched in the yard door. He lurched up when he saw them, hissed, "You—"

"No," said Ghu, trying to put the woman behind him. "Not she, not your traitor. She saved Hadidu. They're gone. Safe away over the roofs." He hoped.

A blast of hot air rolled down the stairs, following a noise like thunder.

"Roof coming down," said Ghu, heading for the yard door, leading Ivah by the hand, catching hold of Nour's shoulder, shoving him out.

They all fell together, picked themselves up, scrambled for the gate. The fire roared overhead now; the last crash had been part of the roof, caving in, as he'd thought. In the distance, there was a lot of shouting. He could see people up on the roofs of the nearby houses, small fires being beaten out.

Ivah pulled free of him, tucked her sabre under her arm, and stood just outside the gate, fingers weaving what looked like a game of cat's cradle. She looked up, looked around at the fire, and pulled a string loose with her teeth. The rest of the roof of the coffeehouse, the weight of plaster and the brick and stone of its enclosing wings, collapsed, the burning beams of the roof and the uppermost floor crashing down, and down, right into the cellars, a pyre roaring into the heavens, scarlet planks whirling from the galleries it shed, window-screens flying, painting a tracery of light against the night. The sound was deafening and the heat unbearable; they'd be roasted where they stood. Ghu took her sleeve to drag her on in pursuit of Nour, who, stiff and slow, was plodding along the back alley towards the one that led up from the market.

"Burn the bodies!" Ivah shrieked in explanation, over the roar.

"Even the bones. If they can't count them, they won't know that anyone escaped."

But a fire that burned even bones would seem unlikely in a house like this.

"Let's go," he said wearily. "Catch up with Nour." Ghu hoped he knew where he was going. It was all very well to believe the neighbours had been willing to help and hide Master Hadidu, but he and Ivah were strangers, foreigners, and terrifyingly battered and bloodied figures, he rather suspected.

Ghu saw Nour stop and look back, waiting, but there were more figures, a gleam of firelight on helmets beyond him.

"Devils damn!" Ivah swore. "Stay here."

"No, don't—" But she shed her bundle and ran, fleet-foot, nearly naked, hair streaming behind her, flinging out a hand that trailed knotted ribbons and launched an arrow of fire that died on a Red Mask's armour.

Just the one. It was enough. The white staff flared and crackled as the long-dead wizard struck her on the side of the head. Nour fell, swarmed by shouting human guards. Too many for Ghu to kill, unless he were Ahjvar, as mad as Ahjvar, and he tripped on Ivah's dropped bundle, staggering to run to them anyway, hit his head and lay stunned and breathless and for a moment dead to everything. When he picked himself up to hands and knees the world was tilting and swimming like the sea in a storm and the guards were retreating, dragging—prisoners. Bodies. He couldn't tell, couldn't feel them, couldn't feel anything beyond exhaustion and failure and loss.

The fire roared. It was too close, too hot. They were gone. He sat up, rubbed his face with a hand that was sticky-slick with blood from the arm Nour had slashed. There were voices. Men. Shouting. Another house had caught beyond saving. He picked up

Ivah's bundle, because it was there, staggered up, took a shuffling step, holding the wall. His foot kicked against something that for a slow, stupid moment meant nothing except that he was too tired and too mistrustful of his ground to take another step, but then he thought, *Sabre*, and that Ahj wouldn't leave something of use lying, so he picked it up too. Besides, it was better than no prop at all, as he hobbled onwards. The alley was deserted now. Dark, silent, dead. He turned away from the Sunset Gate market and went, without thought. Bad foot and sabre down, quick hop, pause for breath, weight on the good leg. And again. And again.

CHAPTER X

Zora Tu'usha caught the edge of the well and vaulted out, to land gracefully on the lip of stone. She had trained grace into nerve and sinew, after all. It did not desert her now, and the strength of her body was . . . deceptive, she decided, was the word. Deceptive for those who thought strength was meant only to be used for force, for the sword's blow or the spear's strike. She thrust wet hair dripping back from her face and smiled around at her priests and priestesses. Shocked, silly, stupid faces.

"Now," she said, "*now* you hear the Lady's voice rather than the Voice of the Lady."

"Zora, dear," the Mistress of the Dance said, hesitating, "Revered Voice, will you let the dear sisters take you to your apartments now?"

"To my prison, you mean?" She had never been comfortable with the way Revered Shija watched her, Shija who had never married, who laughed and made jokes about the clumsiness and sweatiness of men, even when the boy dancers were there to hear.

"In the Lady's name, put a robe on her and take her away, if the Lady has no more to say to us," said Rahel. "Use the smoke again if you have to. That's certainly not the Lady's voice or the Lady's manner; it's the girl, taking undue advantage of the honour done her to put herself above us. Shija, since neither Revered Mina nor Revered Dur is in any fit state to resume their duties, I suggest you stay with the Voice for now. The Lady may speak again, when her Red Masks return with the priest and the wizard."

"Oh, I think not," Zora said. "Did you not listen? Do you not hear, when I speak? I am the Lady. My voice is my own, and no priestess now will stand between me and my folk."

"Zora, dear, please," protested the Mistress of the Dance. "Be a good girl, Revered Voice, and come with me." And she reached to put a hand on Zora's arm.

Tu'usha hissed and shaped the ghost of her sword from the air, sliced off the offending hand.

"Do not any of you think to lay a finger on me again!"

Shija didn't even scream. She clutched her spurting wrist to her breast, mouth stupidly agape, and sank grey-lipped to her knees. Tu'usha frowned down at her a long moment, resting the sword tip-down on the floor. The priests bunched back. She raised her head and glared, no smile now. They froze. The Beholder of the Face, Rahel, was the first to bow, deeply, abjectly, Ashir only a breath behind her. Some even sank to their knees, faces to the ground.

"Zora . . ." Shija whispered, staring up at her. Tu'usha slashed her throat and, hoisting her sodden hem in one hand, sprang lightly over the pooling blood, letting her sword dissolve again to memory as she did so.

"Come," she ordered her priests. "Leave that; the Red Masks will deal with it." She started for the stairs. Her champion took a torch to light her way, preceding her. She swept the priests after her with a gesture, the Right Hand and the Beholder behind her. "Ashir," she said over her shoulder, "after I eat and find fitting attire I will ride out and see my city, present myself to my folk. Arrange it. Find me a suitable horse, and one for my champion as well."

"Your . . . my Lady?"

"The captain of my Red Masks, old man. There used to be a festival procession, didn't there? At harvest or some such thing? Weaving through all the wards, ending up at the senate palace? Yes, I'll address the folk there this afternoon. See that the word goes out. Yes," she agreed with herself. "That will serve." Careful. Zora ordered her thoughts. *We do babble, these days, don't we?* The palace was destroyed, she had not forgotten that, but a long, broad flight of steps climbed up the steep hillside to its portico, now a long platform of tilted paving slabs and the stumps of the black pillars. That would be a fitting place from which to speak. Her folk could fill the plaza, and all would be able to see her, to hear, to worship their Lady. Yes.

Her champion . . . He had not quite died in the well. Some goddess claimed him to a sacred service and held him in life for it, but that didn't really matter. The soul was what mattered, and the soul was hers. Easier to take it from a dead man, that was all; it was not quite necromancy and not quite possession, but she held him, and she did not think the strangely knotted soul of him would reassemble itself to anything of the man he had been, to fight her. The only strange thing was that he was wizard, and she could not reach his wizardry for her use. Something to do with his goddess. She would find a way around that in time, and meanwhile, she had plenty of others.

She would have more soon. She had lain quiet within Marakand long enough. Now the folk could see their Lady ride among them. Now their Lady could command them in her own voice, not the broken babble of her Voice. Now they would know her true strength, and love her, and worship her with their whole hearts, and she would not any longer have to walk softly, fearing the wrath of the deserts and the cities of the coast. No wizards in Marakand. Soon there would be no wizards in the suburb. The suburb was Marakand. Marakand was hers. The wizards would be hers, all hers. Soon.

Ashir, puffing, fell behind, into the crowd of priests trying to follow close on the stairs, but not too close. None, she was certain, would dare to look back at the body of the Mistress of the Dance.

Her champion did. He turned a moment on the stairs, looking back.

She frowned again, quickly smoothed it out, pushed him on with her will and almost thought she felt . . . anger, from him, quickly stifled. She touched the surface of his mind. Faint echoes, grief and anger, bright splashes of joy. That was what the mind always held. Nothing to alarm her. Perhaps he had heard some mutter she did not; his function was to guard her. He, none of them, were entirely puppets. They had some freedom to act within her will. So many senses she did not quite yet understand, that she, that Zora had not yet grown into. So many threads to hold. She would learn; she would grow into herself.

Some urgency tugged at her, but no, it was a lack of tugging, an emptiness. There were Red Masks, dead, in the city. A Red Mask slain at the Eastern Wall, the past morning; she remembered that. What could kill a Red Mask? What, in her city, could tear them from her? Fire? The ones she had sent to the Doves had burned. The Doves had burned. Oh, Hadidu. He should have had the sense to flee the city, he and all his family, years ago. She felt a sort of tired sorrow for the loss of him, the loss of all her father's friends, but it was necessary. If she were opposed, Marakand would be nothing, a rabble ruled by a bickering council of old men and old women, who would fall over themselves in their haste to crawl to her brother's feet when he came. The Doves burned. They were all dead, the last of Ilbialla and the Red Masks together, but the Red Masks should not have waited to be burnt to ash and bone, they should have retreated and brought their prisoners with them, they should . . . that whisper of wind, of cold, of mountain air around the walls of the city, yes, did she remember that or was it a dream of the well? A memory of her champion's, a trailing gossamer thought, a halfling god, was it? A ghost who haunted him. No, the memory was gone. A forgotten dream. Hers? Hers-Zora's, hers-Tu'usha's, a dream-terror of mad Sien-Mor, a shadow of fear, of her brother grown great . . . The well held many fragments of dream.

Zora hesitated at the top of the stairs. The light from the dome's eye was dawn-pale. How long had she floated, suspended without thought, without time, in the Lady's waters, while Hadidu burned? An age, an age of ice, of . . . nonsense. It had been minutes, at the most, a quarter-hour. Surely the priests would have grown restive, begun to talk of dragging the sacred well for her corpse, if she had been drowned an hour or more. Surely. But they were very devout.

"The priest of the Doves is dead," she said sadly. "Dead and lost to me. The priest of Ilbialla burned. I'm sorry for him. But the city will be safer, stronger, for it. Rahel, Ashir—today will be a day of peace, of celebration. Tomorrow . . . we shall see what comes tomorrow."

"Yes, Lady. Lady, what of the Praitans? They've murdered your Voice. Your Red Masks killed the assassin, but if they go unpunished—we've had word the high king is gathering the tribes to march against Ketsim, your captain-general. This murder was undoubtedly done to his order. If words gets out in the city, if the folk learn that the Praitans have dared . . . And when we have only tonight put down an uprising of the loyalists of Ilbialla . . ."

Two children, taught to revere dreams, taught to wait in secret, forever and forever and forever, as she had been, later on, and they grew into fools and dreamed their parents' dreams, never daring, because without their gods, what were they?

"When I," she corrected gently, "have only tonight revealed a conspiracy, yes, of apostates, loyalists of the weak and forgotten gods. It was hardly an uprising against the Lady. Don't give it more weight than it deserves."

"You must not allow the temple to appear weak, Lady," Rahel persevered. "They murdered your blessed Voice! Word of this will give the Praitans heart, and it will be in the suburb by tomorrow, and flowing the length of the caravan road, growing with every mile. A faithful captain could be sent with reinforcements. Captain Ketsim has clearly failed in his rule of the Catairnans, for this to have happened."

"Do you suggest Ketsim is not a faithful captain, Revered Beholder? You don't expect him to know what every lone Praitan plots in the night, do you?"

"He has been very lax about submitting the tribute due. As you no doubt are aware, Lady, in your wisdom and knowledge. He has not sent any message at all in a month."

"He dreams he will be king," Zora said sadly. Strange, how the knowledge came to her, not as vision, which she might have imagined, but just the knowing, upwelling in her heart. "Poor fool, he is only a pilotfish, feeding on the scraps."

"I beg your pardon?"

Zora waved her away. "You will of course suggest a captain, Rahel?"

"I thought perhaps—"

"The captain of my Red Masks will ride to settle the Praitan rebellion, with a company of the Red Masks. That is all I will need."

"The captain—" Rahel swallowed and bowed. "As you say, Revered Lady. We didn't know there was a captain."

She brought him forward to her side, out of the shadows. The priests moved back. As they should.

"My champion," she said fondly, and put a hand on his arm. She felt his muscles bunch. "He will avenge the death of my beloved Voice. He will bring not only the Duina Catairna but all Praitan to kneel at Marakand's feet. *My* high king will rule all Praitan Over-Malagru. Understand, Ketsim was a tool, and he has served. The Duina Catairna is taken, and that the Praitannec high king Durandau cannot possibly endure. He lingers only to gather his kings about him before he makes war on us in the Duina Catairna. Marakand will defeat him, and my champion will be crowned king of the seven tribes. The cities of the coast and their vassal tribes—" she waved a hand, "—can be dealt with another year. Do the kings of Praitan wear crowns? No matter, we will find the proper form, and he will be—" She shook her head, wet hair flying, and ordered her thoughts again. She must make Marakand great, and safe, and strong, yes. Enough. They did not need to know more. She understood the danger, and it sickened her; she understood what drove Tu'usha now.

"Come with me, all of you," she ordered.

Rahel bowed, then scurried to catch up as Zora strode off again. Ashir grimly elbowed his way through the priests overtaking them, put himself at her other side. She smiled, turned to him, ignoring Rahel now.

"I'll be a guest in your house, Revered Ashir, until the senate palace, yes, that seems fitting, can be rebuilt to provide your goddess with a suitable dwelling. And I need clothes. Not a priestess's robes, or a dancer's. White, I think, will be my colour now. The priests of Gurhan wore white when they walked in the festival procession." And saffron for the Lady, and blue for Ilbialla, all the senior priests together, her father had told her.

She saw, out of the corner of her eye, Rahel's lips move soundlessly, shaping, "Priests of—?" and pinching together again. Had she spoken that thought aloud?

"And order a meal for me, Ashir," she said firmly, "as well as for yourself, your wife, and those senior priests and priestesses you think most deserving of the honour."

Most useful, most loyal, most loving, least likely to dig in their heels at change and require messy decapitations in the dining hall. Zora Tu'usha trusted Ashir understood that. It would be a useful test, at any rate, to see if he did.

"Except for the under-master of the dance. He will be arranging the procession." He was not among those who had come to find a new Voice. "Send to tell him so."

That of her that was still Sien-Mor thought a few more priests and priestesses would have to die, before they learned to obey their Lady, but Sien-Mor had a taste for the dramatic. Sien-Mor, Zora Tu'usha thought, had always enjoyed it a little too much, when the need to hurt others arose.

"You honour us, Lady," Revered Ashir said.

"Yes," Zora agreed. "See you earn that honouring, if you please."

But there was one Red Mask, one still living—she called it that—of those she had sent to the Doves. He had gone circling through the maze of alleys, watching, lest the priest flee. A wise man, he had been, and a cunning. He had that quality still. They were not utterly puppets such as Ghatai had liked to make, once upon a time. They had, if not will, if not memory, still some shape of themselves, some remnant of what she thought most valuable in them. And their wizardry, of course. Her servant brought her prisoners, now.

Wizards.

Nour.

"I will see the captain of the guard company that went to the Doves, first. And the prisoners."

The priests looked at one another. They had not known the guards were returned, how could they?

"The prisoners have been taken to the Hall of the Dome to await the Voice," Zora said. "But the Voice is no longer necessary. I will see them."

Strange, to walk between the black marble pillars where she had so often danced, across the circling black-and-white mosaics of the floor that had measured her paces. The high pulpit of white marble, carved into a festival procession with priests and priestesses and offerings of fruit and grain, was for a moment a loathsome thing, the throne of Lilace's degradation and shame.

Nonsense.

A throne. The Lady should have a throne. Here or in the palace, once it was rebuilt for her?

"The Lady," said Rahel loudly, "has chosen to walk among us in the body of her new Voice. Show her honour."

The guard captain, who had been following her with his eyes since she entered the hall, gaped, bowed, and flushed, looking down at his sandalled feet. She should kill him for looking at her so, her nipples dark against damp white cotton. But he, to be fair, could hardly have helped it.

Her champion, prompted by her thought, offered his scarlet cloak. That was better. She adjusted it serenely around her shoulders.

"The Red Masks I sent with you burned," she told the captain, as she climbed the tight spiral of the stairs. No, that was not right . . . But she could not see, something slid aside . . . *they burned*. Yes. "Your lieutenant was burnt with them. A faithful woman. And you bring me two wizards, when I sent you for a priest and a leader of rebellion."

The captain went down on his knees. "Lady," he said uncertainly.

She smiled encouragement. "Lady, the wizards laid a trap, and the Doves was burnt, as you say, but nobody escaped. We—the Revered Red Mask—took these two fleeing in the alleys behind the house. There were no others."

"How do you know?"

"The street guard of the ward know Master Hadidu of the Doves, Lady. I ordered them—the fools sounded the bells for fire and stirred the neighbourhood up, but some I sent back indoors and some I arrested and had sent to the lock-up at Sunset Gate—I ordered the street-guard captain, Jugurthos Barraya is his name, and I will note his resistance to my orders in my report—to have the all-in curfew rung again, and I set street guard searching house to house, all around the market, for this Hadidu and his household."

He had taken longer than he would have liked her to think to assert himself over the street-guard captain. Silly rivalries. Why did the temple guard have to play such games? They ought to have more confidence in themselves as the chosen of the Lady, superior to any mere thief-taker, ward-captain, gate-captain, or even a warden of the walls, for that matter.

"You shouldn't have allowed street guard to have anything to do with the matter."

"My Lady, I didn't mean to. They just showed up."

"I see."

Grudgingly, he added, "They were helpful, in a small way. They did organize the folk of the neighbourhood to keep the fire from spreading."

"I see," she said again.

"I permitted it." He flushed again. "But the captain nonetheless disobeyed my orders."

"You did not permit it," she said. "You went along with it. You failed to keep control of the situation. You allowed a street guard to defy you. You failed to use the power and protection of my name to assert your right to command, and you failed likewise to clear the gawking rabble from the streets."

Would he argue that there were mothers and children among them, and devout householders whose only thought was to prevent the fire from spreading to their own homes? It was not an argument she wanted to hear from her officers. They needed to be strong. The city needed to be strong, and discipline was necessary for strength. A few beaten back would have sent the others indoors of their own will and won more respect for the temple guard than allowing them to witness his reluctance to clash with the street guard. That was what he had feared: riot breaking out and himself blamed for it, for fighting with street guard. Fool.

He bowed his head to the floor. "Forgive me, Lady."

Was it useful to do so? Should she make an example of him? She shuddered at the thought of blood staining that polished floor where she had danced. She had not liked how he looked at her, not at all. But he was afraid, honestly afraid, devoutly so. He recognized her godhead, and he feared it. He thought she was beautiful. He wanted to worship her. But discipline was necessary, as well, and he was weak and foolish.

"You've been captain of the second company only two months, is that not so?"

"As the Lady says."

"Yes. And you are the nephew of our beloved Beholder of the Face?"

Rahel made no protest, no plea. Her heart did not even leap in apprehension. Cold-blooded snake.

"You'll return to the rank of common guardsman. I'll appoint a new captain myself. A new lieutenant, as well."

Silence. Then, "I only want to serve you, my Lady, however you think best."

He seemed to think he meant it, but it was the Red Masks who were the shape of his fear.

"You're dismissed," she said, and waved a hand. "Revered Beholder of My Face, you will invite the commander of the temple guard—" who had sent this company captain rather than going himself as she had intended, and perhaps he had earned a term as a mere company captain himself, "—to dine with me. Now, these wizards, these enemies of my peace, these enemies of the peace of Marakand, these schemers . . ." Babbling. Stop it. Yes. She smiled. "Let me see them."

Those standing near the prisoners drew back, leaving only guards by them. The woman was feigning unconsciousness still. Nour was only half aware, weak with loss of blood, with exhaustion. He had escaped the Red Masks once inside the Doves. She remembered. Someone had slain them, freed them. How? Ilbialla had no way to reach into that house. Ilbialla was sealed in her tomb.

How? Pay attention. Ask him. Reach inside and rip the knowledge from him. He saw. He knows. Wake him. We need to know, I need to know.

But it didn't matter. Once he was hers, once he was Red Mask, she would know. She would take him apart, then, as she killed him.

But he's Nour. He gave me a silver bangle for my birthday, when I was five, was it, or six? In her father's last year she had sold it for the rent, but he had been kind to a little girl who had few treasures. *He was my father's friend.*

She saw him, saw herself, arms about him, pulling him into the well, pulling his soul from him, like ripping out a heart. Less mess, less blood, no need for the stink and the shrieking and the— Great Gods, but Sien-Mor was insane. She felt sick at the thought of embracing him, kissing him, flesh to flesh as he died, as he drowned.

There were other ways to kill him and take what she needed,

make what she needed, of him. Cleaner ways. The end result would be the same. She had lost five Red Masks this night and one during the day past. She had a war to fight and no wizardry of her own. Moreover, though a living wizard might be deceived for a time, a wise wizard would know she was no goddess. A wizard, a scholar, would puzzle over words and bindings and maybe, maybe—no, the very tongues were lost, no scribes recalled, all gone to dust long ago and she had burned the books, the ancient books of the east, they would not find any trace, any memory, that could puzzle out those bindings and prise the gods from their slow decline to death.

No one could hear, no one could know the Lady was not the Lady was she was the Lady, Nour would not know, he would not see, he would love her and trust her and serve her, his friend's dear daughter—

Stop that.

No wizards in Marakand. She needed them. She needed servants, wizards to be the extension of her will, needed their thin, weak-watered power of the divinity of the earth, lest she break the earth and leave it burnt and dead, releasing her full strength in the world. She remembered the dead lands, the wastelands, the abomination they had made . . . Wizardry, they needed, to temper themselves. They had not come to destroy the earth. Wizardry to be controlled, wizardry that could not seek to control her, not taint her, corrupt her . . . strange that she felt so reluctant to be wizard herself again, when she had had so many, over the years, she could have chosen from. Some among them would have agreed, though few had been great enough to be worthwhile. Her champion, maybe . . . to be a man? Her stomach turned. She felt an almost physical fear, not of him in specific, but of taking another such strong soul into her own—or was it deception, was it Sien-Mor's jealousy, not wanting to share

Tu'usha's soul . . . but Sien-Mor was dead. It was her own wisdom had prevented her joining with a new wizardly soul. It was better to control, to rule, than to risk the taint of another will. Zora could be ruled. She was Zora. She did not need to be wizard. She had more wizardry at her command now than Sien-Mor had ever wielded.

Zora's fingers circled her wrist, remembering that child's slim hoop of silver, how sorry she had been when it would no longer fit. Her father said, "Put it away for your own daughter, someday," and she had, thinking, smiling, of Nour, who had brought her other things, later, a carved and lacquered cat, a tambourine. But that bangle had been the first pretty thing she had ever had of her own, because they were poor and Mama didn't like charity from her father's friends. Nour had been *kind*. They had been like family, like uncles, he and Hadidu. Sharp-tongued Beccan who owned the coffeehouse had been an auntie who fed her sweetmeats. She thought of Beccan roasting, twisting in fire, but she had seen no wife when she was the Voice, when she said when she saw the Doves would burn. Dead already, yes, she saw that now, saw infants dead and babies lost before they were ever born, and finally one who would live, had lived, and Beccan bleeding white in a white bed . . . So she hadn't killed Beccan, at least. Not her fault.

Suddenly the other wizard prisoner rolled to her knees with her fingers wound in her own long hair, twisting, and the pair of temple guard standing by, like proud cats over two dead mice, dropped as if clubbed. The woman came to her feet, bolting for the door. The Red Mask who had captured her struck her again. She fell heavily and did not move.

Blazing tawny eyes in a shallow pale face. Zora had never seen her before, Tu'usha had never seen her before, but . . . did she know those eyes? Grasslander, that was it—that was all. It went with the knotted cat's-cradle of hair.

She needed them. There were wizards to be fought Over-Malagru. There was danger stalking in her city.

Zora swallowed bile. She couldn't. Not today. Not Nour. He stared at her with wide, hazy eyes, uncomprehending.

"Oh, Nour," she said. "You should have fled Marakand long ago. Poor Nour. I am sorry."

They were waiting for judgement, all the priests, the guards. They knew the Voice would judge, declare them free of wizardry, and innocent, or wizards to be taken to the Lady in the deep well. But the Lady stood before them, and she spoke no judgement. She must.

"Red Masks will deal with them," she said in disgust, mostly with herself. Coward, weakling, who had never had to make such choices before. "Ashir, Rahel, come with me. Has anyone done anything about fit clothing yet? Or a meal?"

Ashir babbled apologies and snapped at a minor clerk, "Why haven't you seen to this?"

Rahel, with a triumphant look aside at her discomfited spouse and the bowing, apologetic clerk, told her, "I'll see to it at once." Zora left the Red Masks to drag the bodies—living bodies—of Nour and his comrade down to the cells beneath their barracks. She had had them excavate it, long ago. A couple of them had been folk of the silver mines, with knowledge of such things still left to them. Who had died there? A senator or two who had worked against her in more recent years, after the executions in the palace plaza. A brother and sister who had raised all Greenmarket Ward in riot when the wells of half the ward went dry. Temple guard and street guard had died, then, a priestess sent to speak to them in the Lady's name had been pulled from her carrying-chair and kicked to death before the Red Masks came and their terror quelled all except the fires. That had been just after Zora joined the temple; she had forgotten about that, but the smoke had blown into the dormitory window, she remembered now. She had considered ordering them sent to cages in the plaza as the defiant senators had been but had decided for a quiet disappearance, a quiet, slow, lonely death in the dark, where she could go herself to see them, to let them know their folly and how slow their deaths would be. They rebelled against her for water? They would never taste it again, and their souls would never find the Old Great Gods' road, trapped underground unhallowed. Too many of the rebel senators in the cages had been given some token earth; only a few had lingered, fading, forgetting, their bones going chalky in the sun, and even their ghosts were gone, now. Who else? A priest who dared cry out in condemnation of the parents who brought a wizard-born child to her, accusing their own. Poor child. She had left the priest to die, with much time to think of his sin in defying his goddess, but the child she had killed. He was no use to her, too young, nothing in his mind but fear and childish lessons and the frightening discovery that his dreams held foreknowledge. Had he not foreseen this, the betrayal of his parents, or had he not believed his own foreseeing? She had drowned him, swift and merciful, out of pity.

Yes. Fitting. Nour and his fellow wizard were likewise rebels. If in her mercy she spared them the death of the well, the living death of the Red Masks, their ghosts could learn to thank her. Meanwhile, Red Masks could seal them in, somewhere down there, leave them to deal with at her leisure. She might change her mind. It was merely sensible, to wait until she was more—more settled. She didn't have to take pleasure in what needed to be done. She wasn't Sien-Mor. It still needed doing, just . . . with a calm mind and cool head. Later.

Meanwhile, she had her city to claim. And she was hungry for her breakfast. It had been a long time since she had tasted food.

CHAPTER XI

The baby, as babies do, was fussing. Hungry, as babies are. The girls were sleeping with Auntie in the other room, so Talfan had the luxury of a bed nearly to herself, but she pulled on a caftan and went out into the screened porch, where there was more air and the scent of herbs hung to dry. Rain pattered on the roof, dripped in the leaking corner. The night air smelt clean, made her think of the mountains, always seen, never noticed, to the south. Her husband had seen the mountains, gone up into them, too, nearly got himself killed in a war there that had nothing to do with him. One of his friends had family there, he said. It seemed an unlikely reason for a caravan-gang to end up in the mountains. The gang was going out as mercenaries and not bothering with trade, was her guess, and he didn't want her to know he was sliding down to one step above a desert brigand. He was certainly shifty on that point. Next time he was home, she'd try harder to worm it out of him. No baby, this time, at least, while she was still nursing. He'd been gone long enough he ought to be home soon, certainly before this one was weaned. She'd been expecting him back a month now.

The rain pattered, the leak dripped, the baby sucked and smacked and made noises of contentment. The night was hers. Sitting on the cushioned bench where her solitude-loving eldest daughter so often slept—the wretched girl was going to turn out a poet, or worse, a wanderer like her father, if she wasn't careful—Talfan stretched out her legs, leaned back against the wall, and shut her eyes.

There was the scent not only of rain on dust from the lane below but smoke, coming in eddying gusts. Something was burning, somewhere in the city. Had she heard distant ward bells ringing the alarm for fire in her sleep?

Talfan shifted the baby to her other breast and was heading indoors to climb the stairs to the roof when Watcher, the old brown bitch, set up a great clamour in the courtyard. Not any mild bark to let her know some cat had dared perch on the wall, either. Talfan went down the stairs to the kitchen behind the shop sure-footed in the dark, deposited the now-wailing and angry baby in the cradle there, and grabbed the lead-weighted cudgel that hung by the curtained door into the shop. But Watcher's attention wasn't on the house, and nothing rattled the latch of the street door. She went to peer through the tiny, deliberate crack in it to be sure. Silence. And street guard would come with lanterns.

Temple guard would come with torches and Red Masks and great shoutings that she should open in the Lady's name, she was certain. Back through the kitchen. The baby was screaming and Auntie calling from upstairs to know what was wrong, little Iris wailing in half-awakened sympathy.

"Come take the baby!" Talfan called, for what good that would do; Auntie didn't have what the little mite wanted. She fastened her sash and unbolted the yard door.

Watcher was at the far end of the long, narrow enclosure, over-looked by Talfan's own walls on two sides and a neighbour's on the other, filled with laundry lines, the cistern, a weedy vine that got no light and never bore fruit. The doorway in the high wall there let out onto a narrow alley, overhung with porches and dark even by noon. Very private. She got close enough to see Watcher up on her hind legs, clawing, before something came over the wall, slithering down to land with a bump and a muffled noise that she realized was a sob even as the dog, her bark changed to welcome, jumped and knocked the small figure sprawling.

A child, cold and wet and reeking of smoke, shaking, and he flung himself against her, weeping, choking. Talfan knelt and gathered him in.

"Shemal? *Shemal?*" Sweet gods, Hadidu's Shemal. "Where's your papa?" she asked urgently. "Where's Hadidu?"

Hard to make out a coherent word, but a flung hand indicated the door. She could have figured out that much; little Shemal would not have been scaling her wall on his own. She put the boy behind her, waving back Auntie and the girls, the whole clan turned out by now, and lifted the bar of the gate with one hand, the cudgel ready in the other. In case.

Hadidu slipped in and had it barred again before she could even be certain it was he, except that Shemal abandoned his grip on her to seize him.

"Red Masks," he said. "They came for Nour. The Doves is burning."

She felt as if the beaten earth of the yard beneath her feet had given way, and she was dropping into some pit.

"Girls, come inside," Auntie ordered briskly. "Bring the little boy. We'll make some coffee."

But Shemal clung and wouldn't let go, till his father knelt, arms about him, whispering. Then he let Jasmel take him by the hand.

Hadidu stayed where he was, on his knees in the rain, once Auntie had firmly shut the door on them.

"You weren't followed." Old Great Gods, if Hadidu had been followed . . . but he wouldn't have come here if he thought that. "I'm sorry." She put a hand on his arm. He wore only a caftan pulled on hastily and was barefoot and shivering. Shock, she decided. He needed sweet coffee and dry clothes as badly as his son. "Tell me quickly, before we go in. The girls don't need to hear the worst." If they hadn't already.

"They came for Nour," he said, never lifting his head. "Broke down the door. I shouted to him, but—I never saw him. He didn't answer. I don't know where he was. They all knew what to do, the servants, the way over the roofs. I took Shemal—I had to take Shemal, I couldn't look for Nour—but there were temple guard and Red Masks coming behind. They pulled him from me, Shemal, and—my lodger, you know, the scribe, she rented a room—she was a wizard, and I never knew, she attacked the guardsmen and held the stairs—against Red Masks, Talfan—while we got up to the roof. But it was on fire and—we got over next door and along until a safe house and down to the back street. Master Farnos took the servants and was going to pass them on, get them away right over the wall to the suburb before dawn if he could—"

Master Hadidu at the Doves always took on other people's waifs and strays, the unwanted bastards, the stammerers, the simple, the deaf, the birth-marked (Talfan looked after such things herself—amazing how a raspberry-blotched face kept most people from ever seeing beyond the mark), and gave them a bit of work before they drifted off into worse trouble or better positions. Next-to-free labour it was and considered by some charity on his part and by others sharp practice—except they were the wizard-talented youths of Marakand,

and when they vanished, it was with a caravan of the eastern road or a merchant of the Five Cities, and the Five Cities was where they usually ended up, apprenticed here and there, scattered. Marakand's wizards in waiting. Some, of course, were only what they seemed, and it was his charity, and he did train them well and find them better positions. But for the last month, awaiting the right caravan, he had had three, all very young, one runaway fortunately found by Jugurthos and two whose parents had heard rumours of rumours of a refuge.

So those children were safe. Maybe.

"Nour may have gotten away too," Talfan said. "He must have. Surely."

Hadidu shook his head. "I saw Jugurthos, briefly. He hadn't seen Nour. And Ivah, the scribe—a mercy if she died before the Red Masks took her."

Talfan didn't want to say it. She'd seen how he watched the woman as she sat at the table by the door, brush or pen in hand. "Hadidu, if anyone betrayed Nour . . ."

"Betrayed us both," he said faintly. "They were shouting about the priest, too. They knew who I was."

"She—"

"No. No, Talfan. Ivah didn't know anything. She fought them."

"A wizard, to turn up lodging at your house. You don't take lodgers."

"I liked her," he said. "We have—we had the space. Convenient to the market." He got to his feet, wrapped his caftan tighter. "I won't stay," he said. "Varro isn't home, is he?"

"No. But I started expecting them last month. It could be soon, Old Great Gods willing."

He nodded. "Keep Shemal for me? Hide him? I don't know, dress him as a girl, maybe nobody will notice, among all yours. And send him away. Out of the city. Maybe someone in your husband's gang has family that would foster him, away west." He sounded like he was arranging for the boy's funeral. "Just—let him forget Marakand. Worship the god of the land he comes to and be at home there."

"Hadidu!"

"I can't bring him up like this."

"You're in no state to make decisions tonight, and if they've followed you, we're all as good as dead anyhow, so you might as well stay."

Watcher, who'd settled down to sleep again, leapt up in renewed barking. There was a glow of lantern-light beyond the wall. Nobody would carry lights but the guard. She ignored the dog, gestured at the wall. Hadidu, after a moment, caught on and made a stirrup of his hands to boost her up. As she'd expected, the guards, two of them, were staring at the door, watching, listening, not looking up. One was a stocky man with officer's ribbons trailing from his helmet, the other a short and very comfortably curved woman. If she'd had a big rock . . .

Talfan slid back down and dropped the bar. Captain Jugurthos and his adjutant Tulip surged through, seeing, like Hadidu, to the barring of the door themselves.

"What are you doing, running around with lights?" Talfan demanded. "Idiots!"

"Patrolling," said Tulip. "We sent the rest along the alleys on the other side. Not bad sorts, but no loss if they get lost."

"Out of your ward? This far out of your ward?"

"Pursuing fugitives," said Jugurthos, and embraced Hadidu. "Sweet gods be thanked, you're safe, at least."

"Nour?"

"Yeah," Jugurthos pulled off his helmet and dragged a grimy hand through his hair, standing it on end. "Hadi, I'm sorry. I didn't know, when we met at the baker's, but they got Nour in the back lane, him and the scribe both. Just one Red Mask, but he had plenty of temple guard to help him. They've been taken to the temple. There wasn't any chance. If I'd gotten to them first—I had some trusted patrols out searching—but we were too late."

"We're all dead," Talfan said.

"Nour doesn't know me," Tulip said.

"Much good that'll do when they take Jugurthos before the Voice," Talfan observed.

Nour couldn't be saved. Nour was dead, even if he still breathed. Talfan made her heart stone. That was done. Over. Lost. What could be saved? That was what she needed to ask. The children. Auntie. They had plans, they had always had plans, she and her aunt, who wasn't really any kin at all, but who had been nurse to Jugurthos when he was small, in the palace-like Family Barraya mansion in the eastern shadow of Palace Hill, before the earthquake took his grandparents, and his parents were murdered by the temple and he was dispossessed, to drift up, a grudged fosterling of the distant cousin who had grovelled to the temple for the Barraya inheritance, in the street guard. They had plans, and part of the plan was that Talfan didn't know the plans. Because they'd always known this might happen.

The baby would have to stay with her, though. Watcher— Watcher had better go with Auntie. Protection for the girls. They could muzzle her till they were out of the city. There was a way, a house built against the wall not so many streets distant, with a tunnel in the cellar. It emerged under a neglected Family Barraya mausoleum, in the long stretch of private cemeteries and tombs between the city and the ravine where it plunged down from the southern mountains. The brothers that owned the house would have to disappear too, since they were known to her and to Jugurthos, though not to Hadidu and Nour . . . She was ticking points off on her fingers. Hadidu seemed to have lost the will to move. She tugged him up by the arm.

"Inside," she said. "Something to drink and clean clothes. Ju?"

"I should get back to the fort," Jugurthos said. "I can't do any good here. There are people to warn. Things to clean up."

"Things to burn," Tulip said.

"That too. Hadidu, old friend, I'm sorry. You and Talfan stick together, make your own plans after we're gone."

"If the temple guard come for you—"

"We won't stick around to fight and be taken."

"We won't?" asked Tulip. Jugurthos gave her a long look. "Oh," she said. "Yes, it'll have to be that way, won't it? Why did I ever let this man talk me into bed? Well, they say a ghost can keep its secrets in the face of the gods themselves, but I intend to haunt the fortress. The men's barracks, I think."

Talfan saw them out, barred the yard gate yet again, and urged Hadidu into the house, where Shemal was already asleep, wrapped in a quilt on the floor. Jasmel and Auntie were packing a bag of food; Iris and Ermina, already dressed, sat side by side on the bottom step, solemn-eyed. Talfan squeezed her eyes shut a moment.

"I listened at the window," Auntie said. "I'm very sorry, Master Hadidu. Master Nour was a good man. Jas, you go get your clothes on, and bring down Ermina's from last year out of the yellow basket for Shemal."

Too soon—Watcher whining and pawing at the improvised muzzle, Iris scrunching her face heroically against wailing, Shemal silent and almost stunned, and Jasmel and Ermina being self-consciously grown-up and brave, they were gone, a little band of shadows flitting down the alley in the night.

"Where are we going?" Hadidu asked. He was dressed in clothes left behind by Varro, with the cuffs rolled up, and a pair of Auntie's old sandals with the soles worn paper-thin. The sweet coffee had put some life back into him.

"We stay here," Talfan said. "There's a cellar, from the house that was here before the earthquake. The street got shifted over a bit when they rebuilt, and in my front wall, under the shelves, there's a block that can be moved. It doesn't bear any weight. The cellar beyond's half-filled with dust and rubble. You can't stand upright. But it's dry, and it's hard to find, and if the house seems empty— we'll leave the yard gate unbarred—they'll think we've fled. Ilbialla and Gurhan willing."

In the night, the past was very present. Hadidu sat unsleeping, thinking of Shemal, keeping company with his ghosts.

In the coffeehouse called the Doves, by the Sunset Ward market, Esau, son of the hereditary priestess of Ilbialla, his playmate Nour, and Nour's annoying, hair-pulling toddler sister Beccan were all swept down the stairs to the cellar by Nour's father at the first rumble and shudder of the earth. It may not have been the most sensible place to hide, but the Doves did not fall. They cowered there, crying, while the grown folk, family and guests alike, prayed. Hardly able to tell what was street and where the neighbours' houses had stood, they emerged into a sunset of bloody dust and a landscape of ruin. Ilbialla, the goddess of the well in the market square, walked amid the rubble as a white-haired old woman, though Esau knew she was young and beautiful, really. She showed them where to dig, setting glimmers of a sacred light over the living, so they could shift stone with whatever they had, spades and forks and broken sticks, bare hands. Even Esau, escaping the crippled grandfather at the Doves who was minding all the little children of the street, tried to dig, tugging on stones he was too small and weak to lift until his nails were torn away and his hands stiff and black with blood and grime, until Ilbialla herself came and picked him up, carrying him off to his mother. Their house was gone. Grandmama sat by the low wall that surrounded the shallow steps down to the sacred pool in the corner of the market square, rocking his baby sister. Mama, grey-faced, set bones and wrapped broken bodies amid the ruins of the market booths. Esau's little dog was dead. So was Papa. He had been standing in the door of his cobbler's shop on the ground floor of their house when the earth flung the street skyward and dropped, and the lintel came down on his head.

Time blurred. He didn't know how many days it had been, but people came from the temple in the night, and in the morning there was a square tomb built over the steps down to Ilbialla's well, and the goddess was silent. The folk of the ward, and folk from Riverbend Ward as well, gathered, with pick and hammer and chisel, and set about bringing it down, but lightning snapped over it at the first stroke, and the builder who had wielded the first pick dropped dead, and then the carpenter's apprentices, and while they all stood, while Mama, weeping, called and called the goddess, the Red Masks came, priests such as the city had never seen, their faces hidden, and guardsmen in red tunics, and the crowd fled shrieking, and Mama, who didn't flee, they hacked to pieces where she knelt before them.

Had he seen or only made the pictures from the stories? Hadidu thought the former. He thought he had been there. He remembered running, running to the house, which was a ruin, but Grandmama was there with the baby, filling baskets with what could be salvaged and carried over the Doves. Did he speak, or did he simply sob and shriek? He didn't remember. Did she cry out? She shushed him, he remembered, but the baby, who was teething, wailed and wailed. Grandmama boosted him up, and he slid scraping down into the cistern. It had cracked in the earthquake and all the water had run

away, but it was wet inside still, and dark, and the sides were slimy. The
wooden lid fell closed above him.

Outside, the baby cried, and Grandmama sang over her.

There were sounds. He couldn't see out the crack that had let the water
run. Voices, so he knew now, it had been temple guard, not Red Masks. Or there
had been temple guard with the Red Masks, anyway. And Grandmama had
shrieked and the baby had wailed and then there had been horrible sounds,
and the baby had not cried, and Grandmama was silent. Then nothing. He
had muffled his mouth in his tunic and sat, and sat, and waited. When the
lid slid scraping aside it was dark, except for a little dim lamplight, shaking
and unsteady. A voice called him, softly.

"Esau? Esau, are you there?"

It was Nour and Beccan's father, from the Doves. He had hardly dared
make a sound, even then, but the master of the coffeehouse must have heard
something, whimper or gasp, or seen a shadow press back from the light,
because arms reached and he was hauled out, his head muffled against a
caftan so he wouldn't see—what he struggled to see, what the small lamp
held by another neighbour, the grumpy baker, showed, which was—was
pieces—was—but Nour's father folded his head into the breast of his caftan
and muttered a whisper about the lamp and they took him away.

He was never called Esau again.

Hadidu didn't much like sitting in the close, quiet dark of the
hidden cellar. He did not.

The Red Masks didn't come to the apothecary's house that night. In
the morning, Talfan left Hadidu hidden and went out briefly, feeling
as if she walked to her own execution, to hear the rumours of the
streets. There were plenty of them. Rebels and heretics had set fire to
Sunset Ward. A secret priest had prophesied the ending of the Lady's
rule and the return of Ilbialla. The Voice had been assassinated and

a Praitannec army was marching on the city. The Lady had emerged from her well in human form and would show herself to the folk of the city. That one grew and grew, as she returned home to make a pretence of normalcy, opening up the shop, until in the afternoon it became, the Lady was coming, the Lady was riding through the ward, on her way to the plaza below the palace.

Surely not. Surely . . . after a word with Hadidu, Talfan locked up the shop, and, baby in a sling and a sharp and slender knife in her pocket against the worst, the pointing the finger, the cry, the veiled heads of Red Masks turning her way, made her way out to the main thoroughfare of Clothmarket Ward, to see for herself.

Ghu sat up, cold and stiff and aching, blinking at daylight. Day. He had crept into this ruin as the drizzle died and dawn began to paint the streets in misty light. Now the sun shone. Noon, more or less. He stretched, sitting, loosening the muscles of neck and back. The cut on his arm hurt; he'd forgotten about that, but his foot didn't seem quite so bloated. That was from lying down. He should stay lying down, with his foot up on something. It wouldn't heal if he kept running around on it. Why had he woken? He felt rather as though he had been running, hopping, crawling ever since Ahjvar's nightmares woke him. No food, either, but sleep, sleep was like warm arms, a deep and resonant voice, enfolding him, calling him. But Ahjvar . . . Something was wrong, something bad. He had known it in the night; he had told Nour . . . nothing. He knew nothing, had nothing, just the hollow heart of loss, a sense of great wrong. And he needed to be . . . out, not here, not within city walls. Sun. Horses.

Nour would be dead by now, and Ivah, Old Great Gods receive their souls—but the Gods could not. They would be broken and scattered, lost even to themselves, not even ghosts, like the poor soul-remnants of the Red Masks in the Doves. Not his doing, not his betrayal, but he felt as if he carried their deaths anyway, because he hadn't saved them. One Red Mask too many, and they were dead and profaned. Red Masks, dead and enslaved by a necromancer devil.

He could do nothing for Nour and Ivah. If ever he met them again, well, they would try to kill him, and he would free what was left of them then, but if the Lady was a devil, and the Northron storyteller was likewise, he was certain he had sent the little bard Deyandara riding out Over-Malagru with a third. That was a responsibility he carried as well, and what ought he to do about it?

Ahjvar . . . that was where cold thought failed him. He should admit Ahj dead as Ivah was dead, as Nour was dead, dead and lost, and he should go back to his road. Maybe follow the little bard. Maybe go west, chase the sun to the great ocean's edge. Maybe. The shape of sun and horses and green hills tugged at him. Back to the Praitan hills, then. Turning towards Nabban. The need to be outside the city pressed at him, the same need that had put him in Ahjvar's way, and before that, set him on the road to the Golden City, sent him to the harbour, and the islands . . . No, he told it. *I don't want to go on. I want to find Ahjvar.*

Whatever he did, he needed to know where he was. A ruin, that was in his mind, a hazy memory. Wandering aimless, only to get himself away from the stir and the fire. He thought he had wandered north, passing through a narrow, gateless opening in a wall. Clothmarket Ward, perhaps, where the wool warehouses and the workshops of the weavers stood shoulder to shoulder. He had found this ruin, unroofed, a pit with walls head-high along a narrow lane and overgrown with raspberry canes within. He had crawled down through a broken gap in the wall. It smelt of dogs and rubbish, and, as he crawled, bruised leaves. No beggars, not this rainy night.

The knots securing Ivah's bundle were odd. Maybe some Grasslander magic lay in them. He freed them easily enough and unrolled the coat that was the outer wrapping. It had all been tied so that the scabbard was the core of the roll and its mouth was uncovered; the hilt would be hidden within the roll. She could have set her hand to it without needing to untie anything, plunging it between the folds at the top. Clever. He cleaned the blade on raspberry leaves and wiry grass, and his own knife while he was thinking about it and sorted through what else he had carried off. Short, recurved bow and a decorated quiver, a silk purse and a leather one, the former light, the latter heavier. He did not open either. Boots, a cylindrical leather scroll-case, a folded packet of clean cotton rags—women's necessities, that—a skein of red yarn. For her string-weaving wizardry? Clearly it was what she had held to be the bare essentials, anyway. It seemed Ivah had always slept ready to run, to vanish into the night at a moment's notice. But she had not chosen to do so, in the end.

She had carried no food. No more had he; it was all with Deyandara, save Ahjvar's precious coffee. The raspberries were ripe but few remained. Birds had been at them, and the rain in the night had left them grey puffballs of spores. After a moment's consideration, Ghu bandaged the cut on his arm with a couple of the cloths, wrapped his headscarf more in the manner of a turban, for what that would do to change his looks, and traded Ivah's caravaneer's coat, grey, striped with creamy white, for his own. Not only did it change the colour he had last been seen wearing; it got rid of the slashed and bloody sleeve. Her coat was a fine one and fit him not too badly, only a little tight across the shoulders. He transferred the contents of his pockets to hers, found them already full of string and ribbons and leather cords, as well as a sheathed knife. He rolled his coat around her boots and weapons and left that bundle deep under the raspberries, with his blessing for what beggar found it and a hope the finder would not have Nabbani-black hair, but he added the rest of her belongings to his own bundle. String was always useful, and the scroll-case could be pawned or sold, if need be. He was no archer, and the sabre he found too cumbersome.

Last, he bandaged his ankle again and gritting his teeth, forced his boot on. It would swell, but a barefoot caravaneer would stand out. He clambered to his feet.

Bad. Bearable. It would have to be.

Ghu chose the best moment he could to limp up onto the street, yawning and scratching, a man who'd been enjoying the city maybe a bit too well, who'd found himself without coin or time enough to seek better lodgings, when the curfew rang. Nobody paid him much heed.

This lane met another. He followed it, turned up an alley he thought he remembered, squeezed—a big man would have to turn sideways—past the corner of a building set on a different alignment, some earthquake survivor. It broadened, climbed several uneven steps, and came out on a proper street, or as much of one as Marakand seemed to manage away from its warehouses, so narrow that two carts could not have passed. It must be a main thoroughfare, though, since the ground-floor rooms all seemed to be small shops rather than blank house-fronts. He stood for a moment, leaning on a wall and getting his bearings; it was crowded enough that he was just another passer-by up from the suburb, not an intrusion among neighbours.

There seemed an unusual tension among the folk. The crowds around the shopfronts huddled close. Their talk was low and urgent. Someone would break off, move to another with speed and purpose. People went in and out of houses, and every time one went in, more emerged when that one came back out, some hastily pulling on caftans, fastening belts or sandals. He was watching a tide of news flowing up the river of the street, a running fire's edge, Ghu realized. It was hard to read their faces. Cautious reserve, excitement, eagerness . . . the younger they were, the more excited. Children were racing up and down the street, louder than all the rest, crying out to one another, screaming, squealing with what seemed an excess of excitement and outright joy.

"Are they coming this way?" he thought he heard and "The Lady is coming! The Lady! The Lady is riding to the palace steps!" but mostly they spoke a babble, a mix of the two mongrel languages of Marakand into a third, and he had to fish for words. As he fished, though, they came.

Two girls, older ones, almost grown, hugged one another while a third clapped her hands in excitement, seized both her friends, and led them all running hand in hand away, weaving through the ever-thickening crowd. A gang of boys chased after them, calling out. They caught up, merged, and whirled for a moment, into some dance, laughing and shouting, the boys circling, the girls in the middle. A few older women darted in to join them, swaying and stepping, hands in the air, and men, too, different steps, hands low, gesturing, and more women, and then the three girls who had begun it led off down the street and the ring turned into a line, spinning off into other knots and songs. He watched, bemused, while about him the talk rose in intensity. But the excitement that was spreading was not setting them all alight, no. There were wary faces, worried faces, doubtful faces, but very few of those so much as whispered together. Mostly they smiled and nodded. Only their eyes spoke of doubt or fear. Only a few put heads together and slipped away altogether, indoors or down narrow alleys. Reed blinds were rolled up in porches and galleries overhead, carved screens folded open. Whatever the cause of the stir was, they expected it to come this way.

Not, possibly, a good thing for a fugitive so weakly disguised. And then, while he was hesitating over retreating down the alley at his back or crossing the street and striking out towards the central ward, whatever it was—Spicemarket?—the crowd began to flow. Initially it was a drift, not in the direction the dancers had gone but towards the south. "Market," he thought he heard. "Maybe the market . . . she'll speak there, too, maybe . . ." It started with a handful, going purposefully, others peeling away from their own clusters to join them, as when a few on the fringes of some flock of gleaning starlings grow uneasy and take flight, and their flight draws more after them until suddenly the whole sky is black and all are in the air, rising and wheeling above the field as one. The whole street seemed at once to be in motion, a flowing river, hasty strides lengthening to a run. Ghu backed against the wall.

Not everyone ran. There were still people up on their balconies, still the clusters in the doorways and among the baskets and trestle-tables that spilled out of many shops onto the street. Ghu struggled to keep himself at the rear of the crowd, against the wall, as a surge of bodies engulfed him. He winced as someone brought a foot scraping down his ankle. Someone else caught his elbow as he staggered, impersonal kindness that almost made him yell, the slashed arm a brief agony. The man, not noticing the suppressed flinch, let him go with a nod as he found his balance again. The crowd that remained cleared the centre of the street, piling up on doorsteps and into every alley mouth; it stood and craned and jittered with its nerves. He spared a moment to be amazed there were still folk of the neighbour-hood left to stand and stare, after the great outpouring towards the market, but they were gathering from all the ward, rushing to this thoroughfare. That was good. It meant the faces of strangers would not stand out.

"Priests," muttered a black-haired woman to his other side. "Ashir and Rahel themselves. And Red Masks behind them." She subsided, chewing her lip, and carefully shaped a smile, jiggling the baby on her hip. Ghu gave her an innocent smile in turn and looked away again. The priests came on, singing.

They walked, men and women in yellow robes. Most were carrying long yellow silk banners, with characters black on white medallions that looked like simple Nabbani, though he hadn't the faintest notion what they said. In the midst of them a group of girls and boys in facepaint and scarlet robes played flutes and drums, while others danced before and through them, figures far more complex than those the spontaneous young people of the street had performed, all moving as one girl, one boy, bells on their ankles sweet and silver.

Behind them came Red Masks. They were veiled, not armoured, and though there was a tightening up of the crowd, a more concerted pressing back against the walls, people did not react with the limb-loosening terror he had seen even temple guard afflicted with at the coffeehouse, though the woman with the baby clutched it tightly to her breast, a hand up as if to shield its head from their very gaze. As if that wasn't protection enough, she then sank down on her heels, head bowed over the little thing, whispering to it. Ghu wanted to see, but he had to crane and twist, bobbing up and down to find any clear line of sight; too many taller folk in the way. Following the Red Masks were two riders. One was another Red Mask, armoured, a spear braced in his stirrup and a saffron banner with three tails trailing from it, the other a young woman dressed in a white tunic and leggings of leather, with her head uncovered, soft black hair rippling unbound over her shoulders. She had a lovely face, like a desert woman without tattoos, dark and narrow, the line of her nose a perfect parallel to her brow, her eyebrows flying up at the outer corners, like a lilting laugh in ink. Her keen eyes searched the crowd, with a smile for every person whose gaze she captured. No laughter on her lips. None in her eyes. Some cried out, reaching hands to her or fell to their knees, weeping. She rode a coppery chestnut stallion that sweated and rolled its eyes, chewing its bit, not a horse that should be in the midst of a crowd at all, and the mounted Red Mask's black mare was sidling and fidgeting, held on too tight a rein, showing the whites of its eyes as it tossed its head. Frightened horses, constrained by more than leather and iron and human will. No goddess frightened horses or tolerated those who mistreated beasts of any sort; no sane god of the earth would view kindly any human who did so. Ghu felt in his own knees a little of what the Red Masks seemed to inflict on those nearby when the red light of the Lady's power touched them.

The Lady began to turn, looking his way. He bowed his own head, a simpleton child, a stray of no account. There were enough taller folk before him that he would have had to make great effort to see her face again. He felt her eyes, though. They passed over, moved on. He did move a little aside then to watch her passing, the slender shoulder, trim waist. Not, he thought, a rider. That stallion would have her off and be into the crowd and probably killing in its angry panic if she let the grip of her will on its mind falter. The Red Mask, though . . . the armoured Red Mask like a captain at the Lady's side, he rode well, if only his horse were not so terrified.

The Red Mask wrenched the horse's head savagely around, and it wheeled, reared and struck out, scattering the second group of Red Masks who followed close on foot, though they moved only so much as was needed, without fear, even without urgency, while ranks of spear-bearing temple guard behind shouted alarm and the onlookers shrieked and shoved back against those behind. But the horse plunged trampling in place, mouthing the bit, and was hauled around again even as the Lady glanced back. The Red Mask took station at her side once more, her dumb shadow.

Ghu was on his knees, and as the crowd, exuberant in the aftermath of its brief alarm, surged past, pressing against the temple guard, crying out for the Lady's notice, he wrapped his hands over his head against their kicking and shoving. Darkness. Snow, and wind, and the mountain night. The cold depths of the river. His mother had drowned him.

Ahjvar.

Ahj had died and died and his soul was chained to his body and Catairanach's curse twisted fate and chance so that he never was free to die. Ghu had known since last night, he had known it, if he had dared to chase what he heard in the silence; he had felt the hollowness, the place where Ahj should have been, become an emptiness in the world. She took wizards, and if she drowned them in her deep well as the city said, she did not discard them afterwards. Living or dead, ghost or monster, Ahjvar was a wizard, and so was the thing that possessed him. If he could not reach his magic, that did not strip it from his blood. He was a wizard, and the Lady had taken him and severed his soul; it was not the freedom, not the death he had longed for. It was possession worse than Hyllau's murderous-mad ghost; it was perversion worse than any slavery, an abomination, a defilement of the dead and a torment of the soul that could not escape the world's pain.

It was beyond weeping for. Ghu stayed where he was, curled up in the darkness, shivering, with the blizzard of Father Nabban's mountain thrusting fingers into his bones. There were distant voices, but they passed, faded, a tide ebbing and leaving him, the street clearing, pursuing the Lady. Someone touched his shoulder once and spoke kindly but went away when he did not stir. Someone, less kindly, tugged at the bundle still slung around his body, but someone else shouted and footsteps ran clattering away. Vague voices poured over him, something about awe of the Lady taking them that way, sometimes, leave him. They went away.

Another touch came thrusting at him, butting. Beyond weeping, but there were tears, and something found the salt on his face, two muzzles, one licking, one sniffing, each shoving at the other. There was no spring blizzard, and if there were, he had still the mare and foal to find, and there was no voice of the god, no whisper of his goddess, only the need to get up, to go on, because he had been lent life and it was not his to throw away, was it?

Ahjvar was not his, only something he had found for a little time, and there was still his road to follow. He could do one more thing, though. He could destroy the body and unchain the last rags of the dismembered soul. He was sorry for Ivah, sorry for Nour, but Ahjvar had the greater claim on him.

The dogs flinched back when he pushed himself up, sitting on his knees. One crouched and growled. It was a gaunt, dun-coloured dog with a black stripe down its back and black wolf's ears, which flattened when he looked at it, changing its growl to a whine. A second shadow, paler, mottled ash and silvery like sand under moonlight, flitted around behind it, tail stirring, ears folded back. It rolled over, exposing its belly. All legs and ribs. He leaned back against the wall, tilted to find the sky, blue and clear and beyond human reach forever. He could drown in the sky. Maybe he did. The sun moved, and the dogs disappeared. People hustled up and down the streets, talking, uneasy, excited. The Lady came to them, rode among them warning of danger. Their enemies gathered strength in the west and in the east, their land of Catairna, their province, given to the Voice of the

Lady by the desperate goddess there, who had been beset by wizards and so sought her sister's aid, rose in rebellion and sent assassins into the city. The faithful Voice was dead, murdered. No one was safe. Enemies, wizards prepared to assault the city. An enemy gathered strength far in the west, but the Lady would make Marakand great once more. They must all be prepared to fight when the day came, or the men must. The women had a greater task. Marakand needed folk, true-born Marakander folk, who could go out to the new lands they would win Over-Malagru, to serve the new king, the Lady's chosen, who would go to Praitan to teach and civilize the seven Praitannec tribes. Young men went to the palace plaza, to take an oath to join her militia, to be assigned companies by ward, to learn to stand and fight for when the fated day should come and Marakand would close the bronze gates of its Western Wall. Ghu slowly drifted down from the sky and frowned across the street. Shadows stretched out, the sun turning towards setting.

He understood, he thought. Ahjvar *was* his. To this last.

The feral dogs came slinking back, crouched, both of them, in the mouth of the next alley along, watching him with the patience of stalking predators, yet most unpredatory. The pale one carried a dead rat in its mouth, waiting to be noticed.

Half-grown strays, with sores on their faces and the tawny one with a dirty, blackened bite on its shoulder.

A one-eyed cat watched from a porch roof, watched *him*, not the sparrows that hopped, took flight and circled only to return farther along. They, too, watched, with their shiny lacquer eyes, twittering at him. He drew them. He didn't want to, didn't mean to. Not here, not now. Not yet. If even the sparrows saw him, what else might?

Red Masks. The storyteller. Lady Deyandara's wizard.

Not Red Masks. No, not Red Masks, yet; the Lady hadn't seen

him, not with her own eyes to see, and he had been lost in the crowd. But Ahjvar, Ahj . . . had seen him. Ahjvar had seen him, and yet the Lady had not turned back.

He drew a long, shuddering breath and felt sun reach through the dying storm, thought, a blessing on Catairanach's curse, a binding in the white-hot rage and fury of a goddess, a mother . . . a curse no other god, and there had been other gods asked, could break.

The Lady was . . . mistaken, perhaps, in what she thought she held. Perhaps.

The pale dog crept nearer, on its belly, dropped its rat and gave the slightest wag of its tail.

He had eaten rat, raw, on his first ship, when he was stowaway rather than crew, but this one had been dead too long. Both dogs turned and ran when Ghu went to hands and knees, pulling himself up by the wall. His ankle throbbed and he swayed, dizzy. Hungry, but not enough for the gift of bloated rat.

"Thank you," he said gravely, because it was well to be thankful for gifts, all gifts, when they came from a clean heart. The dogs had turned and crouched again, staring. The pale one had dark eyes; the other, amber-brown. "I think, not now."

The sparrows took flight in a twittering cloud. The cat stretched, blinked, and slid fluid along the roof and away. The dogs sat up, staring fixedly.

"I don't think I can give you anything in return," he told them.

An old woman clearing away a tray of coloured threads from a tiny shopfront little wider than her door laughed at him, not pleasantly, went in and came out with a broom. Both dogs vanished. "You get off," she said. "Or I'll send for the street guard. I've been watching you. Overcome by the Lady's presence, hah! We don't need dirty opium-smokers from the Five Cities hanging around here, begging and stealing." He gave her a wide-eyed, dream-hazed look. Maybe he did seem so. He felt half-wrapped in dreams, still. "Go join the blessed Lady's militia and learn to be a man, why don't you?"

He shook his head and limped up the street. "Come on, then," he called softly, as he passed a crack between two buildings, shoulder-wide, no more. "If you will, come."

If Ahjvar were dead and could only be killed as Red Mask and freed, Ghu had still a duty of friendship to do so, and set him free. And after . . . and after . . .

It would be a long, lonely road home to Nabban. There was nothing else for him here, now.

His dogs slunk out to follow. It would be good to have company on the road.

There is a storyteller's cycle of tales, and they begin like this:

Long ago, in the days of the first kings in the north—who were Viga Forkbeard, and Red Geir, and Hravnmod the Wise, as all but fools should know—there were seven devils, and their names were Honeytongued Ogada, Vartu Kingsbane, Jasberek Fireborn, Twice-Betrayed Ghatai, Dotemon the Dreamshaper, Tu'usha the Restless, and Jochiz Stonebreaker. And these seven devils escaped from the cold hells, where the Old Great Gods had sealed them after the great war in the heavens.

And in the days of the first kings in the north, there were seven wizards. Two were of the people of the kings in the north, who came from over the western sea, and one was of a people unknown; one was of the Great Grass and one of Imperial Nabban, and two were from beyond far Nabban, but the seven were of one fellowship. Their names were Heuslar the Deep-Minded, who was uncle to Red Geir; Ulfhild the King's Sword, who was sister to Hravnmod the Wise; Anganurth Wanderer; Tamghiz, Chief of the Bear-Mask Fellowship; Yeh-Lin the Beautiful; and Sien-Mor and Sien-Shava, the Outcasts, who were sister and brother. If other singers tell you different, they know only the shadows of the tales, and they lie. These wizards were wise, and powerful. They knew the runes and the secret names, and the patterns of the living world and of the dead. But the seven wizards desired to know yet more, and see yet more, and to live forever like the gods of the high places and the goddesses of the waters and the demons of the forest and the stone and the sand and the grass.

Now the devils, having no place, had no bodies, but were like smoke or like a flame, and not of the earth at all. Some folk even call them kin to the Old Great Gods, though this is heresy. And these seven devils who had escaped the cold hells hungered to be of the stuff of the world, as the gods and the goddesses and the demons of the earth may be at will, and as men and women are whether they will or no. But they did not desire loving worship and the friendship of living men and women, as do the gods of the high places and the goddesses of the waters. They did not watch and judge and cherish the souls of human-folk after death, as the Old Great Gods are said to do in the land beyond the stars. The devils craved dominion as the desert craves water, and they knew neither love nor justice nor mercy. They made a bargain with the seven wizards, that they would join their souls to the wizards' souls, and share the wizards' bodies, sharing knowledge, and unending life, and power.

But the devils deceived the wizards, and betrayed them. The devils took the souls of the wizards into their own, and become one with them, and devoured them. They walked as wizards among the wizards, and destroyed those who would not obey, or who counselled against their counsel. They desired the homage of kings and the enslavement of the folk, and they were never sated, as the desert is never sated with rain. They would have ruled the earth and the folk of the earth and its gods and its goddesses; they would have devoured the spirit of the living earth and turned the strength of the earth against the Great Gods in their heaven.

So the kings of the north and the tribes of the grass and those wizards whom the devils had not yet slain pretended submission, and plotted in secret, and they rose up against the tyranny of the devils and overthrew them. But the devils were devils, even in human bodies, and not easily slain. Only with the help of the Old Great Gods were they bound, one by one, and imprisoned—Honeytongued Ogada in stone, Vartu Kingsbane in earth, Jasberek Fireborn in water, Twice-Betrayed Ghatai in the breath of a burning mountain, Dotemon Dreamshaper in the oldest of trees, Tu'usha the Restless in the heart of a flame, Jochiz Stonebreaker in the youngest of rivers. And they were guarded by demons, and goddesses, and gods. And the Old Great Gods withdrew from the world, and await the souls of human folk in the heavens beyond the stars, which men call the Land of the Old Great Gods.

It is said that the seven devils did not sleep but lay ever-waking within their bonds, and they worked against their bonds and weakened them, and they worked against their captors and their gaolers slept or they died, as even gods and goddesses can die, when the fates allow it.

And a devil came to Ulvsness of the Hravningas in the north, when Ragnvor was queen, and a devil came to Lissavakail in the Pillars of the Sky when the last human incarnation of the goddess was a child, and there was fire, and battle, and death. The skalds of the north have long sung it; now the bards of the Western Grass begin to shape the tales; the soothsayers see shadows of what yet may come when they cast their stones. The waking devils walk the world again.

PART TWO

PART THREE

CHAPTER XII

Catairlau dreamed. He thought he had been dreaming forever, but Hyllau knew that was not true. There was a girl in his arms, slim and sweet, her head snugged against his shoulder. The girl had been there forever where no one should ever be, wrapped in the same dream, the two of them, lying in deep water, and the girl's hands on his body, which was *hers*, were an abomination. The girl's hand over his, fingers laced into his own, pushing it down the curve of her breast, across her belly, through the curling hair and between—*no*.

She found a memory. He clutched a corpse. Miara, that square, plain, middle-aged wizard who had dared try to claim him. Thought of Miara stirred something in him, the wrongness of it. Too light a weight, too perfumed, too clinging, her fingers pushing his, caressing . . . Not a corpse; hot and alive, burning against his skin. He moved to hurl himself away and was still dreaming, still drowning, unable to move, and the water was so heavy, holding her down as well. She should have slept longer. She was meant to sleep; her mother had meant her to sleep, to drift in soft dreams of gentle water while her Catairlau carried her safe through the years, till the time should come when she would find her rightful place in the world again.

This wasn't the gentle water of her dreams; this was dark, deep, and cold, and her dreams were soft but tormenting. She never slept quiet. The terror of the great empty void, the maw of nothingness that waited to claim her halfling soul never allowed her the dreams her mother would have sent. Always there was the burning, the hungry fire that woke her, the knowing that she was fading into the void as the stuff of her soul fed Catairlau's unnatural life. Her mother had unwittingly cursed her when shaping this refuge, had made her his prey, and as a sleeping man's body, with the assassin's cord around its neck, wakes to defend itself before he is even aware that he fights for life, she, too, would wake, and fight as she must for the breath of her life, the fire of the soul's breaking with its body, as it tore itself away to the long road.

This was a different threat, nightmare, but she stirred and could not wake, as he could not. She was dreaming of herself, of her Catairlau, of the girl who was fire and water and hungry eyes rolling astride him, with thoughts of a child, a king, an emperor Over-Malagru in her mind.

Mine! she hissed, and woke herself with her own fury to take him. She flung the girl aside with Catairlau's strength and followed, seizing her to snap the neck, and drink the fire of her souls, but the girl twisted free of him and struck him down, with a sword in her hand. Hyllau had not seen her draw it. It burned in the air; it was of the air, iron and fire, and the girl smiled seeing her behind Catairlau's eyes and said, *Little death that sleeps in him, I said I would feed you. Shall I feed you on him, and watch you both die beyond any hope of the Old Great Gods?* And she pushed Catairlau down to lie where he had fallen, so that he looked dead, dead and empty, an abandoned corpse, not even breathing, but his eyes were open.

The girl breathed, rapid and shallow, and her eyes went wide and dark in the light of the gilded lamp that burned in a niche by the door. Shocked. Her hand stole down to cover herself, and the sword was gone; Hyllau had not seen it dropped. The girl snatched a blanket from the bed and wrapped herself, wiping her mouth on her arm.

Silly virgin fool. Hyllau could show her . . .

But as she gathered nerve and sinew again the girl crossed the floor in three brisk strides and knelt, a hand spread over Catairlau's chest. She sang, foreign words, high and wavering. Power flowed through them.

The waters of Hyllau's dreaming wrapped about her again.

The Lady would send the commander of the Red Masks, her champion, to aid Ketsim against Durandau the high king. She had said it; it would be so. She had not meant it to be so soon, when she said it, but—it was better so. Yes. Deal with Praitan and have it done. Then she would ride east herself and crown her captain king, and she would—yes.

In the pale twilight before dawn, they assembled to march away. The priests, those who had woken at the stir through the sacred precinct and naturally Rahel and Ashir, whom she had woken with her own early rising, were with her to witness their marching. Zora had ordered Rahel to dress her hair with white flowers, scented jessamine and lacy mist-on-the-river, some twisted into a braid about her head, some loose, coiling down her back. She enjoyed the tight-lipped obedience of the Beholder, reduced to lady's maidservant. She called a little of the haze of the morning to trail about her hems, the white goddess with the breath of the well clinging to her.

Thirty Red Masks. Perhaps she should not send so many away, but she wanted the Duina Catairna settled, not breaking out in new pockets of rebellion every time her back was turned. Finish it, leave them broken, too terrified of Marakand's Lady to dare further resistance, leave the six other kingdoms kingless if possible, if their rulers had joined the high king as they should. Weakened by her divine terror embodied in the Red Masks, the Praitannec warriors would be easy prey for the militias of Marakand, to teach them their business, build their nerve, before she turned her gaze to the Five Cities and the fleets of the coast.

Thirty Red Masks, ten patrols of temple guard—fifty men— under the new lieutenant of the first company, and a young priest greatly in love with his Lady, Revered Arhu, named the Lady's Voice in Praitan, with an appropriate handful of attendants. Not enough, counted as bodies, to make much difference in Praitan and a lot of bother and clutter for her Red Masks to have trailing after them. The Red Masks were all she really need send, but for the look of the thing, for her captain's honour, she wanted a larger escort. She had ordered the commander of the guard to choose men who could ride, and Arhu came of a caravaning family; he knew, she hoped and had made clear she expected of him, how to travel swift and light. Her captain of Red Masks, she told him, had orders to leave behind any who could not keep up, living or dead, as seemed right to him. She should have left some of the Red Masks their voices, to obviate the need for Arhu, but though she meant to discard Ketsim, grown irritatingly ambitious, the men and women who had followed him were still of use. Someone had to speak to them for her, and her own lack of foresight had ensured the Red Masks couldn't do so.

The horse of her champion sweated and stamped, jerking its head against the servants who held its bridle. Her own horse was brought up as well. She would ride with them as far as the gate, to see them on their way and send them east with her blessing, as the Lady of Marakand ought.

They looked a small company, three abreast, silent. Ominously silent. Did not the priests wonder why the Red Masks never made use of the dining hall and the bath-house, why no servants attended them in their barracks, not even to sweep the floors, why nothing was ever drawn from the treasury for their provision, except the entries in the account-books for their armouring and the red cloth of their uniforms? Zora had wondered it. Even if they, humble ascetics that they were, did their own mending and cleaning, ate frugally, and did their own cooking, there should have been some accounting, some trail to follow, of bread and vegetables at the very least, some smoke rising from a kitchen in the forbidden barracks. Zora had spent a furtive festival day, ostensibly ill with a flux, going through account-rolls in the empty office of the temple bursar. Not a sack of meal or an onion had gone to the Red Masks' use since the order was founded.

Zora had had no one to tell. If she had been wise, and not a child confused, loyal to her unfortunate father's diseased fears, Hadidu and Nour could have used that information, used a spy within the temple—

No.

The soldiers and priests behind tried to be silent, gratifyingly sensitive to her mood. She smiled at them, remote and austere. Now it was time to ride. She took four Red Masks as her own escort, to see her back through the city, and a double patrol of temple guard as well, for the look of the thing. The priests who had turned out to see them off she dismissed. They would only slow her down, puffing along at the Red Masks' heels.

The city was not yet stirring and the streets were clear. Even the professions permitted to keep the second curfew, two hours after sunset, had no licence to be abroad before dawn. Only a patrol of street guard near the gateway between Templefoot and Fleshmarket

Wards disturbed the echoing silence, falling to their knees in adoration as she passed. She smiled at them, looked back to see them rising, whispering, eyes wide. They had seen their Lady. For a moment she thought she saw something moving, away down the street near the mouth of a dark lane, but while she blinked and frowned she realized it was only a dog, scrawny and pale, standing ghostlike in the shadows, staring after them. Her champion turned to look back, too.

She regretted—she did not. She put the night from her mind. There was time enough. Later. Better to send him away now, to deal with Ketsim. One thing at a time. But her champion worried her. The mad and hungry soul bound wormlike within him, echo of herself, no, not that, she was never that, she was different, and she no longer hid within the goddess of the well . . . But he was warm. She held him, she had killed him, and he had not died. Useful. Dangerous. It made no difference. Made him different, valuable, made him the father of kings, yes, of emperors, and she was not some foolish virgin girl to shriek and mew and shrink from doing what was so eminently right and meant. *But I am, we are. Silly child.* She smiled to herself. *And we are not his. We will never be his again. When he comes again, the Malagru will rise in a wall of fire against him, and he shall never pass beyond.*

East Ward was the easternmost corner of the city, but it ended at sheer cliff. Fleshmarket was protected mostly by cliff, but at the southernmost side dropped down and Drovers' Gate let out onto a road that wandered away southerly into the foothills. There was no road that turned north and east to join the caravan road; the ravine lay between, and before it a steep fall of bare, stony hillside, but there was a track, and her captain could get a horse down it and over the ravine, she was certain. Arhu and the living men would have to do as well, or be disgraced before they ever started. They would cross the ravine and take mounts at the fortress of the Eastern Wall. She had sent her orders in the night, several hours ago. The street guard commander of the Eastern Wall would have had plenty of time. Dawn, was the message she had sent. They must be ready saddled by dawn. If the wall-captain had not obeyed, if he had delayed or protested, or if he attempted argument, if he had not been firm with the horse-dealers of the suburb, roused from their sleep to face the appropriation of their best, her captain would deal with him, and she would appoint a faithful temple guard officer in his place.

No farewells. A refreshingly silent company. Revered Arhu took his lead from the Red Masks. Most of her priests were forever asking questions. Do you mean . . . ? Shall we . . . ? Are you certain, Worshipful Lady, that we should . . . ?

The street-guard captain of the Drovers' Gate turned out with her hair all sleep-tousled and the neck of her tunic pinned askew to oversee the opening of the gate, her guards drawn up in an untidy array to honour them. Zora, for the look of the thing, raised her hand and sang a blessing as the little company marched away, her champion's horse fretting and prancing.

She regretted sending him from her side now, wanted to summon him back, but it was necessary. He was aware what he had to do; he would do it and give her not only the Duina Catairna, free of rebels and ambitious mercenaries who forgot their place, but all Praitan. And after, she would drag that worm of death from him and let it howl and fade and be forgotten in the dark; it would be useful in Praitan, maybe, for the fear he could carry with him and let loose among his enemies, more terrible because more base and animal than the spell of awe and terror she allowed the Red Masks to wake when they had need, but she did not want it at her side forever, nor in her bed.

Her foolish cheeks heated at the thought. Silly child.

Turning back to cross the market, with its pens and lanes marked off by hurdles, she felt a chill touch her, a breeze from the snow. She looked around, seeking its source. Nothing. A shadow. Another dog, black and brown, slinking along the side of a butcher's hall. Nothing to send her warnings. Only the morning air stirring, cool off the mountains. The dawn was creeping yellow into the sky, with the high haze that promised a sweltering day taking the edge off its clarity. She would break her fast with Ashir and Rahel in attendance, then grace the morning dances of public worship with her presence. Perhaps afterwards she would ride again across the city and look over the ruins of the temple palace herself. She could see it rising, white and golden, to be a fit home for the Lady of Marakand, but perhaps it would be wiser to finish the repairs of the Eastern Wall and the Western, especially the Western, first. Still, she could survey it and make her plans. The folk should see that their goddess was great, and glorious, and living as a guest in the simple house of her chief priests like some mere priestess herself would breed nothing but presumptuous familiarity. Besides, the air of suppressed bickering between Ashir and Rahel was intolerable. She would order them to move out to the unmarried priests' and priestesses' dormitories, to give herself some peace. They should have divorced years ago.

But first the dancing, and she swayed to the rhythm of the opening patterns, humming to herself. Perhaps someday, the folk would see their goddess dance. Yes. When there was victory in Praitan, she would dance for them on the palace portico, a thanksgiving in praise of herself. Yes.

CHAPTER XIII

Mikki's hand was on her waist, a warm, familiar weight. Moth turned into him, pressing close. He made some incoherent noise, breath stirring her hair, and tightened his grip on her as if she might melt away.

"Breakfast?" she suggested against his chest, which won another grunt from him.

Through the first part of this night the full moon had dappled their camp in the ruined compound of the priests of Gurhan, silvery light striking down through the leaves of the scrubby plums and cornels that had sprouted amid the ruins of the sprawling house and its outbuildings, a thorny thicket rich with the promise of ripening fruit. The moon would be setting now, away over the deserts to the west, with the tree-grown bulk of Gurhan's hill between them. The hill wasn't a knee of the great young mountains to the south at all but some folded and twisted remnant of an older land that even the gods could not recall, fissured with gullies and abrupt ravines, worm-holed with caves. Mikki had been exploring them over the past few days, trying to find any lingering trace of the bound god of the hill, while she ventured into the city proper. City folk, and the peoples of the south in general, were not so easy with the demons of the wild as the Northrons or Grasslanders and mountain folk, and she did not think Mikki would be politely respected; he was more likely to be seen as a monster. She might be wrong. She had been before. Still, Moth wasn't ready to draw the attention of the Lady to other powers stalking her land, not yet.

Dawn was creeping over the horizon. Moth felt what she could not yet see. The birds, too, knew it, stirring into song, and the great flock of feral parrots, colonists of the hill escaped long since from the menagerie, ascended in a squawking swarm to descend on the fields of the great manors along the roads that rose through the foothills south into the cloud-sweeping Pillars of the Sky.

Mikki tried to bury his face in her hair. She poked him in the ribs.

"Breakfast," she repeated, sitting up away from him.

He opened one eye. "Is there any?"

"Not much," she admitted. "A loaf and an egg. You can have it." The folk in the markets had been too stirred up about their goddess emerging from her temple yesterday, after who knew how many years of speaking only to her priests through her Voice, to care much for old tales of the devils' wars. She hadn't seen Ivah about again, either, and the coffeehouse the wizard had dragged the Nabbani—man— into when the street guard came after him two days before had been burnt to the ground that night, along with the houses on either side, the Sunset Ward market the only one subdued and fearful amid all the city's hysterical stir. She should have followed her own impulse to intervene and claimed him after she'd wrapped herself in the shadows and faded from sight. She rather feared she had lost the both of them now. The man wasn't any of her concern; if he'd drawn the temple's attention, that was his own look-out, but Ivah—she owed Ivah nothing and yet . . . and yet she was the daughter of Tamghiz, a second daughter reared to worship him, but trying so damnably hard to be something else, motherless . . . Mikki would laugh at her, the devil Vartu coming over all maternal.

She hadn't found any trace of either Ivah or the young man in her wanderings through the city yesterday, shadow-veiled except when she tried to both earn a few coins and reawaken the old memories of the seven devils in the mind of the folk. Stories prodded one to remember, to think, to ask, what is a god and not a god? To recall, perhaps, that folk had in the past dared to stand, weak and mortal though they were, against what seemed to them omnipotence and was indubitably tyranny. Only, though, if one was prepared to hear. Some had been. She wasn't the only storyteller singing those songs, either, not now. Being old and half-forgotten, they had the attraction of novelty. If someone at some point said, there is a devil in the temple, this rule of the city cannot be the true Lady's will, they might recall Tamghat dead in Lissavakail the previous summer, and the rumours that said he had been the devil Tamghiz Ghatai. They would have the older, far older tales fresh and alive on the streets. Perhaps, because of that, that there was a devil in their city and a lie in their temple would not be so unthinkable after all. There was a place in those stories for they themselves to be the heroes and oppose the devils, as others before them had done.

What troubled Moth almost as much as Ivah's disappearance was that until the previous night she had not been certain she could detect any breath of power, divine or otherwise, in the temple, but on the night after she had met Ivah, when there had been a rainstorm off the mountains, power had emerged, far from being a small goddess of the earth. She did not think that it was in response to any doing of hers—a few stories meant to wake memory should not have woken *that*—but she could not discount vision and foreknowing, either. She might be anticipated. Something had troubled the supposed goddess enough to draw her out of hiding. It might have only been that the Praitans dared to murder her Voice; it might be more.

Mikki crawled naked after Moth from their shelter, a lean-to of woven branches built against a ruined house-wall, head-high. It hadn't done them much good in the heavy rain, but it kept the dew off, and that was preferable to the stuffy goat-shed, the only place still intact. He stretched, yawning; a giant of a man with a shaggy beard and hair of barley gold, eyes the black of sea-coal, gold-furred chest and limbs, too—by night. *Verrbjarn* of the north, Mikki was only a halfling demon, his father human. His mother had been a great bear-demon, guardian of the Hardenwald. Eye-teeth too large for a human, disconcerting to those who thought him so. He caught Moth in a shoulder-crunching hug a moment, held her with his chin on her head.

"Going into the city again?" he asked. "You could come see my caves instead. They're quite nice."

"As caves go," she said drily. "I've spent enough time underground in my assorted lives and death, thank you. Enjoy yourself."

Mikki grunted. "How long are you planning to spend here, playing skald in the streets? This hill is dull. I may go up into the mountains to hunt, if you're not going to try to unravel that binding spell on the gods yet. And if there's neither god nor devil in this city after all . . ." He didn't finish that thought. "I'm not only bored but hungry, my wolf, and this folk doesn't seem to know how to honour a skald. Or to pay her."

"They don't know I'm feeding a bear."

Moth had not told him yet what she had felt the night of the rain, or that something had emerged from hiding after all. Why, when he already knew that the runes she had cast sent her here, that she had come here to kill, that the sword sent her nightmares and drove her wandering?

Because she would rather he went away, hunting, safe? Because she would rather he was not by? She could pretend it was the justice of the Old Great Gods she carried; Mikki thought so. When they hunted Ogada it had been justice in the Northron way, vengeance for murdered kin, as well as the command of the Old Great Gods; Ghatai had planned a great wrong against the earth in the fate he had prepared for the goddess of the Lissavakail, and here, in the murder of wizards and the death or sealing away of Marakand's three gods, great wrong was worked again, but next time . . . and next time . . . when it was someone wandering quiet and inoffensive, when it was the Blackdog, come at last to the Old Great Gods' attention, not one of the seven but stray kin to them—someday Mikki would have to ask, How far, how long, do we go on? It was not the Great Gods' justice but their revenge that the sword Lakkariss served. Someday, when she could not hide that from Mikki any longer, he would demand the reason of her.

"And if there's neither god nor devil here after all, why do we stay?" he persisted. "Something sealed those gods away and they should be woken and set free, but if you can't free them, and if it's gone, whatever did it, we should follow. We do no good here."

He found the skin of water she had hung on the branch of a plum last night, brought from the spring that had its birth up the gully past the rockslide-buried, spell-sealed mouth of Gurhan's cave, drank and sluiced water over his head. The big blue-roan stallion came pushing in. Mikki fended him off.

"You don't need it, you're dead. Moth?"

"I'm going to the temple," she said.

"Ah."

The sun, unnoticed, climbed the horizon, and he was a great bear of the northern forest, not a man, barley-golden in the dawn. He nosed into the thin grass by the well, from which they were not drawing their water, filled as it was with the bones of murdered priests, and found the egg, set there last night to keep cool. He cracked it and lapped it up, a few swipes of the tongue, and dealt with the loaf in as few bites, taking her at her word.

"So there is something there after all?" he asked, stretching, forepaws out, yawning again.

"I . . . am not sure. Yet. I'm going to find out."

"That's all?"

"Yes, cub, that's all. You think I'm trying to charge off to get killed without you?"

"I think I'm happier when I can keep an eye on you and watch your back, and that unless you want to go in pretending to be a . . . a juggler with a dancing bear, you should wait for nightfall. Come prowl caves with me instead."

"Seductive offer."

"Well, if you like . . ." He grinned, fangs gleaming.

"I was thinking of the dancing bear, not the caves, but no, I'm scouting. Something changed yesterday and the folk of the city say their Lady has appeared to them. I didn't see her. I made damned sure she didn't see me. Now I want to find out who and what she is, that's all."

"And you didn't see fit to mention this last night."

"I wanted to consider what it might mean, first."

"You wanted a good excuse to leave me behind in safety." Mikki sighed and came to butt at her with his broad head. He was right, of course. Last night, human, if she had told him of a newly emerged goddess who had never before left her well, he would have insisted they both go to the temple to investigate. "Fine. If you're truly only scouting. Going in as a worshipful pilgrim of Marakand? See if you can raid their kitchens while you're at it. I bet the priests eat well. Such folk usually do. Steal some pies."

Moth laughed and pulled her boots on, unrolled her byrnie, and shrugged into the mailshirt, jingling. She didn't need armour. She'd had neither helmet nor shield for years, but the old ring-mail hauberk was a reminder, an anchor. Memory of the King's Sword of Ulvsness and all she had been meant to be.

Last night she had crawled from Mikki's side to cast the runes by moonlight, waiting like an angler to see what rose, three by three.

Devil. Water. Devil.

Water. Boar. Sword.

Devil. Death. Devil.

Water she read here for a goddess of the earth. *Boar* was for protection. *Death* and *Devil* and the *Sword* spoke for themselves, generally. And literally, the devil meaning not misfortune and plans gone awry or contrary fate, but just what it said, and the sword betokening not war or violence, not when she cast the runes, but Lakkariss. But devil and devil, devil and devil, any reading, any crossing that touched the corner-posts of the square . . . two? Together? In opposition? Herself? She did not usually think *Devil* told her of herself, but for there to be two others in the city . . . who? It told her nothing she did not already know. She had carved this new set of the soothsaying runes in slips of birch while Mikki slept the mountain winter away, but she had not used them. She did not remember that she had carved so many with the rune that signified devil and meant ill-luck.

Moth had turned down all the carved slips of wood, hiding the faces that drove her, all but the boar, and sat a long time contemplating that, while the leaves stirred and the shadows walked, and the bone-horse Storm, solid flesh most of the time, seemed to fade to moon-shadow and leaf-dapple in the darkness, no more substantial than the thin night-mist where he stood, hip cocked, head hanging, tail switching at midges in his dreams. If he dreamed, being little more than memory and dream himself.

What was the boar to her now, she had asked, when she was no longer Ulfhild the King's Sword, the king's captain, but Vartu Kingsbane? And if she hadn't killed Hravnmod with her own hand, as all the sagas said, then at least she had doomed him, the brother she was sworn to protect . . . long ago in the days of the first kings in the north, as so many tales began.

The *Boar*. That which protects. The guardian. The armed warder at the king's door. None of that was the Great Gods' will for her.

And she had looked aside at where Mikki slept, or pretended to sleep, pretended not to know she was restless, casting the runes again.

The *Boar*. A reminder. Perhaps.

But when she had crawled back into bed beside Mikki and he had turned to put his arm over her, she had slept, and she had dreamt the dreams that had haunted her in the mountains. She dreamt she came upon Mikki, dead, gutted, his paws cut away, the teeth smashed out of his skull so some Great Grass warrior could swagger with fangs in his braids. She dreamt his head stared at her, wordless and weeping, from the cave of skulls where the old bear-cult had carried out their most secret rituals.

She had dreamt Sien-Shava, who had become Jochiz, the one erstwhile comrade she thought might make her fear, wrapped her in arms of golden fire and drank her, and left Ulfhild's bones shattered under uncaring stars. That one had not seemed warning sent from the Old Great Gods, threat to keep her to her bargain, but something else.

Out in morning's new light, Mikki snorted. "Mail, wolf? You said you were scouting."

She gave him half a smile, belted on Kepra, Keeper, her own ancient sword, a royal sword, the hilt gold and garnets and the blade cut with runes. *The Wolf made me for Hravnsfjall. Strength. Courage. Wisdom.* Not so much of the last of those, in her long life. There were words on the cross guard, too, which she preferred to forget. A curse, a blessing. Hard to say which. And she would take her feather-cloak rolled small, tucked through her belt at the back.

"I am scouting."

"You'll jingle."

"I won't."

"I'm coming with you," Mikki said. "If you can hide yourself walking armed through the city, you can hide me. You're hunting the Lady, and I'm not letting you go alone."

"I'm not. I'm not even certain this Lady is one of the seven. There are other powers in the world, you know. I'm sure I met one of them two days since—"

"You're not going alone—"

"I am." Lakkariss leaned against a broken stone. Waiting. Watching her, she could feel, sometimes. Hungry. The sheath was covered in black leather, cracked with age, though recently oiled, and the grip of the silver and niello hilt wrapped in braided leather as well, hiding the twining inscription in letters that belonged to no folk of the earth. Curse and invocation, or maybe statement of fact. She preferred to keep it covered, to not feel it against her palm, striking cold to the marrow. She caught it up, holding it out across her hands.

"Here." Even the scabbard felt cold. "Keep Lakkariss here. I am not hunting the Lady today, I swear it. I'll go quiet and soft as a cat—"

"Jingling," he said, but his lip pulled up over a fang, reluctant smile, not a snarl.

"She'll never know I'm there, whatever she is, and then we'll know . . ."

"We'll know what?" He swiped the sword from her hands with an ivory-clawed paw and knocked it to the ground at her feet, one heavy forefoot holding it down.

". . . whatever I find out, I guess. Who and what and—and what I want to know is *why?* This killing of wizards is *senseless*."

"*Senseless* bothers you more than *wrong*, princess?"

Moth shrugged, not certain herself and not about to answer. "Keep it safe. It would probably just draw the attention I'm trying to avoid, if I took it into the temple, anyhow. I'll try to bring you something for supper."

"You'd better, or I'll be reduced to gnawing old bones."

Storm blew down his nose and moved away.

"We have plenty of them." Moth grinned, leaned in to kiss his soft and bristly upper lip. "I'll take care. Don't worry about me. Don't get yourself trapped in a rockfall."

"The earth is quiet enough here now, anyway. You—quiet as a cat, you swore. Don't go hunting trouble without me." He followed her as far as the fern-grown dyke into which the old compound wall had settled and stood atop it, still there watching every time she glanced back, until the greenish-white trunks of the thick poplars of the Palace Hill forest hid him.

She was only scouting, and Mikki was not foresighted; he had inherited nothing of such powers from his demon mother. She shouldn't feel such an urge to turn back.

The old keeper of the once-famous Xua menagerie was out already, pottering in his vegetable garden with the only remaining beast, an elderly black moon-bear who seemed to be his pet as well as his charge, nosing about for grubs at his side. Moth slipped by among the ruined and empty enclosures like nothing more than a stirring of leaf-shadow. The bear only raised her head, turning it from side to side to catch the wind, sneezed, and went back to her grubbing. The old man reached absently to scratch the bear's ear, leaning on his hoe a moment, and did not look up at all.

A zigzagging path of many steps led down the north of the hill from the menagerie to the far corner of the palace plaza, a walled, empty place of blowing leaves and dusty stone, decorated less than elegantly with caged old bones along the south-facing wall. No ghosts, whatever the folk of the city believed. Some brave few must have defied the Voice to give the senators the mercy of a handful of dust, long ago. Pity the mass of the city folk hadn't nerved themselves to the greater mercy and freed the men and women so tortured before sun and thirst killed them. But there were the Red Masks, always the Red Masks, as the excuse for paralysis and submission. She very much wanted to meet one, but Mikki would probably look on that as hunting trouble.

Yesterday afternoon the Lady had addressed her folk here, while Moth was over in the Fleshmarket Ward where the butchers and the livestock dealers congregated, singing for pennies. The pavingstones were still scattered with recent rubbish, lost sandals and scarves, trampled fruit, dog dung.

The city woke as Moth passed through, market traders setting up, produce-sellers streaming in from the manors of the south hill roads with donkeys and oxcarts, and the white-kilted free Malagru hillfolk with their own language lilting on their tongues. No one turned to watch her, exotic and armed Northron though she was; thought and memory slid from her, shadow in the corner of the eye, no more.

Templefoot Ward was thronged with folk. She found out why when she drew near the gates and found herself part of a flowing stream of humanity. Young men, old women leaning on their sticks, moneyed Family elders in closed chairs, their chairmen sweating, bare-shouldered. Beggar-children in ragged short gowns, most likely with an eye and a half on the purses of the rest. Prosperous-looking citizens too, decent in clean caftans, nervous, expectant. But mostly young men in packs, noisy, elbowing, yelping at one another. Recruits eager to sign up for the new city militia, she gathered, and the rest were queuing for admission to the morning's public service of worship, in hope that the Lady would again appear.

"She watched the dancing of the evening prayers last night," one chairman assured an old woman. "My grandfather made it in and had a place at the front, even. The most beautiful lady you've ever seen, he said."

"I know that," the old woman said. "I saw her yesterday when she rode through the Greenmarket. She blessed my grandson and he hasn't cried with colic since."

They talked, too, of the company of Red Masks that had marched out early that morning. "Hundreds of them, going to fight a rebellion of the barbarian Praitans," as though they were some long-conquered province. "No, it was a dozen." "It can't have been so few." "My cousin watched through his shutters. Fifty Red Masks, that was all, ten patrols." The militia would soon be following, was the general opinion in the line, and the young men boasted of glory to be won, and wealth, because everyone knew the Praitannec kings hoarded gold in their hovels, though their folk were only poor tillers of the soil and herdsmen.

Moth sidled amongst them, putting herself into the fastest-flowing current, leaving not a few quarrels and at least one brawl in her wake as this person and that accused another of shoving.

The entrance to the temple was a gatehouse like a pillared shrine, at the head of a deep, dark passageway that plunged down through a rock-cut tunnel. The temple grounds were below the level of the city, nearly at the level of the bottom of the ravine. Built in a sink-hole, was her guess. There were no priests in sight, only ten guards uniformed like those who patrolled the city, but with red tunics, armed with broad-bladed spears. They lined the head of the passage and fed the people through the one open side of the double-leaved, gilded doors. One kept a tally on an abacus.

"Tell them we can take fifty more, and that's it for this morning," said a man with a black ribbon depending from his helmet, leaning over the abacist's shoulder, and one of the guardsmen shoved his way upstream to bellow at the crowd, with predictable results. Moth felt the surge coming and dodged ahead of it, through the gate and down the cool passageway. Behind her, shouts and cries rose to a roar, and the officer shrieked above it, "The gate, close the damned gate!"

The eager stream flooded into sunlight, a grassy courtyard with a paved path crossing it. Here there were priests, a young man and a woman in saffron-dyed gowns.

"Through the doorway in the wall ahead, please, good people, and to the right past the gardens to the Hall of the Dome. Through the doorway . . ."

"Will the Lady come to the dancing?" someone asked.

"The Lady's will is her own," the priestess said. "Perhaps she'll favour us in her physical form, but it's not for us to know beforehand. Her spirit fills the city. Be blessed in it."

An answer got by rote and repeated too often, unheard now. Both young clerics were wondering that very thing themselves, and were no more contented than the folk to be told to be satisfied with the Lady's spirit alone, Moth guessed. Once through the next doorway, into another courtyard formed by the walls of buildings, she followed to the right but turned aside into the first garden, all herbs in square beds, bay trees in the four corners, where she waited till the sounds of people passing faded away.

The temple was a complex of a dozen or more great halls, most in poor repair, a scatter of lesser buildings and some outright ruins. Courtyards and gardens seemed trapped between them. The Hall of the Dome, into which the last worshippers were hurrying, had a pillared portico like those of the palace and library, but on a much smaller scale. Even its dome did not lend it grace. It crouched against the earth, toadlike. Powerful and earthbound.

Power did move there; the folk would have their wish and see their Lady. As two companies of scarlet-gowned youths, boys and girls, met and ran together with a chiming of bells and rattle of tambourines through the wide doors of the Hall of the Dome, Moth skirted it on its cold and shadowed north. There was another power in this place, a thin, weak thread of it. She followed, as if it were a scent in the wind, along a well-used path, down a few steps into a sunken yard, along the wall of a newer dun-brick building that looked like nothing so much as a warehouse, only a few narrow windows letting any light into even its upper floors, and to a miniature of the Hall of the Dome, square, squat, grey, with a pillared porch and its own dome. Carvings decorated half its doorframe, old and weathered: laden camels, sheaves of grain, branches of fruit, but part had been redone in plaster, without skill. Thick and hasty mortar showed much repair had been done to the formerly fine wall. New cracks ran jagged up to the roof. The temple extracted tolls from the caravan road to the most it would bear, levied tithes on every member of every guild, the streets grumbled. Only the Families were able to buy themselves freedom from the net of licences and fees and fines that ate up the earnings of the working folk, but where did the money go? Into the treasury of the priests? This certainly looked no nest of an exceptionally wealthy priesthood. Grasslander mercenaries and the rebuilding of the Eastern and Western Walls of the pass might account for it. Or someone was hoarding gold against some greater need foreseen. Ketsim's rabble were not so numerous as all that, and even to defend the pass for long against a determined enemy would require the arming—and provisioning—of a much larger force. If it were Moth ruling this city, working to make it a fortress, as seemed the Lady's idea . . . She would not undertake such a thing. Driving humans to your will was more frustration than it was worth. If they wanted to follow where you led, well and good, but this was not how to win followers worth having. Cattle. Better to be a lord of wolves.

City and village folk were different, of course, than the scattered and independent folk of the steadings of the north. Cramped in their souls from living too tightly together. Mikki would call her an arrogant and prejudiced Northron, naturally.

The door of the smaller domed hall was locked. The rune of *Day* opened it, deliberate wizardry. She had promised Mikki . . . but she wanted to see what would follow. The Red Masks, Ivah had told her, could smell wizardry. Well then, let them smell her runes. There was something unpleasant and most definitely dead, snared in a web of necromancy, in the ugly warehouse overlooking this sacred hall.

She left the door unlocked behind her and, having circled once the chamber within on the unrailed gallery about the central pit, finding nothing of interest, started down the stairs that clung to the outer wall. The light grew twilight-dim and the air cool, cellar-like.

Something followed before she was halfway down, not warily at all. Boots. The curve brought her to where she could see them, two men in red robes and face-concealing veils, armed with white staves. She could see the reins that bound them too, poor corpses, and the soiled light of the torn remnants of soul woven into what they had become. A cold, deep anger stirred. Even Ghatai, who had found the dead apt tools in his time, used only the bodies. He might have been indifferent to the fate of the soul, with no compunction about leaving ghosts trapped in the world, had done so to punish his enemies, but he had never debased them, destroyed them past all hope.

Moth leapt over the edge of the stairs to land on the uneven, water-stained floor, mud and stone and the rotting remains of a small boat. The Red Masks ran, taking the stairs two at a time. Light flared and leaked, a muddy red, as if they burned beneath their veils, and white sparks fizzed on their staves.

Childish display, meant to inspire awe and fear. There was a spell working, a will brought to bear, that said, *You are nothing, you are already dead*, a weight of terror and despair. They were woven around with other spells, protection against metal's bite and the force of any arms, against spell and human will. If she listened, she could catch the echo of the words, singing; the power that fed the spells came from a great weaving, a mighty net of song and wizardry, in which their own power was bound up.

No wizards in Marakand, no. They went to feed this working, knotted into it like so much thread, slaves beyond death.

Kepra's edge would bite them, with her hand behind it. Moth didn't bother, caught the upraised staff of the first down in her hand, earthing the fire of it, and wrenched the binding of the wretched, broken thing away. It fell. She swept the rags of soul together in her hands and asked, "Who were you?"

But there was little left. A scent of roses and wood-dust, memory of a woman, tumble of brown curls, an infant's hand clutching his finger. She breathed on them and they burned away, clean, at least, and the animal wailing that had been the thing's existence years it could not count was silenced. The other she burned, body and spells and broken soul and all, and set the white fire to eat the first body too, lighting the chamber as if by trapped lightning. The thin struggling weeds that grew beneath the eye of the dome shrivelled and fell to ash; the rotten boat steamed and followed them. Mist rose from the well. The place seemed dark to the eye afterwards, small and close.

Mikki would not call that quiet as a cat, no. Not human wizardry, either, and she had been noticed, oh yes, she might as well have walked into the Hall of the Dome behind the dancers and shouted her name. Not much time now.

The mist on the surface of the water wavered. She walked to the brink of the crack, knelt there, a hand in the dark water.

Lady of Marakand?

Something was there yet, hidden in the water. Something stirred, drew away in fear.

Lady of the Well. What is the Lady in the temple?

Barely a whisper. *You.*

Not I. What has become of Gurhan and Ilbialla? Can you see them? Can you reach them?

Gone. Lost. Dead.

Not dead. What has she done to you? How does she hold you?

The Lady of Marakand dreamed of worms, devouring a fish from the inside out till it was nothing but husk, a swimming, rotted corpse that would fall apart and release the bloated worms to find a greater host and feed again. Moth herself, maybe. Or Moth had come to devour what was left of her.

No, Moth told her. *Not that. Who is it? Give me the devil's name. Tell me what this devil wants of you.* Such half-hearted conquest made no sense, ruling a city as a hidden goddess, but doing nothing beyond its walls save the recent and again half-hearted small war against a small tribe. Madness, a child's play, begun and forgotten, or a dotard's feeble fumbling after the self that age had robbed away.

But it might be a deliberate game, a pretence of folly, hiding a trap, as the folk of the marshes of coastal Tiypur had once used tolling dogs, to lure waterfowl into their nets. In which case . . . Moth had come wandering in under the net as tamely as any goose drawn by curiosity about the frolicking dog. She still didn't know why the Lady, goddess true or false, would have woken so few days after her coming, when all she had done was walk softly and tell stories.

It might be that Lakkariss stirred in dreams other than her own.

Or not a trap at all, but someone's pretence at being a goddess gone mad, small and cruel, but of no great danger to the larger world, and so not worth the attention of the Old Great Gods, not with Tamghiz Ghatai threatening to make himself a god of the earth. Cunning, maybe, and sly. She—or he—had had long years left in peace to do—whatever it was she or he did, after all, till Ghatai drew the Great Gods' attention to the western caravan road and the neighbourhood of Marakand. And until the Old Great Gods woke the sword and set Moth wandering again.

She didn't know, she did not know. She wanted a clear enemy and a clean fight. And to go home with Mikki to the north.

What does she intend, this devil hidden in the heart of Marakand?

A cringing fear was her only answer, the terror of a small and broken thing, cowering, near-mindless. There was no trace of another power that she could find, only the one in the temple, aware of her now, wavering, drawn, but uncertain.

Do you remember your name? Moth asked. *You were not always the Lady, small and weak in your well. There are echoes in your waters of older times. There is strength to carve the mountains. Do you feel it still? Shall I show you? Do you want to remember?*

Could she? Maybe. Even the greatest rivers trace their waters, through many channels, many streams, many gathering lakes, to the smallest springs. Every ocean holds, deep and distant, memory of the ice on some mountain's peak. What had the Lady of recent years been? They called it the deep well, but this cavern had been a pool, a cave half-filled, not so many years since. The signs were all about her, the boat she had burned, the stains on the wall, the change in workmanship on the lower stairs. The reservoir had sunk away, drained into the rock, as the goddess's strength and will faded, as the false Lady fed on her. But before that . . . Moth reached for deeper, older times. The echoes were all around them. Strength, maybe, to break the other prisoned gods free, without need to decipher and unravel stroke by careful stroke the spells binding them and to set her wizardry against the great chain of power and will that the inscription only anchored.

The Lady of the temple drummed fingers on the railing of her pulpit as the dancers whirled, flutes rising over the bells, the drums running. She frowned, clenched hands to fists, spread them carefully, smiled. Two Red Masks, her escort, stirred as well, no longer statue-still, alert, uncertain. *Send them, keep them close?* The Lady's lips moved. Fingers drummed again.

She is no longer within you, is she? Moth picked memories free, delicately, offered them back to the goddess. *She has seduced one of your own . . . priestess . . . not your priestess. A girl born to the service of the god on the hill. I see her, almost. She kills in your name, Lady of the Deep Well, Lady of the*

Dead River, Lady of Waters that Once Were. She profanes all that you built with your folk in the long slow years. Do you remember?

No. That was clear suddenly, and bitter, desperate. *I do not, I do not, she has taken it all, it is all gone. I am lost, I am lost, I cannot find my way . . .*

Take my hand, Moth said. *Let me see, and I can show you, now, before she comes here. Remember the strength of your lost days. Help me. I want to free your fellow gods of this land.*

No! Water roiled and the goddess, the godhead in the water, recoiled in a mindless terror, beyond all reason, animal madness. Stone screamed and shifted. Moth swore and lunged and seized water, seized in immaterial fire immaterial soul and held it tight as a panicked, flailing child, a wounded animal, plunged through the water into darkness, dark water, a cavern of cold memory. She could find the way, she could see it, the path of the water, dark and secret, the tide of the years. She showed the goddess, drew her into it, a current pulling them, falling.

Do you see, Lady of Marakand? In this place you are strong. Your heart is still here, if you can reach it again, remember . . .

The ground shook. Plaster cracked. In the Hall of the Dome, the patterned blue glass of the eye, which scattered flakes of light like butterflies when the sun was high, rained down in biting shards and twists of lead. Dancers scattered, shrieking, worshippers yelled and shoved and trampled as the Lady fled her pulpit, white veils trailing, hands outstretched, screaming words that none in the temple knew, but wrapped in black water Vartu heard them.

She is mine! No gods but the Lady in Marakand and I am the Lady and she is mine and you dare—you dare—you dare, kinslayer, murderer! I see you now. This is my place and she is mine—you will not have her he will

*not have her he will not have me again you will not betray not be his death
my death traitor heart in our midst the sword of the night bringing death the
long night of the ice will be your death not mine not ours not the ice I will not
we will not we are not she you cannot take us traitor back the Lady is mine
and I am the Lady—*

Moth fell, holding the Lady, and Tu'usha burst the timbers of the door
of the Dome of the Well. She hurtled down the stairs and plunged
like a kingfisher into the water, clutching close with clawed hands as
Vartu pulled the Lady into her own lost memory, drew her through
days and ages to the years of her strength. Water, lightless and cold,
flowed into them. It could not quench their fires, but it wrapped
them, held them close, and the Lady whispered, whimpered, not
so mindless, not so panicked as she had seemed, triumphant in her
terror, *I have learnt, this much I have learnt from within your madness: to
hold, to trap in my turn.* She drowned them both in her waters and told
the devil holding her there, *Now I know you, now I see you for what you
are. You are mine, you have made yourselves mine, to die here with me in my
lost days, and my city is free of you.*

The city was white and golden in the sun, and shrank, and dwindled away, and rose again. The goddess whispered words that came
from the heart of the mountains and secret springs beneath the high
ice, holding them, enfolding them, chaining the devils in the waters
of memory.

Darkness, cool and flowing, and the silver light on the rippling
current, the quiet murmur of the waves on the shore, the moon
pouring from the sky, the river of the stars carrying them, the road
in the black night . . .

Vartu thought it might not be so bad a thing to lie forever in the deep
waters under the stone, fire bound in water. Thought slowed, stretched

long, the flood and ebb of the river's cycles, snowmelt freshet and summer's drought, the churned mud of autumn rain, the high waters locked in ice and the hoarfrost on the reeds, snow sifting to fade into black water, the spate of the river's joyous wrath when spring came round again and freed the locked and frozen valleys high among the peaks . . .

But there was the demon, waiting. The cub, whispering stories to her bones . . . the young man who went wandering with his searover cousins but came back always to the heart of the forest, to his mother's den, carrying tales of the changing world to the bound and sleeping devil the great bear guarded . . .

Sleep, the river murmured, but the bear's cub lay by her, waiting, keeping watch against the darkness that threatened to eat her heart, keeping her from falling, from drowning in that darkness, now and always, and if she turned away from her road they had sworn to slay him, the Old Great Gods of the distant heavens . . .

She reached for him, but he was not there, of course not. The river had drowned her deep, wrapped her and held her. Water flowed over her, but for a moment she found herself; she was not water. Neither was she thought and flame and old bone, but Moth. She remembered. Black eyes and golden pelt, and he named her Moth . . . She opened eyes to water, water filling the tunnels and the wormholes of its own slow gnawing, the secret courses of the Avain Marakanat, that river was. It wrapped the city called by its name, and the city was the queen of the empire that stretched from the western border of the Stone Desert to the coast of the Gulf of Taren, whose soldiers marched armed with bronze, because only now were the folk of the forest beginning to work the grey iron and the wizard-smiths of the forest kept this secret from the enemy to their south, from great Marakanat, goddess and city and empire. And this lightless water held, too, even older, the little scattered village on the shores of that river, the place of the three gods, where the traders came up from the hills of the east to take away the flint of the desert; the tools the folk of this age used were bone and stone and fire to clear the forested hills. The water shifted with the tide of the Lady's memory; the village built a wall against the raiding tribes of the Stone Desert, and they spoke a language even the devils did not remember, but now the words in the mouths of the city folk were the speech of the Malagru hillfolk, slid twisting through the years, and the slow pulse of the Lady's tides pulled her down again, whispered, *Quiet, rest, sleep, as I promised you, we will sleep together and fade here, until even the water forgets . . .*

Not I, she thought, *You promised me nothing. I promised you I would show . . .* but she was water . . . There was a song in the water, arms about her, holding her fast. Not Mikki, not dead Tamghiz, her husband whom she had slain. Arms of fire, and they burned, as her nightmare had burned, and Sien-Shava said, *You will all come to me in the end, Vartu Kingsbane*, but the singing voice was not Sien-Shava's. High and clear as a child's, it drank in the magic of fourscore wizards or more. How many more? She could not hear their voices, not see the fire of their souls, dark and twisted and broken as they were. The voice drank their magic and spat it out again in words of weight and power, light and strong as silk.

Human wizardry. The Old Great Gods did not fear human wizardry. They hardly took thought to notice it, but the seven devils of the north had learned to wield it. It let them work in the world, beneath notice, till they grew too loud, and it did not wound the world, as the unleashed full force of their own will and soul might. Too many such scars on a world and the walls of it weakened, and the annihilating void waited, hungry . . . They had nearly broken the world, long and long ago, and Tiypur in the west bore the worst scars, a godless land, with hills where all life perished.

Thunder that was stone, a roof falling. The weight of stone came down, entombing goddess and devil. Real, illusion, dream of the sinkhole falling that had been . . . it held them.

Darkness. Deep water.

Traitor, the Lady whispered, Tu'usha whispered into her slow and sinking mind. *You brought me to this. I followed you out of the cold hells, Vartu, and you brought me to mad Sien-Mor. She is dead, and I am the Lady of Marakand. Sleep here with the nameless goddess, till even your souls fade from the earth and you wail like her, a nameless ghost. Sleep here, until you die the final death and are forgotten even in the sagas you shaped yourself, Ulfhild Vartu.*

CHAPTER XIV

The entrance to the cave that felt as if it had been the root and anchor of the hill-god Gurhan's presence in the world had been mostly buried in a landslide, long enough ago that the slope of scree was bound in place with tall poplars, suckers grown to a leaf-shimmering grove. What was left had been closed with stone and mortar and sealed with a deeply cut inscription in letters Mikki didn't recognize, though some looked a little like the writing in an old Pirakuli almanac they'd once owned, and some uncomfortably like the inscription that twisted like vines on the hilt of the obsidian-bladed sword of the Old Great Gods. Digging away the fallen rock was not going to undo that binding. Even if he did find some shaft or passage that led into the cave from behind or beneath, he would hardly find the god waiting, laid out in deathlike sleep. Gods had no physical form in the world but by their own choice and at their own will.

Gurhan's steep hill was not a clean and simple upswelling, some foothill of the Pillars of the Sky but an older stone, ridged and furrowed and closely folded, a knot of hills pressing together, worm-gnawed within by forgotten waters, covered in forest which the folk of Marakand either feared or revered; they left it uncut, unharvested, almost untrodden, not venturing far under its eaves even in search of summer fruit, though there were raspberries and currants ripening in plenty over the stonier ground where the trees were thinnest. Mikki made what second breakfast he could off of such fruit and stalked and killed a couple of fat red squirrels, which was better. There didn't seem much point in further exploration of the caves and tunnels. He had found all that a bear of his size could get into and, by night, most of those that would allow a man passage. Nothing below ground held any lingering trace of the god. It was up to a wizard, which meant Moth, to make some counterspell of unbinding. All a demon could do was call. He had called; he couldn't make himself heard and wasn't answered. He couldn't go down into the city, and no matter what he threatened, he wouldn't go back to the mountains leaving Moth restless and evasive behind him. The Old Great Gods drove her. He didn't think she would ally herself with whatever old comrade it was who had taken up this sick-minded cult of wizard-murder, and he didn't think she had any ambition left to move the tides of human affairs, but—they should have gone to the temple and challenged the Lady to come out, to justify herself and face justice if she could not. Called her out, in the old Northron way, and had done with. Scouting, hah. Moth was working herself into a state of paralysis again, as she had hunting Tamghiz, and that she had once loved the man, and that he had been working spells against them to keep them wandering, she said, had been some excuse, but here, no. What mercy for such a butcher and an oppressor of men, whatever friendship there had been once between you? They had come to carry out the Great Gods' justice; they should do so and be gone, and maybe Lakkariss would then leave them in peace another score or century of years. They could retreat to the north, to the pines and some loon-haunted lake.

To the south, the unreachable white peaks of the Pillars of the Sky floated, a distant dream of snow, above the blue of their slopes, fading again into blue. Even in the deep gullies of Gurhan's hill the day was already hot. Mikki was making for a cool gully where a trickle of water found its way down an old, man-made channel when a deer leapt up almost at his feet. A small deer. A decently supper-sized deer, and surely after dark it would be safe to make a fire, when night would hide their smoke. He wheeled about after it, crashing through thickets of raspberry cane and hazel, down steep ferny plunges and up through poplars again, to where the ground was broken and treacherous, all rubble beneath the deceptive green, and the pillars of the palace porch stood like survivors of a forest fire. The deer bounded lightly through it all, not breaking a sapling-thin leg in a crevice as it ought to have, and darted away into the woods beyond with a taunting flash of its tail, but he knocked some ill-balanced stone loose and started a rock-fall, clatter and rumble into an unseen opening, and had to swerve and land stumbling, nearly twisting a shoulder, when he smelt almost too late the rank scent of blistering blister-vine at his feet. By the time he recovered, the deer was gone and he was already panting, dizzy with running in the heat. Bad idea. The Salt Desert had almost killed him; he should have learnt from that. He didn't belong in the cursed south.

It took most of the rest of the day, circling the ruin, stalking through the thick woods of precipitous western slopes, to run down his deer again. He gutted it where he had killed it and ate what offal was worth eating, dragging the carcass back to the camp on the far side of the hill, his mind running on roast collops of venison and stewed marrowbones, and whether there would be much left worth drying over what smoke they dared; it was not a large deer at all. He could probably finish it before it went off. Pity they wouldn't have time to cure the hide, as well. Wasteful. He was tired of wandering.

He climbed the dyke around the priestly ruins with the weary contentment of homecoming after a fair day's labour. No one to greet him. Moth wasn't back, but he'd known that by the absence of her scent. No sign of Storm, though, and it was hard to lose a large and very solid horse, however dead, in a small enclosure. He dropped the deer by their fire-pit and sniffed the air. There was too much bone about this place to distinguish Storm, and besides, he and the butchered deer reeked of blood. Flies were settling on the both of them.

"Styrma?" he called, unease growing. "Hey, horse?" No ghost-shaping crashed like a boar out of the tangled cornel trees to give him an indignant and unhorselike glower.

Lakkariss was where he had left it, shoved under grapevine along a ruined wall a few courses high. Nothing had disturbed the camp, human or beast.

He found the horse-skull in the far corner where poplars had invaded the fruit-thicket; it lay amid trampled ferns. The marks of an unshod horse in the dirt were real enough, but Storm was a bone-horse, spell and memory bound to his skull. That he was not mere bone-memory, and that he seemed to grow in cunning and will every time Moth drew him into the world again, was not usual, but he was still only a bone-horse, one of the less sinful necromancies, and without Moth's own will behind the beast, he was nothing even a hungry dog would bother with.

Mikki nosed at the skull. The rune, drawn in blood between the eyes, was brown and faded, with older traces staining beneath it. Impossible to say when it had fallen to the ground. Ghosts he could see, but Storm wasn't a true ghost, lingering trapped in the world. There was nothing he could call, and the horse could hardly answer if he did.

He prowled down towards the menagerie, and then back and down the much more overgrown path of many stairs that led down to a fallen gateway and the blind end of a shabby street into Silvergate Ward, but did not find Moth returning by either route. Methodically he rolled in the mould of fallen leaves beneath the trees some way from the priests' compound to clean the drying, sticky blood from his coat and end the torment of the flies and then in the dust of the path from the menagerie, which finished the job. He drank from the trickle of water that came down the bottom of the gully beneath Gurhan's cave and cached the deer high in a poplar in Storm's favourite corner of their camp. Paced again, waiting, feeling the tide of night gathering in his blood. The shadows grew too slowly, darkness pooling in their enclosed dell, but the sun, hidden behind the rise of the hill, still struck fire on the crest of the hill above.

No Moth. When he sought, he did not feel her, like distant sun warming the blind and seeking face, in the city at all. She was not dead. He would know if she were dead, how could he not, when she was sun and moon and the throne of his heart? But she was gone, and he did not think it was by her own will; she had said she would return by evening, and of all the world, Ulfhild Vartu would not break faith with him. Even in the small things. Perhaps especially in the small, on which all else was built.

Bats flitted overhead and a fox yelped. Down in the city, the bells began to toll, the first curfew. They were early by several heartbeats. But sun did set. Moth had not returned, and when he shut his eyes, not even thinking, just reaching . . . she was not there. So. As methodically as he had cleaned his fur and stashed the deer against later need, deliberation and careful movement keeping the urge to run shouting and roaring well leashed, he found his tunic and his double-bitted axe.

Better to be a man breaking curfew than a beast by daylight. He would probably get farther before he had to fight. Fewer people about, as well. He took the path down to Silvergate Ward, knowing only that he had to go north from there, through several wards and gates, but that the gates within the city were never closed, where they existed at all.

He still smelt of deer's blood. Probably he had blood yet in his beard. It didn't much bother him. Anyone close enough to see was going to have other things to worry about.

Two patrols of street guard had not seen him, a demon passing wrapped in night; one had, but Mikki had swarmed to the top of a yard wall and gone away over porches and galleries into another street and left them shouting and ringing their handbells far away. The temple, when he found it, could be nothing else, a silent wall, a gatehouse where strangely nervous guardsmen stood together in the red light of pitch torches, hands too tight on the shafts of their spears, twitching at shadows. Mikki went over and found beyond the wall a crumbling cliff-face, dropping into a shadowed dell, easy enough to scramble down. He dropped lightly to his feet, axe in hand, in what seemed to be a garden, cool and sweet-scented with herbs. A patrol of ten soldiers passed, murmuring and too tightly huddled together. A gap in the wall took him into a stone-paved courtyard, narrowly avoiding another patrol, and he passed in quick succession through a musty-smelling hall given over to storage of books bound and in scrolls, and a bath-house, empty, its pool dark and still, its rooms smelling of human sweat and soap and oil. There seemed to be guards everywhere here, marching in clattering patrols or standing sentry duty at corners and alleyways and the doors of buildings, where lamps still burned behind the screened windows and every now and then a shadow paused, looking out. The place looked as though it thought itself under siege. No sign of Moth. Mostly he managed to avoid the temple guard by scaling the walls between courtyards. Once, growing frustrated, he knocked one on the head from behind and dropped his partner with a blow to the jaw as he turned. That got him through into a narrow alley alongside a massive, dark hulk of a building, beyond which he could see torchlight.

Quiet as a cat, hah. Something had certainly stirred up the temple. He headed for the torchlight. In a sunken courtyard, a handful of guardsman . . . armoured priests . . . no, walking corpses in scale armour, stood before the smashed door of a squat, domed building.

A broken door and the air of a holy place beyond, guarded by a necromancer's slaves? That was his road.

"Damn it, wolf," he muttered, and strode down into the courtyard. By the time the necromantic guards reacted, drawing weapons, swords and short staves, he was running.

One of the helmet-masked corpses struck at Mikki with her staff. It snapped the air like lightning. He blocked the blow with the haft of his axe and roared at the flare of pain that for a moment blinded him, losing the grip of one hand as an edge of white sparks touched him. The rest of the Red Masks closed up in the doorway.

"You—are—*dead*," he snarled at the bodies in his way, and the one who had struck him blocked in turn the swing of his axe with her white staff. She should have been flung off-balance, if not right out of his path. No human woman came near his weight and the strength of his shoulders. Instead she rocked a little, and his blade slid and turned. Wizardry, rooted and bound in them. His snarl had no words in it, then as he turned and with his next stroke, his whole strength in it, found the threads and the weave of it, the flow of will behind its making. He cut through the spell and took head from body. The next in his way he split like a baulk of timber, broke a sword and flung aside another, not swiftly enough to save himself a moment's searing pain on the hip, as if he'd been struck with a red-hot iron, smell of scorched wool and meat. Not heavily enough to kill, either. The dead man found his feet again, but Mikki was through.

Stairs, down. Three came after him, so he turned and threw them off. He could smell now that Moth had been here, but some time ago. The moon had risen high enough to shed some light through the dome's eye; a crack of water gleamed with the dull lustre of pewter and stirred as he drew near, but no godhead woke to acknowledge him when he knelt and dabbled a hand in it.

Mikki was rising to his feet when a blow to his back sent him staggering forward. He caught himself on the lip of the crack, turning, following the sweep of his axe, and the Red Mask fell headless, the helmeted head rolling into the water with barely a splash, short sword falling by the outstretched hand. Wet on his lower back, and cold. He went down on one knee to steady himself, breath caught in his chest, leaning on the haft of the axe. The other two Red Masks were broken from their fall but crawling towards the well, like blind kittens seeking their mother's warmth.

The headless one did not bleed, only leaked a dark sludge. No ghost that he could see, nothing but a faint and fading keening, as if someone, far away and long ago, wept. Mikki heaved himself up and aside, beheaded both, which seemed to sever the spells binding them to their false life, and half-knelt, half-fell again. His back ached; the blood was flowing too freely when he pressed a hand to it. It might kill a man, depending on how deep the thrust had gone and what it had opened up inside, but he wasn't a man, and he thought maybe it was not so deep as all that, anyway. It slowed under the pressure of his hand. A weak stab from a failing arm, he told himself, and sat still a while, listening for the stir of feet, of more Red Masks sent to the aid of their comrades. Nothing. The bleeding did slow.

Hurt, though, and he would get stiff with sitting. How long had he been there, slipping half into sleep? Found the whetstone in his pouch to put some edge back on the blade while he nerved himself to stand again. Stone was no good chopping block. He rocked to his feet again, cloth tearing from his burnt and oozing hip, shut his eyes against a moment's dizziness. There was another way out, a tunnel opening towards the north. He limped to it warily, sliding around the corner. No ambush waited and no scent of Moth, either.

The ground beneath Mikki's feet shivered, just enough to make him put a hand to the wall. The roof seemed sound enough. He went on in the dark till he found narrow stairs rising. The main passage continued on. Up or onwards? He couldn't guess. He didn't think Moth was here at all. The stair smelt of Red Masks; some private way to the well, perhaps, for the dead. He passed the narrow opening by.

The passage seemed now to be rising. He could smell bodies, living bodies.

A rough door in the wall swung to his weight on an empty closet. Cell. Another, on the other side. Neither had housed prisoners, at least not recently; he felt his way around them and found them utterly bare. Another, and here were bones, a child's, he thought. No ghost, though he called softly, in case it merely feared him. A last, and the door was bolted. When he put a hand to it he felt some wizardry stir, something gathering itself. He didn't wait for what it might do; his fingertips came away with a slick of dust that felt almost oily; rubbing them, he could smell charcoal.

"Anyone in there?" he called softly. No one answered, but there was a scrabbling noise. Not, he thought, rats.

Then a voice, too low to make out.

"Stay back," he warned, and struck the door a slicing blow, splintering away a slab from the surface of one of the broad boards in the centre. Iron and a demon's hand and will behind it. He felt the spell shatter, words torn away. Freeing the gods wouldn't be so simple. This had been a little human spell, the sort of thing Moth might set with a simple rune or two. Good enough for a prisoner who couldn't reach it. The bolt pulled easily. Mikki dragged open the door.

CHAPTER XV

*Z*ora stood, her white gown wet and clinging, on a ledge of rock at the edge of a dark pool. Sien-Mor's sword was in her hand. Ulfhild was here; she could almost . . . there. Standing, her gaze fixed on some distance Zora could not see, sword drawn, hands resting on the hilt. There was nothing to see but the water and the far wall, curved, ridged and rippled, gleaming a little in what could not be moonlight, because they were underground, and yet something held her. Zora looked again. Nothing. The Northron woman had vanished. No, she was still there, that upthrust rib of stone . . . tree, pine leaning out from stone, and the river below, gleaming sleek in the moonlight that had lit the cave, white where it clawed the rocks. Its murmuring and the faint thrumming of the current around the rocks filled her head. Only a tree, dead and broken. Not Ulfhild. Stone. She floated in the depths of the pool, and was that shadow . . . ?

Vartu! she cried, and raised her sword.

Ulfhild turned like a sleeper, slow and heavy in the water, but that was illusion of the shifting dream, maybe, because her blade was there to block Zora's rage-wild swing and strike the next moment, unexpectedly vicious.

She leapt away and turned to see hanks of her hair curling, coiling, falling away. The river churned in flood beneath them and yet the hair fell as if in water.

They were friends, she thought in outrage. How dare Ulfhild try murder in what was a friendly bout in the hall, a trial of skills . . . *Don't*, Sien-Shava had said. *You're no match for the King's Sword unless you mean to sing against her. You don't need to make a fool of yourself before these foreign folk.*

I don't have a brother, Zora told herself, backing away, and for a moment the sword was heavy, unwieldy in her hand, unfamiliar and terrible. She wanted to fling it from her. Revered Shija, staring at her severed wrist.

They had gone laughing down to the beach after, playing ducks and drakes like children, and Sien-Shava, whose stones always flew farthest and skipped most, had laughed with them and told Ulfhild that next time the hall wanted to see the Northron sword set against the blade of the south Nabbani coast, she should spar with a master.

And Ulfhild had said, Ulfhild had said, with the grey, sea-gazing feyness that came on her at times, *Not till we seek one another's deaths, my lord.* She, Sien-Mor, had laughed, to make it a joke so that the cold anger would not swim up behind her brother's eyes, and he had laughed, carefully, because she did, and she was always his guide in such things, smoothing his way among the folk he would otherwise offend. Ulfhild had looked at them like a sleeper waking, saying abruptly that the evening was cold; she was going back to the hall and the fire.

Sien-Mor was not so poor a swordsman as her brother told her, Ulfhild had made her believe. It was only that she moved among masters.

Water bound her, slowed her arms, her thoughts. She danced

in water. No. There was stone beneath her feet, and Ulfhild was where she had not been, sword sweeping for her legs. Zora leapt back again, found stone at her back. The blades rang and clashed, no water slowing them now, sparks flying. She raised her head and sang, weaving words of defence about herself and hesitation, the fatal moment, against her enemy.

Ulfhild's eyes were focussed now, cold and undreaming. Ulfhild, Sien-Mor had always thought, found joy in that place where there was nothing but the sword's edge and the red blood, always blood under-lying the Northron magic, that was what they had gone seeking, the mystery of it, a new folk come out of the sea. Ulfhild's lip curled in contempt at that falling-back on magic maybe, and she sketched runes in the air with her left hand, but Zora's songs held strong and true. Wizardry to wizardry, she was Ulfhild's match, yes, and perhaps her master. She drew power to herself to bind Ulfhild in chains of air, and Ulfhild stumbled, but it was Zora who was bleeding.

Blood stained the air like smoke. No, it coiled in water. There was no riverbank, no ledge of stone in the cave, the Lady's underground reservoir. The Lady held them both and whispered of their deaths, drowned in her water, slow fading, long dying. Ulfhild seemed to pay heed to nothing but Zora before her, and for all the spells she set to wrap herself in safety, the blows came like hail and her arms ached countering them. This body wasn't trained for such work, and water or not, the Lady had them believe they stepped on stone, herself forced back and back, and she felt it broken and treacherous under-foot and knew Ulfhild's blade would be her death—

Something fell past them, dark, flash of white, turning, rags wavering. Helmeted skull, rotten flesh pale, gone to mush in long immersion, shredding away. Hers. Her Red Masks, her wizards and their wizardry was in her. She was Zora, not the wizard Sien-Mor, she was Tu'usha, new Lady, true Lady, she was Marakand. She was wrapped in the Lady's soft embrace, her own shaping turned inside out, but the Red Mask had been hers too long; dead and empty it might be, but the path it had made as it fell into the Lady's waters was a pale thread burning in her mind's eye even as it faded, and she remembered she had no human magic of her own. What she did she drew from her servants, and that thread, those many threads, that great weaving she held wound about her heart. She sang a great, calling darkness, the blindness of black night, about Ulfhild's mind, and she rose through it, an arrow slicing back up the path her servant had made ready for her, last unwitting service, tearing through the cocoon the goddess wove.

Ulfhild she left, lost and dream-drowned in the Lady's embrace.

CHAPTER XVI

Nour sweated and shivered in alternate fever and chills. Two days, had it been, or five? Ivah was no longer certain. Surely not five. They would be dead. Maybe only one. Better, maybe, to be forgotten, to die of thirst, than to end up drowned in the Lady's well. Water seeped down the wall of the cell, but she doubted licking it would keep them alive for much longer. Maybe it was a game and servants of the Lady would come bringing light and water, to find them grovelling in gratitude for that mercy before they were taken to their deaths.

No light. Ivah had never minded darkness, because she had never thought she could be without light at will. When she had come round, with a sick headache and a swollen lump on the back of her skull, she had tried to call up a flame, first with the hexagram of *The sun comes forth from the palace gates* drawn out on her forearm and then, when that failed, by weaving her fingers through her hair in a cat's cradle. She felt the magic gather, both times, and then it was as though it leapt from her, lightning seeking the earth or the heat of some tiny spark lost in a mountain of ice. She had panicked then and run into the wall in a moment's blind terror that she had been buried alive. Only smashing her hand into it and the belated realization that she stood upright brought some sense back. She had resorted to feeling her way around on hands and knees and discovered that the floor was roughly hacked stone, two walls masonry and two carved from rock, the door splintery wood, windowless, and that the body in the last corner, which had sent her bolting back again with a stifled shriek, was too warm to be lifeless. Nour, of course. He woke some time later with a worse headache than hers, which meant he did vomit and didn't have the strength to go blundering around the cell battering himself on the walls trying to find a way out. He did try to work a spell, of course, with no more success than she.

They'd gone through shouting at one another and accusations of betrayal, but after that Nour had said in a weak voice, "You came after me, in the street. I did see." And he had added, "That was stupid of you."

"You're welcome."

"I meant, thank you."

She had heard him moving, groping towards her, and after a moment reached, catching his sleeve, not the one that was stiff with blood. They had sat pressed together, for what comfort that could give.

"Is she coming for us, do you think?"

She told him what she remembered of the Voice she had seen in the pulpit, lying eyes slitted, playing dead, or whatever they thought she ought to be, and how the girl had claimed to be Marakand's Lady in the flesh, to the shock of the guard captain.

"I remember. Like nightmare, all scraps. No words. I saw her. She saw me. I . . . she was the Lady and not a new Voice? She said so?"

"The priests were all terrified. Yes."

"I thought she was—she looked like someone I knew, once. Samra, her name was, but she died years ago. It *was* Samra, her face in her youth . . . the first time I saw her, the most beautiful woman.

She died but . . . her daughter looked like her even as a child, you could see how she'd grow. Lovely . . . tall. She disappeared, she and her father. She'd be twenty now, maybe, the daughter. Zora, her name was. This Lady was taller than Samra." Ivah waited, but there was nothing more about the Lady. "No way out, without magic, unless we can kill whoever finally comes for us," Nour said at last. "I suppose they'll take us to drown in her well?" Another pause. "You'd better kill me."

So they had argued about that, and she had ended up, stupidly, in tears, because she wasn't going to strangle him or smother him, which were his only two practical suggestions.

"I know where Hadidu would go, and you don't," he had said. "Great Gods, Ivah, you risked your life and ended up here by saving Hadidu and little Shemal and the servants. Don't destroy the good of that. I know too many names of the loyal folk of Ilbialla and Gurhan. I have to die before they take us to the well for the Lady."

"We've already been before the Lady. She's already got that knowledge, or she can't get it."

"Any goddess can know a man's mind. She's playing with us like a cat with a mouse. She'll send for us again. You have to do it, Ivah."

"I can't!" she screamed. "Don't ask me. I can't murder you, I won't!"

"Then what did you get involved for in the first place? Why didn't you just run? You're betraying Hadi and Shemal to her just as much as if you'd led the Red Masks to the Doves yourself, if you let the Lady have me."

"I can't! No!"

Nour had huddled silent in a far corner after that and had let the matter drop. He had been quiet, calm, friendly even, as they had tried to work out which was the most downhill corner to relieve themselves in. They quickly found they had gotten it wrong.

He had tried to strangle himself with his shirt the first time she fell asleep. Ivah woke, hearing a wheezing, squeaking sound. Nour vomiting again, she thought. The hangover of the Red Mask's staves still lingered. He gasped horribly, breath squealing, and she flung herself to the sound, groping, finding the twisted rope of cloth, dragging his hands from it. He clawed at her weakly, then more strongly, gasping for air, getting his hands on her own throat, thumbs pressing. She kneed him in the belly so that he lost what breath he had, and his hands fell away. She gasped for breath herself and rolled him over, half-lying over his back, pinning his hands above his head. She got hold of the twisted shirt and hurled it away, and he just lay there, not struggling. Not dead, either. His ribs heaved under her. Defeated. His wounded cheek was pressed to the floor. She let him up, and he still didn't speak. Maybe he couldn't. He was shivering, face wet, though she couldn't tell if it was tears or the oozing burn or the unclean dampness of the floor, as she held him, cheek to his good cheek, muttering, "Don't, oh don't. Don't leave me here alone in the dark."

Nour had said nothing, but his arm went around her, clutching, only for comfort, not to try again to throttle her. They sat so through what might have been the rest of the night, but for all they knew, could have been a sunny afternoon.

After that Ivah hadn't dared sleep.

Nour was quite justified. What right did she have to prevent him, if it was all he could do to save his kinsman's life and the lives of his friends, before the Lady got around to questioning him? But she still couldn't allow herself to sleep, staying wakeful for as long as she could, pacing, pinching herself, sitting so that she was too uncomfortable to do more than nod. By then Nour's hand and slashed arm were swollen and hot, as were the seeping burns on his face where the white fire had flared from a Red Mask's staff. He alternately sweated and shivered. Ivah tried what spells she could think of and felt their virtue snap away from her like snatched threads. All she could do was wet his shirt in the seepage down the damp wall and try to cool his forehead with it. She didn't dare wash the wounds; Great Gods knew where the water came from, and her father had always sworn dirty water was deadly to broken skin. Pointless precaution; they drank it, licked it from the wall, and sucked it from the shirt.

It was too late anyhow. He'd lain with that cheek to the filthy floor, and her own weight pressing him into it.

Sometimes he raved and muttered and cried out for Hadidu and someone called Kharduin, or Shemal his nephew, and flailed as though he sought them through the fire.

"Hush," she would tell him then, catching his hands in the dark. "They're safe, everyone's safe. Go to sleep." It would be a mercy, she thought, to kill him in his sleep, as he had said, before it grew any worse or the Lady remembered them. This was going to be a long and agonized death, whether through wound-fever or thirst. Once she wadded up his shirt and pressed it over his face, but as he stirred and gasped and tried to turn his head she flung it away and held him instead, crying.

Coward.

Sometimes he cried out that he had to warn Talfan, warn Farnos, warn Jugurthos against Zora. Ivah knew all three of those names; Talfan was an apothecary from Clothmarket Ward, married to some outlander caravaneer, who came around for private coffee in the kitchen every month or so and whom Ivah had assumed to have an interest in Hadidu that went beyond coffee, given the absent husband and all. Old Master Farnos was the baker a few houses up the street and a good friend of Hadidu's. Jugurthos might be Jugurthos

Barraya, who was gate-captain of Sunset Ward, though she had never seen him in the Doves except having coffee in the front parlour, like any other street guard of that garrison. Now Nour's death wouldn't save his friends after all, unless she could bring herself to kill both him and herself.

It didn't matter anyway. The damned goddess, whether she was really this girl Zora he had once known or not, had forgotten them. The Voice had executed people who defied her by that means before, denying them water, but in public. The senators who defied her had died so, in cages in the palace plaza. Maybe it was how every single wizard had died, hidden, forgotten in the darkness, not drowned in the deep well after all. Maybe there were cells beneath the temple compound full of rat-gnawed bones.

Ghu had said the Red Masks were dead. Necromancy. Corpses woken to serve the Lady. Great Gods, no.

The floor beneath her feet trembled, dying away before she was certain she had felt it.

"Nour?" she whispered. He didn't answer.

If the building above collapsed in earthquake, they might escape. Or die, trapped, but they were already doing that. Another great quake, please, Old Great Gods, to leave the city in rubble, priests and goddess and all, a wasteland, forgotten, a tale of the road, no more . . . but maybe she had imagined it. She was dizzy and dreaming, that was all.

Water from the wall wouldn't keep them alive forever. Nour would die first, as his wounds festered. Then she could eat him. She hadn't thought that. She had not. Besides, what good would it do? She tried again to open the damned door, to blow it thunderously across whatever open space lay beyond, as her father might have done, to pull down the masonry walls or delicately tease the lock or bolt outside to open, which would have been her mother's approach. She tried to shape a dream to call to the devil Vartu, to Ghu, whatever he was, to anyone who might hear, but she still felt the magic flow away like sand between her fingers as she shaped it, and she knew nobody heard.

But then there was sound. A Northron voice called, which was a dream, but she woke and reached, found nothing, scurried for Nour and grabbed him, checking that he was alive. He moaned and clutched at her. Soft scratching at the door. She didn't dream the sound. Better to die attacking Red Masks than to be taken to the Lady's well.

"Nour," she croaked, and dragged him to sit against the wall. "Wake up."

He groaned.

"They're coming. I think we should—we should make an end of this."

Nour understood. He said nothing but crawled to arm and knees, and then to his feet, swaying. Ivah helped him to get propped against the wall, stood at his shoulder, thinking: face, throat. Rip the veil away and hurt the bloodless—thing—at the very least, before it could summon up its divine blessing and knock them cowering down in unreasoning terror. Enrage it so that it struck with fire on its staff and they fell dead as the city folk said rioters and rebels had in the past.

Cleaner to have stayed and burnt in the Doves in her own fire.

There was a voice again, and the door slammed and thudded.

And opened. She felt the draft of it, the change of air, clean. She clawed up at where a face should be, punching with the other hand, but she was weak and slow. Her fingers met no veil, her fist no flesh, nothing, and she lurched off balance, was caught and held. Nour simply flung himself and fell into the open space beyond.

"Easy, easy!" the man said in the Northron of her father's favourite *noekar*, his vassals and tent guard, "I'm a friend." And then, as he lowered her to the floor, "Eh, it's the daughter of Tamghiz."

No red robe, no veil. There was light, coming dim and distant, enough to see shapes. A tall, broad-shouldered man wearing only a tunic. He set down a long-hafted axe and reached a hand to Nour, who found his feet and put his back against the far wall of what was a roughly cut stone passageway.

Ivah lunged to put herself by Nour. They were out. And the door was only bolted outside, not locked, one shove and they could shut the man in. Foolish thought. It would be like shoving a mountain. She huddled against Nour, trying to frame a coherent question. The man was Northron, and—and the light wasn't his. She felt stunned and stupid, as if her thoughts were mired in spring clay. Someone else was coming.

"What's going on?" Nour demanded, sounding like a truculent child woken suddenly from sleep. "Red Masks?"

"Coming," the stranger said, taking up his axe again. A few Nabbani characters ran across the door in smudged black lines, partially splintered away. In some access of anger, he struck the door another blow that left it wrenched and broken on its hinges. "Sorry, I think they knew when I broke the spell on the door. No idea where this goes, but get going, that way. Up. I'll deal with these and follow you." He wasn't a caravaneer; the Northron accent was heavy on his tongue, and the words came slowly in the speech of the desert road. "Can he walk, Ivah?"

"Yes," Nour answered, but she doubted it. He staggered, trying to stand. She put an arm around him and started up the passage, into utter blackness, around a curve. She hoped that they weren't heading for the deep well, but she did think the uneven, toe-catching floor was rising, ever so slightly.

After a while Nour, breathless, said, "Friend of yours?"

"No."

"Knew your name."

"No—" But he had. And her father's, too, his true name, which she had only learned at the end of everything. "I don't know him." Not one of her father's followers; he certainly wasn't a man you'd forget, once seen. "Don't talk," she gasped. Her knees felt weak, trembling, and where were they going, how far, and how long could even an axe-wielding giant stand against Red Masks?

When the faint silver glow, flickering like moonlight through wind-tossed trees, came sweeping towards them, she barely had time to be alarmed before the dog appeared, a clotted shadow of night.

Of course the Blackdog had been going to come for her sometime. She had always known it. She shoved Nour behind her. "Go back!" she screamed at him. "Run!"

The charge faltered, and the silver fire touched her but did not burn, slithering water-cool over her upraised arm. "Leave him!" she tried to plead, but what she felt was worse than the terror the Red Masks could inflict, because it was truly her own, and she deserved whatever the Blackdog did to her. Nour did not, but the Blackdog was mad, her father always said, mad and unreasoning, not a man at all. "Just me, he's nothing to do with me, Holla-Sayan, let him go— Old Great Gods, please . . ."

CHAPTER XVII

Gaguush mumbled in her sleep and turned over, catching him in the ribs with an elbow. Holla-Sayan had been lying wakeful anyway, despite the weariness of the last long haul of the road. They'd unloaded, tended the camels, sent messages to their contacts, the merchants with whom Gaguush usually dealt. They'd been to the bathhouse, ended up dining well in a wineshop, those of the gang who hadn't taken themselves off to their Marakander families in the city, Tihmrose and Northron Varro, whose wife Talfan was an apothecary in Clothmarket Ward, and Judeh the camel-leech. The others were asleep down in the arcade room with the larger bales of goods, except young Zavel, who had disappeared after the wineshop and would no doubt stagger in tomorrow or the next day, surly and bleary-eyed, his pay spent and wanting to borrow against the next trip. Gaguush was running out of patience with him. Not Holla's problem. He'd keep the boy in line on the road, but he wasn't Zavel's uncle or his brother, to be chasing him in the city. If Zavel wanted a man's privileges, he had to take on the responsibilities of one.

Holla-Sayan ought to be sleeping. He felt as if he could have slept even propped against a rock. But sleep wouldn't take him. He folded himself around Gaguush, brushing lips over neck, but she didn't stir again. She was so damned tired, she complained. Nobody had told her being pregnant made you so tired. Nobody had told her morning-sickness could last all day.

Nobody, including herself, had expected her to end up pregnant now, to be having her first baby when most women were having their last. She had been divorced as barren when she was, in Holla-Sayan's Westgrasslander opinion, too young to have been married anyway. If she had ever pined for children in all the years since, she had never let on to him, and he had been her lover, off and on, since he had come over the Kinsai-av from the Western Grass and been hired into her gang. On their last trip south from At-Landi he had finally persuaded her to cross the river, to stand with him before his god Sayan, and, even more importantly, his mother and father and brothers and their wives and their sons and a scatter of other kinsfolk, to marry him. Going up into the mountains to Lissavakail to tell the goddess Attalissa and their friend Bikkim, her mortal husband, had been Gaguush's idea, which he had taken to pointing out whenever she tried to blame him for her current state.

"My blessings," Attalissa had said. "It's about time." She had kissed Gaguush's forehead and winked at Holla. "Take good care of her, Blackdog. She's earned it, putting up with you."

They were carrying only Gaguush's own goods, and some for kin of Varro's the Northron was acting as agent for, not escorting any merchants, so they had lingered longer than a caravan could usually afford to, honoured guests of the temple. Holla-Sayan had fled temple and town after two days to run wild on the mountain, rejoining the gang only as they left. He was not Attalissa's Blackdog any longer, and if the man he had been was glad to know his foster-daughter well and happy, that man had been possessed by an enslaved and soul-damaged spirit, and now that they were—he was—something whole and entire, and *free*, neither part of his twinned soul was particularly glad to be so near the goddess for long. The rest of the gang, those who had survived the battle at Lissavakail, enjoyed the leisure and the luxury of heroes, the goddess's chosen companions in her exile, her saviours.

But now they were come at last to the caravanserai suburb of Marakand in the rift between the Malagru and the Pillars of the Sky, and Gaguush, who had thought she was poisoned by bad water or falling into some desperate illness, had finally, snarling and cursing, agreed with Tihmrose and Thekla, the other two women of the gang. She was, miraculously, pregnant. And it was, of course, all Holla-Sayan's fault.

"I certainly hope so," he had said to that as they loaded up just this morning, out in the Stone Desert, for the climb to the pass of Marakand. He'd had to duck a flying halter. "Is it so bad?" he had dared to ask. His own reaction was an urge to wander around grinning like an imbecile, singing happily and telling everyone he knew, an urge he heroically resisted as liable to result in things heavier or sharper than halters coming his way. "Gaguush, how was I to know Attalissa would decide you—we—needed a child? It's not as if she asked me, and you can't expect me to know what she's thinking."

"Of course I can't, you hardly talk to her anymore and after six bloody years hardly letting her out of your sight—"

He couldn't try to explain that to her. The gang didn't understand, really, what he had been. What he had become since.

"Don't stand there trying to look so sympathetic, you don't understand, you can't understand, you're a bloody *man* . . ."

She ended up clutching him, sobbing on him till his shirt was wet through, while the rest of the gang pretended not to see.

He had untangled Gaguush's words from the sobs, all choked in his shirt, eventually. Simply. "I'm scared, Holla."

Afraid of the responsibility of a child, after so long resigned to childlessness. It was as life-changing as a death. And afraid, naturally enough, of all that could go wrong, and did go wrong, far too often. "I don't think Attalissa would have wished your death on you," he said, and hoped—trusted, because Attalissa was still Pakdhala too, still the girl he and the gang had raised—that the goddess had seen so far ahead. Gaguush seemed less jagged with nerves after that reassurance.

"We could call her Pakdhala, if she's a girl," she had even suggested, when they made up their bed among the bundles of Northron furs and amber and sea-ivory in this upper room of old Master Rasta's caravanserai. They had an appointment come morning with a Family Xua elder, who would probably take the lot, though it would mean a day's hard bargaining to persuade the man of that.

"We could not." Holla knew she hadn't been serious. "Try again."

She had fallen asleep muttering over names.

In the night, colour washed out of her tattoos. The jagged Black Desert geometry in red and black made a pattern different than what daylight showed, to vision that wasn't human in the night, which saw the flow of life in her, the memory of stone in the pigment, echoes of desert, sun, snow, in the blanket woven of camel's wool. He ran a hand down the curve of her side, but she still didn't stir, so he pulled the scattered bedding over her and rolled away, chin on arms. He couldn't sleep and wished that either he could, or that Gaguush would wake up for company, because then he could be distracted from worrying, at least about things that shouldn't be any concern of a landless caravan-mercenary. Even a heated debate about baby names, if nothing else was on offer . . .

When they'd ridden in that afternoon, grey with desert dust, the camels' long strides swinging up the road with the same even pace at which they'd left snowy At-Landi in the north, they had found the suburb stirring like a trampled hill of ants. The caravanserais and coffeehouses and taverns were all talking of nothing but the Lady, who, following the assassination of her Voice by Praitan rebels and traitors, had left her well at last the day before. There was more than a little doubt in the suburb, at least among the folk of the road, of the divinity of the beautiful girl the Marakanders were in such a ferment over, though some of them had gone into the city the previous day to see her, as she rode in a procession through the wards of the city.

Attalissa had never felt there was any goddess in Marakand. Holla-Sayan wished the caravan had arrived a day earlier, so that he could have seen the alleged goddess. There was something lingering in the air of the city that he'd never . . . smelt . . . felt . . . before. Not here, at any rate. It took him back to the temple gate-tower at Lissavakail, with Tamghat on the shore. The same scent of ashy stone and tang of metal . . . no threat to Attalissa, who was not his any longer. It had not even been he who stood there, but Otokas, who had been the Blackdog's host before him. It was the scent of Moth, of himself, maybe. Not even a scent. He simply had no words. If he shut his eyes, he thought, *fire, iron, ice, starlight.* It had ebbed with the coming dusk, a fresh breeze off the mountains blowing it away.

It was not the air of a god of the earth.

So what, then, had come out of the temple's sacred well to ride through the city?

"Devils take it." Holla-Sayan could laugh at the oath even as he whispered it, groping for his clothes and his sabre.

Gaguush flung out an arm, reaching for him.

"Can't sleep," he whispered over her. "I'm going out to run in the dark."

She'd heard that often enough before, this past year. "Don't eat anybody," she mumbled, without ever fully waking. Old joke by now, and a bad one, but she couldn't say, *I love you, come back safe, what's bothering you?*—not Gaguush. He kissed her cheek and left her.

No curfew in the suburb. The caravanserai master's own porter let him out the little door set in the greater gate with a nod and thought whatever she might think about a man creeping out from his wife's side in the night. Not her business to think. There were men and women still out and about by the light of the moon, just past full, caravaneers, mostly, and mostly, from the smell of them, on their way back from taverns. He kept his head down, avoided any noisy clusters, and left the main spread of caravanserais and inns behind, passing the Gore where the city's paupers were buried and the pens of the various dealers in beasts. Watchdogs growled warning at, not of, him but did not bark alarm. Horses snorted and stirred as he passed. Camels were more phlegmatic, grumbling where they lay. He dropped down into the ravine where it curved against the road, startled a pair of feral swine and followed their pattering hoofbeats along a path through dense willow-scrub. Holla-Sayan found the hard-beaten path used by guardsmen of the Riverbend Gate, patrolling for rebels or thief-gangs or whatever they thought might lurk there beneath the trees. The wall of the temple precinct was high; it would take the dog to leap it, but buildings backed onto the ravine and there was a faint old scent, diffused by rain. Not human. Rancid olive oil. Puzzling. He went exploring up the stone ledges and found a door beneath bruised leaves. Recently oiled, and it wasn't even locked. He slipped inside.

There had been humans in this house, or whatever it was, but not in the past couple of days. The deep well was a great underground pool with a shrine of some kind over it, according to his friend Judeh, whose father had been a priest of the Lady before his death in the earthquake. He wouldn't find the well in this outbuilding but more centrally, yet . . . here was a door, and a faint cooler air seeped beneath it. He opened it. As he had thought, the air of a damp cellar gusted up to meet him: musty staleness, rotten wood, musky beast, scent that was not scent but memory of cool green, earth and leaf, pines. Blood and, faintly, humans.

Her.

The Blackdog plunged snarling down the stairs, claws slithering, marking the stone. Changing shape was only an echo of the bone-cracking agony it had been when he was human and possessed, or maybe it was that, chest shattered, mortal body half-consumed and remade in the fire of the devil's soul, the pain didn't have such great weight anymore. He still didn't shift form except when the dog was strong, the wordless passions of the wounded and broken devil's soul too much to shape to coherency, or the threat too great or too sudden for spear or sabre to quell. A cellar, deserted, cluttered with abandoned baskets and broken shelves and jars, squeaking mice, but another stair, narrower, led deeper, to where the walls were stained with pale lines of lime, and damp seeped through the cracked corners. It was all abandoned, rooms empty save for some mouldering, rotting wood, whatever furniture or tool it had once been long past knowing. The scent of her was strong, and very recent. Blood, too, and terror, and diseased flesh. The scent of the woman was before him, running ahead of her on the rising air, up through a narrow, stone-cut passage that sloped down before levelling out. The floor was damp and uneven, lightless. He could call up a light, though Holla-Sayan was no wizard. The Blackdog did such things, odd powers half-remembered. He flung light ahead of him, silver, hunting streaks of fire. The stone had its powers and life, and he would not trip or run into walls, but true vision made the world real.

She was ahead of him, a pale wisp staggering forward under the weight of a large man who sagged against her, arm over her shoulder, head hanging. His snarl rose to a singing howl, and the arrowing streaks of light circled like live things, falcons stooping, showing her gaping face as she looked up, screamed, and hurled the man away from her.

She didn't run but fell to her knees, gasping as if punched below the ribs, a hand up to shield her face. "Go back—run!" was her first coherent shriek, more of a croak, and then, "Leave him! Just me, he's nothing to do with me, Holla-Sayan, let him go—Old Great Gods, please . . ."

The Blackdog came to a skittering stop, and the man, who had fallen behind her, came crawling back. A caravaneer, but he smelt of smoke, not camels, and blood, and pus, and with a shaking hand he tried to scratch what looked like Nabbani characters on the floor, while the silver light faded to something tenuous and slow, winding around them, circling the Blackdog, fading to rest on his fur, like a snowfall.

"Can't run," the man said. "Go. I'll hold it here." But whatever he was trying to build was like a weak breeze pushing against an ancient tree, and the Blackdog surged forward, grown to the size of a yearling yak, a paw obliterating the crooked marks. He shouldered the strange wizard sprawling aside. The woman made no move to defend herself, only shivered, huddled small, staring up at him. She might have tried to speak, but her teeth chattered beyond controlling.

He could grab her by the throat like a rat. One shake, hurl her into the wall. She'd left Bikkim lying with his throat cut, and if it hadn't been her hand on the knife, it had been done by her order and her will. That Bikkim had survived was no lessening of the treachery.

She'd bespelled Holla's friends into trusting her, bound his Pakdhala helpless through wizardry and handed her over, sacrifice to a devil who would have consumed her to take on godhead himself.

She shivered like a rabbit and did nothing but wait.

Holla-Sayan flowed back into man's form, brushing the light from his hair, flicking it off into a hovering fog, and with his sabre's point under her chin forced her shaking to her feet.

"Ivah," he said, and it was still half the wordless dog's snarl.

Nour came stupidly trying to defend her, trying to scribble some syllables of defence, and the dog swelled into something twice the size of any natural hound and spurned the spell with a paw that looked taloned like a lion's. Shadow roiled, and he was the man Ivah knew, with a greenish peridot fire still blazing in his eyes, as if he were some shell encasing light, a lantern only, but the steel against her throat was real enough, and she staggered to her feet obedient to its pressure as he rolled light into a silver mist hanging about them in the air. A Westgrasslander caravaneer, dark-brown hair in the many braids of the desert road, tattooed owls curving from temples down under the eyes, snakes coiling on his cheeks, a hint of the cheetahs twining and knotting on his forearms visible on the backs of his hands.

He wasn't supposed to be a wizard. He had spoken no word, made no pattern of power in any folk's magic. She was weeping, she thought. Stupid, and coward. Her father's daughter shouldn't weep, didn't weep. But she had decided not to be her father's daughter. She wouldn't be shamed if her eyes wept.

Holla-Sayan blinked, entirely human now. He looked, if anything, confused, and Ivah tried to slow her panic-gasping breaths. She was going to faint and cut her own throat on the point of his sabre. Holla-Sayan lowered the blade, just enough, and Nour swayed to his feet, put his good hand to the flat of it and pushed sideways. It didn't move.

"What have you done to him?" Holla-Sayan demanded hoarsely. Ivah shook her head, wordless.

"She's a wizard." Holla-Sayan snarled the word at Nour. "She bespells trust and then betrays it. Stand away from her."

"My friend," Nour said.

"I didn't," Ivah protested. "Great Gods, Nour, I didn't, not to you, not to Hadidu, only to make him think of offering me the room, that was all, just the once and it was so slight an impulse, it wouldn't have worked if it hadn't been half in his mind already. I needed a safe place to live, I needed to be there, to study the tomb, and he liked me before that, he wanted to like me, and I only, I only, Old Great Gods be my witness, I never betrayed you or him, it wasn't me!'

"Know that now," he said. "It was little Zora. Her mother's face. Knew you'd messed about with Hadi, though." He frowned almost drunkenly. "He wouldn't be so stupid, otherwise, 'cept he was ha'f in love with you, 'a course, but it didn't seem like he was getting anywhere with that."

She fell to her knees again, bowed as one might to the emperor, face to the ground, or to an executioner and couldn't find any words adequate. She shivered and thought, so she was a coward at the end. At least it would be the sword and not the beast.

"Bikkim lived," Holla-Sayan said.

"Please. Nour . . ." She herself didn't know what she meant, a plea for Nour's forgiveness or help, or that Holla-Sayan would save him once he had killed her. Her voice trembled so the words squeaked and stammered.

"Something's back there," Holla-Sayan said flatly, "and it smells

. . . dead." His fingers dug into her shoulder as he dragged her to her feet. "Here." He pushed past her, tossing his damned sabre back as though it were a stick, but she managed to snatch the hilt rather than the edge as he surged into the Blackdog's form again, something half-mountain-mastiff, half-wolf, black and shaggy, just the faintest suggestion that for a moment he was nothing but formless darkness, a distillation of deepest night shot with starlight. The silver mist settled on him like dew and vanished.

Something dead but not rotting. Cold, bitter with a power that was not wizardry, but it smelt of wizardry as well, that trace of the earth's magic that ran in such folk from whatever long-forgotten god-ancestor had so blessed them. The thing had been a boy once, gangly-thin, on the cusp of manhood; now it was a shell, with chains like cobweb lace binding it to some other will, and rags of its soul pinned, still struggling, to the husk, the rest lost, drifting in the dark, name gone, heart gone, memory a jumble of meaningless fragments of image, as if someone had painted the boy's life on a beaker of glass, then smashed it and swept half the shards away. One of the fabled Red Masks, his face hidden to hide it from anyone who had known him in life. He strode along the passage, sword in one hand, a short white staff in the other. Searching for Tamghat's thrice-damned daughter and her friend.

Sometimes the instincts of that ancient true dog, unfortunate parasitized first host to the broken devil's soul, the anchor in the world it had taken in its dying desperation, were to be trusted. His growl rose to a snarl of rage at the wrongness of the thing, slavery beyond death and the destruction of a soul that should have long gone to the road. The Blackdog leapt, seizing the Red Mask by the throat as if he had been a terrier and the boy a rat, and hurled him into the wall and out of the web that bound him, out of the false perversion of life. The body fell and rolled, empty, nothing but a weight of bone and flesh now. The rags of the soul fled it; he waited, half hoping the boy might yet find himself, draw himself together as drops of water touch and merge, but they were lost in the dark.

Grunt and muffled curse, and the smell of fresh blood, which he had been smelling, smell of—damn it, bear.

Mikki?

"Blackdog!" the man bellowed. The dog barked, deep, angry baying, took off running again. If he'd been paying attention to anything but the scent of Ivah . . .

The bear-man was hard beset, with his back to the wall, three Red Masks at his feet, unmoving, but his own neck bled, and though one staggered, shoulder half carved away, the axe caught in the armour and slid from Mikki's blood-slippery grip. A fallen torch still burned on the floor. Holla wove through them, grown without conscious will to the size nearly of a bear, bit through the back of a neck, smashed another into the wall. The last suddenly turned and ran. Mikki hurled his recovered axe after it and split the skull.

"One got by," the demon gasped. "Ivah?"

Not by me, it didn't. And I haven't killed her yet. He had no speech when he was the dog.

"Don't. Moth likes her."

Damn Moth.

Mikki came down heavily on one knee, shut his eyes a moment. "What was that, six? And I killed five getting this far. How many are there supposed to be, in all?"

"No idea," Holla pulled himself back to man's shape, took up the torch, and offered the demon a hand up. "Let's get out of here. Or are you waiting for Moth?"

"Is she here?" Mikki asked. The demon limped and staggered. Sayan help him, he couldn't carry all three of them out.

"You are, I thought she'd be too. But—" Holla-Sayan reached out, searching, "no. Did you think she was?"

"She went to the temple this morning. Scouting, she said. Quietly. Promised, quietly. Said she'd be back by evening. Wasn't. I came to find her."

"She's not here. Nothing's here. They say there's a goddess, but where it passed through the city yesterday it smelt like a devil to me. But it's *gone*, now."

"So's Moth. She didn't take Lakkariss."

"Not good."

"No."

After a while Holla-Sayan said, "If it comes back, and Moth doesn't—"

"I nearly got killed last time I tried to fight a devil on my own."

"I did," Holla said drily. "Not that you'd notice. What do we do about it? I'm not touching that sword. It wants me."

"Moth will come back."

"If she can."

"She will." Mikki staggered into him. Holla steadied him, a hand under his elbow. A nice mess to take back to Gaguush, and to take Ivah—no.

Holla-Sayan had gone, and Ivah was blind again, with Nour somewhere by her. He touched her, and she gasped, flinched, found his arm with her left hand and clutched him there, so he couldn't stumble in front of her, now that she was armed.

A rib-shuddering growl rising into a snarl, a man's shout, a thud. Great Gods, not the axeman, Holla-Sayan hadn't met and killed the axeman. Silence again, except maybe there were voices she couldn't quite catch.

Cold hells take it, anyway. She turned Nour loose. The Red Masks already knew there were wizards down here. *The sun comes forth from the palace gates*, pressed with a nail into her own right arm, and Great Gods, the relief when light bloomed, like a memory of sun, before her chest. She gestured it higher, pointed Nour down to where wall met floor. He nodded and slid, clumsy, to crouch there, not protesting, out of the way if more enemies appeared. She took a few steps back down the tunnel, her light gliding with her.

Light met her, red torchlight. No need for the sabre; it was Holla-Sayan, human again, supporting the Northron by the arm. He was even taller than she had thought, head and shoulders above the Westgrasslander, and alarmingly pale, as if he'd bled nearly to death.

"Red Masks?" she whispered.

"Dead," said Mikki. "Or something. They were already dead."

"I know," she said. She couldn't take her eyes off Holla-Sayan. He could kill her. The Northron wouldn't stop him. Nothing would. He hadn't, but he could, he would, so she had to tell him, because someone had to know, someone who could do something to stop the Lady. "Ghu—a boy, a man I met, he killed one with a touch." Her teeth still chattered, but the sabre in her hand, Holla-Sayan's sabre, was steady, as though that arm belonged to some other woman whom nothing could ever rattle. "I saw him do it. He said they had to be . . ." A lifetime since. Was Ghu here too? She had not even thought to ask. ". . . to be cut off from what was feeding them. It's some kind of necromancy." She swallowed. Her voice croaked, parched.

"Killing them enough they know they're dead seems to work, too," Holla-Sayan said, and his mouth twisted, as if at a foul taste. "How did you end up here?"

"Red Masks," she answered, and heard her voice sink to a whisper again. "I think that's what happens to wizards. Maybe the Voice— the Lady, locks them up to die first, like us. Holla-Sayan, are there any other prisoners here? Ghu—when they captured us, he was behind. He was injured, lame. He wasn't in the temple when they took us before the Lady."

Holla-Sayan studied her. She resisted the urge to wrap her arms tight, to hide herself. She stank. Even as a man, he must smell as well as a dog did, to have smelt the Red Mask coming. He was a man now; the yellow-green light had faded from his eyes. They were green-flecked hazel, she remembered. She'd always liked his eyes. Wanted them warmer, when he looked at her. Remembering that shamed her now.

"Bones," he said. "The only humans down here are you two. And the bear."

"Bear?" she asked, wondering what she'd misheard. Ulfhild had said something about a bear when they spoke by Ilbialla's tomb.

"Me," said the Northron. "Dog, stop glaring at her, you're scaring her out of her wits. Let's get out, as you said. Moth's not here."

"Who's Moth?" Ivah asked.

"Ulfhild," said the Northron.

"Ulfhild?" Ivah wouldn't have thought she could know such relief at that name. "Is she here?"

"No, she's not," said Holla-Sayan. "His name's Mikki. And he belongs to her."

"Hah, other way around, foolish dog."

"Yeah, you can say so. I'm a married man now; I know how these things go." He put a hand on Ivah's arm, just a touch, which made her shiver, but he only wanted his sabre back. A glance at her light, and he stubbed out the torch on the floor, left it lying. "Take your friend and go ahead. I'm sure we haven't killed, or whatever you want to call it, all of them yet."

"Wasps," said Mikki, a bit indistinctly. "Reaction, I think, like wasps. I've broken into their nest and so some followed me, but they won't come hunting now we're out of sight and memory, not until their maker comes back to set them going with her will."

"You go ahead as well," Holla-Sayan told him. "You're no more use than the other two."

But when they came to stairs, endless stairs, Ivah thought, Holla-Sayan took Nour's weight from her and left the Northron Mikki to guard their backs, or perhaps he could smell there was no pursuit. Up and up. Nour stumbled on a step, and Holla-Sayan lifted him bodily to a landing, saying, "Catch your breath. There's a ways to go yet."

"Kharduin's gang," Nour gasped, the first he'd spoken in some time. Ivah wasn't certain he even realized he was with strangers. "Shenar's caravanserai."

"So you can die of wound-fever there? Yes, all right. I'm certainly not taking *her* anywhere near my gang. It'd be throwing a rat to the dogs. What were you doing in Marakand, Ivah? Looking for a new master?"

"Dog," Mikki rumbled, in what sounded like reproof.

"I—I was studying Ilbialla's tomb. You must have seen it, in Sunset Market."

"Yes. What is it?"

"A prison, Moth thinks," Mikki said.

"I can't even translate it, I can't read the writing, except a few words that might be really old Imperial Nabbani written out by sound in some Pirakuli script. Holla-Sayan, the Lady—she's the same as my father, isn't she?"

He stopped, and she staggered into him.

"*Father?*"

"Father?" Nour asked, but she ignored him. Old Great Gods save her, bad enough he knew what she had done to Hadidu. And she'd thought, since Holla-Sayan knew Ulfhild Vartu—

"You didn't know I was—" She could hardly even whisper. "Tamghat—Tamghiz Ghatai—was my father."

Nour, lost in some fog of his own, had missed that and was muttering, "I never man'ged to read any words in't a'tall. Wish we'd known wha' you w'rup to."

After a moment Holla-Sayan tugged them both onwards, leaving Mikki to follow. And the stairs were at an end. Her knees shook on the blessed flat; she had to lean on the wall to catch her breath. Holla-Sayan batted at her light with a hand, and it was quenched, as if he'd crushed a spark. Darkness returned.

"I've never noticed that there's anything in the tomb in the Sunset Ward market," he said, as if that last exchange had not happened, "but maybe I don't know what I'm looking for. I've never bothered to go sniffing around it. Marakand has no gods that I've ever noticed, though, and none Attalissa ever knew of, either."

She tried to moisten her mouth. "That girl." She realized he would never have seen her. "A girl in the great hall of their temple. They took us there, for judgement by the Voice, but they didn't call her the Voice. They said—she said—she was the Lady herself, and I believed her. She wasn't any priestess. Is she one of—of the seven?"

"Probably," he said, and Mikki growled, "Yes."

They couldn't fight a devil. Even the Blackdog hadn't been able to—it was Ulfhild who had killed her father, she knew, despite what the songs on the caravan road said, and Ulfhild Vartu wasn't here. Great Gods, please, let there be water, somewhere.

"What," Holla-Sayan asked, "will you do now? Is Ketsim yours? They say he's the temple's man, ruling the westernmost Praitannec tribe. Will you go to him? Claim your rights as his lord? Take rule of that tribe from Marakand?"

"You can kill Ketsim, for all I care," she croaked. "You should have killed him at Serakallash, when you lot killed everybody else. I don't want to be a damned Great Grass chieftain or make myself a warlord."

"What do you want?"

"I don't know!" She was shivering again. Old Great Gods save her, he was still thinking about killing her. Trial and judgement, staggering in the dark.

"Don't shout. There's nobody in this house that I can smell, but don't shout anyway."

Nour slipped and hung a moment from Holla's grip. Ivah hauled his other arm over her own shoulders.

"Water," she said, as if that would produce it.

"Bring back the gods," Nour rasped. "Raise the city. Need the gods." Each word was an effort now. "Can't read th' inscriptions. Been to Nabban, imperial wizards. Nobody knows. Can't break the walls. Tried, long 'go. Hadi's mother died. Red Masks came. Killed e'ryone. But i' kill Red Masks—Ghu—an' if you can read the spell and take it apart—"

"Hush," Ivah said without thinking. "I can't, I said I only thought I could read the script, a little, a few words. There are letters like nothing I've ever seen, as well. But we'll talk about it later. When you're rested." Great Gods, she sounded like somebody's mother. Not her own.

"Goin' die. Know it. You tell Hadi. Ghu. Got to be now or never. Get Ghu to kill the Red Masks. No Red Masks, city won't fear the

Lady. Pro'lem is they love her. Make them know her first. Make them remem'er wha' she's done. Make them hate."

Ghu's dead, she wanted to cry. *I never even got to know him, and he's dead, because of us.* Why should it seem suddenly to hurt so? "You're not going to die. We're going to get a physician." A surgeon? Amputate the festering arm? A wizard-physician might save him, but if there were any among the caravans, only their own gangs would know it.

"Am," he said. "Blood poisoning. Seen it on th' road. You go to Hadidu. He needs a wizard. Promise. You promise, Ivah."

"Yes," she said.

A door. An ordinary door. Beyond, clean outdoor darkness, with starlight and the moon sinking towards the west and the ending of the night. Pure, sweet air. Getting down what was a small and crumbling cliff with Nour—and herself—so weakened and clumsy was a drawing-out of the nightmare. Mikki managed on his own but didn't have the strength to help either of them. She kept hearing things, a branch, a leaf, a rattling stone, and thinking she saw a flowing black shadow coming out the door after them, the Blackdog, veiled Red Mask, something that was both, her father wearing that girl's white veil over his hair . . . Holla-Sayan had his hands on her waist, lifting her. He'd already more or less carried Nour down, though the Marakander was no slighter man than he.

"Why aren't you in Lissavakail with your goddess?" she asked, leaning on him without meaning to do so. His body was warm and solid, strong as stone to hold her up.

"I don't belong to Attalissa any longer." He didn't quite drop her on the broken rocks of the old riverbed, but he couldn't get his hands off her fast enough, that was certain. Oh Great Gods, she hadn't meant—it was only that for a moment he had seemed safe, a great sheltering wall. "I'll take your friend. You follow. Stay behind and try not to leave too much of a track. There's water, not far. Mikki, you all right to watch behind?"

The man Holla claimed for a demon grunted.

A long, weary stumble in the dark followed, broken only by a halt at some tiny reed-fringed puddle, where she drank, sucking the water like a horse, and then tried to get Nour to drink, cupping the water up in her hands. Much of it dribbled down his neck. He couldn't hold his head steady. Holla-Sayan didn't quite swear at them but muttered in his native Westgrass tongue and eventually put her aside and pulled Nour up again. Ivah started counting steps in her head with the rhythm of her breath, just to be sure she took the next one. Despite his wounds and the slow care with which he'd climbed down from the temple's door, the Northron behind her moved silent as some great beast, only his breath, panting a little, or now and then a hand giving her a shove over some upheaved stones or sprawling willow trunk, reminding her he was there at all. Through bushes and brush, under trees. Branches snagged her and dragged at her hair. Ghost of a riverbank.

The earth shuddered again, and Holla stopped so abruptly they all ran into one another; he flung up his head, eyes gleaming.

"Ya," the demon said, in answer to something Ivah must have missed.

"What?" she demanded.

"Something in the temple."

"Ulfhild?"

"No," Mikki rumbled. "Dog . . ."

"Leave it. I know. And we've probably left a trail even city folk can follow. Probably working wizardry against pursuit would bring Red Masks down on us that much faster." He snorted and led them on.

Soft churned earth of a road, cobbles, earth again, houses, a stone wall against which she leaned while Holla hammered with the handle of a knife. Light, and someone took her arm, exclaiming.

"Sun and moon and Old Great Gods. Nour! Kharduin's been having kittens. Where'd you find him, man, a brothel? She really doesn't look his type."

Ivah blinked at a woman's swaying face a moment, all blurry golden lamplight and shadows, then hauled off and punched it.

The woman caught her wrist easily, as if she'd been a flailing child.

"Easy! Gods forgive, I'm sorry, it was a joke and a bad one, girl. Come on, come in, you're safe now. It's all right, safe."

Arms about her, the strange woman all unheeding of how dirty she got, how Ivah stank. They were into the gatehouse of a caravanserai, a brick-vaulted stairway angling away into darkness, the arcaded courtyard before them. A man holding a cudgel hovered but was waved away by the woman.

"It's Nour, safe back at last, porter. Lock the door and shout for us if anyone comes following him." Whispered debates, the woman and Holla-Sayan and, running down the stairs, a bushy-bearded man exclaiming in bastard Nabbani with the accent of the road, not the city, while Mikki slid down to sit, eyes shut and axe at his feet, with his back against the wall. Holla-Sayan hauled him to his feet, and they all staggered up the stairs and around a gallery. She missed something, woke gulping salty broth, insisting, Nour, where was Nour? She had to see Nour. He had vanished. They would see to Nour, they said. A crowd of faces, curious, horrified. A wizard of the caravans, saved from the deep well. They meant her. She was wrapped in sacking over the rags of her shift. No one wanted to sully their own clothes by giving her a coat. Only the women touched her, the rude one and a very young Grasslander and a dark desert woman with hawk-tattoos. Something important they wanted to know. She remembered agreeing, Yes, do it, but then couldn't remember what she had agreed to. A tattoo? No, silly. She was dreaming, strange dreams, mortifying dreams, naked with the Blackdog.

She woke up, ashamed, with the weary, dragging weight of sleep still on her. She was clean. She did remember a trip back down the stairs into the yard, two of the women with a pail of warm water, a rough cloth, soap, scrubbing at her as she crouched naked behind the camels, too weary to stand. Someone else's clothing, just a long, loose shirt, the sleeves rolled up, and a quilt, and warm bars of sunlight slanting in through the slatted shutters onto her. Itchy fire, oozing blisters on her arm. She'd run into blister-vine somewhere along the way. Enough to drive you crazy. No right to complain, nothing like Nour's face. But Nour . . . Nour was dying. He might already be dead, but she did not think she had been sleeping long. If she only shut her eyes again she could slide away for hours, days, she felt, but she wanted to see Nour. Ivah sat up. Her head felt light, dizzying.

They'd cut her hair off.

What? Ivah put a wary hand to her head. Gone. Cropped short and ragged, sticking up all over.

"It looks—well, it will grow back," a woman said, equally wary. "It was filthy, matted up and full of burrs and sticks and sap and worse. You'd never have gotten it clean, and, ah, it was my bed you were going to be sleeping in."

Ivah considered, slowly and carefully, just what her hair might have been like, unbraided, long as it was, and what manner of filth would have matted it. She very carefully put both hands in her lap, clasped together, where she sat in a room with scattered bedding on the floor, random untidy bundles of caravaneers' personal belongings. Hair did not matter. It had been her mother's obsession. A Nabbani imperial daughter did not cut her hair, but Ivah was not that, no matter what her mother had been. Her head felt absurdly light, and she wanted to cry. Stupid. Cry for Nour, if she cried for anyone. She had been crying too much lately. She was dry of tears.

Yes, and she was alive and safe and free, against all expectation. Her lips were cracked, but her tongue was alive again, no longer a stiff and swollen baulk of wood in her mouth.

"Nour?" she said instead.

The woman, a Northron with sandy hair in desert braids to her waist, tilted a hand this way and that. "Better, a little. Old Great Gods willing. We had a wizard-surgeon in who was travelling with my cousin Ragnar's gang. Holla-Sayan wouldn't let him take Nour's poor arm off and talked Kharduin into backing him somehow, so the wizard didn't hold out much hope when he left, but he's a Westron. What does he know of demons and their blessings? *We* think Nour's certainly not any worse, and anyone can see that the poison's ebbed more than a little, down the arm, which I don't think any physician could have managed, wizard or not, it was so far along. Your friend Holla-Sayan says he's no wizard, nor demon, but there're some uncanny rumours going round the gangs about him, you know. Anyhow, he's done something, he and the *verrbjarn* between them."

"Where is he?"

"Nour? Next door with Kharduin, of course. They all are." The woman offered a hand. "Well, not Ragnar's Westron wizard, he'll be on the road; Ragnar was heading out today. And Holla-Sayan said he and his boss had a meeting with some Family elder in the city to get to and took himself off not long ago. I'm Guthrun, what passes for a camel-leech in this gang. Nour's sleeping, but I'll take you to see for yourself."

Guthrun kept a hand ready to seize Ivah's elbow, but she found she was steady enough, even if she did hobble. Her torn feet hurt. The next room along the upper gallery was warm and golden with morning sunlight, the shutters drawn open. Nour was straight and neat on his back as if laid out for burial, hands resting on his chest over the blanket. One was wrapped in bandages and marked with words in some stiff alphabet Ivah didn't recognize, painted in thick ink, and three more beaded dark on his forehead. His left cheek was a mass of black crust, but he was neither pallid nor flushed, and he breathed deeply and easily.

The man leaning against the windowsill must be Kharduin, the caravan-master, a burly man with black hair in desert braids, gold rings in his ears, and a thickly curling beard. Blue eyes were startling in his dark face, and black scorpions were tattooed on the insides of his wrists, no folk's mark that she knew, but he might be from the eastern deserts. He came at her like a bear, lifting her onto her toes, squeezing the breath from her. "My thanks," he said gruffly, and turned away to the window. Ivah blinked. Not, she thought, merely Nour's gang-boss.

"I haven't done—" she protested. "Mikki freed us. Holla-Sayan got us—"

Guthrun grinned and put a wary hand on her arm. "Holla-Sayan says you were practically carrying Nour out when he found you."

She shouldn't have gotten up. She was going to faint. No, it was the floor trembling, not herself. She clutched at Guthrun, who braced a hand against the wall and looked up at the ceiling, as if expecting its imminent collapse. A cobweb danced and trembled, then hung still.

"It keeps doing that," Kharduin said, and turned back, shrugged. "Maybe the city will fall and change the temper of the Lady again."

And what she had hazily thought to be heaped bales of furs spilling along the far wall heaved to its feet, stretching into a huge dusty-gold bear, bigger than any her father had ever taken her hunting on the northern edge of the Great Grass.

Her ears rang, and everything went red and distant. Kharduin caught her as she started to crumple.

"Mikki's a demon," the caravan-master said. "Didn't you know?"

She shook her head, swallowed, and blinked till her ears stopped ringing. "All right," she said, and managed a weak smile. "How— uh, how are you?"

"Half-demon. I'll do. I generally heal quickly."

"You speak!"

"Well, yes." He ambled over and gave her a light shove on the shoulder with his nose. "You're thinking of Holla? He's a thing. A monster, if you like. Why shouldn't I speak? I'm natural, I was born this way."

"That must have been, um, a bit of a surprise for your mother."

"She was a bit taken aback with the whole naked pink screaming baby thing happening every night," he said, and grinned, which made him look as though he'd just seen his dinner, and she was it. "But she got used to it eventually."

"Oh."

"Put some clothes on, now you're up," he advised. "We're not staying."

"Nour is staying, Lord of Forests," said Kharduin firmly. "He's not fit to be moved."

"Do you want him to be here when the Lady comes to smash your door in? I should take him and Ivah and a couple of your gang to carry a litter, and head up into the Malagru, for his sake as well as yours."

"The Voice of the Lady never paid any attention to the suburbs. We're fine, here."

"We're not. The Voice of the Lady is dead, and the Lady is a devil set on murdering wizards so she can bind their souls and use their corpses for necromancy. We destroyed a dozen of her tools last night. She's going to want to avenge that, if not to replace them."

"You can't go dragging him up the cliffs into the hills. You'll kill him."

The door banged open, and they all grabbed for weapons. The Grasslander girl strode in, with Holla-Sayan grim behind her.

CHAPTER XVIII

Zora broke the surface of the water and breathed deeply. The cave was dark, but the eye of the dome was not quite so black as the shadows. Dusk. She had fought daylong. Small wonder that she felt so weary . . . No. She felt it, her Red Masks knew it. She had dived into the well in pursuit of Vartu and the goddess in the morning, and morning overtook them again. It was the first faint lightening of the coming dawn she saw overhead. Her body ached. Her arm throbbed, and her breast. She pressed the palms of her hands to the ugly parted lips of flesh, leached of colour by the water, and sang of healing, until the flesh knit again and the pain had mostly ceased. Both gashes left a white line of scar; her gown had not rinsed clean of the brown stain even in the well.

Ulfhild did not follow. Not yet, but Zora would not trust to the darkness of her spell or the slow dreaming of the true Lady to hold Ulfhild Vartu forever. With a thought, she brought Red Masks down the stone-cut stairs from their barracks. The empty shells of four others lay in a neat row by her well, killed with brutal strength, but carefully set with mangled limbs and severed heads in their proper places, arms folded on the chest, awaiting her—repair. The Red

Masks did not leave their dead out to be seen, but these were beyond saving, even in the well. They were empty, useless. The head of one was missing. She knew where that had gotten to. These weren't the only ones who had been ripped from her binding, though. She sought after them. Empty corpses in the tunnel that led to the Voice's hospice and a lingering trace of some power.

The Red Masks didn't know what it had been. None of them had seen and survived, and what knowledge they held in common was confused. Fire and darkness, high snows and stone; a forest in the mind, leaf-rustling, moss-deep, green-scented. Fear, and longing; they would seek . . . whatever it had been . . . if they could.

"You will not," she said aloud. "You are mine."

It was outside the city. It had passed through the empty hospice and into the suburb, and the cell into which she had shut Nour while she delayed settling his fate was shattered, empty as the husks of the Red Masks were empty. He was hers, and he had been taken—

She brought her mind back to the task in hand, found long strides had taken her halfway to the tunnel. So—the prisoners were gone, more Red Masks had been slain in their liberation, and whatever power it had been, she could not go chasing it this moment. Ally of Vartu's? Ghatai? No, the road said he was dead. Ogada, perhaps, or Dotemon. Later. She would deal with this second enemy who stole her wizards from her later. She must secure what she had first. Her temple, her priests, would be wavering, doubting her divinity, deserted.

Red Masks escorted her up the stairs. Foolish to feel a little trepidation. What tale had the worshippers carried out to the city of their goddess fleeing in the midst of the morning dances? Zora was no truant girl to be quailed by Revered Rahel's tongue.

Two Red Masks still stood guard at the broken door of the Dome of the Well, good and faithful servants, obedient to her overruling intent that they should always protect her and the well and their own secrets. They had come to replace the first who had fallen and carried the bodies below and taken their places. She would have them relieved by others, lest any wonder at priests, however ascetic, who could stand a watch of a day and a night, but there was no point until someone was nearby to witness the change of guard. For now, they could continue to stand.

Singing echoed faintly from the Hall of the Dome. Zora went to it, wet as she was, torn and bedraggled. She carried her sword naked in her hand again. More Red Masks came from the barracks to stride ahead of her and fling back the doors with a bang. The singing faltered.

Faces looked around, shadowed beyond reading in the feeble light of the lamps that burned about the walls. The fading of the sky that was the harbinger of dawn, much brighter now and not merely the hint of the night's fading, fell through the broken window of the dome, but did little to relieve the shadows. She drew fire to the lamps, set pillars of golden light climbing from them, strode through the hastily parting dancers—they had been performing "Tempest on the Mountain," a plea for the Lady's aid in times of peril and weary they were of it, reeking of sweat—to the pulpit.

"The Lady," she said in a voice that carried to the far corners of the hall, "knows all your prayers, those you make together in the harmony of word and body, and those you tell over in the silence of your mind."

She let her gaze pass over them, lingering on certain ones. Ashir. Rahel. Ashir flushed, and Rahel's mouth thinned. The woman was afraid.

"My enemy—Marakand's enemy, who dared to profane my sacred waters, will trouble us no more." She brandished the sword, which exposed the slashed bodice of her gown. No matter. "But there are others. Even as I fought in the darkness of realms you cannot tread, allies of the wizards who threaten us dared breach the defences of the temple to assault my sacred Red Masks, who have died, some of them, protecting me as I strove against my enemy in the well."

They cried out at that. She swept on, ignoring the doubts, the running voice of her mind that said, *No weakness no doubt no you say too much but better they fear and fearing follow fearing obey, and they may have seen, some may have seen the Red Masks lying broken before others carried them down to the well, too many windows look out, too many . . .*

"Lady, they have attacked temple guardsmen too! None were killed, but one still lies senseless, and the other can't say who attacked him. It was some foul wizardry, that they were overcome and their enemy passed unseen."

"No one is safe," she said solemnly, "not even within the sacred precincts of the temple. For not all within the temple are faithful."

Silence, then.

"Did not the Beholder of the Face urge you to enter the Dome of the Well, though the Red Masks barred the way?" That, she knew. The Red Masks remembered.

"Revered Lady, I feared for you," Rahel said.

"Feared for me. For *me?* And this is why you allowed the worshippers of the morning to return to the city carrying tales of the Lady's flight—"

"I said—" Ashir coughed. "Lady, I spoke from the foot of the pulpit and I said that without doubt the Lady had become aware of some danger and flew to prevent it! I assured them, you would protect us, and I ordered that we should all sing the prayers for protection of the city."

"And did you?"

He shuffled. "Many left, Lady. We couldn't prevent them."

"You have the temple guard!" she shouted. "What do you think they're for?" Zora swallowed her sudden rage, terrified by it, and made herself smile. "Have many worshippers returned?"

"The folk gather at the gates," Ashir confessed. "We haven't been admitting them, not knowing—not knowing what your will might be."

"And meanwhile, Rahel urged that you violate the well, though my Red Masks were guarding it."

The assistant master—now the master of the dance—shifted his weight nervously from foot to foot. "She said—" he began, and his voice broke.

"She said . . . ?" Zora kept her voice sweet and serious. "What did she say?"

"She—" The man could barely speak.

"Yes?" Zora said, encouraging as though she already knew the answer.

"She said that you—forgive me, Lady, that the—the former dancer Zora was only the Voice, grown mad and deluded through being weak and unfit to bear the goddess, and that we must find you—her, if she had not already drowned your-herself in the well, and—and free the Lady from you, so that a new Voice could be chosen." The man went down on his knees. "Forgive me," he whispered. "I'm only repeating what she said."

"Rahel?" Zora asked, with sorrow in her voice. A goddess must be a merciful mother to her folk. And a stern one, when need was. "Did you say this?"

The Beholder of the Face raised her chin. "I was wrong."

"But you were among those who insisted that Zora was the chosen of the Lady, that the Voice-that-was had spoken of her as the Voice that would be. I remember," she said, so gently. "And so quickly you doubted my fitness?"

"I thought I had misunderstood the Lady's Voice. I thought to correct my mistake, to serve the Lady. I—I know I was wrong, I see that. I never intended any—"

"I am the Lady, and you thought to serve me by murdering an innocent girl, whose form I have chosen to wear when I come among you? You sought to persuade these virtuous men and women to my murder?"

"Lady!" Rahel went down on her knees, not out of any true contrition. Did she think Zora did not see the bitter anger in her heart, the hatred of—of the Lady, of the temple, of the Voice Lilace who had all unwitting and unwilling stolen her husband's love, long before her mind broke under the—when—*It was not my fault she was too weak and went mad.*

"Oh, Rahel," Zora said, and let the sorrow in her voice deepen. Some of it she even truly felt. Poor, bitter, lost soul. "You should have been stronger in your faith. Take her away," she told the Red Masks. "The times are too dangerous. Mercy for the weak in faith is a luxury I cannot afford."

"But—" said Ashir, and then fell to his knees, his face to the floor. By ones and twos, and then whole swathes, the priests and musicians and dancers did likewise. Zora alone stood, and her Red Masks. "But where—?" Ashir mumbled.

He was weeping and trying to hide it. She ignored his question. Where indeed. Not the deep well; she did not want to disturb its waters, not with Vartu trapped within. A cell, to await her judgement, as a few others, that wizard-child too young to make Red Mask, brought to her by his own parents twenty years ago, had waited? No, she did not want to risk any other incursions freeing her prisoners, when she did not yet know what exactly it was that had trespassed. No. She knew what. What else could it be? *Who*, it was only *who* she did not know.

Two Red Masks took the priestess, and when Rahel screamed and tried to pull away they put on the blessing of the terror of the Lady and dragged her half-senseless and wailing, all control over her limbs lost, from the Hall of the Dome, through the cowering, shivering, weeping, and moaning priests.

Zora didn't have time to deal with these petty matters. There were real enemies at her very gates. She had the Red Masks throw the Beholder of the Face from the top of the stairs to the well, while she remained behind to order Ashir to his feet.

"I have no time for traitors and the faithless," she told him. "Summon the captains of the temple guard to my house. My enemies hide in the suburb," she added, leaning forward in the pulpit, sweeping them all with her eyes. The columns of flame above the lamps climbed higher. "The Lady has shown too great a mercy to them, too long. As of today's dawn, the law of the city runs from the Eastern Wall to the Western, and no wizard found there will be permitted to live."

She heated the flames from yellow to white, scorching the stone, and let them die, left the still-cowering priests and the dancers blinking after-images away in the darkness as she paced from the hall.

"Ashir," she called back. "The captains. Now!"

A muffled choking escaped the Right Hand of the Lady. He rose and scuttled after her, his clerk trailing behind.

CHAPTER XIX

Ivah stumbled and fell halfway down the stairs, and without thinking Holla-Sayan pulled her up, an arm around her waist. Kharduin's gang had rushed to find her clothing, giving up their goods as if she were one of their own. There were gangs that were master and hirelings, and gangs that settled into families. Kharduin's, like his own, was one of the latter, and Ivah had brought Nour back to them. They would have given her more than trousers and coat and someone's newly purchased, bead-trimmed felt boots; she could have had a camel to ride for the Western Wall and the fifty-mile journey down the pass to the Stone Desert, far out of the Lady's reach if anyone had thought she had the strength for such a journey.

If she would have taken that gift.

Uncomfortable thought, that she would have turned down the offer of escape. But Holla-Sayan thought she might. She'd thrown her life onto the table for Nour three times now at least, by his count. That wasn't the woman he knew. She had nothing to gain from Nour, so far as he could see, nothing worth her very life.

Maybe she didn't think her life worth so very much. Not a comfortable thought, either. Great Gods who'd damned him, he was not still in some corner of the Blackdog's soul shaped to be a protector of girls. Ivah didn't like his hand on her any more than he did. She pulled away once they were at the bottom of the stairs.

"If you're going to have to carry me, better to leave me on the street," she snapped, and the young Grasslander woman, Nasutani, running after them, pulled Ivah's arm over her shoulders instead.

"I'm to go with you," she said. "Kharduin says so."

"The fewer the better," Holla said.

"Mistress Ivah's too weak. They've been days without food or water. She'll need help on the way, and whatever you and Lord Mikki are thinking about hiding in the hills, if anyone does follow, you'll want an archer."

"Kharduin says that, too?"

"Kharduin's coming with us," she said, matter-of-fact. "He says if they take Nour again, it'll be over his lifeless corpse."

"It will be. How many others?"

"Vardar and Seoyin to carry Nour. Vardar's Malagru hillfolk. He knows mountains."

"So do I," Holla-Sayan growled. "Why not bring the whole gang and some banners and trumpets to see us off?"

"Are you and the lord demon planning to carry both the wizards up the cliffs on your own? Don't be a fool."

"More a fool than walking through the suburb with a bear, right." But the girl was right, he and Mikki, with or without Kharduin, couldn't get a semiconscious Nour and Ivah so weakened up the steep sides of the pass themselves. Though if Mikki would let Ivah ride . . . he snorted. Ride a bear up a cliff, yes, without saddle or stirrups, forget that.

Hells and hells and hells damn them all. He shouldn't be here. He should be in the city with Gaguush, drinking syrupy coffee and keeping his mouth shut, looking decorative, had been her words, while she and the Xua merchant talked polite and effusive circles around one another. Instead she had taken Kapuzeh and Varro, and left a message that he thought Thekla, using as excuse her poor command of any language of the road, had softened far beyond what Gaguush would have wanted. If he wasn't too busy, could he perhaps meet her at Varro's wife's house, where they were dining after the meeting with the merchant lord? Sarcasm that was diffused by Thekla's conciliatory smile, but he wasn't going to make it. He started on his way and met a frantic pair of Red Desert sisters he knew slightly, one a minor soothsayer, who'd left their gang and were heading for the Western Wall, fearing to find it sealed against them. In the early hours of the morning the captain of the Eastern Wall had sent soldiers through the pens and paddocks of the horse dealers, expropriating mounts and gear. They'd been sent into the city by their gang-boss to find out what the stir was about, only to see from the Gore the splash of red that was a company of temple guard, with armoured Red Masks at their head and a woman in white, with a shirt of red scale armour over her robes, riding at their head.

He'd gone to investigate, heard the uproar, and found the lanes of the suburb and the road itself filling with people, wild rumour already rising; the temple was seizing horses and camels, conscripting by force fighters for its war in the east, arresting all Praitannec folk, hunting the assassin of the Lady, sending Red Masks through every inn and caravanserai to sniff out wizards, carrying off children to serve in the Lady's ritual dances or for worse fates . . . People on the rooftops shouted down that it was true, they could see the red of the temple guard. He hadn't pressed on any farther but had run back for Shenar's. His own gang were safe enough, so long as he kept clear of them. Assuming, that is, that wizards, assassins, and invaders of her temple were the Lady's prey, and not camels, but Master Rasta's, where they lodged, was at the western end of the suburb where it thinned away to dusty stone and thorny scrub. The soldiers would have more camels than they could hope to manage long before they ever got so far, if that were their object. Thekla and Django were no fools; they'd hear the stir and find out what was afoot soon enough. But he wasn't saving wizards, even Ivah, from the Lady's torment only to stand by and let her take them back.

Shenar, the stout master of the caravanserai, pushed past him up the stairs, shouting for Master Kharduin.

"What?" Kharduin snarled, standing to block the man's way.

"I've turned my back and shut my eyes," Shenar said, puffing a little. "But I've got my living to think of, not to mention my life, and last night's goings-on—my porter says Red Masks are loose in the suburb along the Gore. You tell me they're not coming straight here for this man of yours and the strangers you've brought in."

A Nabbani merchant, dressed in brocades for the city, came flying out of a room farther along the gallery, a small chest in her arms, two of her gang running after her with larger bags. One paused to shout down into the yard, ordering someone else to ready a camel. Someone who had something she didn't want the temple finding. Even if the street guard at the Western Wall hadn't been ordered to seal the pass, any alert captain was going to take it into his own head to start searching and questioning very closely, when a sudden rush of lone riders without caravans began to flow past him, especially with so many folk of the eastern road among them—what would such folk do, faced with the Stone Desert?

Not Holla-Sayan's problem. His fault, maybe, but if he'd stayed dutifully in bed, Mikki would nevertheless have gone killing Red Masks and would nevertheless have freed Nour and Ivah, though whether any of them would have then made it out to the suburb . . . And Mikki, having been seen leaving this place, was going to have every tongue up and down the street wagging. Holla-Sayan took Master Shenar by the arm, pulled him from the stairs.

"Problem," he said. "Do you have a side door?" Few caravanserais did. They were meant to be defensible. "A window looking out the back, someplace we can lower Nour from without attracting so much notice? You need him out of here as swiftly and secretly as we can manage, right?"

"Oh, so they can decide he's still here and tear the place apart looking for him?" Shenar gave him a scowl. "And whose gang do you belong to, so I can get the damages out of them? You're the one brought them all here."

"And here I thought we were all such good friends and brothers." A stocky Nabbani man with iron-grey hair put an arm around Shenar's shoulders. "Dear, dear Shenar, you know what the reputation of any caravanserai owner who rats out his loyal caravan-masters to the temple for smuggling books or dodging tolls or harbouring wizards is going to be, once the dust settles?" He grinned at Holla-Sayan. "There's a window looking north from a room on the back range. Mistress Sa-Sura has her bales of silk in it, but my son had a word with one of her girls and we, ah, have the key, for a bit. Nothing behind but a narrow alley." He raised his eyebrows. "Very narrow. We can lower Nour down; they're making a litter for him now. And—what's that place beyond the lane, Shenar, a goatshed? Yours? Your sister's, oh. It looks like a good strong roof, and not too great a leap for a large animal."

"What does the roof matter?" said Shenar. "What animal? You don't need to talk like I'm about to betray you all, though any fool of a wizard who goes into the city deserves what he gets, in my opinion. I'm just saying I want the wizards and these strangers out, I didn't agree to sheltering wizards, and if you've snuck them in they're your look-out, and I don't like the brawling rabble of the western road—"

"Good, good, so the sooner you help us be gone, the better," said the Nabbani. "Where'd Nasutani go, Holla-Sayan?"

To the vaulted gateway—hells, the two women had already left. "I'll catch them," he said. "Grab a couple of waterskins for us, would you, and see someone has them; you can't put Nour and Ivah through another day without water."

"Already done," the man called, as Holla turned away and ran for the gate. The porter was just shutting the inset door again.

"The Grasslander women?" he asked, and the man nodded, sighed, and raised the bar.

Ivah and Nasutani walked arm-in-arm like two friends out for a stroll, nobody paying them much heed. He caught up in a few strides. "Where are you going?" he demanded. Sayan help him, it was the dog, wanting everyone safe and under his eye, and he'd given in to that instinct without being aware.

"Kharduin said to go now, and we'll meet up after, if we can," said Nasutani. "There's a place where some cedars spill down the slope, just past a windmill; he said aim for that. Attract less notice, he said, if we're not all one crowd together leaving the caravanserai. Especially with Mikki. But maybe you'd better go with Nour."

"Mikki can fight the—them," he said. "You two can't." Three friends out for a stroll? The Nabbani caravaneer had been right; Mikki could surely manage a leap from a window—if it was large enough—to a goatshed roof, and Kharduin had plenty of bodies to help in getting Nour out. He fell in beside Ivah.

Gaguush was on the other side of the temple's soldiery and undead wizards. Maybe forever. How many Red Masks could he kill before the Lady killed him?

He was going to be a father, a real father—his son among the ferrymen of the Kinsai-av didn't count, Kinsai claimed her own—and before he ever saw his baby, undying devil or not, he was going to be destroyed, the human soul he might no longer even have certainly rejected by the Old Great Gods, if it had not already perished. And for the sake of a woman whom yesterday he would happily, eagerly, have slain himself.

"You don't have to do this," Ivah said. "Go to Gaguush."

He said nothing.

"Holla-Sayan!"

He whirled, hand going to his sabre. Zavel. The youngest of Gaguush's gang, whose parents had both died because of Ivah's father. The boy's eyes were bloodshot, squinting against the day, and his face had a yellowish cast, his braids dishevelled and unravelling. He stank, too, of stale wine and rancid body oil.

"Take your hangover, go home to Rasta's, and pray Django doesn't skin you to save the boss the bother," Holla-Sayan advised, turning away again.

"Holla!" Zavel clutched at his coat. "I was looking for you. I've been back to the caravanserai. Thekla said you'd gone to Shenar's. Listen, uh, Gaguush told me to tell you to advance me some money on the next trip."

Gaguush had said this was Zavel's last chance. Every town they came to, the drinking was worse, and so were the sullen tempers in between. In Serakallash he'd started a fight with a sept-chief's guardsman and nearly gotten himself killed; Gaguush had only been able to bail him out at all because of who they were, and respect for past valour and sacrifice wasn't a coin you wanted to overspend, especially not for a fool who'd brought his immediate troubles on himself. Zavel wasn't the only one who'd lost close kin; everyone found their own way of carrying their grief, but his, she'd told him, seemed to be to destroy himself out of spite at the world, which childishness she didn't have the patience for.

"I don't keep the strong-box. Go back and wait for her."

"You must have the key," Zavel wheedled. "She's your wife. Look, Holla, she said it was all right. It wasn't my fault, I was robbed—"

"Sure you were. And if you really were, what do you expect, going with those poor little fools the city 'uncles' send to market in the taverns? You're lucky they left you your boots. And if I had a key to the strong box, which I don't—"

"Well, maybe it was her purse, then, maybe it was a purse she said you had. I forget. My head aches. You know how it is. Anyway, she said you could advance me something on—"

"You haven't seen Gaguush, Great Gods damn you, do you think me a fool? You've pickled your brains to the point you can't even come up with a good lie! Thekla told you Gaguush was gone. What were you planning to do when she found out, if I did rob a purse for you?"

"I was joking! Sera bless, Holla, you can't take a joke anymore. Well, lend me something, then. I owe—"

"I'll think about it, if when I get back I hear from Django you've put in a fair day's work, all right? Now get lost. I'm busy."

Zavel sneered. "Does the boss know you've dodged her to run after pretty girls?"

"What do you think? I said get lost." Damnation. He walked away, striking off the hand that clutched again at his sleeve. The few passers-by were looking at them but swinging wide around, smelling a fight. Kharduin's girl had waited, damn her, and though Ivah had limped ahead a few paces, now she turned and glanced back, urgently beckoning Nasutani on.

Fatal.

Maybe it was the line of her jaw. With her hair cropped and her face so haggard, Ivah didn't look much like the shy Nabbani coin-thrower in whose company they'd travelled so far, but the fool boy knew her.

"Holla . . ." Zavel's grip tightened on his arm. "Ivah! You murdering, bastard whore of the Lake-Lord, you—"

He dove past Holla-Sayan, knife in hand. Holla jerked him back by the hood of his coat and, as Zavel's knife-hand came around at him, laid him senseless on the mucky street with a fist to the jaw.

He took Ivah by one arm, Nasutani by the other, and dragged them on, not looking behind.

They didn't wait for Kharduin and Mikki where the suburb faded away into a fringe of shacks and sheds but carried on over the rising, stony ground. The sides of the pass reared up in broken, fissured cliffs and slopes of scree, here and there patches of trees clinging with roots like claws. A dry streamed took them to where Kharduin's cedars spilled down, and in the sweet-scented shade beneath they waited. Farther to the east, a man ran from between the sheds, turning to make expansive gestures at nothing. The air between him and the buildings shimmered smoky a moment. The red-armoured figures who pursued ran through the shimmer unslowed, and the man dropped to his knees, arms wrapped over his head. They beat him so he sprawled on his belly, then dragged him away by his arms. There was Kharduin, spear on his shoulder, and two men with a litter made of spears and a blanket swaying between them. Mikki paced behind. Nasutani nocked an arrow. Ivah had her eyes shut.

"All right?" the Grasslander girl asked her.

"They can be killed, I've seen it. But I still don't see how. We're not strong enough. Nasutani, if they come, if Holla-Sayan can't stop them all—"

"Thank you," he growled.

"Don't let them take Nour again, or me. They say wizards are drowned in the deep well, but it's not true. The Lady kills them and enslaves them as Red Masks after they're dead. She's not a goddess; she's a devil—"

"What? No—"

"—and a necromancer. Kill us first and then—then at least she can't take our souls. Please."

"She's out here because she wants us, but she's hunting wizards as she comes," Holla-Sayan said. "How many in the suburb, do you think? I know of a couple, just soothsayers, no one with any real education or power, but there's always a few scholars travelling to Nabban, or other wayfarers."

"Nour and Hadidu take wizard-talented children out of Marakand, if they can find them," said Nasutani. Her voice shook. "There's kids now that showed up after the fire; Nour was supposed to bring them, but Master Hadidu sent them on their own. They'd been living in his house as servants. We passed them on to Lu's gang that runs down to the Five Cities. They usually put up quite close to the Eastern Wall; Lu's a horse-dealer."

Ivah had shut her eyes again. Hadidu's servants. She could see their faces. "We can't just sit here and let them—"

"The Lady's a devil," Holla-Sayan said. "Mikki's not invulnerable, you've seen that. Neither am I."

"Where's Ulfhild? She could stop this. Couldn't she?"

"Maybe dead," Holla-Sayan said. "She went into the temple looking for the Lady."

"And Ghu's dead too."

Whoever that was. The thought seemed to give Ivah some resolve. She gave a long sigh and opened her eyes, began peeling long strips of stringy bark off the nearest trunk.

"Wizardry will attract the Red Masks."

"I know." She began braiding the strips, making thin ropes a yard long. "I'm just . . . thinking. Do you have a knife?"

He handed one over from the pocket of his coat. She nodded,

checked the blade, single-edged and sharp, sheathed it again and slipped it into her own pocket. Nasutani watched uneasily.

"I held off a Red Mask for a little while, back in the Doves," Ivah said. "I don't know how. Mikki's father was human."

"Yes."

"He's a demon."

"Yes."

"Am I human?'

"You're certainly no demon."

"What are you? What's the Blackdog? What's that mean, when people call it a mountain spirit?"

Nasutani's lips moved, repeating *Blackdog*, wide-eyed, but she said nothing.

"That was never true. I'm—" None of her business. He glanced at Nasutani. "Like the rest of them. You've guessed? A lost one. From an earlier war. Weaker. Wounded, she says." No need to say who. "Crippled."

Ivah watched her braiding fingers and asked, low-voiced, "So if you had a child, would it be human, did she say that?"

That felt like a punch in the stomach. "What?"

"Am I human?"

"Of course you are."

"Are you sure?"

"You don't smell like a devil." She didn't. That was that. She was human. So was his child.

Nasutani put a hand over her mouth, eyes showing white.

"Oh," Ivah said, sounding almost glum.

"Old Great Gods! You should be relieved!"

"You don't need another wizard who can't fight the Red Masks. You need something else." She looked up. "But I'm not that. You need the gods of Marakand."

"They're gone."

She nodded, coiling up her braids of bark, as Kharduin and the men with the litter came in under the trees. Nour lay limp. Mikki shambled up and snuffled him.

"Now what?" he asked.

"Up," said Kharduin. "There's a dry stream cuts a way down under these trees, lots of fissures and crevices and caves up there. We get Nour into one we can defend against whatever comes and wait it out. And if they don't come, we wait till it quiets down and he's fit to ride, get what carriage we can even it's no more than a few bales of camels' wool for the Five Cities, and get the hell out of Marakand."

"Every wizard they take in the suburb is another Red Mask," Ivah said. "The problem with fighting Red Masks isn't only that they're already dead and so wounding them doesn't stop them. They have too many layers, the fear, the way spells run off them. The fear's the worst. It means people just collapse and don't fight any further. Who knows, a wizard might find a way through their other defences, if someone had a clear head and could try. If there are Red Masks among them, the temple guard doesn't even have to fight. If you take a shield from an armoured man, he still has his armour, but he's that much more vulnerable. If taking his shield meant you could go on standing on your feet and fighting . . ."

"Can you?" Mikki asked.

"I don't know. I wonder. Now that I know what they are . . . The suburb would fight if it could."

"The Lady's there," Mikki said.

"I know. Holla-Sayan?"

"You know," he said. "What you asked, Ivah, earlier? Gaguush is pregnant."

Ivah looked down at her hands. "I'm sorry," she whispered. "You should have just killed me."

He cuffed her shoulder.

"We need to go," said Kharduin. "It's all very well, but we can't save everyone. We do what we can and don't throw our lives away for nothing."

"There's no one following," Mikki said, low-voiced, looking at Holla-Sayan. "These should be safe enough on their own. When the Lady works her way to Shenar's, they'll be set on our trail, not before. No one's going to keep secrets from her, however much they want to, and I would think she could track you, dog, if she tried. We'll be fighting them all anyhow, one way or another."

Unless we just abandon these and run. He sighed. *Sooner rather than later, you think?*

The two of us together might have a chance, even against one of the seven.

I doubt it. It was a handful of human warriors killed the last Blackdog. It didn't take the Lake-Lord himself.

He wasn't what you are.

Maybe not. Moth's still missing? Mikki, is she dead? I'm sorry, but what else could hold her?

"Not dead," Mikki said aloud, quietly. "I'd know. But gone. Like the gods of Marakand."

"Nothing we can do about that here and now, then." *And if the Lady overcame her, what hope do we have?*

None, although—she went without Lakkariss. She went not wanting to fight. She might have done something stupid, trying to talk to this Lady. They were friends—she had friends, you know. I could see her being taken unawares.

And what about Ivah?

She should stay here, Mikki said. *She's only a human wizard, no matter what her father was, and half an idea about one part of the Red Masks' spells is not any use at all.*

Maybe. But she had stood against Red Masks. What other human wizard had managed that?

"Ivah," said Holla-Sayan, "a vague inspiration's no good. Can you break their fear?"

"I don't know. I won't know till I see it again and try. But to try, when I'm not fighting for my life—maybe."

She was desperate. Desperate to die, maybe, in a cause she thought would redeem her.

You've paid for Bikkim. Her eyes widened. She did hear. *Stay with Nour. You don't need to do anything more. I'm not going to come back and kill you. Probably not going to come back at all.*

"No," she said, and, "I can't walk all that way. I'll be too slow."

He considered a long moment. "Mikki can carry you."

"Do I look like a camel?" the bear rumbled.

"No!" said Kharduin. "Are you mad, the lot of you?"

"I am," said Holla-Sayan. "Just ask the storytellers. Take Nour, hide, defend him as long as you can and kill him when you can't. Nasutani can tell you why. He'd ask for it if he were awake. Like Mikki said, we can fight them in the suburb, or we can fight them here, eventually."

"Up there's a lot more defensible. Height and a narrow place."

"It'll come to the same thing in the end."

"But Ivah—!" Nasutani cried. "She's—"

Ivah stood up. "Look after Nour," she said. "Old Great Gods defend you."

"I think you should ride the dog," Mikki said.

"I think she shouldn't." Holla-Sayan cupped his hand for Ivah's foot and heaved her up to Mikki's back.

CHAPTER XX

The demon's shoulders bunched and stretched under her hands, and Ivah tightened the grip of her legs, unloosing her fingers to make loops of the braided bark. She was a child of the Great Grass, riding nearly before she could walk, but a bear was not the same as a horse and she was so weak and weary. Hungry. But she needed her hands free.

She was going to die. It was a calm, remote, strange thought. She had been living inside death delayed for days now, ever since she chose to stand and fight for Hadidu at the Doves. Red Masks, the Lady, slow starvation, the Blackdog, now the Lady and her Red Masks again. It didn't matter when she died, early or late. Every breath was an unexpected offering from whatever gods held her in their hands, every deed she lived to attempt a repayment of that gift.

The bear's rolling lope slowed, and he turned after the Blackdog down a dusty lane between walls of dusty stone. What had Kharduin and his people made of that? Nobody had warned them. Holla-Sayan had flung himself down the slope of the rising cedars, a black mountain dog, quite ordinary-looking, between one stride and the next, and she had clutched at the long, thick hair of Mikki's shoulders as he bounded after. If there was any cry behind, she hadn't heard it.

She felt for the knife in her coat pocket, eased it partially from its sheath, and, not without a wince, closed the heel of her hand over the edge of the blade.

Her mother had not believed one should mix together rituals foreign to one another, the way her father always had, but for breaking a devil-created spell of terror she had no carefully memorized set of characters with their layers of meanings, from literal through to the most secret known only to imperial wizards, declared by long tradition to be correct. No Grasslander string-weaving on its own would carry much weight against a devil's will. What she needed was hidden in some deeper place, in the marrow of her being.

Ivah felt she was floating, not in water but in the sea of grass, one of her earliest memories, standing, a little child, and the wind running towards her. Almost it had seemed a horse, a great silvery sky horse running, hooves touching the tips of the blades. The wind, of course, and a small girl's dreaming. Now it was the delirium of exhaustion, but maybe it was also the trance her father had sought with his drugs and meditation, which had always eluded her. She floated. The waves of the grass were green and silver, shoulder-high, and she rose on the wind over them, hovering like a kestrel. The grass-waves and the wind and the racing white clouds, small in the burning blue depths of the sky, hung about her, and she could feel the shape of the world, the balance of being and not-being, the fire in the heart of life, and the dark and the cold poised against it, a breath, a shadow's barrier, between. And this weaving of disparate strands was right, was hers.

Her hair was gone and what was left too short to use, but blood was hers to her last breath, and the Northron wizards used their own blood to colour their runes. She wrote Nabbani characters, smearing the blood from finger to finger, on the inside of each wrist. The words rose from the grass, rained from the blue sky of her birth.

Mother Nabban, great river holds me.

Father Nabban, great mountain strong beneath my feet.

And on her forehead, *Grass, sky, I float to strike, the kestrel between.*

The flow slowed and oozed, but last she drew the three loops she had made for the Grasslander cat's-cradle over that hand, staining her braided bark strings, and only then pressed the wound to her coat, blinking against the ache of it, falling back into the world, and clutched again at Mikki's fur, dizzy. They were on the main street of the suburb, the caravan road itself, and the Blackdog had grown again, more giant wolf than guardian mastiff. A caravan was just emerging around the corner from a narrow lane, camels stepping with their deceptively slow, ground-eating pace, bells shrill. The leading rider shouted and caught up his spear but then swung it erect, reining his camel aside, and they passed unchallenged.

"The Blackdog of Lissavakail!" she heard someone cry out in the accent of Serakallash. "That'll teach the Voice of the Lady to shelter the Lake-Lord's murdering *noekar*-men!"

There were people abroad on the streets, Marakanders, caravaneers, merchants, but more pressing west than east. The Marakanders yelled and fled before them down the lanes or indoors. Caravaneers, though, clustered armed and alert around caravanserai gateways. You saw things, in the deserts and the wild places . . . demons, gods. They watched, warily, as they had been watching, listening to the growing rumour, before the beasts ever came. You didn't ready a caravan for the desert on an hour's notice. They were trapped here, many of them. A horde of warriors waiting to be roused . . . No. Caravan mercenaries. They wouldn't fight for any but their own.

A cordon of temple guard blocked the street ahead of them, facing inwards, making a living barricade. Ivah could see the logic. The main road of the suburb was like a spine, and its alleys and lanes sprang off between the caravanserais and warehouses like ribs, with no other street running parallel to the road for long; cut off a segment of the suburb, subdue it, capture what miserable wizards or soothsayers you found, only then extend to the next. Where could any wizards go, if the Western Wall was held against them, as it must be, if the Lady were not utterly a fool? There were message-riders in the temple and swift ponies. No one could hide on the sides of the pass for long, whatever Kharduin believed, and not many of those caught nearest the city walls when the Lady rode out were likely to have had the time to flee to the Eastern Wall ahead of her or to take the road south to the silver mines. No escape. How many wizards? A handful, a dozen, a score? Was she going to throw her life away trying to save half a dozen folk who should have known better than to be in this place? She had been willing to offer it for one. How many folk in the suburb, how many wizard-born in a thousand, how many—her mind was wandering into nonsense, dizzying spirals, and her belly ached.

"Leave you here," Mikki said, each word a grunt with his stride.

"No." Great Gods, no, she needed to be far away, to have run far, far, sold her services to the emperor of Nabban, who might or might not be her grandfather, to be some dutiful, useful, obedient, unthinking servant of power, the weight of decision deferred to broader shoulders. "Find me a corner you can defend."

Damned fool. That was Holla-Sayan, the words, not the sound of his voice but the flavour of him, somehow, forced into her head. *Keep down and hold on, then.*

He gave no warning, and the fools were maybe the outward-facing soldiers who only gaped and then shouted and thrust back into the threefold ranks of their fellows, starting a panic that at first had no idea where the danger lay. He leapt on a man, knocking him flat, grabbed the one beside and hurled him by his spear-arm. By then the whole rigid line had broken up into screaming confusion. One shouted, trying to rally them, but they were panicked as a mob of children. Her father would have executed half of any troop of warriors who broke like that at the first sign of the enemy as an example to the others. Or had one half execute the other. The Blackdog singled out the shouting commander, a lieutenant's single black ribbon on his helmet, and brought him down by the throat. Ivah shut her eyes as Mikki took the shortest way through, which was over the officer's still-thrashing body. They were both sprayed with his blood.

Holla-Sayan and Mikki hesitated then, slowing, maybe discussing something silently. The street here was deserted, but now doors opened, a wary crack here, another. A straggle of people emerged from a wineshop and sidled along the wall until they were past the demon; then they ran, scattering in twos and threes once they were beyond the line the temple guard had held. Over-Malagru tribesmen, Ivah thought . . . She forced her mind to focus, to be ready for some spear or arrow. The guards themselves had mostly taken refuge in an alleyway.

"Get indoors!" some shrill-voiced one among them shouted, as more people emerged. "Inside, in the Lady's name. The Red Masks are coming."

And then you'll be sorry . . . ? He didn't seem willing to enforce his own orders now, and that alone started a rush down the road to the west. Screams broke out, closer to the city. Mikki leapt forward, Holla-Sayan keeping just a little ahead. Here the street was deserted again, and five-man patrols of temple guard stood scattered along it. She wouldn't have expected the suburb to be so tractable, but the Voice had only ever condemned wizards and rebels against the Lady. If you weren't that, what did you have to fear, so long as you scurried indoors from the Red Masks and their divine terror? You could emerge later and tell yourself, *Well, anyway, I'm safe, and they brought it on themselves* . . .

Smoke rose away to the north-east, and another plume, nearer, just off the road. The screaming came from there, like nothing human. They swerved that way.

A man on his knees in the dust, alone. A dead Marakander lay before a caravanserai's gateway, a cudgel by his hand. The porter, no doubt. The double leaves of the door had been thrust inward, torn from their hinges, but were dragged back into place and wedged with their own bars, wedged closed from outside, and a sign scrawled on the gate in charcoal. *Traitors*, it said. Ivah thought hazily that she smelled the scorched air of wizardry, like a lightning strike, and wondered at that, because she had never noticed magic had a smell before. She could see it, too, like light on the edge of vision, colour without a name. The eyes of the horse of the sky, burning. Delirious. Raving in her weakness. It was the caravanserai burning. The screaming was nothing human. Some beast in terror of its life.

"Get up." Holla-Sayan, human, had the kneeling man by the shoulder. "Come help me."

The man looked up at them, eyes as empty as death. "They took her," he said.

Blood matted his scalp, soaked down his desert-braided hair and stained the half of his face. Salt Desert tattoos.

A patrol of temple guard came nearer but only to huddle in the shadow of a porch, bristling with spears but advancing no farther.

"Mikki . . ."

"I can get down," Ivah said, but Mikki shook his head and lumbered to the door, muttering something about his axe. A few swipes of his paws clawed the jamming boards away and they forced the broken gates. The wooden galleries of the caravanserai burned, and a stack of fodder smouldered, while men and women passed water from the central watering trough. Bodies had been left where they had fallen, a Salt Desert woman, a Black Desert man, a Marakander boy, a dog. Horses and camels were going mad with terror of the smoke, but it seemed the folk of the place might get it out.

"Dog!" Mikki bellowed. The temple guard had gathered courage to charge them. They scattered and ran as Holla-Sayan shifted form again. Someone within shouted at the man kneeling in the street, too, cursing him for bringing a wizard among them, for even trying to fight, for trying to follow and leaving them to be sealed in and burned.

"Fools," Mikki grumbled under his breath, and then roared, "Call yourselves free folk of the road? There's nothing out here now but coward temple guard. Hiding like slaves and children while your comrades are dragged away to die . . . Where are the damned Red Masks, dog? They've been here. The stink of them's everywhere."

Away down the lane to the south, quartering back and forth, Holla-Sayan said.

"Come!" Ivah shouted at the kneeling man as they swerved around him, slowed now to a careful stalking pace, sniffing the air, reaching with whatever other inhuman senses they had. "Come and fight them!" She didn't think the caravaneer heard and what would he think, a mad Grasslander riding a bear? What use would he be, anyway?

The lane was narrow, and every door marked with a sign in charcoal, a hasty "Clean." Clean of wizards. They were searching house by house in the area the temple guard held, and—and a hole-in-the-wall herbalist's burning, smoke pouring from its reed-thatched roof and "traitor" written again on its door, which was ajar. Holla-Sayan shouldered it wider, backed out, nose wrinkling.

"All dead," Mikki said. "Old woman and a young man and children."

Burning where they found what they sought, which might prevent folk opening their doors even to their neighbours, after they had been searched once, in case the guard came back. More temple guard watched the street but fled before the Blackdog. Why bother dying? The Red Masks would deal with them. The lane looped back to the main road and there, dragging two bodies now, a woman and an old man, strode Red Masks.

They paused and turned, horrible to see, a unity.

"Down!" Mikki roared and stood erect, so Ivah slid down over his side and somehow landed on her feet, her back to a wall, knees shaking. A corner, as she'd asked for, where a stone house abutted a caravanserai wall. She hadn't meant it literally, but what did she expect, an impregnable tower?

Holla-Sayan was a man again, but his eyes belonged to nothing made of flesh and bone. "They're coming," he said hoarsely. "I think they've noticed us. Someone has."

Ivah swallowed painfully. Her lips bled when she tried to speak, so she nodded. She was a fool. She couldn't do this.

A sudden surge of people poured by, a house marked "Clean" emptying, heartened by the flight of the nearest temple guard or panicked past breaking by the Red Masks' turning back. Their cries were empty of meaning, a flock of birds, wheeling and rising. She shut her eyes and saw them, black, flowing from the grass, seeking the blue, turning on the wind. Fell to her knees and felt Holla-Sayan seize her arm, shook her head. She couldn't stand; she was too weak. Better to be on the ground to start with than to fall. There was nowhere safe to run anyway. She draped two of the loops of bloodied bark-twine over her shoulders, ready to take up when she needed them, wound her hands into the other, felt the characters in blood on wrists and forehead warm as the touch of the sun.

I am, she told herself, falling into her mother's Nabbani. *I am strong. I have no gods, but I am of the Grass and the wind of the grass danced for me as a horse sky-silver, and my eyes and no other saw. I am of Nabban that I have never seen, and the strength of the river and the mountain of eternal snows is in the truth of my tongue and the womb that bore me. I am . . . a thread of fire in the heart of the ice, even that, I am. He carried me on his shoulders, so I could see over the grass, and he was my father and I loved him. And all these strengths are in me, and I make them a wall against the devil of Marakand.*

She opened her eyes, weaving figures, seeing her fingers only hazily, as if they were shadows in a dark mirror. Terror. The Red Masks carried terror like a stench. It struck at the animal inside the head, the little, scared, trembling animal that knew a mighty predator stooped over it. She wove encircling river and fortress mountain, kestrel and the wind, stone and grass. That was her safety. And the mountains of the southern fence below the deserts, the Pillars of the Sky, and the forests, because they guarded her now, and Holla-Sayan's hand rested on the crown of her head.

This place I am. This place is mine. They cannot touch me here.

She heard boots pounding, opened her eyes on advancing Red Masks. Two of them, while four stood over the prisoners flung to the ground.

The second strand, and she had to use teeth as well as fingers to pluck and pass and turn. Mikki's low growling rose to a snarl, and he was gone from before her, charging out, swiping, crushing, and wheeling back, and one Red Mask lay broken. Another, fallen, staggered to its feet again.

"Break the neck," Holla-Sayan suggested with remote interest.

The four who had hung back charged now, senseless prisoners abandoned. Sullen fires played over the eyeslits of their helmets. A dog within some building whined piercingly, and a baby wailed. Ivah was able to look at the Red Masks, not to fail and faint. But she felt the pressure of their fear pushing at her, pushing back her defences, gnawing like rats on a corpse not quite dead, and her breath quickened. She forced it to slow again, but her fingers shook and she faltered, dropped a doubling of the thread. No. She could sense the shape of them, the unity of them in what made them and bound them, see it as it might be if it were a Grasslander weaving, too vast, too manifold to comprehend, and yet a little . . . she echoed it. Fear. Drew in the third loop, wove it under and over, and they rushed forward, six together and the wounded one limping slow behind them, because Holla-Sayan and Mikki would not come out.

She saw what followed only dimly. The Blackdog ripped them from their Lady's web, and Mikki turned back and forth before her, so sometimes there was only a golden-furred flank and sometimes a great paw and once, twice, red-dyed boots and a white staff burning, a desert sabre striking when a Red Mask forced past the Blackdog, but the demon was always there behind him, between Ivah and her death. Claws raked or teeth tore and like the dog, Mikki dragged them dead from the chains that bound them. Ivah was knotting, twisting, tangling her threads now. She forced herself to slow down, to pick carefully, thumb and fingertip, sobbing with every breath, hands shaking. She felt as if she were being beaten down to the earth and yet was numb. There were more of them, more than six destroyed, and yet more came, wasps drawn to defend their hive-mates, to kill by a hundred stings. Mikki stumbled, sides heaving, head hanging, in a moment when she saw the Blackdog fall, but he rose up shaking free of them, and she had it, the shape of that one spell; she caught it and held it, and the threads of it led away though all the nest of them, to the queen herself.

The spell could be rebuilt, word by word, but not quickly; it was a song, she thought, in its making, but she saw it as cat's-cradle, and cat's-cradle was what she held to the sun in the moment when she was kestrel, between sky and grass.

She called fire, with the character held in her mind, no hand free to write it. Fire answered. White fire, the light of the stars. Her ribbons of bark burned, and the Nabbani characters in blood on her skin burned with them, cool as water, as starlight on snow. Her cat's-cradles fell away into ash, and Holla-Sayan was again a man, slashing a Red Mask down, shouting something. He had been trying to tell her something for a while now, Ivah thought, but she had walled herself against him or made him into her wall, and she had not been able to hear till he spoke aloud.

"Wizards," he said. "We might still save them. You've done it, haven't you? The light on them's gone out."

She nodded, tried to find words, and even her whispers broke, rasping and choked as sand in the throat, swallowed and tried again, managing, "The fear's broken. That's all. Still can't kill them."

"All?" he said, and something else maybe, to Mikki, that she could not catch, but he was a dog again, loping away around a dune of bodies. Nothing stirred, except the hem of a red cloak in the wind.

And a man, Salt Desert tattoos, bloodied head, with a spear in his hands, running up from behind and nearly flattened by Mikki.

"Where have they taken them?" he asked. Two more men and a woman drifted up. They all looked ragged, tattered and beaten; her eye was seeing not the body but something of the heart. Tattered and beaten but on their feet again. They smelt of smoke. Caravaneers, armed and grim. "My lady?" the stranger asked. "They took my wife. Where?"

Ivah pulled herself up by Mikki's flank. What did they take her for? Why ask her? She wanted to weep. She had nothing left. The demon turned his head to nuzzle her shoulder. For a moment she leaned on him, face buried in his fur.

"They had her there," she said. "I didn't see . . . more came."

"Some took the prisoners and ran," said Mikki. "We can follow. You can't fight the Red Masks." The desert man didn't flinch. His mouth thinned. He meant to. "But you'll stand when they come. This wizard of the Grass has torn their terror from them. Set your spears against the temple guard. They've hidden behind the Red Masks long enough. Ivah, up." He crouched, and she mounted again, thinking, no, no, she couldn't, not again, she'd done enough. But there wasn't any such thing as enough, was there?

She found her voice. "This Lady of Marakand is a devil," Ivah told the caravaneers. The more who knew that, the better. "She's no goddess. Kin of the Lake-Lord of Lissavakail, and he died, you remember, he died for what he dared against the goddess of the lake. This devil from the well is a necromancer, and the Red Masks are dead. The Red Masks are what becomes of the wizards she takes."

Grim faces grew bleaker, and for a moment she thought the man would weep, but he only swallowed and stepped near, reaching to touch her, to touch Mikki, as if to assure himself they were real. When Mikki broke into a lumbering trot they followed, all but one. Afraid and hanging back, Ivah thought, but when she looked back, too weary to be angry or sorry, that man was pounding on a tavern door, shouting, "Come out! Come out and fight! Are you humanfolk or rabbits? There are demons killing the Red Masks and a devil has taken the Lady's place!"

When she looked back again, she had a dozen armed people behind her. Not all folk of the road, either.

Dead temple guard and another pair of Red Masks unmoving in the street marked Holla-Sayan's passage.

"Come out!" the Salt Desert man began shouting. "Come out and fight! A devil has taken the temple and the city. Come out and stand against her, save the wizards!"

"A great wizard of the Grass has come to fight her!" a woman called. "Even the Red Masks fear her. Come out and fight!"

What?

Mikki gave a cough that she realized after a moment was a laugh. They were surging ahead now. Someone carried a Red Mask helmet on their spear, brandishing it like a banner.

Hurry up, bear. She heard that.

Mikki broke into his rolling lope again, and her followers ran after her, still growing. Some word was spreading, but the Old Great Gods alone knew how it might be changing as it ran. If they flung themselves against the Red Masks . . . and the Lady herself had done nothing, yet. Ivah knew she should have told these people to run away. She couldn't save them.

The street here was very broad, a place where a market might spill out before the shops, but beyond, it narrowed between warehouses again. In the distance, one blazed high. Temple guard barred the near end of the street to them, and Holla-Sayan paced back and forth before the line of their spears. They had a bunched and shuffling look, as if it would not take much to send them into retreat, but behind them were Red Masks. The Lady was using her living guardsmen to guard her Red Masks. No wave of nauseous fear hit Ivah, except what was due the moment, and that was bad enough. The Lady rode a horse that looked beaten and broken to the strange vision she still held, though to the outer eye it was sleek and spirited. The Lady. A girl younger than Ivah herself, very slender and beautiful, white surcoat, white silk scarves fluttering over a Red Mask's armour, bare-headed. Among the Red Masks were those who swayed, silent, but in unison. The Lady's lips moved, equally silent.

Singing. She worked her spells in song. Something was being prepared against them. Ivah shut her own eyes, found the place of grass and sky within her, floated on kestrel's wings, and faintly, faintly she heard, but the words eluded her. Fire, a rain of stones maybe. Something. The Lady made the shape of the spell, and the Red Masks poured themselves into it.

They're going to attack us, Holla. A spell. The swaying ones. She didn't know how she did it.

I feel it. It's in the earth. Do you see the wagon?

The wagon. There, a wagon drawn by a team of oxen, Red Masks about it, and bodies tossed onto the bed like gathered faggots of wood. They were trying to back and turn it where the street narrowed, and the oxen blew and stamped and pulled against one another, trying to break free of their yoke, fearing the scent of the dead.

"We'll take the wagon, dog," Mikki said. "You stop the singing, if that's what it is."

And the Lady, meanwhile . . . She watched, eyes half-shut, lips still shaping voiceless words. But Holla-Sayan paced forward, snarling, slow and inexorable, throwing his own aura of terror onto the massed temple guard, whether he knew it or not, and they fell back a little, edged sideways, thinned their centre, while men in ribbons tried to hold them firm.

"The prisoners aren't dead yet," Ivah told the men and women nearest her, hoping it was true. "We'll fight the Red Masks. You deal with the temple soldiers, get us through to them."

The street vibrated beneath them. Ivah shut her mind to the singing, drew Nabbani characters in the air, setting protections on herself and Mikki. All she could do. Holla-Sayan charged the line. Temple guard scattered or died. The caravaneers, Marakanders of the suburb among them, poured ahead of Mikki, roaring to give themselves heart, making for the gap the dog had made.

The street crumpled and rucked up as though something stirred beneath it, flinging men off their feet, and walls cracked, swayed, fell in on them, on temple guard mostly, but screams came from within the buildings, and fires rose swifter than any cook-fire should have spread, beams blazing, tiles cracking in the sudden heat. The Lady spread her hands and brought them together, and the flames were drawn out and together as if she closed a gate, but most of them were through. Ivah had no weapon and hardly the strength left to wield one. She crouched low, clutched Mikki's fur, and tried to weave more protections with her mind alone, imagining the pull of ribbons on her fingers.

Holla-Sayan was not bothering with the silently singing Red Masks. He killed one, she saw, but another nearby took up the swaying, and the words still flowed in some undercurrent of her mind, lightning, she thought, and thunder, and she looked up to a sky where black cloud boiled into life from nothingness. Old Great Gods, she had nothing to set against this. The air smelt raw, metallic.

The Lady flung a hand against Holla-Sayan, and the street erupted beneath him, hurling him sideways, but he rolled and then she lost sight of him as Mikki flung himself at the Red Masks around the wagon. The oxen bellowed. The wagon had gotten wedged lengthwise across the street.

"No teamsters among you?" Ivah shrieked, almost laughing, and she raised a hand, not able to spare both, to sketch characters of breaking and severing. The bows of the yoke splintered. One ox wrenched itself free, lowered its horns, and charged, temple guard

and caravaneers scattering alike to let it through. The other tried
to follow, stumbled on the centre-pole, wheeled around, and tossed
a Red Mask, galloping a few yards before slowing to a purposeful
trot. It didn't look likely to stop till it reached the Eastern Wall,
and good luck and blessings on it, Ivah thought. The Red Mask
it had hurled into the wall did not rise again. Make them know
they're dead, Holla-Sayan had said. But all the while, she kept up
the shield in her forefront of her mind, and the thrusts and blows
that came at Mikki glanced aside. Mostly. One Red Mask only was
left of those who guarded the wagon, and despite that the caravaneers were already swarming over it, pulling the senseless prisoners
out, dragging them like dead things in their haste. This last was a
swordsman, some warrior-wizard whose fragmented soul still held
its old skills fast. The demon was wounded, moving without grace or
speed, barely holding his own, even with her shielding . . . if only she
had a weapon. The Salt Desert man clutched a fish-tattooed woman
to his side, standing legs braced on the wagon bed, and hurled his
spear into the back of the Red Mask. It struck armour and fell aside.
Ivah let go her grip on Mikki and slithered to the street, groping for
the spear, found the strength to stand and darted sideways, found
her moment and thrust for the back of the leg, below the edge of the
skirt of plates, felt the head bite deep through leather and tendons,
hamstringing him neatly, so he folded down, and Mikki with one
movement raked his helmet off and smashed his skull against the
dust-covered paving-stones.

"Get up, get up, girl!" Thick and lilting Northron, urgent.

Ivah hadn't realized she was down, crumpled on the road. She
clawed her way up the demon's side again, standing, couldn't find
the strength to pull herself to his back, but everything had gone still
and calm around them. A back was against hers, a hand reaching

from the side to steady her, another wiping at her cheek for her, bleeding from some flying chip of stone. Dust made a golden haze in the air, and the sky was clearing.

"The lightning," she said. "The lightning—" But there was none. The bolt had never fallen. "Where's the Blackdog? The Lady—" She tried to pull herself to Mikki's back, merely to see, but she shook too badly. Many hands heaved her up, folk standing, hands on the demon as if he were some talisman or maybe a horse that needed steadying. One or two of the rescued wizards were even on their feet, megrim-grey, and a few more awake enough to be on their knees, vomiting.

She still couldn't see. Temple guard had mostly fallen on their knees, not sick but likely to be dead unless some law of honourable war prevailed, which wasn't looking likely. The slaughter of the sur-render had already begun. Some protested, Marakanders and folk of the road both. She croaked a protest herself, she had to, but nobody paid her any heed now. At least some guardsmen were hustled away, hands on their heads, prisoners, though to what fate she couldn't guess. The roof of a small workshop, burning, fell in, and the smoke coiled about them, choking and acrid. Motionless Red Masks were stripped of their helmets, and an old man in a caftan silently wept, rocking, clutching a Red Mask's limp body, a woman's brown hair lank over his arm.

Mikki's ribs heaved beneath her.

"The temple!" one of the caravaneers shouted. "The devil's fled to the temple!" And they surged up the road, flowing past, even those who seemed to have appointed themselves for a time her guards and Mikki's.

So many had not actually been here to fight. The folk had poured out, following those who had dared to follow her. Now they formed a pack, hunting, shouting of devils and victory and the treachery of

Marakand, the murder of caravaneers. They left murdered temple guards in their wake. If they went in such bloodlusting riot through the city . . . murder and rapine and no warlord to command and control them.

"The temple is your enemy!" she shouted. "Not Marakand! Not the city!" But they didn't hear or didn't listen.

Others remained, pulling stone and brick and timbers aside from the walls and roofs that had fallen when the Lady raised the earth against Holla-Sayan. Voices cried beneath the rubble, but there were enough hands, she thought, to free them, those who still lived. She couldn't find the strength to move from where she lay over Mikki's neck.

The Lady had vanished.

Something came, like a sandstorm from the desert. It sought her, and it hated, hungry. Zora felt it, and for a moment the Red Masks faltered in their searching, as she almost—almost pulled them all back to her.

No. She was not some child, some weak little girl, some naive dancer. She had walked among the stars when Marakand was a village of a dozen huts. She would not run. And there was nothing in this land she needed to fear, not now that Vartu the traitor was captive in the well. Some small power of the earth, that was all, some traitor beast of the Malagru hills that thought the suburb its own and would soon learn otherwise.

She carefully marshalled the words that rose, jumbling. *We must retreat not risk ourselves not risk our city leave the Red Masks to search leave the guard to hunt to learn to stand to die not us not me. No, coward child, it is nothing you cannot withstand reach out your hand it dared the temple it killed the Red Masks it stole Nour from you from us from me it must break and bow and learn my mastery I have we have we not have we broken gods?*

Hush, hush, hush. She smiled at nothing. There were no priests to see, coward priests, more trouble than use in such a day. The search was going well, Zora thought, carefully. She had not found Nour, but he could not have been in any shape to run far. She would come to him, as they cut off the suburb, lane by lane, searching every inn and caravanserai, every shop and hovel. Temple guard made certain the folk knew what would come to them, if they dared open their doors again after they had been searched. The Lady would know, they said, and the Red Masks would return. Once the Red Masks had been in, with her divine blessing glowing in their unseen eyes, there was no danger any would be so foolish as to offer shelter to a fugitive. The terror of her divinity would make a man bar his door to his brother. *Bar the pass to her brother, hold safe the east . . .* Besides, the temple guard promised that any who did shelter wizards, whether scholars or caravan guards or tramp soothsayers, would burn. Praitans, too. Even the temple guard could execute Praitans, assassins who dared defy the Lady, to keep her from her own. *Poor Lilace.* They had fired a Praitannec-owned warehouse over the body of its master and his servants when they first marched from the gates, a carefully calculated gesture. The Lady was merciful, but the Praitans had presumed too far upon her clemency. She was *unhappy* with Praitans, at present. She did not think of her beautiful champion, leading his mounted company of Red Masks east. She did not.

Lane by lane, they moved through the suburb. The temple guard fought with a gang of caravaneers hiding a wizard in their centre. The caravaneers forced their way free, so she sent Red Masks to haul out the wizard and scatter in terror all who defied her. The temple guard were useless. Bully-boys who thought their lot in life was to accuse her folk of blasphemy and take bribes for overlooking it. Time they learned otherwise and earned their bread with their sweat and blood, yes. She sent more of them to seal off the perimeter within which the Red Masks searched, and hoped there would be more escape attempts to try them. Those wizards who tried to hide or to weave defences about the places they hid only revealed themselves as if they had lit a bonfire. She took eight, and then ten easily, though most were minor soothsayers, coin-throwers, and smoke-readers who barely understood their art and had not the strength to work any but the smallest spells, fools who told themselves they were not truly defying the decree of the Voice, because they were not wizards, but there was still half the suburb to search.

The Red Masks were the twigs of her nest, woven close about her, and something ripped one away. She hissed and reached after it, but the remnants of its broken mind and soul flickered through her fingers like darting fish, minnows eluding a child's snatching hand, and faded into nothing.

Another. She felt each loss, as if her own nerves and sinews were being plucked away, and the pain of the loss burned. *Kill it, kill my enemy, tear it from the world in turn.* Zora shouted aloud in her rage, "Kill him!" and a householder already on his knees on the threshold of his workshop, a saddler who had opened his door willingly, was run through by a patrol-first of the guard.

Her horse tried to rear and back away.

"Not him!" she snarled, and struck down the idiot soldier herself, her hand opening on a bolt of white light drawn not from the Red Masks but from within herself, while inside the man's wife wailed.

Something touched her spells, wound will into her words, made an echo in the undying song she had so slowly and carefully built, soul by soul. Some wizard dared think . . . it was a demon who defied her, was it not? She couldn't see. Zora shut out the howling of the woman. When she reached for vision, the Lady's vision, the Voice's vision, there was only darkness. Snow. Wind. Then a sun burning white and blinding. And Red Masks kept on dying. She began to sing, hands raised, eyes shut, seeing the knotted web of them, binding them more tightly, but there were gaps, missing knots, threads running loose, and . . . the woman by the workbench beyond the open door, the saddler's wife, raised her head. She no longer quivered and blubbered. She wept, yes, but there was hatred in her eyes, and her thoughts were of her husband again, not her raw and animal self. Her hand reached for an awl.

The Lady's blessing on the Red Masks had been destroyed. The soldiers who had cowered like the woman and her servants, helpless, useless, straightened, eyeing one another, prepared to swagger. Let them.

The saddler's wife rose to her feet, and they did not see the awl in her hand. Blind idiots.

"Kill them all," she said.

The guardsmen hesitated. Their patrol-first had died for such an order. "Yes, her, those there, kill them, burn the house."

The woman got her awl into a guardswoman's eye, before they hacked her down.

Zora knew she should be sickened with this, disgusted, horrified. She was strong now, as she had never been. But she had always been strong. She had simply never known it, till she dared refuse her brother.

Zora left the temple guard to their business and rode to the wagon. Three Red Masks had fled from the demon's slaughter with, great triumph, two wizards, one a furtive scholar disguised as a caravan mercenary, a daughter of the ferrymen of the Kinsai-av in the west come to hunt lost secrets in the library—but she had burned those books, burned them all, they would not be found. The other was an old man who read the leaves in the Praitan way and mostly told his patrons what they wanted most to hear. Even the first-taken wizards lay still, unconscious, ill as death, they looked. No weakness this time. She needed them. To rebuild the fear . . . she could not, not as it had been. She had woven all together. Her foundations shifted now. She must patch and cobble, inelegant. She would choke the life from this defiant, destroying wizard of wizards with her own hands, when the Red Masks brought her, and make her know every moment of her lingering death, make her know what would come, make her watch as her soul was shredded away and bound into the harmony of the Red Masks. This wizard who dared, who had the strength to see and break even the Lady's spells would be made a great captain among them, a thing of terror and dread to all Marakand, and she would know it, as she died.

They came, the wizard and the darkness and—some power of the earth. Zora rode to where she could better watch, better command, flung Red Masks across the narrowing of the road to hold, there, while she prepared a trap. What, what, she could not see . . . *what is it? I don't know.*

It had the shape of a dog, but it burned within, ice in its marrow, fire in its eyes, and it paced, awaiting something, some sign, some gathering of strength. Or did it fear her? Did it now, at last, hesitate?

Where's Vartu? it asked her.

Her stomach lurched. Not *him*. Not her brother—she had no brother, not Sien-Mor's brother, who was nothing to her, nothing. *Don't be a silly child, you would know it, will know it when he comes you will learn to fear him as you should as we—no, we are strong and we are safe and we will stand hush hush hush he will hear be still be silent be strong be—*

Vartu is dead, she told the dog. The road said Ghatai was dead. He was not her brother, this false mountain demon, and not female, he had never been a woman, she knew it. *Jasberek*, she guessed. But he was changed, so changed. So was she. He laughed at her, showing teeth in what looked like a snarl.

Liar, he said. *You couldn't hope to kill Vartu even in your dreams.*

Death he is death he is—he is nothing he cannot kill me he is not the sword—"Get the prisoners back to the city!" she screamed aloud, and her inmost thoughts swelled loudly so that the pacing dog must hear, *Don't let him hear don't show him don't be so weak before the guardsmen silly fool.* She could feel the watching eyes, behind every door, every window, and the saddler's workshop burned. They were afraid, all those eyes, but they were not beyond thought, not reduced to cringing animals, and they dared to hate where they should love. She moved her Red Masks to take her captives to the city now, to go, now now now before the demon took them from her.

She would kill the demon's wizard slowly, embrace her in the well and make her know her death, yes.

Or . . . she would be a more fit mate for Tu'usha's soul.

Yes . . .

No! I am Tu'usha I am Zora I am the Lady of Marakand I cannot die—

—I can burn you can burn as Sien-Mor burned and we will take this one and be strong, stronger than any, strong to hold the east—

She came, a wild woman riding a demon bear, the amber-eyed Nabbani wizard taken with Nour, architect of his escape, maybe, having summoned her demon to the temple her fault the Red Masks died her fault and she should die she was not beautiful she was hard and haggard she was no Lady the folk could love *we don't want her I don't want to be her I don't want to die you promised I would not die—*

Zora was Tu'usha was no fool. Did they think her one, that they dared come against her so openly? She had a trap laid, the Red Masks building the spell. She would raise the earth against them and crush them, gather the fires of the sky in her hand, she would break them and leave the suburb a scar by which it would remember, year upon year, its punishment, forbidden to rebuild, she would finish her search and take the Nabbani wizard back to the city and subdue her and—

Red Masks died, and the weaving faltered. The earth broke, walls fell, wind roared, and the cloud tore apart in chaos. The force of her will was broken too, staggering, and she felt her own her Red Masks' strength slipping from her—

Fool! No! Damned fool! They will die you will die weak and powerless you are nothing in yourself the Red Masks bear us up they are our nerve and sinew we cannot unleash our own my power against the world for long you know we I know even to stop him it must not be the world cracks and breaks and dies even against him I must not I must be strength of this earth to stand on this earth I must be wizard be Red Masks hold Red Masks stop them killing stop them protect the wizards you need the wizards get them to the city go go go—

The dog ignored the Red Masks rushing against it and came for Zora. She changed her sword to a broad-bladed boar-spear, made it burn like molten steel, rode against him. At the last moment he twisted aside and brought her horse down by the throat, but she saw that moment and swung her leg free, sprang clear, and flung Red Masks between them, because even the spear would not stop him; he was a mad beast, he would gut himself to come at her throat, she could see it, feel it, she could hardly breathe with the fear that shook her. *Damned coward child he is nothing to us kill him.* But it was she who was mad. She was only Zora. *I should never have been in the temple at all Papa save me take me away Gurhan hear me I didn't mean to I didn't want*—She broke the road and flung it between them, felt the world tear a little, felt the deadness creep in, so she gathered the strength of the Red Masks in wind and fury and even the stones rose and flew, and she turned with Red Masks about her and ran.

This was no safe place, not her place, not her walls, her fire, her fortress. They had snatched her Red Masks and her victory from her, the wild wizard and her demon, and the wizards were waking, her wizards escaping, wrath rising in the suburb which did not love its Lady she needed Ketsim no she needed her champion her king she must recall him—no she must make him king and bring all Praitan to her the wild tribes the warriors who would teach these Marakanders what it meant to fight she would purge the suburb and make it a desert she did not need the road once she had Over-Malagru once the Five Cities were hers and their fleets and the great sea—she was of the sea.

She hid herself in light and passed into the city to unveil from her concealing spells in the forecourt of the gate fortress, where she ordered the gaping captain of the Riverbend Gate to close it and hold it against the rebels of the suburb.

"Ring the warning bells for the closing of all the gates of the city. A wizard of the Great Grass leads demons against us," she told him. "Don't open this gate again without my word, on pain of death in the cages for you and all the street guard of your command."

But the temple guard, the Red Masks still in the suburb . . .

There was the old water-door of the hospice, the weakness in the wall the assassin had discovered. Zora reached for her Red Masks still in the suburb and set them to gather and march to that place. She would seal it, after. She should have done so before now.

"Temple guard, those still without, don't trust them. Do not open to them, if you value your little life." *They failed us. They are undisciplined cowards.* Any who had the wit and the courage to follow the Red Masks, those she would admit and welcome back to her service. A test. Yes, it was a test, all a test. She learnt by it. "Send couriers to every gate with those orders. Now, man, now!"

The gates closed, hastened by sight of the dog. She drew her sword from the air so that she stood there defiant, slim and fragile and beautiful, steel and fire, in the narrowing gap, defending her city to the last, and turned away once the bars dropped home, to smile with the radiance of godhead on the white-haired gate-captain.

"He will not pass," she said. The devil-dog was wounded, she had seen. Her spear had bitten. He was not a fool. She would destroy this gate and every life in this ward to hold the gate against him, and she made that image in her mind, held it for him to see. He stood, panting, checked at last. He knew it for truth.

Whatever he was, he had a strange mind: half beast, thoughts without words, shapes and smells and emotions. He knew the broken dead places of the world better than she, and yet he could not understand them, only feel them, know the horror of what she prepared to do, flinging human wizardry aside, standing as naked devil alone, if he defied her further.

It was enough. He turned away.

"Where's Holla-Sayan?" Ivah asked.

Mikki lifted his head, sniffed the air. "Don't know. I didn't see. The Lady didn't go past us. Did she fly?"

"Fly?"

"Feather-cloak?" he suggested.

"I don't think so. She . . ." Ivah hesitated. "She was using the wizardry of the Red Masks. Not her own."

"They're all wizards, the devils," he said, and began to walk. People gave way to them but didn't follow now and didn't try to touch.

They found the false Lady's horse dead in a pool of blood, the great veins of its throat torn away. Oh, Holla-Sayan, she thought, and found her eyes stinging for this, of all things.

Mikki nosed at it, though what sniffing it could tell she didn't know. Maybe it was just the demon's animal nature, maybe a blessing. Maybe it had been the only way to come at the Lady. Maybe he was hungry. Mikki padded on, down a lane between warehouses. Another dead Red Mask. The Lady had retreated around them and the captured wagon blocking the main road, that was all. But Ivah should have seen when she crossed again.

There was a strange light over the city, a brightness, shadows gone wrong, along towards the temple. Some new devilry brewing? She didn't think she could face it. But there was Holla-Sayan, walking slowly up across the graveyard of the Gore. He looked almost as terrible as she felt, grey under his tattoos, his coat and leather jerkin beneath torn and dark with blood. He crossed to them and leaned on Mikki's shoulder in silence.

"I have defeated the mountain demon," Zora announced, and the gate-captain, after a moment, bowed. Mountain demon, that was a good name for the creature. She would not give him his true name. She did not want the folk thinking of devils, no, and she smiled at the street-guard captain, smiled to make him hers. "Hold fast here. Admit none. Marakand will not fall while it holds true to its Lady."

He offered to send for a horse or a chair and bearers, but she smiled gently and shook her head. "Do your duty here," she said. "That's all your Lady needs of you now." She walked then, escorted by Red Masks, and the folk went silent to see her so, dirty, bloody . . . yes, that was fitting. A victor in a hard battle, with the true war yet to come. Yes.

They would love her the more for the blood she shed for them. Yes.

But she must make the temple safe, safer than the walls could ever be. Walls would not keep the devil of Lissavakail out for long. If the Blackdog had abandoned that lake in the mountains, having defeated Ghatai to keep it, it could only be because he sought some new seat of power, a great fortress for the heart of his empire, not a backwater far from the road and the pulse of the world. He would try again to defeat her, to seize her city from her. Or he might know himself overmatched. He might retreat, leave her in peace . . . to ally himself with the greatest of her enemies, who would turn all the world against her if he could?

She would build the walls of fire, as the little demon, the sala-mander of the undying fire, had shown her when he guarded her. In the heart of Marakand, she would build a fortress of fire, and within it she would await her champion, her king, her emperor Over-Malagru, and her Praitannec army that would be.

Then when her champion came to her again, the suburb could burn.

ACKNOWLEDGEMENTS

Although I don't usually include a long list of acknowledgements, *Marakand* really needs one. So . . . many thanks to my usual gang: Tristanne, Connie, Marina, April, and Chris, for reading so many drafts, variants, and abandoned chapters. Thanks to them again, and to Molly and Jocelyn, for reading the nearly final draft or portions thereof, and for being there when I needed people to think out loud at. Connie Choi and Emily Suen kindly checked my Nabbani names to make sure nothing was unintentionally embarrassing.

While I'm at it, I'd like to say here what a pleasure and an honour it is to work with Raymond Swanland, who captures the spirit of the stories so well for the covers, and Rhys Davies, who takes my utilitarian maps and makes something beautiful, and who takes so much care to make sure they make sense. Especially, I want to thank Lou Anders, my editor at Pyr, for so passionately championing the world of Moth and the Blackdog.

ABOUT THE AUTHOR

Photo © Chris Paul

K. V. Johansen grew up in Kingston, Ontario, Canada, where after reading *The Lord of the Rings* at the age of eight she developed not only a lifelong love of fantasy literature but a fascination with languages and history which would be equally long-lasting and would eventually influence the development of her own writing, leading her to take a Master's degree at the Centre for Medieval Studies at the University of Toronto. The love of landscape and natural history that appears in her work also traces to an early age, when she spent countless hours exploring woods and brooks with her dog. While spending most of her time writing, she retains her interest in medieval history and languages and is a member of the Tolkien Society and the Early English Text Society, as well as the Science Fiction Writers of America and the Writers' Union of Canada.

Her previous fiction for adults include the Sunburst-nominated *Blackdog* and the short-story collections *The Storyteller* and *The Serpent Bride*. She is also the author of a number of books for children and teens and two books on the history of children's fantasy literature. Various of her books have been translated into French, Macedonian, and Danish. Visit her online at www.kvj.ca.